G i n   L a n e

_____

## Also by James Brady

*The Coldest War*
*Fashion Show*
*Nielsen's Children*
*Paris One*
*The Press Lord*
*Superchic*
*Designs*
*Holy Wars*
*Further Lane*

St. Martin's Press ❧ New York

# Gin Lane

*A novel of Southampton*

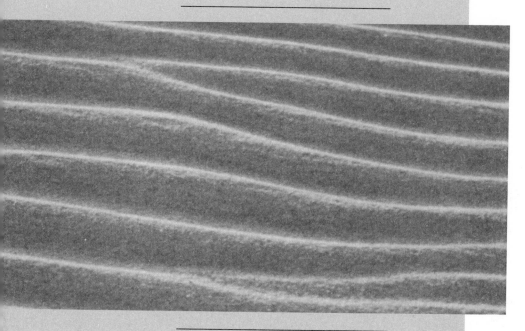

James Brady

This story is for Sarah and Joe Konig

A Thomas Dunne Book
An imprint of St. Martin's Press

GIN LANE. Copyright © 1998 by James Brady. All rights reserved. Printed
in the United States of America. No part of this book may be used or
reproduced in any manner whatsoever without written permission except
in the case of brief quotations embodied in critical articles or reviews.
For information, address St. Martin's Press, 175 Fifth Avenue, New
York, N.Y. 10010.

Library of Congress Cataloging-in-Publication Data

Brady, James, date
    Gin Lane: a novel of Southampton / by James Brady. —1st ed.
      p.    cm.
    "A Thomas Dunne book."
    ISBN 0–312–18579–0
    I. Southampton (N.Y.)—Fiction.   I. Title.
PS3552.R243G5   1998
813'.54—dc21                         98–11950

First Edition: June 1998

10  9  8  7  6  5  4  3  2  1

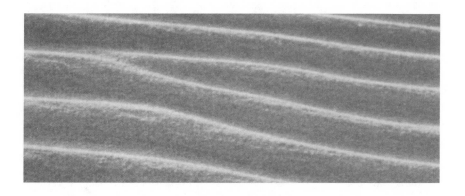

*Men who were always gloriously broke but*
*attached to the top girls . . .*

To write about and understand Gin Lane in Southampton, New York, it is helpful to have lived nearby so that you have at least a passing acquaintance with that rich and famous road and the breed of people who live there. And how this past spring they confronted and coped with what they saw as a threat to their place and their quality of life. It's a lively yarn, quite as colorful as anything in a full-blown and fleshed-out history of Gin Lane, and does credit to only a few of us. Since the cast of characters includes powerful folk who believe they pretty much run the country (and perhaps they do!), much of what happened there on Gin Lane in late May and June with the Southampton "Season" barely under way has been hushed up. No one really wanted it out and especially not the government, neither Southampton's nor Washington's. For most people the president's problems began with the running of the White House interns. But along Gin Lane months earlier, we knew how near he'd come to stumbling into an entirely distinct scandal not of his making;

we'd seen evidence of a presidential skittishness none of us yet understood. Probably you've heard rumors, the snippets of truth, those partial explanations, the outright gossip: about how the president of the United States failed Tom and Daisy Buchanan and, for all he knew, might have broken their daughter's heart. And why the earl of Bute never got to dance at his son's wedding, depriving the old gent of "having a gallop about the hardwood with a bridesmaid!" And grounds on which a celebrated fashion designer was arrested. And who very nearly got shot at Cowboy Dils's house and how A. J. Foyt was asked to save the Bridgehampton raceway and where Mandy Buchanan danced on tables and how the forty thousand honeybees died and why "Nipper" Gascoigne chided his boyhood chum "Fruity" Metcalfe and how Señorita de Playa's splendid pecs were deprived of kayaking on the Nile and why Wyseman Clagett was warning against El Niño and attempting to eat his own ear and just who it was sent the Marines ashore. As well as the role played by the Shinnecock Indians and those Argentino polo players and what it was got *Women's Wear Daily* on the case and why people were squashing lemons into their hair and wearing watches on the wrong wrists and how Nurse Cavell rescued the Dalai Lama's ambassador-without-portfolio and the future of the shellfish hatchery and bad feelings over Magistrate Hobbes's unfortunate seizure and who borrowed Captain Bly's industrial-strength sunblock and why an apparently innocent tango ignited fistfights with the RAF and whether The Eel Lady predicted an early spring.

I realize all this sounds pretty complicated. Maybe I better just tell you how my own good intentions foolishly got me pulled into those and related events along Gin Lane and who was involved and what really did go on this past spring in Southampton. As best I can remember . . .

Further Lane, where my father and I live in East Hampton, is fourteen miles east of Southampton's famous Gin Lane.

And along both of these brief and lovely oceanfront lanes people are forever debating just which of the two Hamptons is better, richer, a more desirable place to live and raise families and enjoy the good life. They also argue just which have been the truly *great* Seasons out here, the vintage summers no one who experienced them will ever forget.

From one celebrated Hampton to the other is but a twenty-minute drive, an easy hour's bike ride along the Atlantic Ocean, and if you are fit, a half-day's stroll in the sun. For places that are so close, the two Hamptons are quite different in style. Book publisher John Sargent, a sophisticated and witty man who long ran Doubleday for Nelson and the family, once attempted in a merry moment to explain about the two villages: "If you're going to dinner in Southampton you wear a tie but no socks; and in East Hampton you wear socks and no tie."

There may be something to that or no sense at all, but there are other, less superficial distinctions as well, I'm sure, and not being either a historian or a social scientist but simply a journalist, I will leave it there. Both Hamptons have their traditions, their accepted ways, their look, and the casual local snobberies that flourish with age along certain roads and at the more desirable addresses. That these snobberies are casual does not make them any less cruel and cutting. Gin and Further Lanes, behind their masking hedges and great, gated walls, possess a haunting beauty, each very lovely in its own distinctive way, and they are linked by a single, narrow road, by the ocean, by a strip of gorgeous beach.

And by money.

When you arrive there on Gin Lane, you find yourself on a narrow, somewhat claustrophobic road with one slim lane in each direction onto which hedges and walls and gates press close. And if you are fortunate, through the gates and thin places in the privet hedge and down the graveled drives, some of the drives so long and sinuous they are interrupted for safety by speed bumps, you may even glimpse the ocean. It is always there, just beyond the great houses and tennis courts and marble pools and rich, rolled and sloping, darkly grassy lawns. But in these precincts, an Atlantic view is exclusively purchased, and even the sand looks expensive. The people along Gin Lane are rich as well, always have been, I guess.

Through the years, and even today, it has been a gorgeous place. Though over cocktails or after golf or inhaling a surely unnecessary final midnight brandy, the subject comes up and the proposition debated by the modernists and those who insist on favoring "the old days": Which really were Gin Lane's best years? Which the best times? The top crowds? The prettiest women? The most lavish parties? The quintessential Southampton Season? Certain glorious years are nominated, specific moments are recalled, various men and women mentioned, this great house or that remembered and eulogized, a road race or a polo match or historic carouse described in exquisite if antique detail, a particularly splendid lawn party praised or champagne breakfast cited. And, inevitably, during these genial exchanges there will be someone who nominates Ten bis Gin Lane (the original Number Ten was washed away in the "great" hurricane of '38, thus justifying the label "bis" on its successor), and others will nod and half smile in aimiable memory, and Number Ten bis will get its share of votes as a Gin Lane address ever to be remembered.

I'm from an old Hamptons family (Beecher Stowe being a familiar name out here), but having been born in France, and for a time working as a foreign correspondent, I'm hardly the fellow to make such judgments, and prefer listening to those who claim to know. Maybe, connoisseurs say, of all the good times there ever were along Gin Lane, some of the best came right after the war, from '46 on; 1946 I mean, since in the Hamptons the good times have been going on for three centuries (of course, bad times occasionally punctuated the good, though these are rarely mentioned). But in 1946 and 1947 the world was at last out of uniform, back home, and at play. Then began the summers when Angier Duke and his brother Tony came home from the war to Gin Lane. Ever since, there've been Dukes at various places here and there along the lane, these days at Wyndcote Farm, but at that time they had their house at Ten bis Gin Lane that people, including the Dukes themselves, good-naturedly and with youthful, self-deprecating wit, labeled "the Duke Box." From Memorial Day through Labor Day, what Southampton calls the Season, the house was never empty.

As an agreeable chum of Tony and Luly Duke (Luly is Tony's wife, and you probably know the man I mean) remembers the house even now, half a century later: "It was always filled with pretty girls, out from Manhattan, and White Russians, dashing fellows who worked in PR or sold expensive fragrances to Saks and Bergdorf or were trying to get jobs with E. F. Hutton or Merrill Lynch, plus a few clever men like Serge Obolensky (a prince who had actually served and knew the tsar!) and his comrades Count Vava and one Sasha, a Guards officer whose last name none but Sasha could pronounce, and then but marginally, as well as other men who were always gloriously broke but attached to the top girls in a time when the really top girls looked better than women ever had. Remember? There was Audrey the Conover Girl and Faye the Powers

Girl and, in from Hollywood, a couple of Goldwyn Girls called Mona and Jill. A French lounge pianist named Jacques Frey, invariably addressed by the Goldwyn Girls as 'Monsieur Pierre,' dropped by in June and stayed the summer, reminiscent of poor Gatsby's 'Mr. Klipspringer,' camping out there in the sunroom playing piano, the show tunes everyone could sing and to which anyone could dance, the tall windows opened to lawns and sprawling patios and dunes and the beach beyond and the ocean's surf, so there was music everywhere, indoors and out, and the laughter and voices of the girls as well..."

Tony and Angier Duke had enjoyed splendid wars, and so had many of their friends, including the Russians (they were OSS mostly and had been parachuted into dicey places where they did deadly things), and now all of them felt obliged thoroughly to enjoy the peace. Which they did from the end of May to early September, when, in the week following Labor Day, the Southampton house was tidied up and shuttered and they all, Russians and girls and Monsieur Pierre, plus Count Vava and Prince Obolensky, and various Duke boys, returned to Manhattan, simply moving the party from Gin Lane to El Morocco and the Stork.

It was that house, that "gentleman's estate" (in the stuffy, pretentious phrasing of real estate advertisements), which Leicester "Cowboy" Dils bought for $12 million a year or two back and in which he briefly, and flamboyantly, lived until what happened this past spring, at the very start of yet another Southampton Season. Until then, Cowboy had been enjoying himself and delighting his friends, less elegantly but every bit as fully as the Dukes did so long ago, even while scoffed at by his "betters," men who clucked at the very idea of their new neighbor. While the Duke boys' parties inspired rhapsodies of memory half a century later, Dils's contemporary gatherings invited privileged, local scorn.

"Cowboy Dils on Gin Lane? Preposterous." And probably it was. Yet who was there to tell a wealthy American such as Dils that he couldn't buy this piece of property or that and live wherever he chose? Even if he did entertain odd friends and loudly. And was forever threatening to "have a fistfight" with someone. How strangely soothing and old-fashioned the phrase "I want to have a fistfight with you!"

It occurred to the few of us who actually liked him that with Dils, even his hostilities were comfortable and homespun.

I mentioned the differences between East Hampton and Southampton, the distinctions between our Further Lane and their Gin Lane; mentioned as well the links they share: the narrow road, the lovely beach, the ocean on which both front, and the money.

Cowboy Dils understood the money part, I guess, but not much else about the Hamptons or the Season. He was a queer duck with all the usual tics and neuroses, but he had remained very much the westerner, and had a westerner's open, easy, joshing ways. Where he came from, traditions began a few decades back and a hundred years was a long time; here in the East we counted by centuries. There are local people who can count back twelve generations of Hamptons residence, to the 1660s, when Connecticut still owned some of the Hamptons. And from the very moment he moved in, much of what Gin Lane was and stood for eluded Dils. Despite this, there were in Cowboy's time glorious days and nights at his mansion at Ten bis. "Good Gawd A-mighty!" he cried in considerable if primitive exasperation. "I was only trying to make people happy."

It was what Cowboy Dils didn't understand about the place and its traditions that in the end drove him from Gin Lane and emptied that wonderful house which used to be filled with music and laughter and the top girls and dashing Russians, the place at Ten bis Gin Lane they once called the Duke Box.

# t w o

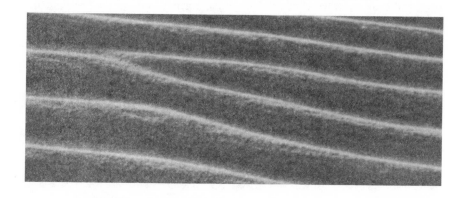

*What it is in spring that turns men and women*
*reckless, no one could say.*

In the good years—and despite our latitude, 41 degrees north, this promised to be one of them—spring comes early to the East End of Long Island, to what is known generically, and in the gossip columns, as the Hamptons. And with spring each year begins a new time we call "the Season."

Along the beach paths and rural country roads of East Hampton and Southampton and Water Mill and Bridgehampton and Amagansett and Montauk, the old Puritan villages that have bordered the Atlantic since the 1640s, the long, chill winter just sort of vanished this year one warmish, sunny day in mid-April. On Gin Lane and Dune Road and Lily Pond Lane and along Bluff Road and the Old Montauk Highway and on Further Lane, you got those first deliciously teasing hints of a better time: the snow gone, the wind-driven sand no longer abrasive as emery and scouring bare limbs, the ice melted off the brackish ponds. The migratory birds were back and the first silly plants had come up, gaudy with optimistic color in a monochrome land, flirtatious and at risk, daring the last frost, imperiling themselves the way careless men and audacious women do, in passion, or in drink. Credit the ocean for our early spring, the moderating effect of seawater and the Gulf Stream and the onshore breeze blowing across it toward the beaches and over the land. Or so I'm told by old-timers like The Eel Lady, a local seer who sells live baits and predicts weather. That's what she claims warms the East End and propagates and excites our early growths, our premature greenery; what it is in spring that turns men and women reckless, no one can say. Not even The Eel Lady. The way we are, I suppose.

I didn't come back to the Hamptons this year until May. And then, unexpectedly.

I'd been in California to interview an important actress. I won't mention her name here. Not fair, since the interview never came off. But she was one of the biggies with the requisite Academy Award and all that. And good; her Oscar was no fluke. She was as big even as Streep and Close; younger, too. A little younger. A wonderful actress and beautiful woman, and I'd arranged, with her people, to do a piece for the magazine about her new film. And after all the arranging, with her people getting back to me and my getting back to her people (in California, people are always "getting back" to you), when I arrived she wouldn't see me. Didn't even hint she might be "getting back" to me. Just plain sent out word to go away. Something happened. Was she ill? I could understand illness. People got sick and they canceled. No, not that. Well, maybe she'd disliked the new movie's final cut and didn't choose to promote it. No, not that, either. In the end no one ever told me exactly what it was and I never got to see her. But the buzz suggested it was a young man, much younger. They'd been together here and in Europe, France, I believe, and then something happened and he went off. And the joy went out of her and she didn't give a shit anymore and didn't care to hype the film or talk to me or go on Letterman or do those other things actors do. Nor did I find out the young man's name.

So I flew back to New York.

"These things happen," Anderson said. He wasn't happy about it but he said he understood. Anderson is the editor of *Parade*, the largest-circulation magazine in the world, and we were sitting in his corner office at 711 Third Avenue talking about what happened out there in L.A. and about what I might think about doing instead. I'm under contract to write eight pieces a year for Anderson and this was the first time I'd failed to deliver. "Not your fault, Beecher," he said, and of course it wasn't. But neither was Anderson much for trotted-out excuses and labored explanations; few serious editors are. While I was also a professional who took pride in getting the job done. It's no great credit to me, just how Episcopalians and Harvard men were supposed to be, how my father is, how we were in my family. Professionals, who knew the work and did it. Anderson, who'd been a Marine, was that way himself, perhaps one of the reasons we get along.

My new book was out, the one I wrote on terrorism in Europe and the Middle East and North Africa (the king of Morocco having graciously provided a brief book jacket blurb), and doing well with both the reviewers and the *Times* best-seller list, sitting there at an encouraging number six for nonfiction, and until this failed assignment with the actress, I was feeling myself a pretty bright fellow indeed. Anderson was sensitive to mood and didn't want his writers sulking, so to clear the air between us over my failure, he said why didn't I get out of the city. Maybe go out to the Hamptons, now that the weather had turned, to do that piece on the Baymen I was forever talking about, about the last hardcore commercial fishermen we have in our overcivilized part of the world. After all, the *Parade* story I wrote about Hannah Cutting, and how Hannah got to Further Lane, finding fame and wealth, until in the end it all kind of ganged up and killed her, had turned into a pretty good yarn. . . .

"This best-seller about the Gloucester fishing boat that goes down, *The Perfect Storm*, is good stuff," Anderson said. "Same kind of men as your Baymen, I imagine. A slice of America people in the great cities, sitting down to a fish dinner in a first-rate restaurant, never pause to consider. I thought of asking Peter Matthiessen to do the story. He's out there, knows the territory."

"You could do worse. He's very good," I said. "Very."

"So are you," Anderson said, "and you're under contract and he isn't. I prefer to use the writers we're paying already."

That made sense. And who ever said editors considered only the words and not the dollars?

And so that was how a pout on the part of a famous actress who'd lost her boyfriend sent me slinking back to New York unfulfilled. And almost as an afterthought, got Anderson to give me an assignment that, without his intending to do so, would entangle me with Cowboy Dils and whatever demons pursued him.

Not something Anderson expected or I sought. But reporting was the work I did and so it was I found myself getting my bags packed for East Hampton. Anderson was probably right; with the good weather, there was nothing to keep me in the city, and the beach and ocean beckoned. The Baymen idea might work, could be a fine story. They were hard, wonderful, colorful men working a difficult, often dangerous trade. I was already getting enthusiastic about it; I'm that way about a good story. I get worked up, get excited; show me a writer who doesn't feel that way and I'll show you a cynic. Or a burnt-out case. Besides, our house out there stood empty and available, my father, the Admiral, having been seconded by the Pentagon (by the defense secretary himself) to a liaison job at NATO headquarters in Brussels.

"But you don't even like Brussels."

"I know, Beecher," he acknowledged, "but I can't just say no to Bill Cohen. He's a decent man and he called personally and I'm going."

The Admiral wasn't enthusiastic about the post, or the place, but for forty years since Annapolis, his had been a career in which you saluted and went, finding along the way small consolations. So he reminded himself, as the French are fond of saying: "One eats well in Brussels." Thus dismissing the neighbors, as the French are wont to do, with faint praise, and, like Caesar, not all that fond of Belgians, the Admiral shut down his (and my) house on Further Lane, and off he went.

I had additional small consolations as well. East Hampton would be relaxed and casual. It was a place where tradition still meant something; you could go to the bank on that. The Hamptons were traditionally pretty tranquil until the Season began and that would be Memorial Day at the earliest and nothing could possibly happen until then.

Or so I believed.

# three

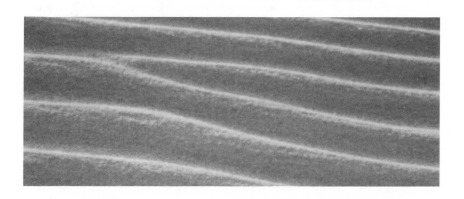

*...and Katharine Hepburn said, "I don't give a damn!"*

There are celebrated people I don't know, exotic places I've never been. But not many.

Which is part of the reason Walter Anderson hired me from *Newsweek* as a roving correspondent for *Parade* magazine and why this was the first time in almost a week I'd awaken in my own bed, jet-lagged from the Coast and then a crash session with the editor over what went wrong. Since that business on Further Lane in East Hampton last September, I'd interviewed Katharine Hepburn over coffee in her Manhattan town house, profiled Lord Attenborough (Sir Dickie to his chums) in London, flown off a carrier with the Top Guns keeping an eye on Castro from Key West, and done Q & A's with both Cindy Crawford and Vice President Al Gore, the latter inside the White House, where I had trouble with my tape recorder and handed it helplessly to Mr. Gore, on grounds he was the administration's point man on high tech (he couldn't get it going either). In the end, his PR woman had to instruct us both: "Gentlemen, there's a button that says On. You might try that."

I even profiled Cowboy Dils, the popular music DJ whose morning drivetime show provided a national pulpit from which he functioned as a political power broker and intellectual gadfly, raunchy and comic, a cult idol to his millions of fans, a daily irritant to the rich and comfortable. Cowboy had a wide range of targets, his prey including Roger Champion, who was his boss and the network's chairman; Ted Kennedy; women in the military; Microsoft's chief executive nerd, Bill Gates; Demi Moore; the Promise Keepers; Garth Brooks; and even the First Family and the president, whom Dils aimiably if outrageously caricatured on-air with a practiced and uncanny mimicry and dismissed airily as (among other, ruder things) "that fat pantload."

I'd spent a week with Cowboy and his broadcast crew doing the *Parade* piece, starting off wary and ending up hooked on his show and admiring him. And I was hardly alone in this. Among his fans were such admirable people as Ted Koppel, Walter Isaacson of *Time*, Brokaw and Rather (though not Jennings, who was not amused!), Hewitt of *60 Minutes*, Maureen Dowd and Mary McGrory, Maynard Parker of *Newsweek*, and Bill Bradley. Sure, he was vulgar and given to tantrums and shallow enthusiasms, but he read everything and had opinions and possessed, in his grouchy, self-absorbed manner, a small but genuine and entirely handcrafted genius. And, in his own idiosyncratic and decidedly flawed way, there was at bottom a strong moral core. You knew you ought to hate him. But you didn't. There were those occasional flashes of genuine caring, gentle moments, as when Marv Albert was arrested and, despite the rich comedic material at hand, he decently refused to air Marv skits. Dils grew on you, the way honeysuckle does in East Hampton, sweet and strangling.

After that, there was an interview with Spielberg about filmmaking, a week in London with the Spice Girls, and the piece I did in Florida with Pete Sampras, the tennis champ. And the abortive business of the actress in Los Angeles.

Anderson kept his people moving smartly; they earned more that way and stayed keen. Any old city editor could tell you, bored reporters drank and played pillow and delved into office politics. And who needed that?

I'd moved back into the city last October into a nice apartment on Sutton Place after those five years as a foreign correspondent and then the turbulent, lethal Hamptons summer that followed. And along with the apartment came Mary Sexton.

"Good morning, Mr. Stowe, and a fine day in May it is." Then, after a thoughtful pause, "May fourteenth, my cousin Ellen's birthday, she's got to be forty-seven if she's a day, my third cousin, once removed, and in addition, summer is nigh."

Mary Sexton worked for me and really said things like "summer is nigh" and kept track of relatives' birthdays. And, more to the point and helpfully, had fetched coffee and the papers. The coffee was instant, Taster's Choice, since I'd finally convinced Mary her own coffee was, in fact, foul. She was a big, strapping, rawboned Irishwoman in her fifties, and a Communist. She'd come to me with recommendations from friends I'd asked about a woman to clean once or twice a week.

"Five days," Mary Sexton said. "I need five days' work."

"I only need someone one or two."

"I need the five days. I have responsibilities and causes. My wage rates are reasonable."

They were and I took her on, though what she'd find to do in a bachelor's apartment five days a week I couldn't fathom. But I learned about the "responsibilities," her "causes." Mary's older brother had been a merchant seaman and maritime union firebrand and as a teenaged girl she converted from Roman Catholicism to Marxism. She belonged to just about every red front committee and organization there was, and paying dues and traveling to protest rallies kept her broke. She even subscribed to the Russian-language party newspaper, *Novy Mir*, which means "New World." That was the only thing Mary could understand in the weekly since she couldn't read Russian. But when I protested this was silly and a waste of money, Mary said she subscribed out of loyalty, "to encourage the lads in these difficult times when the party's out of favor." I wondered how she ever made it through the Joe McCarthy "red scare" days without being arrested; maybe she was too young. Wondered as well what my father would say about her connections, Admiral Stowe, who'd spent such a jolly Cold War jousting with and attempting to break the USSR as our chief of naval intelligence.

"All right with the world?" I inquired idly over the newspaper after taking the first sip of hot coffee.

She expected the question, a ritual, and would have been disappointed not to be asked. So as she fussed, picking up socks and underwear from a chair and emptying an ashtray, Mary Sexton, last of the devout Stalinists and true believers, launched into a brief diatribe about Ukraine.

"I always say 'Watch Kiev!' Those bastards are plotting again and they have their Fascist cadres everywhere."

Otherwise, she said, things looked rather hopeful, especially in Belarus, where the Minsk city council had just voted to restore a plaque and bas-relief of Stalin on the town hall, and in Mother Russia itself, where the demagogue du jour was demanding the return of Alaska and the Aleutian Islands, and, according to her, "rightly so under international law and how the tsar betrayed his own people, the workers and peasants, selling off their patrimony to neo-Colonial and Imperialist interests!"

Punctually each year, on July 16, she celebrated the anniversary of that ghastly business in the cellars of Ekaterinburg when the commissars shot the tsar and tsarina and the rest of the family, even Anastasia and the tsarevich and the other children. Mary conceded it was tough, about the kids I mean, and that ordinarily infanticide wasn't at all to her taste. "But understand the political imperatives, Mr. Stowe. Those were the heirs to power and the throne. Leave even one of the royal tykes alive and you establish a cult of restoration around which revanchist White Russian and neo-Imperial forces would instantly coalesce and flourish. Those little bastards *were* the dynasty; they were the last of the Romanovs! While they lived, the peasants and workers, and the Revolution itself, remained at risk." The jargon, I was sure, came out of books and pamphlets; her passion was genuine.

Mary was an American citizen. I had the impression she didn't take it very seriously.

Because I was healthy and enjoyed my work and, as someone Moss Hart once wrote about, had "emerged from the womb liking the world and everything in it," and even considering the recent disillusionments of Hollywood, I was pretty content. Except for how empty the apartment was. Her Ladyship, Alix Dunraven, was back in London editing books and charming authors to the greater glory of Rupert Murdoch's publishing house, which was all very well but for the vacancy it left in my life. Whenever I began thinking this way about Alix, or otherwise feeling sorry for myself (an emotion with which I had little patience), I recognized it was time for a shower, a brisk one, and I bounced out of bed, unwrapping myself from the sheets as Mary vanished swiftly from the bedroom and fled into the kitchen, lest she be compromised.

The shower did its work, and besides, my piece about Hepburn would be on the cover of the magazine this coming Sunday. That always made a reporter feel good. Especially how it came about with a woman who shunned interviews, an occasional East Side neighbor (her real home was in Connecticut) who'd passed by wordlessly on several occasions. Until:

"Why, aren't you that fellow in the Sunday paper? You look younger than your picture."

So it was that a chance encounter on the East Forty-ninth Street side-walk led to an interview over coffee in her town house, where I asked, "Do I call you Miss or Ms.?" and in reply, Katharine Hepburn snarled sweetly:

"I don't give a damn!"

I was fully dressed when Mary Sexton returned, the mail in hand, on top a familiar-looking envelope addressed to me and, oddly, bearing French stamps but, not at all oddly, redolent of a scent I knew well. Her scent. Inside, as I tore it open, risking paper cuts in my haste, was a single sheet of foolscap covered with numbers. Numerals. Not a single word—until the last!

And yet . . .

Suddenly, who cared if movie stars in Hollywood had gone AWOL? It didn't matter that Anderson was sending me to Long Island to inter-view fishermen. Nor could I be bothered about the Fascists in Kiev or plaques in Minsk or whether the ozone layer were closing in on us . . . or if the mayor of New York won reelection and the Spice Girls' latest album sold.

To hell!

I grabbed the letter and retreated into depths of the apartment from which maids, even ones as favored as Mary Sexton, were discouraged.

"Darling," it read in Alix Dunraven's familiar cipher: "Am roughing it on the Left Bank amid intellectuals, smoking Gitanes, knocking back the old vin rouge whilst listening to Piaf records, and attempting to charm this chap they're all calling le nouveau Malraux. He's got a super brain and is a cert to be elected to the Academie Francaise before age forty. Suave and randy as well. I think I've got him convinced we ought publish the English version of his latest pensees. Dancing until dawn seems to have worn down his resistance. Mr. Murdoch will be so proud. Miss you enormously. If only you too were in Paris sporting about with the new Malraux and me. Were the Hollywood starlets truly voracious? Oh, yes, where is a place called Gin Lane? They tell me it's near your East Hampton. There's a wedding I may be compelled to attend. All love."

The coded message was signed, in Her Ladyship's customary fashion, with the name of an English thoroughbred, one that she thought vaguely might have won the Derby, Original Sin. There was a brief postscript: "If you hear rumors of my being engaged again, dismiss them."

"Suave and randy" and not yet forty! I didn't like the sound of that at all. Nor was I all that delighted about her "dancing until dawn" and wearing down men's resistance. And just what was this about "being engaged again"? She might have given me some rough idea of just when she was coming to the Hamptons and who might be getting married. And why would Alix "be compelled" to be there? She was the most exasperating woman ever! As a rational and reasonably intelligent fellow, I ought to have tossed such rubbish into the wastebasket on receipt. But instead I folded Alix's note carefully and placed it in the handkerchief-and-sock drawer, where I kept all her communications, plucking them out occasionally to reread and to breathe deeply of, inhaling her scent.

The important thing was, for whatever reason, Her Ladyship might any day now be just down the road from me on Gin Lane. Suddenly, the world on this May morning looked even brighter. Then: "Mary! I'm going out to East Hampton for a week or so. Can you pack me some shirts and things?"

Of course she could. And did, muttering Leninist wisdom and hurling imprecations at the Trotskyites and "revanchist sons o' bitches" as she went.

# f o u r

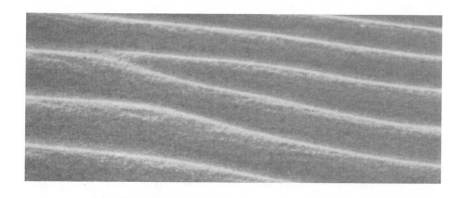

*Naked women dancing, guys in dreadlocks running around smoking ganja*

I had errands to run and a lunch I'd nearly forgotten at Michael's on West Fifty-fifth and a meeting with my agent, Jack Scovil, so that day was filled, but Mary got me organized, and with shirts packed ("plus underwear and socks and a good wool sweater such as peasants and workers wear against the chill, Mr. Stowe"), and shortly after six the next morning, I was driving through the Midtown Tunnel and emerging on the other side of the river into a low, blinding sun rising over the endless miles of Queens row houses and cemeteries, on my way to the east and the Hamptons. Not for the first time, I concluded how nice it was not to be a grown-up with nine-to-five responsibilities and an office to go to and meetings to attend. Journalism was a chancey business and you could make more money in a Wall Street bucket shop or lots of other ways, but it had its consolations. As soon as I got the six-eighteen traffic and weather report over WCBS I switched the dial from all-news to all-manic. To what I was by now convinced was the best morning drivetime show on American radio, the locally produced but nationally syndicated four-and-a-half-hour tossed salad of news, music, weather, insults, insights and laughter.

To, in other words, the daily epiphany called "Cowboy in the Morning."

While I was doing the story on him, I asked Cowboy Dils about his first name, Leicester. "Is that a family name or did your people come from that part of England or what?" A simple, predictible question; the answer was pure Dils:

"No, my old man was in the war with Hemingway's kid brother Leicester. He said Leicester was a big, handsome guy, with guts and good looks and the smarts, and shaped like an ice-cream cone, all shoulders and no hips, and my daddy thought a lot of Leicester and they saw to each other in the fighting, the two of them, and kept in touch after the war. So when I was born that's what they called me, Leicester Dils. The real Leicester, Hemingway, killed himself a few years ago. They're the damnedest family for killing themselves you ever saw. Must be a tradition, or in the genes. A wonder there's any of them left alive."

Dils had brothers with ordinary handles, he said, names of Henry Bob and Joe. Leicester, he thought privately, provided a certain cachet. But you couldn't live with it day in and day out, not in cattle country or on the rodeo circuit, where he put in a season or two, or in the Marine Corps, where he spent a Vietnam year, the name too precious for that bunch, so he became "Cowboy."

Because I'd been all those years in Europe working as a correspondent, I'd lost touch with much of contemporary culture, or what passed for such, in the States. I wasn't up on the television Americans were watching, the songs they hummed, the books they were reading, the latest folk heroes and heroines being coined, the current outrage and scandal. In fact, until I came home last year to recuperate from that shooting in Algiers and to write my book on terrorism for St. Martin's Press, I'd barely heard the name of Cowboy Dils and had never once listened to his show, had never before heard a broadcaster refer to a certain crucial organ of his own anatomy as "Zippy, the love monkey."

Then last winter, after Cowboy had that dustup with the president over just what Cowboy said on-air and during a National Press Club talk about him and the wife and kid, Walter Anderson assigned me to do a cover story for *Parade* on Dils and his show, and on the swiftly building nationwide cult that wasn't content simply to follow the program but came close to canonizing its creator and host. A serious intellectual journal termed Cowboy "a Will Rogers for our time" while a sober editorialist insisted he was "today's H. L. Mencken." Not since Ed Murrow or Arthur Godfrey, to touch opposing ends of the broadcast spectrum, had there been so much debate, much of it heated, about a guy who made his living talking into a microphone. His behavior was outrageous but, unlike a Rush Limbaugh or Bob Grant, Cowboy had wit. Of course, Howard Stern was funny and had his following as well. But Howard was hostile, angry at people. Cowboy found the world, and himself, slightly ridiculous and a constant source of amused irritation, his noisy rage an act to mask vulnerability. His own.

And despite being competitive, he was anything but your ordinary "shock jock," neither envious nor mean. He considered Don Imus "some sort of genius." And he tolerated Stern, telling an interviewer, "It was Howard they invented the V-chip for."

After listening for two weeks to prepare myself to interview the guy, I was as hooked as any cabdriver or cop or Columbia Law professor, all of them typical of the fiercely loyal following that had sprung up around the man and his show. Cowboy was as irresistible as the scene of an accident; you had to stop and shudder at the damage, amazed there were survivors. He was politically incorrect, intolerant of "phonies," which in his world seemed to be most of us, read omnivorously and with intelligence (that he had no social life to speak of and was a famous insomniac helped provide plenty of reading time), had for years kept a collection of rattlesnakes that traveled with him, and was compulsively insistent on performing a daily litmus paper analysis of his own urine, being convinced that it provided an infallible indicator of one's buoyant good health or impending terminal illness. Among his other fixations: jogging, diet, and the near-religious patronizing of very specific brands of photographic film, yogurt, wristwatches, bottled water, four-wheel-drive vehicles, leather gloves, men's drawers, and Korean fruit stands. And he hated Roller Blades, men who dyed their hair, and adults who whistled unless it was for a taxi.

"Good Gawd A-mighty!" he would implore his sidekick, Harry Almond, "do I need whistling along with my other burdens?"

Beyond all that, his various tics and quirks, he had simply the best, most authoritative, reassuring, confidential, broadcast-quality voice in the business. Cowboy, I swiftly came to realize, was contagious.

Which, it occurred to some people, including a small but vicious fringe which truly hated him, might one day make Dils dangerous.

He was about fifty when we met, lean, lank, leathery, ruggedly handsome with a craggy face that was all angles, no curves, long-haired and skinny. He claimed to be six-two and was maybe five-ten and even when he jogged or swam, and maybe when he slept, wore a cowboy hat. But unlike Garth Brooks or some of those other "country" boys, he wasn't "all hat and no cattle." The Dilses were ranchers out there in New Mexico, substantial people, and had been for generations. Cowboy could ride and rope and could, as he occasionally informed his audience to the shock of animal lovers and the more effete city people, castrate a calf with the best of them. "That's what a steer is," he would thoughtfully explain, "a bull without balls," and then launch into a description of ghastly precision as to just how you used a knife to do the deed, a broadcast moment which invariably drew cries of protest from the long-suffering Harry Almond. Such crudities aside, and with all his reading, when he chose Dils could speak a flowing and even eloquent English. Cowboy had been married several times and this seemed an especial irritant so that he rarely spoke of former wives. He'd gone through a "groupie" stage while still drinking at Hurley's, down the street from Radio City, inspiring Almond, famously and on-air, to remark that his girlfriends were so young, "Cowboy drops them when they move on to solid food." Harry, who was happily married himself, had over time grown more sensitive to this aspect of Cowboy and it was one of the few subjects on which he would no longer needle Dils.

His show was called "Cowboy in the Morning" and it had the highest-rated morning drive radio numbers in the country and for about twenty-four months had also been simulcast over one of the big cable channels with automated cameras panning around the cramped radio studio, in essence, taking pictures of people sitting there talking, drinking coffee, scratching themselves, cueing up records and commercials, threatening "fistfights," wearing cowboy hats, eating cornflakes, tossing wadded-up spitballs at each other, and on memorable occasions, a close-up of Harry flossing the Almond teeth. It was the stupidest television ever and people doted on it.

Dils had a small but devoted (except in moments of rebellion and threatened mutiny, which were frequent) team of merry pranksters who, with Cowboy, wrote all the skits, did all the voices, and helped out with such brief distractions as news, weather, traffic and the ball scores, all of which Cowboy, he made quite clear, considered impertinent intrusions into his precious airtime. They went on the air here in the East at 5:30 A.M. and were on until ten, broadcasting from that big broadcast center out in Astoria where WFAN covers sports twenty-four hours a day and Cosby tapes his show, from a subterranean studio Cowboy invariably referred to, and with mingled pride and loathing, as "the führer bunker."

When I went over there the first time to do the story, I met them all: Almond, his closest friend and longest collaborator, sometimes referred to on-air, for his piety, as either "Cotton Mather" or "Parson Weems." Almond was a straitlaced Bible reader and solid family man who wrote some of the gamiest material they aired and who would, on occasion, protest his own lines: "Cowboy, how can you stoop to this?" There was streetsmart Maguire, the producer and rebel, lovingly tolerated; Sal, the engineer; the Sports Geek (he had a name but was never identified except as "the Sports Geek"), who provided the scores; Annie Willow, who was fat and forty and could sound nineteen and sexy, who did all the female voices from Mother Teresa to a whacked-out Courtney Love to the first female cadet at the Citadel (Harry played the entire male student body, all the chauvinist pig cadets singing "Dixie" and stealing her bras); the rotund comic and master impersonator Jersey Fats; a driver/bodyguard, a former New York homicide cop, Ed Guzik, naturally renamed "Greasy Thumb" after the post-Capone Chicago mobster, Greasy Thumb Guzik; and Cowboy's combination secretary/factotum, a Vietnamese boat person known to all, both on and off the air, as Dr. Fu Manchu.

"I used to have a manservant, Abercrombie. Very fine manservant, lent a note of class, did a fine spitshine. Ironed my shirts, as well. But he refused to do voices or be in skits so I sacked him and hired Fu. I don't have to put up with manservants that won't do voices, do I?"

All these people appeared on the show both as themselves and as one or more of its fictional characters. There were literally hundreds of these as conjured up by the fecund (some insisted *warped* was the operative adjective) minds of Cowboy and Harry Almond. Some of the characters were actual or historical figures, others were simply made up, or cribbed from the movies or early radio. In the *Parade* piece that I did there wasn't space to list them all, but I tried to provide a typical sampling:

A drunken Boris Yeltsin, Snoop Doggy Dog, Cardinal O'Connor, Fibber McGee and Molly, Pancho Villa, various inmates of the Betty Ford Clinic on a night of the full moon, Donald Trump, Elvis in Purgatory, Chief Moosejaw of the Totem Pole Casino, Senator D'Amato, Charles Darnay of *A Tale of Two Cities* as portrayed by Ronald Colman, the Dalai Lama, Leona Helmsley, Irabu of the Yankees, Holden Caulfield of *Catcher in the Rye*, Vic and Sade Gook and their son Rush, Colour-sergeant Lejaune of *Beau Geste*, Caesare Borgia, Eva Peron, Betty Boop, Hitler, "King of the Khyber Rifles," Ted Kennedy, O. J. Simpson, the Bogie of *Casablanca*, Joey Buttafuoco, the Marquis de Sade on a bad hair day, all four of Bing Crosby's sons, Cronkite, Katharine Hepburn, the pope, Vinny the Chin Gigante, Duke Wayne, Jesse Jackson, Giorgio Armani, Truman Capote, Ricardo Montalban, General MacArthur, the Mayflower Madam and Bill Blass. Greasy Thumb, hired as a bodyguard, turned out to have a positive gift, flopping in a short-lived skit called "Officer Ed" but flourishing as sepulchral-voiced "Mr. Gloomy," host of "The Bad News Hour" and one of the show's audience favorites, cataloging each day's disaster with solemn glee: volcano eruptions, tidal waves, boa constrictors slithering out of a typical Manhattan apartment's toilet, meteor collisions, outbreaks of bubonic plague, El Niño, killer bees, landslides, global warming, giant tarantulas, Greyhound buses swallowed by quicksand, shark attacks, and "a New Ice Age."

In addition to his other virtues, Cowboy was paranoid. Like the James Thurber character of a long-ago yarn, he had an unreasoned fear of being struck by a comet: "They aim these things at me." So that in a way, the "Mr. Gloomy" character, one of his more manic inspirations, tapped the primal fears in all of us. Especially in Dils himself.

Dils also disliked most of his neighbors: "Oh, I'm sure they're perfectly decent people. But I lack small talk and feel no compunction whatever to discuss the weather. Nor do I like having to smile and shake hands. Or have people come up and attempt to initiate some sort of immediate intimacy. There are four billion people on earth. Am I supposed to say hello to everyone?"

At his splendid new place on the ocean in Southampton on Gin Lane, for which he paid $12 million last year, he already had some glorious feuds raging, being convinced, for one thing, that they rang the church bells on Sunday at St. Andrew's Dune Church not to summon the faithful to prayer but to irritate him. Real guns were not to be fired in the village but Cowboy had an old Red Ryder air rifle, with which he was an excellent shot, and he used the weapon against a roster of favorite targets: the belfry of St. Andrews, local dogs he caught peeing on his lawn, and for shooting out a lightbulb on a shed of the Bathing Corporation beach club because "They shine it at me in the night." Various neighbors, the church, the beach club, land developer Wyseman Clagett and the village brought lawsuits and he countersued in return. All this during the first six months after he moved in. His customary description of the neighbors en masse? "Seersucker white trash." Now that another Southampton Season would shortly be starting up, Cowboy was quite convinced (without the slightest evidence) of plots being laid by the neighbors against his life: "Innocence and boyish joie de vivre didn't save the Lindbergh baby, did they?"

And when the pious Harry Almond attempted to defend at least the local church against his employer's wrath, Dils responded shrewdly, "Then if it's the house of God, why the hell do they have a cannon out front? You've seen it there, rusting and sinister. Answer me that, Parson Weems!"

In these skirmishes he won some, lost some, and suffered the odd humiliation. Surely Cowboy's worst Southampton moment came late in his first summer when ninety-year-old Magistrate Hobbes, hearing a civil complaint brought by a maiden lady who caught Dils cursing as he passed the village cemetery, handed down a ruling that Cowboy felt unfair and probably unconstitutional. And, in an unguarded moment on-air, overriding Harry Almond's cautionary protests, he called the magistrate "that senile old fool!"

Hobbes was neither senile nor a fool. But he was very old, and with exquisite timing, the magistrate took a seizure and died three days after Cowboy insulted him from coast to coast on radio and cable television.

Dils knew a truly awkward moment when he encountered one, and admitted so next morning on the air: "Well, what can I say? This is all very embarrassing." Then, prompted by Almond: "And an enormous personal loss as well."

Denying he was difficult, Dils frequently insisted to his audience that he was a "child of God," claiming to be misunderstood and "the most reasonable of men." He liked to inform listeners, especially those in the Bible Belt, "I love sweet baby Jesus. Out there on the ranch, amid the mesas and Navajos, I was raised to say my prayers every night. And I did, too. Just as I pray now for the soul of Magistrate Hobbes. Even back in that unhappy era when I was stoned, still drinking vodka, and frequenting women of easy virtue, I continued to recite, 'Now I lay me down to sleep...' Evil and sinful as I knew myself to be, I still fell to my knees and was not embarrassed to do so, despite being in the presence of loose women or my drug dealer du jour. And not many sinners out there can say that, I assure you."

But a Southampton Town trustee remarked sourly, "I'd trade Dils away in a heartbeat for a half dozen Martha Stewarts and a player to be named later," shrugging off Martha's own and well-deserved Hamptons' reputation for, let us say, wanting her own way.

Or, as Maguire put it about his boss, "He was born pissed off and got worse." Harry Almond, the only one permitted even under duress to address Cowboy by his given name, did it rarely. "Now, Leicester..." he would begin admonishingly, with Cowboy hurling back, "Don't you 'Now, Leicester' me, you pencil-necked Baptist Bible-thumper..."

He and Southampton were mutually exclusive; each being everything the other wasn't.

Cowboy started out as a disc jockey (back when payola was routine, an honored tradition, and cocaine the drug of choice) who really knew his music, country and western, rock, and jazz. He could tell you the sidemen on an obscure Patsy Cline cut or a familiar Coleman Hawkins, and who arranged this John Coltrane song or that. Dils actually had known Kid Ory and Earl "Fatha" Hines in San Francisco in the Hungry I and Purple Onion days, and down in the French Quarter hung with the Assunto brothers. He knew Artie Shaw and Brubach and Nancy Wilson and Miles Davis and Stan Getz and Sarah and Lady Day and could tell you which of the Dorsey boys was the real stuff. He sloughed off some of the contemporary stars and lionized such long-dead singers as Ruth Brown and Dinah Washington. And he loved country! One morning he had George Jones on and spent nearly the entire four and a half hours playing George's records and reminiscing with Jones about sidemen both had known and gin mills in which both had done a little drinking and about how George packed a Smith & Wesson revolver he used to shoot holes in the floor of a rented un-air-conditioned touring bus to cool it off as the band rolled from one gig to another through the Texas summer. And they yarned about the Marine Corps.

But on the morning I drove out of Manhattan headed for East Hampton, Cowboy was talking about another variety of music. Cowboy had moved the show, cast, crew, engineer and all, to the Hamptons for a week or two, and they were broadcasting from his own house, where one of his Gin Lane neighbors had done or said something grievously offensive to Dils and Cowboy was on the counteroffensive and pondering vengeance.

"Now, Leicester..." Almond began.

"I'll show the bastards. I'll make them sorry they ever tangled with me. Maguire!"

"Yes, boss."

"Get Fu Manchu in here with my Rolodex."

"Right away, boss."

When the secretary arrived with the rolo, steno pad at the ready, Cowboy was already in full flight, all of this on-air, I remind you:

"Listen to me, you benighted heathen lascar, and get it right. I want to throw a party this weekend on Gin Lane. Saturday night. Start making the phone calls, issuing the invitations, providing directions. Get some of the heavy metal groups out here to play. Set them up right out there on the lawn. Lots of amplifiers. Big speakers, industrial strength. Those searchlights they use for movie premieres. Rent a couple of them. Get some gangsta rappers. Lots of guys in dreadlocks running around Gin Lane smoking ganja. Get Puff Daddy and Marilyn Manson to perform. Butthole Surfers and Heavy D. and Insane Clown Posse. Smashing Pumpkins. Good, loud groups. Guys like Violent J and Shaggy 2 Dope. Paul McCartney's in-laws live in East Hampton: the Eastmans. See if Paul's in town. Nine Inch Nails. Tha Dogg Pound. You know that rap group that won the Grammy, Bone Thugs-N-Harmony? They were arrested last year for explosives. They'd fit in with Southampton, wouldn't they, blowing up things and doing rap? Courtney Love if she's on this coast. Are Keith Richards and Mick still touring? Man, think of Jagger and Richards on my lawn, smoked out of their birds and gyrating. Love Spit Love, they're a must! I wish to hell they hadn't bumped off Tupac and Biggie Smalls. Wouldn't that be the best? Tupac and Biggie on Gin Lane! Keep the party going all night. Naked women dancing. U2 out there on the front lawn playing 'Achtung Baby.' Blondes dancing with Tupac and four-hundred-pound black guys in dreadlocks. Daft Punk and Sneaker Pimps. Electric guitars. Sound and light shows. Fireworks! Fu, do we have an entry in there under 'pyrotechnics'? What about Oasis? Are they in the States? Just imagine them here, with Noel and Liam Gallagher out there on the lawn, duking it out, gouging and biting, kneeing in the groin and rabbit-punching."

He paused to savor imagery. But briefly. "Motorcycles. Have we got a PR contact for the Hell's Angels, Maguire?"

"Right away, chief, I'll call Peggy Siegal. She's handling the account, I believe."

"Stretch limos, white ones, double-parked all up and down Gin Lane. Choppers landing and taking off on the front lawn. What about Suge Knight of Death Row Records? He still in jail?"

"Nine years for parole violation."

"Damn shame. Ol' Suge naked out on the lawn two in the morning, that'd be something. I suppose they don't give weekend furloughs?"

"I'll inquire, chief," Maguire promised.

But Cowboy was off on another tack.

"Firing my Red Ryder air rifle. Up on the roof stalking the widow's walk, my own damned widow's walk that I bought along with the house! Shooting at things. BBs ricocheting off the bell in Saint Andrew's tower. And later on, toward dawn, everyone naked, stoned and sleeping it off on the lawn, throwing up now and then to settle their stomachs, with servants solicitously moving among the guests passing around the bicarbonate, the Alka Seltzer, the Rolaids. A fernet branca for the sophisticates. Towelettes and mouthwash for tidying up. I'll show Gin Lane! Senile old drunks out here playing golf and sipping gin and tonic and acting superior in their saddle shoes and foulards and canary-yellow slacks. I'll give them canary-yellow slacks. I'll give them foulards . . ."

A moment later, quite cool and controlled, he was smoothly, persuasively reading a BMW commercial and selling cars at a national rate of $12,000 per thirty seconds (extra if Cowboy read the ad himself). While the unfortunate Fu Manchu, swift and efficient, was being chewed out for having acted rashly, in reckless haste, in prematurely issuing the first few invitations to Cowboy's party and nailing down RSVPs from groups to perform a Saturday night frolic along Gin Lane.

"Just horsing around, Fu. Just horsing around. Don't take me so goddamned literal."

"No, sir, esteemed and honorable leader..."

The Sports Geek was giving last night's baseball scores when I pulled into Gracie's Hots in Manorville, not for one of her famous dogs with kraut and mustard but for the usual Styrofoam coffee with an ice cube in there, so you wouldn't burn your mouth drinking it and go off the damned road. This was the semi-official gateway to the Hamptons, where Gracie did everything but stamp passports and check visas. Here was where you passed through to a greener, jollier place, the other side of the biblical hill. John Bunyan's Pilgrim, in his progress, would have sensed a change as they crossed, he and Mr. Standfast and Mr. Valiant-for-Truth and the rest of them. I'm like that, like a character in Bunyan's allegory, each time I come back to the Hamptons, it's yet again a sort of powerful mystical experience, and I very nearly get religious. Especially when I get to Montauk Highway opposite the Southampton Burger King, and see the church. You know, that boxy little evangelical church with the sign out front advertising that week's sermon or quoting from the psalms. The message on this spring morning?

"Forgive the nouveau riche. They know not what they do."

I meditated on that for half a mile or so, as people in my family do, enjoying a good ponder (might Cowboy Dils be among those forgiven? Okay, Lord. And Donald Trump?) and communing with the deities. Probably that's a genetic hangover I've got, being descended from several reverends on the Beecher side of the clan, but already, you had to admit, the air smelled better.

# f i v e

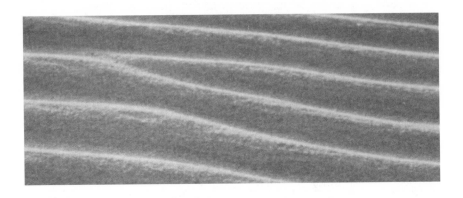

*Molly the cow charging at Christie Brinkley and the children . . .*

I'd not been to East Hampton since last Thanksgiving but it looked fine. A few new houses were going up, big, sprawling ones, the raw wood of the framework stark against the green spring and the deep blue of a cloudless sky, streaked with the thin white contrails of the daily Concorde crossing from Paris. Or London. Perched atop the wooden frameworks were suntanned, sinewy young men up there hammering and sawing and using carpenters' levels.

People who lived here already, who had theirs, hated to see new construction, filling the last empty spaces, what little open farmland we had left. But that was the way of the world; new people wanted places, too. It was also the market, I suppose, with the Dow above 8,000, people had to do something with the money. And it meant jobs. That, too, was important for local folk, the laboring men up there on the framework, hammering and sawing, nailing down shingle or fitting in window frames. Houses were always going up. Good wages and honest work, right here in the Hamptons and not having to commute fifty miles Up-Island to Huntington or Oyster Bay. Oddly, with all the construction, there were more deer than ever and no one could recall when so many red foxes hunted, even on the fairways of the Maidstone Club. Our own place looked in good shape, even with my father in Europe, and there with him as well, Inga the housekeeper. The big house was shut up and since it seemed all right from the outside, I didn't bother finding a key to check. My place was the gatehouse, much smaller and up front, back from the beach and bordering on Further Lane. That looked pretty good, too. Joe Marciniak took care of the lawn and looked in every day in the cold months to be sure no pipes had burst, no vandalisms had been committed. If serious work had to be done, Dale Uhll, our contractor, came and did it. You found a capable, reliable man like Dale Uhll, you stayed with him. The tennis court looked as crummy as it usually did, aging badly, and we just didn't play enough to wear down the weeds coming up through the cracks.

Too bad Leo Brass had been killed during the hurricane last September. I didn't like Leo much, nor did a lot of people, but he would have been the one to call about getting hold of a couple of talkative Baymen. I called Tom Knowles at the police station. But Tom had recently transferred out, they said. He was a detective for the county now, working out of Riverhead. More money and a promotion, I guess.

I walked down to the ocean beach and took my shoes off. No matter the early spring; the water was still too cold to swim. For my tastes, anyway. My old man would probably have been right in there. He's something, the Admiral. Back at the house I sat down and wrote a letter to Alix (in the same cipher she uses and taught me) at her London flat, asking about this mysterious wedding on Gin Lane and when she'd be here. She hadn't included a Paris address in her letter or I would have sent it there. Up in the village there's a stationery store called the File Box and they send and receive faxes for me when I'm in town so I drove up there in the Chevy Blazer and chatted for a time with the ladies who run the store and gave them my fax to send. To them it was just bunches of numbers and not some fairly sexy stuff I'd written for Alix's eyes only. The ladies at the File Box were one reason I didn't buy a fax machine of my own; this way it got me out of the house and into the village to send a fax. That's what correspondence has come down to, E-mail and faxes, even love letters, which was why, exasperating as she could be, it was good getting a genuine letter from Her Ladyship, with actual stamps stuck on and the stationery smelling of her scent, the glue of the envelope flap recalling the lick of her tongue. Then I went around the corner to the Blue Parrot for a Pacifico.

Roland was on the bar, very suntanned. He's the manager and when they shut down every year just before Christmas, he takes off for Puerto Rico to surf, and they'd just reopened. Lee the owner, who has a place in Hawaii, was back as well but nowhere to be seen. Lee keeps a low profile unless there is absolutely no way he can avoid work. I took a stool and Roland opened a beer for me. Things, he said, were pretty slow. Except that Uma Thurman, all six feet of her, had been glimpsed doing pilates on the beach? . . .

"Pilates?"

"Stretching and strengthening exercises. When she isn't doing pilates on the beach, Uma's up at Nick and Toni's smoking cigarettes. I wish she'd come in here and smoke cigarettes. Or do pilates."

That was the kind of woman they liked at the Parrot: hardbodies who smoked.

"And Kim Basinger's raising hell again." Oh, what was that all about?

"Beagles."

Last year Ms. Basinger's husband, Alec Baldwin, had something of a second career writing long letters to the *East Hampton Star*, our weekly newspaper, about the failure of the local trash collection franchise to separate out the various recyclables, newspapers, bottles, cans, organic garbage, and so on. But beagles? That was a new one.

"What about beagles?" I said.

It turned out there was an animal lab in East Millstone, New Jersey ("Nice name for a place, don't you think?" Roland remarked), where they had forty beagle puppies scheduled to have their legs broken so as to try out the regenerative powers of a new drug for osteoporosis manufactured by an outfit called Yamanouchi USA. The plan was to snap the dogs' little legs and then see if the drug did much if anything toward healing the bones. When Kim Basinger and others started raising hell, the Japanese outfit agreed to halt the experiment and give the forty puppies to Ms. Basinger, who told reporters she was ready to take the forty dogs to a waiting plane and fly them to a sanctuary out west where trainers would socialize them and find them homes. "People are waiting with open arms to give them love," she said.

Except that, in East Millstone, the animal lab people refused to give up the dogs to Kim on grounds they'd been raised for research purposes and would not make suitable pets.

Someone had managed to sneak inside the lab, the actress said, and shoot a video of scientists laughing, joking, and putting on "German accents" while strapping down live animals and cutting into them. The whole story was turning into an episode of *Stalag 17*. Or, more aptly, *Hogan's Heroes*. Anyway, I'd heard sufficient of the story and cried, "Okay, Roland, enough!" I'm aware of the need to use lab animals in scientific experimentation but on this one I found myself siding with Kim Basinger. Besides, I was trying to have a quiet beer after six months of not having been to East Hampton or visiting the Blue Parrot, and did I need horror stories? And didn't Roland have a small dog of his own, Little Bit, and should Little Bit be sitting here atop a bar stool nibbling nachos and listening to this stuff? We don't need any more neurotic dogs out here. Though I did wonder, briefly, why "Cowboy in the Morning" hadn't picked up on Kim Basinger and the beagles and done a skit. Fu Manchu could have done the Japanese characters and Jersey Fats the German accents. Surely Cowboy hadn't passed on the material out of delicacy; men who grow up on working ranches are hardly sentimental about animals, even pet dogs. Maybe Annie Willow couldn't do a good "Kim Basinger"; that must be it.

Oh, yes, there were two political campaigns under way. The Democrats were going all out this year to save the shellfish hatchery. While the Republicans were pushing the right to drive on the beach. There were dueling bumper stickers from each party. What else was going on?

Pam Phythian was still out on bail and no trial date had been set in the unfortunate death of Hannah Cutting. Most villagers sided with Pam, even if she was accused of having bumped off Hannah (and suspected of doing likewise to Leo Brass) and there was residual ill feeling on the part of a few toward me for having nailed her. Meanwhile, three writers with impeccable feminist credentials were preparing books about the case, justifying Pam's actions, and at ABC there were reports Jamie Tarses had a miniseries in the works with Sharon Stone penciled in as "Pam," though with the family name spelled as "Fithian" to circumvent the state's Son of Sam law, intended to prevent felons from getting rich (or richer) on their crimes.

As for Leo Brass, fatally stabbed at the height of last September's hurricane, no indictments had been brought. Which was, as Alix might have said, hard cheese on Leo.

Last summer's swami, Mr. Kurt, had been arrested on warrants issued in several states but his acolytes, most of them wealthy local women, expressed their confidence in Swami and were raising a legal defense fund. Martha Stewart and developer Harry Macklowe were at it again. This time it was a disputed fence which Macklowe forces attempted to build in the night only to be interrupted when an understandably irked Martha sped up in her pickup truck and demanded they demolish the damned thing. He wanted her arrested for menacing his men; she wanted warrants against him for trespass. I thought they were both being silly but you had to score Martha a ten on sheer guts.

A local tradesman we all knew had been found wandering drunk on Fresno Place early one evening and told police he had secret information there were plots by the Cali drug cartel to blow him up and he was merely trying to throw off his assailants by pretending to be intoxicated. Jerry Della Femina was intent on selling off some of his properties, though not the house, following settlement of his lawsuit against the village. And the town trustees, men who looked ahead on behalf of all of us, were considering a closure over Fourth of July weekend of Georgica Beach.

"On the biggest beach weekend of the Season?"

"The piping plovers, you know," Roland reminded me.

"Oh, yeah. They nest on the beaches along there."

"But Larry Cantwell, speaking for the village, says such a closure is not enforceable. They may go to law."

Town versus village, yet again, this time over some birds' nests on the beach. "Sounds like a normal spring so far," I said, and Roland opened another Pacifico. Had one himself, too, breaking a rule.

More difficulty as well for Christie Brinkley. "What now?" I asked.

"She's being harassed by a cow. Name of Molly. Seems when she and Peter Cook signed the lease on this Bridgehampton farm, there was a resident cow and they were amenable. Fine, let the cow stay. No problem.

Except, according to Christie, 'Then it started charging at our nanny and my children. It had to go.'"

I was taking this all in. Reporters do that; you never know on a slow day when you might need a story. Roland sucked a quartered lime and sipped delicately from his bottle of Pacifico (the Blue Parrot had its genteel moments as well) and went on.

"Molly the cow was relocated but went over the hill and came back. Charging people again. Even the cops when Christie called. It was getting ugly but Christie denies she ever got to shouting at the cow, 'You're hamburger!'"

Despite their aggro, Christie and Peter were still on the farm and had renewed for another year.

The big news in Bridgehampton dealt, as things usually did out here, with land. Some big developers headed by Southampton attorney and power broker Wyseman Clagett (his partners remained anonymous and were trying to keep it that way) were seeking control of the old automobile raceway where sportscar racing in America pretty much began in the early 1950s. There'd been racing here back in the '20s sponsored by the Bridgehampton Lions, but it was road racing then, through the farms and over the little bridges and down Ocean Road past the little red schoolhouse and one driver was killed and spectators hurt when a speeding car collected them into a potato field, and that did it for the Lions. They pulled their sponsorship and the sport died until after the war, when wealthy amateur race drivers revived it on the Bridgehampton raceway. That was maybe the only big parcel of land left out here in the Hamptons that hadn't been raped. Although that's unfair of me to say. Close by was the Atlantic, the big country club the rich Jews started a couple of years ago. These were wealthy men who enjoyed golf but couldn't join the National or Shinnecock or Maidstone because they were Jewish. Hard to believe there were still requirements like that in America. Or even in the Hamptons, but there they were. I mean, men like Bruce Wasserstein could buy and sell all of us. Spielberg, the best moviemaker in America. The Lauders. Perelman of Revlon who bought the biggest estate we have, the Creeks. Rich men, powerful men, brilliant men. Ralph Lauren, Calvin Klein, Mort Zuckerman, who owned ... well, he owned a lot of things. But they weren't wanted in certain locker rooms. The refreshing thing about it was that the rich Jews, instead of whining or writing letters to the *Times* or organizing committees of protest, did something positive.

They founded their own club. Quite conceivably the best one out here. Charged charter members a million dollars to join. To hell with the WASPs.

As a WASP, I liked their style, rather admired the men of the Atlantic. And now developers wanted to turn a clapped-out old sports car race course into money.

"You know this Karl Lager?" Roland asked.

"Sure, the 'noblest fashion designer of them all.'" I mean that—the guy was so implausibly handsome and dashing, Cubby Broccoli once thought of casting him as James Bond instead of Connery.

"There's talk he and some other old guys are going to pull some wild protest during the Memorial Day weekend."

"What d'you mean, 'wild'?"

"I dunno. Stage an illegal race or something. They're pissed off over Wyseman Clagett's plans to develop the old Bridgehampton raceway."

Here I'd been concluding we were having a perfectly normal Hamptons spring, and the place was starting to sound like Bosnia.

"Lager and Carroll Shelby. A. J. Foyt. Stirling Moss. Maybe King Richard Petty. Baron von Kronk. People like that? . . ."

That pulled me up short. Von Kronk? He was dead, wasn't he? Killed on the hairpin turn at Monza. Or was it Le Mans? Driving one of those big Auto Union cars years ago. Or had he just lost his leg? I can't keep my old race car drivers straight. I'd better call Lager, who had a big place out here with his wife, a farmhouse that would have looked right at home in Nebraska or Iowa, one of those big states out west where they grow stuff. Karl's place was up on a hill off Scuttle Hole Road near the old Bridgehampton racetrack. I guess Lager liked to sit there on his rocking chair and remember. I'd read somewhere he was feuding again with John Fairchild and *W* magazine so I knew Karl would be talkative; problem was to get him talking about the race course and not the conniving and wickedness of fashion editors.

Von Kronk, dead or alive, one-legged or two, was one of the great Kraut drivers. Started with Auto Union. Later drove Mercedes. Karl Lager was a Kraut, too, and a Jew as well, who'd gotten out of Berlin as a small boy when the Hitler time began. Off to voluntary exile in Shanghai, to the International Settlement and all those White Russians. Then to London, where he was enrolled in a good public school. He became a fashion designer next, for Charles Creed or at the House of Worth or someone like that ... came to New York. Got an assistant's job on Seventh Avenue. And then ... when we got into the war, there was Karl Lager, as if put here on earth by God specifically to help FDR beat Hitler.

Fascinating guy. One of the best interviews ever. And think of him in 1941 or '42, a German, speaking prefect *"Ich bin ein Berliner"* German (though what that really meant in the Berlin slang was "I am a jelly doughnut"), and handsome, looking more Aryan than Boris Becker, and here he was ready and willing to do the nasty on the Nazis. So Lager was seconded to the OSS, parachuted into the old Fatherland, and blew up things and shot people, and ended the war a captain. Herr Hauptmann Lager! The whole story was as good a yarn as *The Scarlet Pimpernel* and could have made a swell operetta by Strauss. Or maybe Victor Herbert. And then, talk about anticlimaxes, our hero went back to designing women's sportswear. Successful at it as well, and soon had plenty of the folding, as Philip Marlowe used to put it. He and Bill Blass and Bill Fine, who ran *Harper's Bazaar* and later Bonwit Teller, they were pals. Lager also had enemies.

What was it John Fairchild had against him? Why did *Women's Wear Daily* invariably refer to Karl, if it did at all, as "premium Lager"? I must find out one of these days.

Richard Ryan and Craig Wright and Buddy Pontick and other regulars drifted in now to the Parrot so I had one more. Then Buddy started on his passion, which was growing bamboo, and how certain species bloomed only every century or so but when they did every plant in that species all around the world bloomed simultaneously and then choked on its own flowers and died off.

"It was that which nearly wiped out the giant panda," Buddy said. When Buddy starts in on bamboo and the pandas, I pay my tab and take off. Miss Margaret at the IGA checkout complimented me on the boneless sirloin I'd selected and said it was nice to see me back. I don't believe Miss Margaret knows my name but she's ever cordial. Full of good stories, too, about the hurricane of '38, when green water came up out of the ocean and sloshed up Egypt Lane for a mile to Main Street. Boy, that must have been something to see! Huge elms and oaks toppling and shingled roofs coming off the mansions and people being swept away and the Atlantic Ocean rushing right up for a mile through the center of town! I wonder if The Eel Lady predicted that one.

What has people confused about the Hamptons is they think it's this snob, glamorous, sophisticated place where everyone's famous and owns a private jet and your butler does the marketing. Sure, there's plenty of that; but they don't know the nice people at the IGA or Chris and Yvette who own the liquor store or Bradley the pharmacist or Bernie at Village Hardware or the young women who sell kids' clothes at Punch, or Hugh and J. J. behind the bar at the Grill, or Debbie at the public library or DeeDee who used to manage the Laundry Restaurant and now owns that new place on the Highway, Peconic Coast. Or know anything about the '38 hurricane. Or even about what people eat in the Hamptons. Do you know what the favorite breakfast is out here? No, not Dreesen's dough-nuts; they're great but it's the summer people and weekenders who buy those. The locals have what they call the "Bub Burger": a hard roll slath-ered in peanut butter. And butter. That's right, peanut butter *and* butter!

You eat that for breakfast, chances are you're a Bub.

Not me. My family's owned a place out here nearly two centuries but I wasn't born here. I was born in Paris because my old man was stationed there and my mother was French. Bub? Not on your life! You have to be born here to be a Bub (or in these times of gender equality, a Bubette). The man who owns Santa Fe Junction restaurant, near the railroad station in East Hampton, he and his wife had a baby last year, delivered in a hospital Up-Island. Not here. The parents are East Hamptoners but the kid can't be a Bub. As someone, a strict constructionist on Bub-ism, said, "If you weren't born at home in the kitchen of your own house in Springs, you ain't a Bub. Not hardly."

This early in the Season nights on the ocean could be cool, even chilly, down into the forties, and I built a fire in the den and after dinner and a chilled Brouilly I sat there in front of the fire and read some, imagining Alix back here in her tie silk robe from Liberty of London, with little or nothing underneath, curled up near me on that battered old leather chesterfield couch of mine, reading something, maybe the letters of Evelyn Waugh to Nancy Mitford, or something else amusing and literary, and putting down the book occasionally to light a cigarette or relate some extraordinary gossip straight from London via her Sloane Square and Belgravia chums, while Ella played on the stereo or Lee Wiley or the better Coltrane or anything at all from Louis Armstrong.

I can be awfully domestic and have my little romantic moments like these, as most of us do, can't you?

## s i x

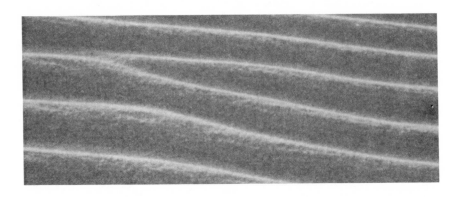

*No one here asking for autographs, Karl. Let's go home . . .*

I was awake by six next morning and tuned in to Cowboy while the coffee cooked. I stuck with the radio; the skits played better without visuals to dilute your imagination. This morning he was railing against a congressman who'd done something to irritate Dils and was being dismissed as "that moron!" and they were testing a new skit that might conceivably become a continuing series, "The Horror of the Fifty Thousand Scorpions."

In this one Jersey Fats played Baba the Sikh holy man who, in attempting to get into the Guinness Book of World Records, and thereby earn contributions to his favority charity (Second Homes for Untouchables), was spending a month in a sealed crypt with fifty thousand live scorpions. As the skit opens, the scorpions are crawling all over his face and head, into his ears and nostrils, and under his shirt and even inside his boxer shorts, while Baba croons soothing rubbish to the scorpions to mollify them, keep them from becoming annoyed and stinging him. Dr.

Fu Manchu, hissing and crackling in irritation, plays all fifty thousand of the scorpions, and every so often Jersey, as Baba the holy man, lets out an agonized scream as if having been randomly stung and interjects sobs, moans, prayers and curses amid the crooning. After about a minute and a half an impatient Cowboy had had enough and out of displeasure blew them all up with his nuclear explosion sound effect. You got the impression "The Horror of the Fifty Thousand Scorpions" wasn't destined to fly as a regular feature on "Cowboy in the Morning" and I took my coffee into the bathroom to shower and shave.

Arnold Leo, who'd taken over as chief of the Baymen after Brass was killed, was away and none of the Baymen I had names and phone numbers for were home and so I called ahead and drove over to Southampton to see Lager the designer.

Southampton and East Hampton border one another, the town line drawn just east of Bridgehampton, which has its own name but is officially part of Southampton, and where Karl and Melisande Lager have their dozen acres, half of it in corn rented to a local farmer.

Sandy greeted me and took the drinks order while Karl and I went outside to talk. "Tell me what it was like in the old days, the Bridgehampton raceway and how it got started. I may do a piece."

Lager liked to tell stories; told a good one:

"They'd discontinued the old Bridgehampton road races back in the twenties. Too dangerous. But in the early fifties some local people, quasi-gangster types who'd made a black market killing in the war, gas station tycoons and the like, decided the Hamptons had a future and why not build a permanent raceway, stands and all, to attract some big auto races out here. Other people joined in, including wealthy amateurs, and they got it open about 1957. Unfortunately, it was very badly built. The grandstands were too small and the road surface was inadequately ballasted and began breaking up right away. But they raced on it anyway. Dave Garroway raced an old Jag painted yellow that he called 'Mother.' Carroll Shelby raced. Stirling Moss. Bob Donner and Augie Pabst. John Surtees and McLaren and Denis Hulme from New Zealand. Charles Addams, the cartoonist, drove a blue Bugatti. Mario Andretti and Dan Gurney and Walt Hansgen. Walter Cronkite raced. You know who John Perona was, operated El Morocco? He owned a couple of Allards. I drove one of them for him for a time. There was a beer millionaire who raced a three-Ferrari team, driving one car himself while his two homosexual lovers drove the others. They were something, those three. They raced boats, raced cars, flew gliders. Fearless, those boys. The lovers are both dead; the beer man's still alive but not racing anymore. Other big drivers came. A lot of the Sebring drivers. Men I knew from the OSS who'd stayed on to create the CIA, fellows who liked to take chances off the job as well, hang-gliding and scuba diving and driving fast cars against other fast cars. They heard about Bridgehampton and came out. For about fifteen minutes it was chic as hell. But when they learned how bad the track was, the good ones, they never came back.

"And racing out here changed from the amateur wealthy to grease monkeys and scruffy types. It would have cost ten or twelve million to fix it up properly so the track never got repaired. Yet it was used over and over. People raced but no one came to see them. Then a man called Robert Rubin bought it a dozen or so years ago. He thought about rebuilding the track properly but that didn't fly so now he's on to building a golf course and putting up houses on maybe twenty four-acre spreads. Nice man. Loves the race course, I believe. He's the one Wyseman Clagett wants to squeeze out.

"By the sixties or early seventies, it stopped being the chic place to go. I walked over it recently with a driver friend of mine, a Brit, and he turned to me and said, 'There's no one here asking for our autographs, Karl. Let's go home.'"

I got right into it then with Lager, asking about this stunt they were supposedly planning for Memorial Day weekend.

"It has a name, an honorable name," Karl Lager said, "it is called 'civil disobedience.'" Far from being annoyed at breaches in security, he seemed delighted their madcap plans were the talk of Hamptons' barroom idlers.

The fashion designer and I sat sipping iced tea on the broad verandah of this wonderful new house on a hill in the open farm country off Scuttle Hole just south of where Lager raced cars in more innocent times. I didn't even like iced tea and rarely drank it but this was his house and his wife had served it, and you sip your tea and shut up. Especially when you are asking questions and trying to get some answers.

"The difference in our definition of civil disobedience is, we don't set ourselves afire or do a Gandhi, lying down in front of railroad locomotives. Not a bit of it. We tug on the old goggles and slip into the cockpit behind the wheel, hit the ignition, and begin to roll..."

Lager in full flight was something; you just had to let him run out of breath. So I sipped my tea and listened as he talked about half-baked plans for a demo to save the old track.

"...an extraordinary range of great drivers. Rednecks from the NASCAR circuit and gentlemen from Formula One. Think of Junior Johnson and Stirling Moss on the same lap. Roger Penske and Paul Newman. We get Newman and we'll have press. Everyone but Nuvolari and Ascari. If only Fangio were still alive. Surely Fangio would be flying in..."

"Realistically, how many do you think will show?" I asked.

"Couple of dozen, if we're lucky."

I arched an eyebrow. "A couple of dozen?" He was kidding himself. But I didn't say that. Instead:

"Karl, they said von Kronk was involved. I thought he was dead."

"Should be, the old bastard. Lost a leg."

"Le Mans?"

"No, Italy. The *mille miglia*. May have fallen asleep on one of those fast turns just past the bridge. Hit a tree or two, took half a forest with him. They had to cut him out of the car. Never had a chance of saving the leg. Damned shame."

"Didn't realize you two were pals."

"Weren't. We played on different teams. He was a panzer officer."

"Nazi."

"No, too much the gentleman for that; and too much the German not to fight. Surprising thing he wasn't scooped up after the assassination attempt in July of '44. That's when a lot of the aristos were pulled in. If you had a 'von' in '44, you were suspect. Hitler was paranoid about it by then, realized that if anyone were going to pull him down, it would be the old Prussians and the Swabians and the barons and Bavarian grafs. It wasn't so much they opposed his policies; they considered him beneath them."

"So the German 'resistance,' such as it was, was a matter of social standing. Snobbery. The old school tie."

Lager shrugged. "That's simplistic. But, yes..." He thought for a moment. "Hitler'd been a good soldier, awarded the Iron Cross First Class, twice. Göring was the only one of them who'd been a genuine war hero. Commanded Richthofen's Flying Circus after the Red Baron was killed. Roehm was an officer but he was gay. Himmler raised chickens. Goebbels was educated, had a doctorate, but he had a game leg and in chasing actresses he passed himself off as a wounded veteran. Ribbentrop sold champagne . . ."

Karl knew this stuff; he'd written books about the roots of Nazism, casual but canny profiles of Hitler's cronies all the way back to the Vienna flophouses and up through the "beer hall putsch." Considering he was Jewish and an exile, and had fought the Nazis during the war, his commentaries were remarkably even-handed, manifesting no personal animus against men like Schacht or Ribbentrop. He let their own words and deeds skewer them.

"Look into the Hamptons phone book. Even today, there's a von Ribbentrop listed . . ."

The Hamptons, clearly, were to be spared nothing.

"But will a demonstration work? Even with all those famous drivers? If the raceway's bought by developers, can't they do whatever they want? They own the land. They'll just pull all you guys in and issue summonses. Southampton jail for the night? Spoil your holiday as well."

"Worth it if we discommode Clagett. Mr. Rubin's a gentleman. Maybe he'll let down the barriers and permit us all a glory lap around the course at thirty miles an hour. Then perhaps a little promenade through town to show the flag, introduce Generation X to the Morgan and the TR 3 and the Dino Ferrari and the XK 120 Jag . . ."

He seemed to be seeing the old cars now, his eyes staring past me toward an empty field. Much as Costner looked out at the corn and saw Shoeless Joe Jackson. Then Lager resumed:

"I've called everyone. Actually got hold of A. J. Foyt down south somewhere. I must have been giddy by then, calling A. J. He'd always been contemptuous of sports car drivers. Called us 'sportycar drivers.' I knew I wouldn't get far with him."

In mixed amusement and exasperation, Karl said he'd confessed to Foyt that the entire business might be a waste of time, that in the end they might simply be tilting at windmills, like Don Quixote.

"That the Talladega fella drives for Budweiser?" A. J. inquired.

Lager admitted to me, "We probably can't win; just a few obsolescent old men in obsolete cars, but maybe we can embarrass them. And the money behind the development scheme is a man who doesn't embarrass graciously."

"I thought it was Clagett. He's the heavy, isn't he? Is there someone else?"

I expected Trump. Someone like that. Icahn. An outsider. But susceptible to adverse publicity. Or Breslin, the Long Island builder. I was wrong. Lager enjoyed telling a reporter something he didn't know.

"You know who Roger Champion is?"

"Sure, the broadcasting tycoon. Old now, but very nearly a great man. Why?"

"The venture capitalist putting up the cash for the Wyseman Clagett land grab to develop Bridgehampton raceway is a man who doesn't need the money. Who, in fact, is widely believed to be 'the man who has everything.' Including as a wife a great beauty named Slim Norris. It's that pillar of Southampton society, the 'doge' of Gin Lane, the 'last true gentleman' in America: Roger Champion."

"But why the hell would a man like Champion...?"

"Haven't the foggiest," Lager said, the line thrown carelessly away as if it didn't matter.

Sandy Lager gave us some more iced tea and then showed me through the house. She was so nice and the house was so comfortable and tasteful, you wondered why, at his age, her husband was intent on getting himself arrested.

He spoke of preserving the pine barrens, protecting the aquifer, respecting the estuary. I didn't buy it. You don't want to be irrelevant, do you? Not even old war heroes who once raced automobiles and made fortunes designing sportswear. I think the only thing Karl Lager wanted to save was memory, be able to sit out here on his porch close to the old track and remember the whine of the superchargers and the heavy throb of engines and the reek of fuel, perhaps even a distant cheer, and recall how it used to be.

I don't think he really gave a damn about the racetrack or the aquifer or anything else. There are touchstones to yesterday and the crappy old Bridgehampton track was one of them. To Lager, the track was nothing; he just wanted to be young again and driving fast.

There was no wind that afternoon and I got out the Old Town canoe and slung it atop the Chevy Blazer and went up to Three Mile Harbor to paddle around for a time. Didn't fall out, even once, and was never close to capsizing. Which was good; even in the bays and harbors, in mid-May the water was still pretty cold. When I got back to the house on Further Lane, sporting the first sunburned nose I'd had so far this season, there was an E-mail message from Alix.

In her familiar and accustomed six-figure cipher cribbed from the novels of John Buchan, *The Thirty-nine Steps* and all that, on which British kids of a certain class were brought up; Buchan and Kipling, *Gunga Din* and *Kim, the Boy Spy.*

"Arriving Thursday. Buchanan limo meeting me JFK. Assume I'll be properly stabled. If not, please change sheets your guest room. Wedding on Gin Lane Memorial Day. Is that May 30 query? I tracked you down through Mary Sexton. Don't be cross with her, Darling. You know she dotes on you. And I did bribe her a bit, promising to subscribe to a wonderful newspaper of hers called Novy Mir. She says it'll broaden my political horizons ever so much and that my old Pa the Earl ought read it as well. Provide him grist for speeches in the House of Lords. All love, Mountain Peak."

Thursday was tomorrow. I hadn't the vaguest idea who was getting married on Memorial Day and who was the Buchanan who sent limos to airports and "stabled" people properly. And where? Why was Lady Alix Dunraven coming to the Hamptons? And why Gin Lane?

Visions of Dave Garroway in a yellow Jag called "Mother," of Baron von Kronk lifting his wooden leg into an old Ferrari, of King Richard Petty in manacles arguing the toss with Southampton cops, of old raceways and new shopping malls, all vanished from the screen. It didn't really matter why Her Ladyship was coming to the Hamptons or who Buchanan was. A. J. Foyt drove better than any American ever had but thought Don Quixote was out of Talladega and raced stock cars, so why should I be expected to know everything?

I hadn't seen Alix since last fall. And was starting to suspect all over again I was in love with her.

Sufficient unto the day, as the wise man says. . . .

seven

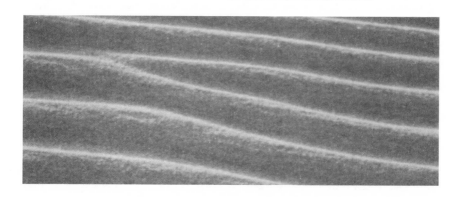

*He'd strolled the Hindu Kush and dived to 150*
*meters with Cousteau . . .*

Mysterious weddings on Gin Lane and the crackbrained plots and exotic conspiracies of Mr. Lager and his superannuated little guerrilla band of fast drivers and assorted spies and other sports were hardly the only social events scheduled to open the Season in Southampton.

Year upon year, no Season began as opulently or with better taste than the Memorial Day garden party thrown at 550 Gin Lane, the great house and stables and sloping, oceanfront lawns of Roger and Slim Champion. You know who they are, Mr. Champion, CEO, chairman and founder of International Broadcasting, and his second wife, Slim, a former stage actress regularly featured in the pages of *Quest* and *W* and *Town & Country,* either here at the Gin Lane place or at the apartment at 834 Fifth or, in its own "season," at Palm Beach, where their winter home shared an ocean with the Breakers to the north and Mollie Wilmot's great cottage to the south.

It would take two days simply to erect the green-and-white-striped marquee and an entire morning just to set out the two thousand flower boxes (the Champions' own geraniums were late this spring for reasons too horticultural to explain) while the caterers and two bands were ordered up and three of Mr. Champion's secretaries at the network's offices in Manhattan were assigned to sending invitations and charting the acceptances (very few rejections were ever called in). Working alphabetically, they heard from (in part, only): Anne Bass, Adair and Bill Beutel, Christine Biddle, the Watson Blairs, Jan Cowles, Justine Cushing, Pat and Marquette de Bary, Alessandro and Cathy di Montezemolo, Carol Dickey, Jeanne Twiname Downe, Ann Downey, Tony and Luly Drexel Duke, Lillian Fanjul, Liz Fonderas, Anne and Charlotte Ford, Ahmet and Mica Ertegun, the Goulandrises, Jamee and Peter Dickey, gorgeous Nina Griscom, Duane Hampton, Katharine Johnson and her new husband Billy who sold advertising space, Kay Meehan, Carroll Petrie, Sally Richardson, Ambassador Felix and Liz Rohatyn, Francesca Stanfill, Peter Tufo, Saul and Gayfryd Steinberg, Jean Tailer, Alfred and Judy Taubman, Lauren and John Veronis, and the Zilkhas.

On all of these, they agreed. There was considerable debate about David and Julia Koch (pronounced "coke") recently and somewhat bitingly profiled (she was from Arkansas, for one thing) in the *Times*. They were rich and had a fine place in Southampton.

"But buying Jackie Onassis's Fifth Avenue apartment and bringing in a decorator whose specialty is the stately homes of England, Slim?"

"Well, that may be a bit much."

"And ghoulish, besides. Like living atop Lenin's Tomb."

"Oh, Roger . . ."

"And their money doesn't talk. As the *Times* said, 'it shrieks'."

In the end, being a man who loved his wife and Slim wanting to see these people up close, Champion gave in.

Cowboy Dils, pointedly, was not invited.

"But he's sure to be fun, Roger," Slim Champion protested, pouting prettily.

"Let him have 'fun' on the radio," her husband sniffed. "He's an employee."

And that should have been that. Except that with Cowboy, one never knew, did one? Nor, it turned out, with the Champions.

Roger Champion disdained many of the people he knew. And most of those he didn't know. And why not? Now in his eighties, Champion had his own teeth and except for shades worn against the sun, didn't bother with glasses and could still do so many things well. And, when younger, he'd done them superbly. He'd skied with Lowell Thomas at North Conway and Tuckerman's Ravine, dived to 150 meters with Cousteau when Falco was still alive, strolled the entire length of the Hindu Kush with Sir Ranulph Fiennes, the man who walked across Antarctica. He'd been an eight-goal polo player and was a member of Augusta National, where, well into his sixties, Roger played to a handicap of an honest four. In the Florida Keys guides still spoke of tarpon he'd caught on a fly rod and of his bonefishing rivalry with Ted Williams. Even now, he was an extraordinary shot, and rarely returned from a hunt with less than a full bag of duck, partridge, pheasant, grouse.

In rare moments of humility, Champion acknowledged, "I might have been really good at something, great even, if only I could have figured out which of all the things I did, I might be able to do best."

On Wall Street, of course, they thought Roger was pretty good at running a major corporation. By his own estimate, perhaps his finest hour had come when he married Slim Norris.

There were those who didn't know quite what to make of Slim. She was beautiful, that was a given. Tall, dark-haired, slender, with great legs and carriage that relaxed at times into a slow, after-dark, pantherish tread, and a professionally trained speaking voice (she'd been a stage actress) that could project across large spaces and crowded rooms or drop to a whispered hush that, well, beckoned. But was she a great lady? Or a talented courtesan? Strategically yawning gaps in her résumé provided tantalizing hints one way or the other but never really answered the question. Men, among them men nearly as rich and almost as famous as Roger, as well as those considerably younger and therefore credited (at least by themselves!) with being more virile, gave Slim Champion a try. How could an old goat, even one as towering as Champion, satisfy a woman who looked and moved like Slim? Naturally, there was speculation, talk, pursed lips and heads together, when she'd vanished through a closing door or momentarily left a room. So men gave her a try. Had any succeeded in luring her for a night? Or even a few hours? In a village as small and inward-looking as Southampton, wouldn't it have gotten quickly out? Men gossip about such things and with Slim the paucity of gossip seemed to have slammed the door on that vulgar but essential question: Does she or doesn't she?

Except that, one night at the Meadow Club, the question was raised aloud. In his cups, a nationally ranked twenty-eight-year-old squash player came to blows with a sixty-year-old railroad baron; one defending Slim Champion's honor, the other boasting "I've been there, damn you!" I was never able to learn which one was the cad, which the defender. And since this was the Meadow Club, the thing was swiftly and with brisk efficiency hushed up.

To some people, the Champions among them, Gin Lane was the last, best place in America. East Hampton, just over a dozen miles away, was light-years different. Proper Southampton dismissed East Hampton as Malibu-by-the-Sea, as Hollywood East. East Hampton with its fashion designers, its filmmakers, its go-go financiers, and especially its writers and artists. All very well for those people to have a place in the Hamptons. Just so long as it wasn't next door to yours.

Southampton, or so Southampton believed, had . . . class. Especially Gin Lane.

Gin Lane was rumpled linens and creamy flannels and two-toned shoes. Men's double-breasted navy blazers sported nacre buttons, mother-of-pearl instead of mere brass. And where less-snooty East Hampton accepted golf (and even baseball!) caps, though never worn backward, Southampton was strictly Panama hats and boaters; yachting caps on the water. If you played polo, you did it in Southampton. Except at the Maidstone, East Hampton tennis was played on Har-Tru. In Southampton, they still played on grass and red clay.

Southampton belonged to the Meadow Club, swam at the Bathing Corporation (founded, as most good things were, by the First Families), worshipped at St. Andrew's, dined at Basilico's on Job's Lane or Savanna's, rather new but good, drank at Barrister's on Main Street (the Driver's Seat was popular but touristy). There was no hotel to speak of but you could put up friends, of the right sort, at the Southampton Men's Club at the end of First Neck Lane (but only if they were men). The Bath & Tennis on Gin Lane was good—very good, in fact—and they might take you if you couldn't get into the Bathing Corp. The Bath & Tennis took

Jews, as well, proper Southampton liked to point out, proud of its own (limited) tolerance.

In winter, people along Further Lane retreated to Manhattan. Or the Coast. Aspen or Sun Valley. Southampton went south. Gin Lane's winters were spent in Palm Beach. Martinis at the Breakers and lazy golf and shopping along Worth Avenue and reading the shiny sheet and bidding on the right batch at the right auction and entertaining and being entertained, yacht to yacht, the polished mahogany tenders shuttling busy as waterbugs between the floating gin palaces, darting this way and that. Palm Beach was Old Money and young wives. Or, if you were less discriminating, you might winter in Boca. Or if you didn't really care at all, on Florida's west coast. Society in Southampton, and especially along Gin Lane, preferred Palm Beach. In winter, in summer, Southampton was in its way as rigidly stratified as India under the Raj.

Only here, widows no longer were burned on funeral pyres and there were no Sepoys to mutiny, and decent working people still knew their place.

Not since Eden had any neighborhood been perfect; Southampton had its garter snakes (not many and rather puny) but again this summer the Army Corps of Engineers, with its civilian allies, would be battling a local "good citizen" group called the Long Island Shorefront Defense Fund over a thirty-seven-year, $300 million project, riddled with dubious assumptions. The army believed that the way to protect our beaches and dunes and waterfront homes from routine erosion, and the occasional, more dramatic major hurricane, was to dump ten million cubic yards of sand on fourteen miles of Fire Island (a barrier island for Long Island itself) and the placement of steel revetments along a mile of country beach west of Shinnecock Inlet. Honorable men differed on just how effective any of this might turn out to be. But the skeptics and suspicious among us were led to wonder whether it was entirely coincidence that Mr. Wyseman Clagett, the local power broker and developer and an enthusiastic supporter of the army engineers' plan, owned the third largest sand supplier in the county and that one of his partners, Thomas Packer, manufactured steel revetments.

Confronted by critical editorials in the local weeklies, Mr. Clagett showed the bully he was, snarling defiance and pulling all his advertising from the *Southampton Press* and the *East Hampton Star* as well as Jerry Della Femina's *Independent*. That was how you broke a small newspaper; pulled the damned ads! His small but menacing driver and aide, the ferretlike Herb Riddle (his local nickname, though not to his face, was "Roadkill"), visited each of the weekly newspaper offices to deliver the bad news personally. That was the way to show those pot-smoking pinko elitists not to oppose the good works of Wyseman Clagett. Hurt them in the pocketbook, pull the ads, punish these modest little local papers and spend his money instead on Channel 12 and in the much richer, more powerful Long Island daily, *Newsday*, with sixty-second commercials and full-page ads denouncing "petty, devious, small-minded radicals who oppose progress and care nothing for the safety of their fellow beach-loving citizens," ads that featured a photo of the huge, hulking Clagett staring out to sea (standing guard against hurricanes? on the alert for tidal waves?) from a Southampton beach while towheaded little children with shovels and pails frolicked and gamboled around his large feet, all innocence and serenity. Since Mr. Clagett was a lurching, deep-chested, heavy-shouldered, thuggish and nearly grotesque figure with a ghastly facial disorder, at the sight of whom mothers grabbed young children and hustled them indoors, both ads and commercials were a marvel of creative art direction, montage and cross-cutting computer graphics. The headline read "Wyseman Clagett and Your Children/Into a New Southampton Millennium," followed swiftly by praise for the Army Corps of Engineers and the American Way. There was no disclaimer in the ad about Mr. Clagett's being a supplier of either sand or structural steel for revetments.

My father, the Admiral, being old East Hampton and professional navy, was contemptuous of Wyseman Clagett. Admittedly, he was something of a snob himself, and having graduated from Annapolis, could be a "ring-knocker" (a "ring-knocker" being a navy man who, in order to gain advantage in an argument over tactics or strategy, might somewhat showily rap his Naval Academy ring against the helm or the desk, just to demonstrate who was the boss). But even he found Southampton, and the pretensions and rituals of Gin Lane, and the schemes of men like Clagett, to be a bit much.

If a "ring-knocker" found Gin Lane a bit much, well, you know what we're talking about here.

# e i g h t

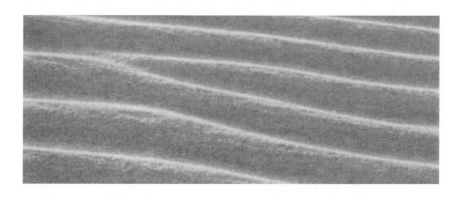

*A fine gold chain threaded erotically through her left nipple...*

Buchanan's limo rolled smoothly to a halt on my father's gravel and paused there, the whisper of its engine, and my own labored breath, the only sounds.

And then, in an instant, this charming little still-life vignette shattered into movement as a liveried chauffeur, moving smartly, was out one door and flinging wide another, and Alix Dunraven stepped down. Oh, yes, I thought, how lovely she is....

"Beecher," she said, with precisely the right blend of intimacy and bonhomie, and aware of the chauffeur's presence, "you are the best, taking one in like this. The very best. If England had men like you, we'd still have that decent chap Chris Patten governing Hong Kong for Her Majesty. And not dispatching Prince Charles to surrender the place whilst doing all that kowtowing to the Yellow Peril."

Yes, I agreed, as she threw arms wide and kissed me, chastely, on both cheeks. Except that wasn't "kowtowing" a Japanese ritual, straight out of *The Mikado*, and not Chinese? I must look that up.

When the driver had been sufficiently impressed, and then dismissed (Alix borrowed two twenty-dollar bills to tip him, not yet having changed her pounds sterling), I lugged her Louis Vuitton matched cases into the gatehouse and provided her a fresh hand towel and the freedom of any of several bathrooms. "I say, Beecher," she interrupted once, "you usually have a goodly supply of tooth string about, and I can't find any." When I got her the dental floss and she was appropriately refreshed, we strolled down to our dunes on the sunny spring ocean's edge where I took her by the hand so that she leaned against me, the whole wonderful length of her, towing the both of us gently back into recollections of last summer. . . .

Having kissed, and less chastely, for a time and properly said hello, and assured ourselves that, yes, the ocean is still out there half a year later, we sat out in the old Adirondack chairs on the lawn of the gatehouse and watched young bunnies cavort, drinking cold Cokes that she'd found in the fridge, one of the few culinary arts she had. Finding things in refrigerators.

"You've got a splendid suntan for this early in the year. That couldn't be Paris?"

"No," she said vaguely, "I was also in Barbados for a week. Staying with friends . . ."

"Friends?" And what friends might those be? I wondered uneasily. But this was hardly the time to do anything but celebrate; Alix was here, after all, and welcome as Christmas morning, wasn't she?

"So you and Mary Sexton have been conspiring in my absence."

"You're fortunate to have her, Beecher. She's absolutely first-rate."

"Also a Bolshie."

"There is that. And on any number of things, we differ. Regicide, for one. I'm totally opposed to the bumping off of kings and Mary's all for it."

"Yes," I said noncommittally, maintaining a neutral position on the matter. Then I brought her up-to-date on my father's adventures at NATO and what was happening at the magazine and then, just to make trouble, I asked innocently about Paris.

"That Frenchman you were wooing for HarperCollins, how did you leave that?"

"He's devastated that I've abandoned him. And France. Threatens to invade America, show up in the night and carry me away. All very Gascon, d'Artagnan and all that."

"With highly dishonorable intentions, I assume. Knowing the Frenchies as I do."

"Quite the contrary," Alix said primly. "He was babbling 'marriage' in two languages."

"Oh?" I said, shaken.

"Yes, but those chaps always do, don't they? My, this isn't bad Coca-Cola if I do say so ..."

I felt better.

"But what the devil's all this about a wedding? And who are the Buchanans?"

"Well, Beecher," Her Ladyship said, getting down to substantive matters, "that's our task, you see, to *derailleur* Fruity Metcalfe's marriage. And since I was once, though briefly, engaged to him, I feel a certain responsibility."

"And Fruity's marrying a Buchanan?"

"That's it. You are keen, I must say. And it's why though they very kindly sent their limo to meet me at JFK, I can't possibly stay with them and consequently am descending on you. Wouldn't be cricket to accept their hospitality whilst I'm hatching plots against them, now, would it? So you'll have to put up with me for a time."

Not that I minded that at all, but I was still in the dark about her hosts. "Just who are they?"

"Tom and Daisy Buchanan. He owns a chain of sweetshops or something and they're just rolling in filthy lucre, and they have a dozen or so gorgeous daughters that they have to marry off. One of them, name of Mandy, has been assigned to Fruity. I'm to be in the wedding party as one of the bridesmaids, Fruity's nomination, of course, but I'm absolutely determined there shan't be a Viscountess Albemarle entered in the stud book quite yet. Wouldn't be fair to Fruity, the way they've swept the poor chap off his feet."

"But he's thirty—"

"Thirty-two, actually—"

"And eventually he'll have to marry someone. . . ."

"Yes, I know. And often I think a first, failed marriage is good for one. Gives one a little experience, you know, running a house, hiring servants, bouncing up and down on the old nuptial couch for a bit. Then he could go on to someone more appropriate to his station and lineage. But the dear boy's a bit muddled, as so many Etonians are, regarding his sexual identity. I fear he'd be very restive with a sensual young beauty as this Mandy is reputed to be, not satisfying her and all that rot, and she'll have to take lovers. Which would be horrid for Fruity, you know how chaps talk at the club. Or over a pint at the pub.

"No, what Fruity needs, and I mean no disrespect at all, I assure you, is a suitably randy old thing of his own class, like Camilla Parker Bowles . . ."

"Yes, I see what you mean," I said, not at all sure I did, and once again slightly out of my depth with aristocratic mind-sets. Ever since poor Diana, younger noble Englishwomen seemed still in a state of shock, and I hesitated out of sheer delicacy to just barrel ahead with questions. Alix went on:

"But meditating on Fruity's plight in the plane from Heathrow, it came to me that even for a first, failed marriage, never mind one that's expected to prosper and endure, an American sweetshop heiress isn't at all the right thing for the son and heir of the earl of Bute. So here I am, prepared and even eager to do devious battle for the soul of a chum." She paused. "And I know you'll enlist right alongside, Beecher, and help me confront the sweetshop billions and foil all those hot-blooded daughters they've foaled. Even if you've got to throw yourself at one or more of them and cool the family's insatiable ardor for yet another titled husband, whilst they take carnal advantage of poor, dear Fruity . . ."

But what was all this about her being engaged again herself? Not to the Frenchman but in England. "You might have let me know," I said.

"Oh, Beecher, I should have, I know. Forgive me, darling. But you're such a hardcase and so admirably cool about such things, I didn't see the need. So many boys I know aren't nearly as sophisticated as adults like you. And when things are going badly for them, and they're in a funk and vulnerable, I can't help pitying them. And it does so cheer them up to see a jolly engagement announcement in *The Times*. Later, when things are going well once again, and they're more chipper, it's the simplest matter in the world just to call it off."

She paused. "Although this last time Nigel Dempster in the *Daily Mail* was rather beastly about it. Kept referring to me in his column as 'the very, very engaging Lady Alix Dunraven.' Don't you think that was snide of him?"

"The cad!" I said, while secretly enjoying Nigel's clever little mot.

To get her off that subject, I told her about "Cowboy in the Morning."

"He even had Reverend Al Sharpton out as a weekend guest." When she asked who that was and I told her about how Reverend Al ran for mayor of New York every four years, she said:

"Oh, they both sound heaven! The Reverend and Mr. Dils both! And with a house right there on Gin Lane near the Buchanans'. Most neighbors turn out dull. I can't wait to meet him. Does he really fire shots at peeing dogs and the church belfry? You do have the best chums."

I explained that not everyone along Gin Lane was feeling all that neighborly toward Dils. That, in fact, relations were somewhat strained and a state of war existed. There was even a Stop Dils Committee.

"Compared to Dils and much of Southampton, the Hutus and the Tutsis are fraternity brothers."

It had become, I explained, a war of attrition and like the Thirty Years War it appeared likely to go on forever.

"He touched it off last year when he first bought the place and started building a helicopter pad on the front lawn. Then he gave an interview to the *Southampton Press* in which he said he'd be commuting daily by chopper. Except that before the pad was finished, the village had a preliminary injunction against it. So it was then that Cowboy warned he had many friends of color in the music business and was likely to be hosting any number of parties during the Season, some of which might be attended by large black men with dreadlocks, arriving in stretch limos and smoking grass. He was only joshing, of course, or at least to some it sounded that way, but Wyseman Clagett, among others, took Cowboy at his literal word."

"Who's he? 'Wise Man' what?"

"Wyseman Clagett, linear descendant, from the pre-Revolutionary time, of the king's attorney for the province of New Hampshire, which is somewhat north of here. This current Mr. Clagett, who is an attorney as well as a land developer, owns a big place on Gin Lane. He's also a dubious and difficult character, in large part because of a dismaying nervous affliction he's inherited from his long-ago colonial ancestor. I looked it up once in a book about the period by Kenneth Roberts and it's so; two hundred and fifty years ago an ancestor Clagett also suffered from precisely the same dreadful tic."

Alix's eyes went wide. She was partial to monsters and so enjoyed the details. "Tell me, Beecher," she urged. "Do tell me about the Clagett tic."

I always enjoyed this part as well and not only described the family's facial problem but tried my best to act it out.

"It seems that in addition to being an enormous fellow, Clagett has bushy eyebrows which, at the moment of distortion, jerk together like two great caterpillars battling, and his mouth, convulsively contorted, is drawn to one side so that he appears to be attempting to eat his own ear!"

Alix put down her can of Classic Coke.

"You're not making this up."

"Not a bit of it."

"But he's a wonder. Does Mr. Clagett ever visit England? I'd love Pa to see him. He'll give a dinner party, have people in. Pa so likes a good fright."

"I'll cable you if I hear of an upcoming visit," I promised.

Then, getting back to Dils, she asked:

"And does he come and go by private helicopter? That *is* posh."

"No, earlier this spring when Cowboy got the injunction dismissed, on one of the first tests of the new pad, there was fog and the chopper crashed. No one killed but both pilots were hurt and people asked 'Suppose it came down on the schoolhouse? Or, God forbid, on the Bathing Corp.?' So for the moment, the injunction is back and the chopper's grounded. Cowboy thinks it's all a plot, maybe even an attempt on his life. Not that anyone takes that seriously. He personalizes and exaggerates everything."

I told her the unfortunate tale of Magistrate Hobbes's seizure and death last summer and explained how the warring sides were now lining up for a new Season: much of the village apparat, the Zoning Board of Appeals, the Ladies' Luncheon Society ("He curses," one member said, "the foulest language. I've heard him!"), the Meadow Club, the Parrish Museum, four of the seven churches, the Bathing Corp., the village clerk's office, and so on, all fiercely opposed to Cowboy Dils. And others took up arms as private citizens. Having seen letters to the editor of the *Southampton Press* and a list of names on one of several petitions, I was able to rattle off for Her Ladyship some of the local people who wanted Cowboy driven from Gin Lane, preferably after being coated in tar and feathers. Not all of them orchestrated by Wyseman Clagett, but some:

"Haverford, who gave forty million to Dartmouth; Da Vinci the jeweler; Jennings Sheeran the magazine publisher; Gulbenkian the rug merchant; Van der Kander the horticulturalist; Dr. Anspach, who runs wellness centers; Gates Penn the railroad baron; John Murphy the machine tool heir, who moonlights by designing golf courses; Leland the Broadway angel; Reverend Halsey, one of the original Halseys; Hawkes of Hawkes Retail; Princess Galitzine the younger; Farris the arbitrageur; Ross, who sails each year in the Newport to Bermuda yacht race; Holcombe Balcony, the biggest thing in pineapples since Dole; Won Hookey, who made his killing in Hong Kong; Emma Faber; Wolfsheim the realtor; Monsieur Francois, who raises and races thoroughbreds; Jelke the oleo man; Signor Frascati, who collects antique Keuffel and Esser slide rules; Fullalove of IBM; Cromer of Chase Bank; Pepi Coster, who once cornered the ball-bearing market; plus the Uptons, the Cheshires, lawyer McKeon of Sullivan and Cromwell, Julia Smythe, the Monteleones, the McGinns, and Saladin the ore magnate . . .

"He's also feuding with the president over things he's said at the National Press Club and on-air about him and about the First Lady."

"Golly! Just think of it. It's like roll call at the House of Lords. Or Nixon's enemies list. Doesn't Mr. Dils have any pals, no defenders?"

Well, he does, I said. "Mostly flawed men, like himself, none of them terribly popular with the town. Ace Gold the mergers and acquisitions specialist, himself under indictment for securities fraud; Count Galli-Curci, who wears an elastic stocking and carries a sword cane; and Onkleman the McDonald's franchiser, who has gout and gets about in a rolling wicker chair of the sort you see on boardwalks. Then there's Tom Goff . . .

"As for Dils's own employer, Roger Champion, he hasn't yet cast his ballot. Champion's a canny type and you never know quite where he stands on controversies. Especially insofar as Dils is one of the biggest stars on American air and obscenely profitable."

"Golly," Alix said, not very impressed by this slim roster of support.

I took her for drinks at the Blue Parrot, where they all made a fuss, and then to dinner at Della Femina's and when we got home there was a bit of an awkward moment when I wasn't sure whether she would be sleeping in the small bedroom upstairs or with me. But that worked out very satisfactorily in the end.

"Oh, darling," she said as she undressed, "I'm still awfully keen on you."

It was then I noticed for the first time a tiny, very fine gold chain threaded erotically through her left nipple.

"That's new," I remarked, furious but trying desperately not to show it.

"Yes," she said, looking down, pleased I'd noticed. "A chap gave it to me and I thought it rude not to wear it."

"Oh," I said, still more than a little deflated and annoyed.

But then Alix started doing things with pillows and moving about a good deal and I realized this was hardly the moment for issuing complaints and there was really no need for me to say all that much. So I just began moving about as well.

We hadn't been together for half a year but eventually even I got the knack of what we were doing.

n i n e

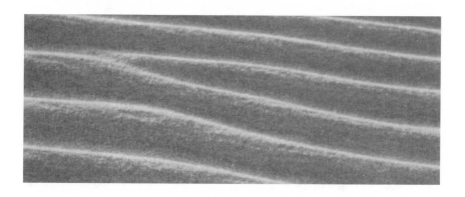

*God sent Job various plagues: boils, hemorrhages,*
*canker, tennis elbow . . .*

I was awake about six and Cowboy's accident was already the second or
third leading news item of the morning.

He'd been out for one of his midnight jogs along Gin Lane in Southampton and had been run down by a vehicle that sped off without stopping. Local police were looking for a hit-and-run driver but had no
suspects nor yet much of a description of the car. Mr. Dils was at Southampton Hospital with a broken leg and other injuries, none of them life-
threatening. Alix was still sleeping the sleep of the just, or the jet-lagged,
so I used the phone in the kitchen to call the hospital and got the floor
nurse. She couldn't put me through to Cowboy, she said. He was sedated
and probably asleep.

"Is there a Dr. Fu Manchu around? Distinguished-looking Oriental
gent?"

"Our Dr. Willoughby is the attending physician," she said officiously, as if Willoughby raised Lazarus from the dead and healed more hopeless cases than Bernadette of Lourdes.

"A fine man," I acknowledged. "They speak of him up and down Harley Street with enormous respect. But Dr. Fu is a specialist in jogger injuries. Flown in for the occasion from Hong Kong."

Just how Fu Manchu would have gotten from Hong Kong to Southampton Hospital when Cowboy was run over only about six hours ago, I didn't explain. But nurses respect the chain of command in medicine and appreciate that specialists rank very high on the ladder of influence.

"There is a tall, slender . . . foreign gentleman here of that description." She was very sensitive, politically correct, almost punctilious about not pigeon-holing Fu Manchu with an ethnic or racial label.

"Please tell him it's Beecher Stowe."

When Fu got on he was quintessential Fu, very calm and cool. Suitably deferential.

"Most worthy and esteemed leader sustains gallantly the most excruciating of pain. The nobility of his spirit has never been exceeded. He rests now, a damaged splendor in human form, under the dedicated care of highly competent physicians and—"

From somewhere just off-mike came Maguire's voice, an aimiable growl:

"He means, the sonuvabitch will live. We're less confident about the doctors."

Fu Manchu passed the telephone to "Honorable Maguire." Who gave me a condition report. The right leg was broken low down near the ankle and had been set, a nondisplaced fracture. There were cuts and bruises, mainly from being brushed off the road into the brush and dirt of the shoulder. They'd tested for concussion. So far, negative. Some water in the lungs, since the car that hit Cowboy knocked him down the slope and into a small lake that bordered the road. Lucky for him, an unidentified-as-yet passerby had tugged him out of the lake, pumped some of the water out of him, and called for help. Cowboy might be sent home by tomorrow if nothing else turned up. He'd be in a wheelchair for a while.

"You talk to him?" I asked.

"Yeah, before they gave him the shot. He's really pissed. Claims it wasn't an accident at all but a cold-blooded murder attempt. Actually saw the car. Swears it was a Rolls, dark blue or black. Told me that privately. Said don't give it to the papers or tell the cops. I dunno why."

"Jogging on an unlighted road at midnight. Sounds like an accident to me. But the guy should have stopped."

"Maybe the driver had a couple of beers on his breath and panicked. You know how they are out here about DWI. Anyway, Cowboy was calling down curses on him and demanding that Janet Reno name an independent prosecutor. It was pretty colorful here for a time. That's when they gave him the shot. Not so much for him, I think, but to spare the rest of us. Harry was here but he got out. Couldn't take it anymore. He's gone off to find a nice quiet church and pray for Cowboy."

"There's a church right there on Gin Lane."

"I know. St. Andrew's. Cowboy hates that church. That's where they ring the bells Sunday mornings just to annoy him. He told Harry he'd burn in hell if he prayed for him at St. Andrew's so Harry's looking for another church..."

Sounded to me as if Cowboy would recover. I got the phone number of Cowboy's Gin Lane house out of Maguire and promised to call there later. If there was anything I could—

"Not that I can think of. Give me your number. I'll call if we need any local connections. But I think it'll be okay. Greasy Thumb knows one of the Southampton cops. Cowboy's in room 308. They've got him knocked out now but maybe later he'd get a kick if you called. Give him one more person to chew out."

I promised to call. When I was only a kid, my father drilled it into me: "Episcopalians visit the sick, we comfort the afflicted, we bury the dead. All the corporal works of mercy. Such things are expected of us whatever lesser men may or may not do." Even when the "afflicted" included Cowboy Dils, I took it.

Maguire asked a few more questions and I gave him the names of a couple of restaurants and bars in Southampton and a few places I knew better in case they ranged farther afield and got to East Hampton. Also my detective pal Tom Knowles's name and number at Suffolk County PD in Riverhead. A hit-and-run Rolls-Royce, just imagine! Although along Gin Lane Rolls-Royces were common as Fords. Cowboy even had one himself. In black. And why was he being so secretive about describing the car? Maybe he didn't know what he was saying.

After breakfast Alix rented a car ("A Range Rover," she explained; "there were no Jags available and, as you know, I'm quite particular about driving British") to visit Southampton and the Buchanans to fob them off with some phony tale about why she couldn't stay at their place with the rest of the wedding party. So I found myself late that afternoon at the bar of the Blue Parrot having a Pacifico beer and listening to people talking about Cowboy's accident when Harry Almond and Maguire and Fu Manchu came in.

"Guzik is outside," Maguire said, "with the motor running, just in case."

"How's Cowboy?"

"They're keeping him overnight, thank God. We get him back in the morning if all goes well."

Harry Almond ordered a sherry, which had Roland the manager delving around under the counter for a time, finally coming up with a dusty bottle half full of Tio Pepe from last summer. "Speaking frankly," Roland told him, "as a joint that specializes in Tex-Mex, we don't get all that much call for sherry."

"Sorry," Almond said. He was the nicest guy. Polite, too.

The rest of the group ordered. I bought. Fu Manchu bowed deeply in my direction and murmered, "Honorable Stowe..."

I bowed back and then, "You find a church?" I asked Almond.

"Very nice. Big stone Catholic church on the main street of town. Cool inside. Peaceful. Prayed for Cowboy to recover; prayed for myself to be more patient with him. I thought about lighting a votive candle but felt that might be pushing the theological envelope."

Maguire shook his head. "He's got a left-footer like you going to Catholic churches? You've got the patience of Job as it is."

"What's a left-footer and who's Job? That the guy they named Job's Lane for in Southampton?" Roland asked, whipping up some margaritas and opening beers.

"Left-footer's Catholic slang for a Protestant. Job was an Old Testament prophet," Maguire replied.

"Said to be the finest, most decent and holy man of his time," Harry put in, "a regular Billy Graham, another Dr. Schuller. Except that the Great God Jehovah must have been out of sorts that year and kept testing Job, killing off his family, even the little tots, and sending him various plagues: boils and tennis elbow and hemorrhages, eczema and paper cuts, cankers and root canal and God knows what else ..."

Maguire scowled.

"They didn't send him Cowboy Dils."

Greasy Thumb came down the alley to the open doors of the place. "A man might die of the thirst in this town. Could you send out a small boy with a large beer?"

Roland said he'd see to it himself. He was a big fan, he admitted, and thrilled to meet Ed Guzik.

"I think Mr. Gloomy is the best thing on the show. I never miss an episode of Mr. Gloomy."

That gave Maguire an idea: "Why don't we have 'Mr. Gloomy Meets Poor Job'? That could be hilarious. 'Lepers with Root Canal' as the opening episode."

Greasy Thumb thanked Roland, pumping his hand. You could see the shoulder holster shifting under his suit jacket.

"Hey, it's Cowboy!"

They had CNN on the television above the bar and there was a file shot of Cowboy in the studio at the radio station and then a doctor standing in front of Southampton Hospital and finally a local police chief. Cowboy was alert and might be released tomorrow. The cop said they were following up a few leads on the hit-and-run. They hoped to run tests on flecks of paint found on Cowboy's bicycle shorts and embedded in his leg.

"Amazing what forensic science is capable of," Harry remarked, shaking his head in admiration.

I was standing next to Maguire and I asked quietly, "Is Greasy Thumb carrying?"

"Absolutely. Especially these days," the producer said.

"What d'you mean, 'these days'? Since the accident?"

He shook his head.

"Cowboy gets warnings. E-mail and regular mail. Phone calls. Stuff on the Internet. It's changed since you interviewed him, gotten worse. The chopper crash scared him whether he admits it or not. So Guzik doesn't go out without a piece."

"But there's always some of that with big stars," I said. "Crank threats. All the weirdos out there ..."

"Sure," Maguire said, but not sounding as if he agreed. He seemed to ponder whether to say more. And then he did.

"It's mostly since he trashed the president down there in D.C. It got worse right after that. More vicious, more specific. Not just the usual sickos. Threats, warnings, abuse—"

"Hey," someone at the bar who was still watching the tube called out. "The president! He's coming here next week! The goddamned president!" And sure enough, up there on the TV screen, Wolf Blitzer or someone like that standing on the White House lawn was confirming the story and reading off a few sketchy details.

The president of the United States? In the Hamptons? And hadn't we just been talking about how Cowboy, now in the hospital after being run down by parties unknown, had been receiving vicious and ugly threats following his National Press Club performance burlesquing the First Family?

Just why would the president be coming to the Hamptons?

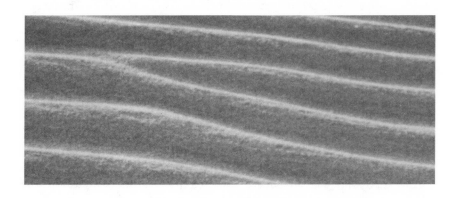

*What happened? The president run out of
Indonesians?*

The "someone" who pulled Cowboy's bruised, unconscious body from
the reedy shallows of Agawan Lake, dragged him back up a slope to the
shoulder of Gin Lane, drained him of most of the lake water through a
competent administering of CPR, and called 911 on a cell phone, was
none other than Jesse Maine. Who didn't hang around to take credit,
sign autographs, or be nominated for this year's Good Samaritan award
or any of the Nobels.

"There'd be no profit in it, Beecher, not like I was running for town
office, for alderman or such," Jesse told me.

"But you're a bloody hero, Jesse. You rescued a national icon. More
than likely saved his life. You deserve his thanks and the gratitude of the
entire—"

"Not likely," the "hero" said. "Wouldn't take long for people to inquire just what mischief a Shinnecock Indian might be up to out there

on Agawan Lake at one in the morning gazing up at the stars and constellations from his simple, homespun birchbark canoe."

Jesse's canoe happened to be constructed of Oltonar/Royalex, manufactured by a factory in Maine, as I well knew, but he had a point.

"And just what were you doing out there?"

"Poaching muskrats, of course. There wasn't much wind, the moon was in the right quarter, meaning the pelts are rich and full, and my canoe was to hand. I am a man who believes with the Latin scholars that when opportunity presents, you damned well seize the day. Or the night, if it's after dark." He paused and thought, then added, "Especially when the muskrats are plump and swimming about."

It was his call, of course, though I told him I thought he was wrong, keeping quiet about it. But I wanted him to meet Cowboy. "At least he ought to know who his friends are around here; he's got enough enemies."

That made sense to Jesse, who understood about enemies. And friends.

Her Ladyship was inordinately pleased Jesse Maine was still in the parish. "I do want Fruity to meet him. There's ever so much a great hunter and angler like Jesse could teach Fruity. About the more practical aspects of Ag and Fish, I mean. The viscount is splendid on the theoreticals, you understand; he's studied up. But how impressive it would be if on his return to London, Fruity could inform the PM during a cabinet, that whilst in the Colonies he actually caught a fish."

I told her I couldn't spend my time nursemaiding Fruity, that I had a story to do about the Baymen.

"Precisely, Beecher, and aren't they just the admirable breed of men the Minister of Ag and Fish ought to be meeting as well?"

She was indefatigable when she got on to something. Just never stopped. And what she was on to now was keeping poor Fruity as far away from his intended bride, Mandy Buchanan, as could decently be done without actually popping into bed with him herself. And if hardworking reporter Beecher Stowe or the Hamptons Baymen or that noble chief (and prominent local poacher) Jesse Maine could be recruited to distract the viscount, it seemed to Alix a shame not to put us all to work.

Whatever story she'd sold Mr. and Mrs. Buchanan had been graciously accepted. "They're far more mystified and anxious about Fruity's whereabouts. I kept telling them he was briefing the cabinet on codfish or closeted with the PM on tariff matters but I'm not sure they're convinced. Mr. Buchanan's a social climber but a shrewd one, and I fear he suspects a case of cold feet on Fruity's part. Buchanan *pere* is very clearly in the business of buying titled husbands for his daughters and takes it all very seriously. They've already got one daughter a maharanee redecorating the palace in Kashmir, another an intimate of the pope and confidant of Vatican officials in dear, *dolce* old Roma, and one who's married to a Graf von und zu Something-or-other in the Tyrol, where she skis and is learning to yodel. An English viscount, son of the earl of Bute and heir to one of the great titles, is all the Buchanans need. They'll be expecting invitations to tea at the palace, grouse shooting at Balmoral, Ascot with the Queen Mum. Fruity would definitely put the icing on the Buchanan cake."

Fine, I thought, if Fruity doesn't show up in the Hamptons at all, Alix won't have any incentive to involve me in transparently absurd plots. But as she chewed her lip, fretting about the lies she found herself obliged to tell, I felt protective of her and, remembering the pleasures of the night, said, "Come on, let's phone Dils's place. If Cowboy's back home on Gin Lane and feeling up to it, I'll take you over there to meet him."

The wounded man was sunning on the patio, propped up on a golf cart he was using in lieu of wheelchair, and when I introduced Her Ladyship he turned on the charm, rewarding her with an enormous and leering grin, and informing me, "Never suspected you had such exalted connections, Stowe. Does you credit."

As Fu Manchu jockeyed the cart around so as to give Dils the full effect of the May sunshine, Alix tugged at my sleeve. "Why, he's wizard. You suggested he was crude and boorish, even ill-tempered—"

"It's early days," I said. "Give him time."

Somehow Alix had been told Cowboy's given name. "*Quel* concidence," she remarked. "My fourth cousin twice removed is the earl of Leicester. I wonder if you and I might, even distantly, be related."

Cowboy said no and told her about Hemingway's kid brother, going into considerable detail, as he was wont to do, about various suicides in Papa's family, the weapons used and particulars of the coroner's reports. He enjoyed the details, Dils did, demonstrating for example how you could fit a shotgun under your chin and then set off the trigger with a toe. "Only one I know of died of natural causes in that bunch was sister Marcelline."

"Pity," she said.

"Oh, well, they live pretty well until they pick up the old shotgun..."

"No, I meant a pity you and the earl aren't cousins. He's elderly now and slowing down but he was a great one for tooling about in roadsters and nipping off to Monte for a go at the chemmy tables. Or getting up onstage at the Windmill Theatre to dance in the chorus line with the girls. A most diverting chap you surely would have enjoyed. Drank a little."

"My loss," Cowboy said. "If he drinks, they probably know him at Hurley's."

Dr. Fu came out assisting a manservant and a platoon of bustling Hispanic maids with trays of chilled fruit and cold drinks and we all took something and lounged about there on the patio, chatting with Cowboy and attempting to take his mind off his woes.

What was starting to worm its way through his fevered mind was the possibility, faint as it might be, that there was a link between the hit-and-run and the helicopter that crashed en route to his pad earlier this spring.

"Oh?" said Alix, as if I hadn't told her already. "There was another accident?"

Dils told her about it.

"I go back and forth on it, suspicious as I am. Probably was just an accident," he conceded. "You get a lot of fog in April. Mornings especially. The ocean's still pretty chilly and the air can warm up in a hurry. There was fog that morning. Thick as hell. Maguire can tell you. Or Harry."

"I wouldn't simply write it off as a natural phenomenon, though," Alix responded. "In at least two Hercule Poirot stories I can cite, the murderer used a supposed earlier 'accident' to mask his later, and considerably more lethal, attack."

Cowboy looked sharply at Harry Almond, as if to say "See, and you think I'm paranoid?..."

Then Her Ladyship got right into it, as she customarily did:

"Beecher tells me you have enemies. The local church. Several of your neighbors."

Dils shrugged. "As Faulkner said at the Nobel presentation, 'Man not only survives; he will prevail.'"

"Hear, hear," Harry murmured. Alix smiled in small tribute and went on:

"I understand as well, that you and the president of the United States have been tiffing."

"Tiffing? Tiffing? You might say that. He has a sense of humor about everything but himself. I may have gotten too close to the knuckle and he resented it."

"Yeah," Maguire said sourly. "The guy doesn't like being called 'a fat pantload.' Hell of a nerve."

"Well, I also said a lot of nice things about him. Gave him air time when his campaign was dragging ass. He knows we do a comedy show, that we raise hell with everyone. Fine with Bubba so long as it wasn't him. I cut him all sorts of slack and then he turns on me, poisons the air, whips up antagonisms. He's as bad at bringing out the weirdos as Rush Limbaugh. I'll bet that hit-and-run driver that knocked me into the lake was a Democrat."

"You said it was a Rolls, chief," Maguire reminded him.

"Hey, on Gin Lane even Democrats drive Rolls-Royces. This place has class and I won't hear people putting it down."

"That's enormously generous of you, considering your leg is broken, not to parcel out guilt."

Cowboy beamed. "Well, thank you, Your Ladyship." He seemed to enjoy using the title.

"He's coming here, you know," Alix said.

"Who?"

"Your president."

"Yeah, I heard something about that, that he's coming to the Hamptons." Cowboy sounded slightly uneasy about it.

"Not only the Hamptons, Mr. Dils," Alix went on, "he's coming specifically to Gin Lane. Not a hundred yards from your front gate. On Memorial Day he'll be at Saint Andrew's Dune Church!"

"Here? He's coming *here*? Good Gawd A-mighty!" Cowboy now looked more than slightly distressed. Was the president of the United States that pissed off at him? Was the chief executive intent on confrontation, meeting his irritant face-to-face? It was one thing to needle great men from the relative security of a radio studio. Or the dais of a black-tie dinner. But to be tracked down here at his own home by the most powerful man in the world? And not just the president, but Saint Andrew's! Talk about being ganged up on, church and state both! This was a side of Dils most people never saw, that he revealed only to his closest friends, the guilt-ridden, somewhat cowardly wretch . . .

"I don't understand why, as busy as he must be, he'd come all this way to . . ." Dils began in a strangled voice.

"I can explain," Alix said, very crisp and controlled, pleased to have information none of the rest of us possessed. "He'll be here on Gin Lane next week attending a wedding at Saint Andrew's Dune Church and the reception to follow at the Meadow Club. I heard all about it at the Buchanans' when I was over there yesterday. They briefed the bridesmaids and groomsmen in considerable detail."

"A wedding? What wedding? Who's getting married?" Cowboy demanded, greatly relieved that he himself wasn't the cause of the chief executive's visit, wasn't the president's prey. And evidently annoyed at having allowed himself to appear intimidated by a mere head of state.

"A great chum of mine and member of the British Cabinet, Viscount Albemarle. He's to wed one of the many lovely Buchanan daughters, Mandy. According to snippets I picked up yesterday, your president owes Thomas Buchanan a favor of sorts."

"Oh?"

"Yes, they were talking about it, the members of the wedding. It seems Mr. Buchanan gives loads of money to the party and to the president's own campaign treasury. For some contributors, there's an invitation to coffee. For others, a night in the Lincoln bedroom. To repay a man like Tom Buchanan, you come to his daughter's wedding."

Made sense. Except that Cowboy Dils was still reducing it to size, coming to grips with the situation.

"What happened, he run out of Indonesians?"

Harry Almond smiled that benign smile of his. Perhaps he was thinking about a new skit along those lines. "The Last of the Indonesians" maybe, starring Johnny Huang and Charlie Trie and Johnny Chung, and even those Buddhist nuns Al Gore called upon, with Fu Manchu playing all of them. . . .

# e l e v e n

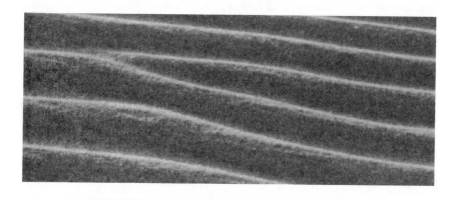

*Rex Magnifico each winter flatbedded his Ferrari to Aspen. . . .*

If the president was strapped for cash and renting himself out as a wedding guest, there was no evidence of equivalent fiscal shorts along Gin Lane.

There was so much money being made last year, men had to invent ways to spend it.

The predictible among them bought racehorses and yachts and third homes and second mistresses. Rex Magnifico the magazine publisher, who each winter flatbedded his Ferrari convertible to Aspen from New York, so that when he wasn't skiing he could be driving the Ferrari with its top down, wearing his ankle-length mink coat and shades and waving to the chicks, had taken up a new hobby: polo. Though Rex could barely sit a horse, he'd invested in a string of polo ponies and hired three Argentinos to teach him the sport. And he'd entered a team in the coming season's matches at Two Trees Farm in Bridgehampton and was inquiring, privately, when he might be considered an internationally ranked player.

Nick Ruggles and his ancient mother took a penthouse on the *QE2* and sailed back and forth from New York to Southampton and never went ashore. "I hate to pack and unpack," said Nick. "Mother enjoys the bingo and I like the ship's cabaret girls." Buddy Pontick had more novel interests, as you know, cultivating a crop of living bamboo on his Hamptons properties. "There are fifteen hundred quite distinct varieties of bamboo. I probably number about one hundred and twenty of them in my collection," he would explain if given the opening. Pontick belonged to the Bamboo Growers' & Fanciers' Association of North America and spent his evenings logging in on the Internet to like-minded hobbyists, exchanging lore and anecdotes. Martha Stewart, over in East Hampton, in between publishing a profitable magazine, hosting a daily TV show, creating a web site, doing radio essays and designing house paints, raised backyard poultry and each summer without fail entered one or more of her prize fowl in the big Avian Fair in the Pennsylvania Dutch country (invariably winning blue ribbons).

There were other prominent local folk who spent a dollar here, a dollar there. We had: Maureen Kirk's annual African safari treat for her scads of nieces and nephews, Cosmo Cosgrove's vast array of HO-gauge Lionel electric trains, and Patrick Ford's elaborate ant farm, all vying for attention with yet another total demolition and redesign of Mickey P. Schulhof's house on Egypt Lane (an almost annual affair), the 1911 electric runabout maintained and driven about the village at a majestic eight miles per hour by Timken the fluorescent bulb magnate, and even more startling, the spectacular one-man hot air balloon flights right off his own beach by Commodore Baghot, the soybean heir and our onetime naval attaché to Nepal. Which had neither coastline nor navy.

Of all these wealthy people seeking ways in which to spend the filthy stuff, Gilbert the Wall Street portfolio manager may well have been the busiest and among the most imaginative.

Needing additional land for his many and varied interests, Gilbert traded in his Gin Lane house for a nice, roomier waterfront place on Mecox Bay in Water Mill south of the highway where he kept his two boats and in the fall did some bird shooting over pedigreed retrievers he'd had expensively trained by experts in South Carolina and which, occasionally, brought back a bird.

Gilbert's true passions were considerably more exotic. On one of his business trips to South America he became sold on alpacas. They were cute, they were clean (unlike llamas, he was assured, convincingly if inaccurately, they rarely spat at you), they were easily raised and there was a thriving resale market in the States. Or so he was told. And believed. And even if there weren't, think of the sweaters you could have knitted up from their wool? Eighteen months after having paid the first installment on a half dozen of the beasts (five females and a male he called "Osvaldo," the females as yet simply numbered), the alpacas were still going through the red tape of the export trade.

"There's an alpaca cartel," Gilbert muttered darkly in explanation, sensitive to friendly joshing that he'd "been taken." He'd had a corral built (which the neighbors regarded narrowly) and had taken husbandry courses in the care and feeding of the damned things, and not one of them had yet arrived! There were now seven alpacas, one of the females having given birth. Osvaldo was suspected of having done the deed, Gilbert said.

While awaiting Osvaldo and the females (and discreetly inquiring just how one went about bribing the alpaca cartel), Gilbert saw to his other, equally expensive hobbies. He grew varietal grapes, both white and red, and had purchased all the machinery and other gear necessary to press and ferment and bottle the resultant wine, spending considerable time designing and having printed up bottle labels to his satisfaction. As for the wine itself, it wasn't very good, he conceded, noting in justification that the Widow Cliquot, Baron Mumms, and even the Rothschilds took a few years to get the vintages right.

He also traded expensive cameras, bought and sold platinum futures, collected antique firearms and marine oil paintings of the late eighteenth and early nineteenth centuries, and invested in bees. Except for the alpacas, none of whom he'd yet even seen, Gilbert's greatest challenge was the keeping of bees and production of honey.

He was a large man, well over six feet and of considerable girth, weighing perhaps 260 pounds, but had a good Hong Kong tailor who'd trained on Savile Row and whose nimble fingers achieved a pleasant drapery that tended to conceal thirty or forty of those pounds. But only when Gilbert wore proper business suits or weekend blazers and flannels. His beekeeping outfits were decidedly off the rack. From the pages of an apiary catalog, he'd purchased a beekeeper's outfit, size XXL, and while providing protection, the getup did little to slim or disguise his silhouette, leaving Gilbert resembling a cross between the Michelin man and Neil Armstrong on the moon.

So now he was properly togged out, his hives were full of healthy bees, and Gilbert was equally full of lore. Except that, the previous winter, disaster struck. Blame it, if you must, on his nobility and generosity of spirit. And rather than being embarrassed by what happened, he regaled men at the bar of the Meadow Club, confessing his own failure and reducing drinkers to hilarious tears.

"I was out inspecting the hives one of the first really cold nights last January. It was my first winter with the bees. I admit my ignorance, my naïveté. The wind was coming off the water, off Mecox Bay, absolutely fierce, and it seemed to me one of the hives was being buffeted more so than the others." He sipped at the Opus One and went on. "Now you know that even in winter, the bees regularly must leave and re-enter the hive. Despite what you may hear, they don't hibernate. Nor do they simply remain indoors, leaping laciviously upon the queen, alternately randy and waiting for spring. So that a good hive necessarily has slots through which the bees can fly in and out. Except that on this fatal night, the mercury was falling so drastically low and the wind was whipping at the hive so ferociously, I feared the entire hive might freeze. Here I was, the caretaker of thousands of little creatures who appeared to me about to freeze to death. I quite literally felt I might be guilty of mass murder if I did nothing to protect what were, in effect, my wards."

So Gilbert got some plywood and a hammer and nails and boarded over the slots. By now frostbitten himself, Gilbert the portfolio manager, the financial whiz kid, the wine maker, the frustrated herdsman of alpacas, the sailor and shooter and hunter, paternalistically protective of his brand-new bees, boarded up their hive against the storm. Forgetting, as he now admitted, "Bees are very clean, almost prissy, and they never defecate inside the hive. That's where they live, that's where they produce their honey, so they are very particular about the need to go outside to defecate. And here I'd just nailed plywood over the only exit they had."

Gilbert understood the value of a pause in a good yarn.

"Next morning, I had forty thousand dead bees in that hive. Dead of constipation, the valiant little bastards," he said emotionally, shaking his great head in wonderment and admiration as he spoke. "Tell me another species that'd rather die than shit."

Few people on Wall Street, or along Gin Lane, were as noble as Gilbert. *Or his bees.*

Roger Champion wasn't. Had he known Gilbert, he might have admired his financial savvy or dismissed him as an aimiable dilettante. Champion would never, at the bar of the Meadow Club or anywhere else, have publicly admitted foolishness. Being human, of course, he made mistakes, backed wrong horses, erred in business or in judging men. But he was never made a fool of, as Gilbert boasted of having been. And certainly Roger would never permit a woman to shame or embarrass him.

Just off the screening room with its forty movie theater–style chairs was the great den of Champion's house on Gin Lane, the room he liked best of the forty rooms, with its leatherbound books, its walk-in fireplace, its silver and pewter, the framed letters from kings and presidents and Nobel laureates, the photos of Roger with such men in cheerful, or wary, intimacy. There was but a single picture of a woman. And it was that painting which dominated the room, that drew the eye from all those presidents and kings. Drew the eye and held it, as magnetically as Jacoby's portrait of "Laura" in the film drew Waldo Lydecker's eye and his chill soul and melted Dana Andrews's more vulnerable cop's heart.

This was the famous Trude Kramer portrait in oil of Mrs. Champion done about ten years ago, shortly after they married. When I was still with the *Boston Globe*, a kid reporter, I'd once interviewed Mr. Champion in that room, saw that portrait. It wasn't a great interview or great journalism and only a routine event for him; it was a great moment for me. I recalled the moment, the room, the interview, the portrait of the man's wife. He owned a broadcast network and its parent company, he owned that house, he owned that painting, he owned . . . her. He was easy and careless in the midst of his possessions, a man in charge, sure of himself, cocky without being smug. You had to like his style, envy his control, admire his grasp. I was a kid. And in something approaching awe.

I saw her portrait on that visit; never saw the real thing. Don't know if Slim Champion was even in the house that day. Servants let me in; servants showed me out. As they would do even now if I drove up and knocked. That was how a man like Roger Champion lived. Still lived, I supposed, cozened by servants.

Except that I didn't realize and had no way of knowing that something had changed. Something rather fundamental and beyond his control.

There were things Champion could no longer do, times and places and situations he was no longer able to dominate and master through sheer will, people he was suddenly unable to cow or manipulate. There were even, though he hated the mere acknowledgment of them, physical and mental gymnastics that were slipping from his capacity to perform. And he realized that his wife knew it. For the first time, there were tensions between them; also, for the first time, there were problems. In bed. And elsewhere. But it was in bed that counted most. And that, more than all the rest of it, turned him to schemes like the raceway takeover, to men like Wyseman Clagett, from whom not too long before he would have turned in contempt, being above such schemes, understanding he was better than such men. Throw in with a sleazy developer just to coin another hundred million? Hardly that. But to impress the world...and his wife...yet again that he still retained his power, his acumen, his authority? Yes, there *was* a possible motivation....

Roger Champion had gotten old. And knew that he had. Knew also that in the way of the world, age was the enemy which might steal from him a wife and lover.

# t w e l v e

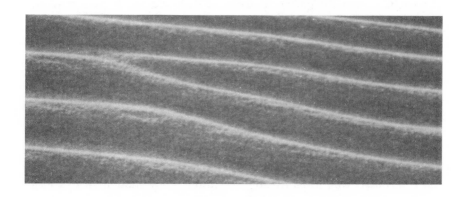

*They've found a clever little woman. Name of*
*Karan . . .*

Dils was back on the air from his Gin Lane digs before six the next morning (they'd aired a repeat show when he was still in the hospital) and in great voice and full flight, with a swiftly cobbled-up hospital skit (the nurses and doctors were all drunk on duty and chasing each other, half nude, in and out of operating rooms and lavatories). There was even a totally new skit featuring an upper-class Englishwoman, known as "the mems'ab," who sounded suspiciously like Alix (Annie Willow did wonders with the accents!), and her faithful Indian manservant Gunga Dils (played by Fu Manchu), who kept the cobras at bay, brushed off the Untouchables, watered the elephants, and served her endless cups of Earl Grey tea. The mems'ab, it turned out, was married to an English tea planter and they lived on his estates near Darjeeling, where she drank a good deal of excellent tea, coped with the snakes (they slithered in and out of the story, ubiquitous as "Baba's" scorpions in a recently discarded skit), and carried on a fairly decorous affair with the young maharajah, who addressed her as "Esteemed Madam." It was pretty good stuff and a very gracious little tribute, I thought, to our Alix on the part of Dils.

I was burning an English muffin and drinking orange juice in the kitchen when Her Ladyship strolled in from the bath.

"You're dripping wet, Alix," I said.

"Yes," she agreed. "I've been showering."

Her hair hung straight and heavy and dark and on all the rest of her, droplets glistened.

She came closer, leaning against me so I could feel the whole length of her wetly through my clothes.

"There I was showering, all dewy innocence, when it occurred to me, mightn't it be fun like this?" she said, dripping on my kitchen tile. "I mean, only if you're at all in the mood."

I was. And it was.

About eight the phone rang. For her.

"Fruity's arriving in America at lunchtime," she announced in considerable animation. "How far is Westhampton Beach Aerodrome?"

As we drove to Westhampton she laid out plans, conspiracies, plots. "I had hoped to be able to consult with Jesse Maine. As a great war sachem and also a renowned hunter and angler, I rather conceived of him as being of enormous assistance to us in rescuing Fruity and fending off the Buchanan clan. Take Fruity lobstering. Teach him about muskrats. Show him the Shinnecock vineyards and their cornfields. We grow maize in England, of course. Raleigh and Captain John Smith fetched the seeds back from Virginia and the Carolinas. But it's nothing like your huge golden ears of bantam corn, sad to say. Things such as that, of enormous potential value as well to Her Majesty's government, and specifically to Fruity's Ministry of Agriculture and Fisheries. But he's being evasive. Where is Jesse Maine?"

Alix knew almost nothing about the Hamptons or about Jesse, barring the two weeks we'd spent together last September, in the hurricane and coping with a menacing and quite possibly murderous Leo Brass and trying to find out who hated Hannah Cutting sufficiently to drive a stake through her heart. But she was right; Jesse was being evasive. Except for saving Cowboy's life by tugging him out of Lake Agawan and summoning ambulances, the great sachem had vanished. Where the hell was Jesse and what was he up to? I was aware that Jesse heard different drums than most of us and frequently went off without explanation, but Alix, desperate for assistance in derailing the viscount's upcoming marriage, was less patient than I in accepting Jesse's absence.

We drove the thirty-five miles to the old air base, reduced now to Coast Guard and radar flights, grass and weeds growing up through cracks in the tarmac, what I imagined the old Eighth Air Force fields in England must look like now, a half century after the Blitz and the counterpunch bombing of Germany. At about eleven-thirty the control tower alerted us. "Here comes that RAF flight of yours, Lady Alix."

"My, my, flying RAF. The PM must have laid it on. Being a cabinet member does have its perks. I am impressed."

Alix made the introductions right out there on the tarmac, the Viscount Albemarle and myself. He wasn't quite the chinless wonder she'd so often described but not far from it, though everyone else seemed to give him enormous respect, his due apparently, as a member of the prime minister's cabinet. Not knowing just what to call him, I settled for "sir."

"Dash it all, you can't go about calling chaps 'sir' like that, Stowe. Everyone calls me 'Fruity.' Have done since Eton."

Then, having good manners, he introduced us to the crew, starting with the wing commander, a ginger-haired chap with a nervous twitch, the co-pilot, and several enlisted men. Fruity admitted he didn't actually rate an RAF plane, "But there was a transatlantic training flight leaving Gatwick and they permitted me a lift. They're to do a fortnight's NATO exercises out of Westhampton Aerodrome with your Coast Guards. Don't know just whom we're exercising against these days with the bloody Russkis totally fini. But not my affair. Awfully decent of the RAF taking me along, not having to go through Customs and such. If there's ever another war I'd join up in an instant, Churchill and the Battle of Britain and 'the Few' and all that." He pondered for a moment. "Bloody Germans, bombing London. Damned Boche. Still don't trust them. Dropping bombs on pubs and Marylebone cricket ground. On the palace and Saint Paul's. The zoo at Regent's Park. I try to be aimiable toward the filthy Hun but I'm not. Can't help it." Then, looking at me, the working journalist, "I say, Stowe, I'd be grateful if you didn't quote me on any of that rot. Prefer not to embarrass the PM, incite the Hun into striking back, by making political representations, y'know."

"Don't be ridiculous, Fruity." I thought of my own dear old dad over there at NATO headquarters, dealing with "the Boche, the Hun," on a daily basis. And not much fonder of them than was Viscount Albemarle.

Then he brightened. "Did I tell you? The wing commander flew jump jets against the Argies in the Falklands War. That must have been jolly, Wing Commander, final gallant gesture of Empire, eh?"

"I was nineteen, sir, and bloody scared of those Exocet missiles the Argies had. Heat-seeking stuff, you know. Lock in on your exhaust and follow you right up the old bunghole!" He stopped abruptly. "Oh, I am sorry, Your Ladyship. Bloody rude of me, language like that. Dash it all!"

"Bloody Argentinos! It's all their fault," Fruity assured him. "If they hadn't stolen the Falklands you wouldn't have been scared and needn't have said what you just did, I mean, about 'up the old . . .' well, you know, dash it all."

Alix told the wing commander he was forgiven and we gave him a few phone numbers and addresses in the Hamptons, the Blue Parrot among them, in case the NATO exercises permitted them a bit of leisure time before they had to fly home, and he twitched a bit more frequently over that. Then we shook hands and boarded my car to head east. Alix got right into this matter of Fruity's wedding. And his bride.

"Just how much do you know about her, Fruity?"

"Well, her pa owns a chain of sweetshops here in the States and major cities 'round the world. Rich as Midas. Name of Buchanan. There are dozens of daughters, all of them beauties. The one I get is Mandy, second youngest. Quite jolly, actually. She's rather stunning to look at, smashing legs, y'know. Met her at a garden party last year. Dances extremely well and hits a very decent two iron. Blond, I believe—"

"Don't you know?" Alix demanded. In matters like that, she was like the medical examiner at the autopsy; she really wanted the facts.

"Well, I don't. You know I'm not all that keen on sex and we haven't yet . . . oh, I say, I do hope I'm not offending Stowe here with these intimacies."

"Not at all," I said, quite cheerful at that admission, considering how much time he and Alix had spent together over the years. She didn't let up on him either, not even after that:

"I simply don't understand, Fruits, why you have to marry anyone. And especially a social climbing heiress from New York. For an Old Etonian, it's all too, too Freddy Eynsford-Hill."

Fruity looked gloomy. "I feel that way, too. A bit. But she is jolly and there are all those sweetshops. My old pa says we could use the money. You wouldn't believe the cost these days of gardening, just rolling our lawns. Next autumn we have to put a new roof on Bute Castle, imagine the bill for that! The earl would hate to have to sell off any of the ancestral acres. So there's the cash. And having a wife would be something to occupy my mind."

"But your cabinet post. Isn't that sufficient?" I asked.

"Well, Ag and Fish isn't precisely being chancellor of the exchequer. I visit canneries and muck about on farms. In between I attend meetings of the Grange and chat with chaps on tractors about crops and such. Stare at prize poultry and suckling pigs and hand about blue ribbons and make polite remarks. Beyond that, Tony—I mean, the PM—doesn't tell me much about what's going on. I'm not even allowed to do the talk shows on the telly. Tony says stick to the garden club circuit and let grown-ups do the telly."

"That *is* rum," Alix said, all tea and sympathy, "not allowing you to go on the telly." While my opinion of "Tony," Prime Minister Blair, rose considerably.

Preparations for the wedding itself were well advanced, Fruity said, and thankfully at little burden to him. "They are a take-charge crew, got to say that. No fumbling about or shilly-shally. Get right to it. Efficient as the chain of sweetshops, I'd guess. They've got the caterers laid on. And the orchestra. Chap called Peter Duchin. He any good? I do enjoy a good gallop about the hardwood, y'know. And Mandy tells me the wedding dress is a smasher. I like Hardy Amies, myself, especially since that poor devil of a Wop got the chop down there in Mee-amee—"

"You mean the late Signor Versace?" Alix inquired tactfully.

"That's the fellow. Great talent lost there, people assure me. But the Buchanans insisted on an American look to the thing. I would have thought they'd go for Halston, if they needed a Yank."

"He's dead, too," I said.

"Pity," Fruity said. "All those talented chaps done in. Anyway, they've found a clever little woman. Name of Karan."

The Buchanans, as they had for Alix, had quarters arranged for Fruity. But Alix insisted we stable him elsewhere. "We don't want you in their clutches, do we? Retain your freedom of movement, Fruits, that's what I always say. Don't you always say that, Beecher? Gad about a bit, see the country, chat up the natives. I know this smashing little place, a bed-and-breakfast in East Hampton. I stayed there myself, although rather briefly, last year. . . ."

I groaned.

"The Mauve House?"

"You have the keenest extrasensory perception, Beecher. It's uncanny."

Fruity spoke up then, sensing a slight tension between us over housing him at the Mauve House.

"Will I like it, do you think?"

I turned from the wheel to nod encouragement. "Just keep the bedroom door locked, Fruity."

He brightened. Being an Etonian, there was a generous dose of voyeur in the viscount.

"Oh, I say, one of those places, eh?"

"You might say that," Alix said, noncommittal and not giving much.

# t h i r t e e n

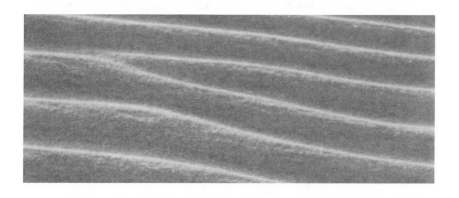

*They ate their captives. Nothing like a plump*
*teenager...*

Jesse Maine finally returned a phone call and joined us for dinner that
night at Monterey Grill, up on Three Mile Harbor. After introductions
had been made and over cocktails on the deck, watching the sun hanging
low over the opposite shore, Alix sort of briefed Jesse on the need to get
Fruity involved in any number of projects and keep him mentally challenged and otherwise occupied (and out of the clutches of the Buchanans,
though this went unsaid).

Jesse sipped at his vodka and Schweppes, considering a courteous response.

"Viscount, old bean, there's nothing I'd rather do than assist your
tutelages in the Great Outdoors here in America. But the timing ain't
good. My days are largely taken. It's the damned Pequots," Jesse Maine
said. "You know those bastards."

"Actually, I don't. Who may they be?"

"The Pequots are the meanest sons of bitches of Native Americans and indigenous peoples we got, Your Lordship. Clever as well and the richest. There's only maybe three hundred of them and each and every one a millionaire. Living like earls and dukes and such live back in your neighborhood. Up there in the woods in Connecticut they got the most profitable casino in the world, with sixty thousand trailer park white trash and other poor souls traipsing through there and leaving their cash every single day of the year. Christmas Day. Good Friday. Patriots Day. Hannukah. Puerto Rican Independence Day. Don't matter. People are up there just emptying out their pockets and signing blank checks, losing millions at the slots and making the damned Pequots even richer than they were yesterday. And close? Despite their millions a Pequot will use a damned kitchen match twice before lighting a fresh one. Nor are they tame, genial fellers like we Shinnecocks. You can negotiate things with a Mashpee Wampanoag or a Shinnecock, share at the campfire, buy a round of Coors. But not them Pequots.

"And now they're down here working the precincts and attempting to get some of our noble Shinnecocks on their side so they can open another casino on reservation land in Southampton! They even gave us two hundred thousand dollars to build a Shinnecock museum here but left us poor local boys to raise the other three hundred grand."

Jesse emptied his glass at a draught and signaled for an encore.

"So that's why, as much as I'd enjoy doing so, I can't guide Your Lordship through the local fens and bogs in pursuit of the wily muskrat and possum and raccoon. My days and nights are occupied with the damned Pequots and the temptations they and especially their chief medicine man, Honorable Autaquay Wilson, dangle before the innocents out here among the Shinnecock Nation."

"Does you great credit, sir," Fruity acknowledged, "though I do enjoy visiting the odd casino at Monte and Trouville, wagering a bob or two on the chemmy. But I see your position. Back home, the Welsh Nationalists feel much the same as you do about self-rule. As do the Scots. To say nothing of the damned Irish! Stand up for one's own patch of turf. Defend the home wicket, I always say, even if such sentiments may run counter to current national policy at Westminster."

"It's why the PM respects you so, Fruity, for your independence, I'm quite sure," Alix said, not at all sincerely, "but isn't it possible that your political acumen might be utilized on behalf of Jesse and the Shinnecocks.

And in opposition to these troublesome Pequots and foiling their medicine man?"

"'Troublesome' ain't the half of it, Lady Alix," Jesse declared in angry tones, almost spilling his freshly arrived vodka and Schweppes. "Did you know their original name was 'Pekawatawog,' which translates out to 'the Destroyers'? They was the most feared tribe in New England and in 1637 there was even a war fought over them, the Pequot War. In that one, it was Pequots versus everyone, the English and all the other Indian tribes. Everyone was in that one but the Latvians and Basques; it was the Muslims and the Serbs all over again. Unfortunately, about three thousand Pequots survived when their fortified town on the Mystic River was bombarded and captured by assault."

"Was that war over casinos, too?" Fruity asked.

"No, sir, that particular war was over furs and pelts, like what I poach out of Lake Agawan and Heady Creek and Georgica Pond and elsewheres today. But you got to go back a bit fully to appreciate what was going on here in them days. In Europe you had your Protestant Reformation and the Thirty Years War and such, butchering the Catholics and skewering the Huegenots; burning heretics at the stake and drawing and quartering the lads down there in Spain, where old Torquemada and the priests was in control. Or even in your very own little country, the Roundheads and the Cavaliers. I read up on such in the winter nights, y'know.

"Why, hell," Jesse went on, "that was naught but gin rummy compared to what was going on here in the years around 1550 when the prophet Hiawatha was out there speechifying and trying to unite the Five Tribes of the Iroquois League. And they needed unifying, let me tell Your Lordship. Scalping and blood feuds and treachery and ambushcades and tortures most fiendish and, yes, even cannibalism! You heard correct, sir; in them days they ate their captives. Men, women, children. Nothing quite like a plump teenager. You roasted them over campfires, basting them from time to time, tucked in your napkin and went right at it. 'I'll have a shinbone rare, Uncas. But hold the sauce.' Eating your enemies was to the Pequots what a covered-dish supper is to the Methodists 'round here today. You wouldn't believe what they was up to in the neighborhood back then, them Pequots and most of the other tribes."

"My word, Chief," Fruity said, "this is astonishing. In England we don't have a clue such things were going on. I assure you, the Colonial

Office should have cracked down, and smartly. You shan't find Tony Blair tolerating cannibalism, whatever the jurisdiction."

"There's more, Your Lordship. Don't go cracking down yet awhiles."

The waitress came, a young college kid, and we ordered. And, to tide us over, she brought another round of drinks. Then Jesse resumed.

"Meantimes, we fellows around here, the Shinnecocks, weren't let alone. No ivory towers for us, no sanctuary nor respite. Here we were cultivating the land and fishing and doing a little whaling right off the beaches. Montauk, back then, was known for producing the finest wampum in North America. We also did some trading and, Your Grace may be pleased to learn, we had good relations with the English, us and them bowing and scraping to each other like we was all cut of the royal cloth—"

"Oh, on behalf of the Crown, I am glad," the viscount declared, happy to make such representations on the part of his government.

"But there was no rest or tranquility for us, not a bit of it, not with the Pequots about and still undefeated. They came down here, looking for control of the wampum trade and, by the by, killing, looting and raping. Begging Your Ladyship's pardon, but there was that as well. Ripe young women carried off, with warriors taking full advantage. A sorry era for we Shinnecocks, I can tell you. After that, following the Pequot War, over from Rhode Island came the Narragansett. If it wasn't one maurauding tribe it was another; there was no time-out nor halftime show for the Shinnecocks, beleaguered as we was, and occasionally eaten, they never let up on us. By 1659 the Montauks had had it and retreated to East Hampton, where they sought refuge among the English settlers. Later on, the Mohegans took over, beating up on us and pillaging. And I might remind you, they, too, have a big casino up there in Connecticut today. Only us Shinnecocks are holding out against the slot machines and that's why I'm regrettably not at the viscount's every beck and call. And if someone could catch that waitress's eye, I could use another vodka before we start in on the victuals."

"My dear chap . . ." Fruity said, clearly moved by this account and by Jesse's emotional regrets.

"I say, Beecher, this is a jolly good spot," Alix said, also cheered by a fresh drink and enjoying the setting sun just to our west across the water.

When we'd dined, and well, and gone through several bottles of a quite passable Merlot, she gave Jesse one more nudge. Alix was like that; relentless.

"Jesse, in the film *Jaws*, the fisherman played by Robert Shaw, the one the shark swallowed whole, tugging him off the stern of the boat, didn't he come from out here?"

"Yes, he did, Lady Alix. Frank Mundus from Montauk. One of the great windbags of all time and a harsh, hard man. But a good fisherman. After the movie, he retired on his earnings and went to live temporarily in Hawaii. Came back a year or two ago. Don't know why. Maybe they had a shark shortage there at Waikiki Beach. But, yes, Mundus lives here on the East End."

"Could we retain him to take Fruity out one day and hunt sharks?"

The viscount got very excited over that.

"Oh, I say, Alix! What a smashing notion! Can one do that?"

Didn't take long for Jesse to deflate enthusiasm. "First of all, May is too early for shark. The water's still too cold for them to come in close enough for a day boat to reach them. Second, Mundus is retired. Thirdly, I wouldn't hire him if he carried us for nothing and advertised free drinks during the Happy Hour."

"But surely, if the sharks aren't biting, something else must be," Alix said, not willing to give it up. "The grunion, for example." Then, to me, "Didn't you explain to me about the grunion last year, Beecher?"

"Yes, I said they have a grunion run every year, but it's three thousand miles away in southern California."

"Oh," she said, somewhat deflated.

Jesse went on to talk about blackfish and mackerel and bottom fish like flounder and fluke and suggested if the weather got warmer the bluefish would be showing up. "Or," he said, trying to be helpful, "you could just charter a boat and go out for the day. Maybe see a whale out there, spouting."

"Good lord, Chief, do you mean that? An actual whale?" Fruity asked.

"Yes, I do. My own direct ancestor Wickham Cuffee, one of eight children born to Sarah Bunn and Vincent Cuffee of the Shinnecock Reservation, was a famous local whaler, going out in whaleboats right off Georgica Beach or Indian Wells or Old Beach, harpooning sperm and right whales, and towing them in through the surf to be rendered on the sand for their oil and baleen and ivory. He lived from 18-and-26 to 19-

and-15 and was, as far as can be determined, a pure-blooded Shinnecock. Most these days ain't, of course, having intermarried with blacks and whites and Asians and Italians and God knows what else. Look at me, Your Worship. I might well myself pass for an African-American gentleman when everyone knows I'm a sachem of the Shinnecocks."

"You can count on me, Mr. Maine, to keep that in mind when I return to London."

"Thank you, sir."

Jesse gave us the names of a couple of reliable charter boat skippers both in Hampton Bays and out at Montauk, just in case we wanted to take Fruity for a sail, and then we drove down to Main Street to have a nightcap at the Blue Parrot.

"Wing Commander!" Fruity cried, clearly delighted to see his RAF crew had made its way safely into town.

"Your Lordship."

The wing commander and his gallant "Few" had fallen in with tootsies who were staying at a local motel while scouting about for a group house to rent for the Season, and had discovered the margarita. At a corner table, down from Sag Harbor, Jimmy Buffet smiled benediction. Jimmy was hardly a regular but he dropped by on occasion and was always welcome. I bought a round and then Fruity bought and then Alix and I bailed out.

It had cooled through evening and when we got back to my gatehouse Alix said, "Might we have a fire? I do love this little house and hearing the ocean through the night and a fire would render it just perfect."

I made a fire and lighted it and we talked for a time about the odds on saving Fruity from the Buchanans, conceding they were slim but she wasn't ready quite yet to capitulate, and then Alix curled up next to me on the old leather chesterfield and kissed me before saying:

"East Hampton is wonderful. And so are you, Beecher Stowe."

I may have told you previously that Alix lies like a newspaper, as the saying goes. But I liked hearing her say that and liked it as well when she got up and led me to the bedroom, tugging her sweater off over her head as we went, and displaying that lovely back of hers to the best advantage as she passed through the door and into my bedroom....

# f o u r t e e n

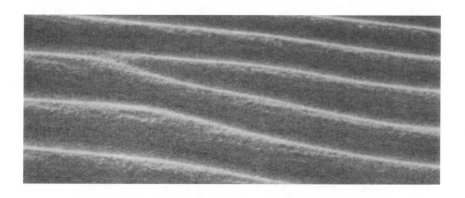

*When Irwin died, Hamill read, and movingly,
from* Girls in Their Summer Dresses...

Even before the Season begins out here there's one party everyone tries
to get to, especially literary people and those who pretend to be. It's the
annual spring book fair they call "Meet the Writers," to honor John
Steinbeck (his widow lives here) and to raise money for the library named
for him at Southampton College. Any writer who's got a new book out
is expected to contribute a half dozen copies and sit at a card table signing
books. The dough doesn't go to the writer or publisher but to the college
library and the most embarrassing thing for a writer in the Hamptons is
if no one buys the damned book and you end up buying back six books
yourself, just to mask shame. The book fair takes place at Elaine Benson's
outdoorsy art gallery and people mill about amid the statuary on the lawn
and drink cheap wine in plastic glasses and check out the chicks (or be
checked out by the chicks). And it's always a good crowd since fully half
the people in the Hamptons are writing books and the other half are
either literary agents or publishers. Ms. Benson herself has a book out

currently, a study of underwear through the ages, which is about as intellectual as things get in Bridgehampton. Alix wore a summery floral dress and a large straw hat and looked approximately perfect.

Bryan Webb came up and I introduced him. He had family money and went to Williams but he was okay despite that, pretty relaxed and having both style and a beautiful wife.

"Bryan and Pat have a great old farmhouse and a super garden," I said, being gracious.

"But north of the highway, Lady Alix. North," said Webb, 'umble as Uriah Heep and about as genuine. "We're obviously out of the loop. Wrong side of the tracks, proletarian when you get down to it. The same house south of the highway would cost real money."

Webb was a wealthy man who voted Democrat and talked airily of raising the minimum wage and opposing welfare reform, all that liberal rubbish. And that business of "north of the highway"? Well, there was something to it, snobbery as well as economics, but personally I thought both Webb and the local real estate salespeople beat it to death.

The usual writers had been rounded up. Bill Sheed and Peter Maas and Plimpton and Joe Heller and Vonnegut and Susan Isaacs and Ed Doctorow and Pete Hamill and Martha Stewart and Budd Schulberg and Michael Gross and Bill Flanagan and Sally Quinn and Ben Bradlee and Nelson de Mille and Gail Sheehy and Clay Felker and John Irving and Marty Gottfried and Rona Jaffe and plenty of others. Everyone but the checkout lady at the local IGA was writing a book. Irwin Shaw never missed the book fair and used to have people back to his house in Southampton afterwards where his son Adam entertained French covergirls who spent their time diving into Irwin's pool while we enjoyed a cocktail, and also enjoyed watching the French covergirls, especially those who didn't bother with tops, diving into the pool.

When Irwin died, that next year at the book fair Hamill read, and movingly, from *Girls in Their Summer Dresses*. I'll never forget that year's "Meet the Writers."

Daly the movie producer came over, and I made introductions again. When you went to parties with Her Ladyship you spent an inordinate amount of time making introductions.

"The president isn't due for another week and can you believe it, the

Secret Service is here already," Daly remarked. "Laying phone lines and looking suspiciously at things."

"Oh?"

"Sure, men in suits and short haircuts going in and out of shops on Job's Lane in Southampton and not buying? What else could they be? Women window-shop on Job's Lane. Not men in business suits."

I wondered if they'd yet gotten around to scrutinizing Gin Lane. Or if Cowboy knew. And decided I wouldn't be the one to inform him. He was sufficiently paranoid already. Let Parson Weems or Maguire confront his wrath. Alix thrilled to the idea of armed men checking us all out. "Do nudge me if you see one, Beecher. We don't have anything like it in Britain and I don't want to miss seeing them."

I promised. Among the regulars at the book fair in years past were James Jones, Truman Capote and Willie Morris. Willie was back in Mississippi, Truman was dead. I wonder what Truman would have thought about Secret Service agents prowling the Hamptons. Probably invite them home for a drink, he would.

Jim Jones was dead as well. But Gloria Jones came to the book fair. And their glamorous daughter; both Jones women writers themselves.

John Sargent was there, the former Doubleday boss, a big, hearty man who was married to a beautiful book editor named Betty Kelly. It was Sargent who got off that line about the difference between Southampton and East Hampton, about wearing ties and/or socks to dinner. But I always forget, which was it?

While we chatted with the Sargents, there was a bit of a buzz at the entrance. Alan Alda and Roy Scheider and their wives. And then there was even more of a buzz:

As Cowboy Dils rolled in on his golf cart, the broken, splinted leg awkwardly out to the side.

"Water for my horses and wine for my men, innkeeper!" he cried out as Fu Manchu cleared the way ahead of him brandishing the sort of fly whisk you might see Sabu wielding in a Zoltan Korda movie set in Calcutta. While Greasy Thumb Guzik and Maguire guarded his flanks, wary of mere people forcing themselves on Cowboy and seeking autographs. Or even more frightening, actual intimacy. Harry Almond caught my eye.

"I warned him not to come," Harry said fretfully. "But he's headstrong and won't listen."

"Well," I said, not knowing just what tack to take.

"I for one am delighted he's here," Alix said, very crisp about it.

"Is it dangerous? Are there risks?" Almond asked. "You've been to these things before, I take it." He sort of shuddered, uneasy with the crowd pressing in so close. "I do worry about him. Too much, I'm sure. But he insisted. He doesn't want people thinking he's afraid. Since the hit-and-run, I mean."

"Don't let him run anyone over in the cart," I suggested. "Beyond a few autograph hounds, and the groupies, I don't think he's in danger."

"We'll be on the alert as well, Mr. Almond," Alix pledged, "prepared instantly to spring into action should events require."

"I do thank Your Ladyship."

She gripped my forearm fiercely. "Was that appropriate for me to say? I know I speak out too freely at times, Beecher, and you're so much more tactful. I do count on your discretion."

"Fine, Alix." Her manners were instinctive; she didn't need lessons.

Why weren't the Buchanans here? I'd have thought this was precisely the sort of social-climbing event that would have drawn them. I considered making our way over to Cowboy but there was a crush. He might not be terribly popular along Gin Lane; here in Bridgehampton at the book fair, Dils was almost Cronkite, "the most admired American." Except for a few people who got him mixed up with rival icons.

"Where is he, where is he?" a woman said, pushing past Alix and me. "Who?"

"Howard Stern, you moron! Howard's here and signing autographs."

I determined to be above such drama and, vaguely, informed her:

"He toils not, neither does he spin."

"But where the hell is he?" the woman demanded.

"He fell into a sulk and left," I said. "You missed him."

"Oh, shit," the woman said, dabbing at her eyes with a Kleenex.

Alix shook her head.

"We have people like that in Britain, too. Appalling. Pa blames the telly."

A man I knew but whose name I couldn't recall came up, having just seen and heard Cowboy in full, rhetorical flight.

"That fellow Dils, that man is his own hurricane!"

I agreed that he was. And took Alix off up the road to Bobby Van's for a cocktail. To our astonishment, Viscount Albemarle and the RAF had already set up a command post at the bar.

"What happened to the Blue Parrot? I thought you chaps were well and truly—"

"We heard there was a party nearby, lit'ry folk, Somerset Maugham and Jeffrey Archer and that lot," the co-pilot said, "but we lacked the current charts and landed here instead."

They were all drunk, or en route, even Fruity. The wing commander, well, let's not speak of that, was resting, his face in the ashtray.

"Wouldn't it be delicious if Mr. Buchanan came in now? With that wife of his," Alix murmured. "A confrontation with Fruity; that's all we need."

"Bring on their nubile daughters!" I shouted, attempting to get into the spirit of the thing along with Fruity and the RAF.

"Don't be vulgar, Beecher. You're superior to all that."

Alix didn't nag but maintained a certain standard; like Harvard or the Episcopal Church, she didn't let you get away with much.

"Sorry," I said, and meaning it. Alix expected better of me than shouts and one-liners, especially when Fruity and the lads, being drunk, had excuses and all I'd had were a couple of cheap wines.

We now had a round of the better stuff with the viscount and his air crew. Alix was all for my drinking provided I didn't shout. The wing commander had been revived with a fresh drink and was going on about the Falklands and what bastards the Argies were. I had the impression his brief war had, at age nineteen, formed him forever, and that whatever age he now was, or would live to, he would always, at the core, be a nineteen-year-old carrier pilot terrified of Exocet missiles and going up regardless. Which is, I suppose, as good a definition of courage as you'd want.

I kept waiting for Cowboy and his entourage to make their way a few hundred yards down the road to Van's. But they never got here. Although, as I scanned the place, it seemed to me there were several men in dark suits, navy or banker's gray, wearing white shirts and muted ties as well, young, useful-looking men, with badges of some sort in their lapels and, some of them, earpieces in their ears, as if they were listening to the Walkman.

The feds, I assumed, silently crediting Daly for being well informed.

Was it possible they were watching for Dils? Or anyone else who might conceivably put the president at risk? Maybe that's why Dils wasn't here; Harry Almond, who didn't drink, might astutely have steered him away. Or was all this simply lively imagination on my part?

Just then, unnoticed by the feds, and by most people, Roger Champion and his wife arrived and were bowed, quietly, to their table against the wall in back. No fuss. Fuss wasn't Mr. Champion, who did things with a quiet, appropriate style, as the old WASP were supposed to do. But he was cordial to the man seating them and gave a small wave to a diner who called out "Hallo there, Roger," and bestowed a good smile on the waitress when she came with the menus. A man relaxed and secure in knowing just who he was.

A few heads had turned to watch Mr. Champion; more had turned to follow his wife moving through the room to their table.

Over a final drink at the bar, joshing with Fruity and the RAF, I watched the Champions and felt slightly uneasy for having done so. Champion was very nearly a great man and most people, myself included, recognized that and admired him. And his wife was still one of the true beauties. A good marriage, people said, one that endured. Yet I sensed a tension between them. Was that, like this sudden arrival of "federal agents," to be blamed on an overactive imagination, fueled by my own drinking? For whatever reason, the ease with which they'd taken their table, smiled their quiet hellos, was gone. In its place, something impossible to quantify. She was doing most of the talking, her voice low, her body language conveying intensity, leaning forward on her forearms, her eyes focused on his. She had a classically beautiful face but it was her body that spoke, an articulate and fluent body, a body you imagined could tell tales. I watched Champion's face. Stone, absolutely stone. His face told you nothing, hers told you, well, what you read into it. What could she have said to her husband that turned him so cold? They were close, they touched, and yet...I felt almost cheap about watching them, listening to the murmur of their voices and trying, without success, to catch their words, to discern the root of that tension. If tension it was. Nothing wrong with working honorably as a reporter; voyeurism was something else again.

"Beecher, are you still among us?"

"Yes, sorry."

Alix had taken note of my wanderings. So as to recoup my sense of self and slough off this faint, unexpected and surely pointless guilt, I whispered in Her Ladyship's ear, "Let's go home. I don't want to compromise the aristocracy by getting pulled over on a DWI."

She stood then on tiptoes and kissed me lightly on the lips.

"No," she said, "we certainly don't want that, do we."

Outside at the curb as we went toward our car, a big Rolls-Royce waited, the chauffeur lazing in the driver's seat, half asleep. Walt, one of Van's barmen, was on the sidewalk grabbing a quick smoke.

"Some car," he said.

"Yeah," I agreed. "Whose is it?"

"That car? Why, that car's Roger Champion's."

Like the car that hit Cowboy, it was a Rolls and it was black. And once more I wondered, just what the hell was Slim Champion telling her husband that turned him so rigid? I started to remark this to Alix but she was saying, "If you'll give me the keys, Beecher, I'll get us back safely. And discreetly as well. I promise."

She did, too.

# f i f t e e n

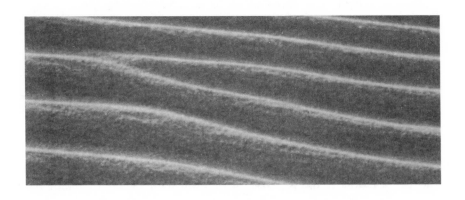

*"Don't try to bully me and the American press, sir!"*

I slept badly and in the morning was briefly restless, and didn't know why. Must have been those final and surely unnecessary drinks. Then I remembered. It was seeing Roger and Slim Champion up close, privy to their private moments at the small corner table near the window. Why was that insight into their lives, which until now held no great interest for me, at all significant? Why it bothered me, I could not even now say. What if her gaze lingered and her voice beckoned and men wondered in drink if she . . . And what if their car were black? So was Dils's own Rolls. So were a half dozen others I could name from here.

A long shower helped and then the sight of a not-yet-dressed Alix bustling about the kitchen pretending to make coffee (she rarely ever committed coffee but liked to threaten), focused me wonderfully, not on unhealthy curiosity about Mr. and Mrs. Champion, or on omens and portents, bad dreams and queasy yesterdays, but on the ripe possibilities of this and other bright mornings yet to come.

Alix had her own schedule limned out and I spent the day down at the Montauk docks watching the fishing boats go out, chatting up mates and skippers, having a beer in the waterfront bars. Talking, listening, taking a few discreet notes. In a primitive way the story of the Hamptons Baymen was coming together. No need to tell Anderson; he didn't want progress reports. Editors want the finished story. That evening, with Her Ladyship occupied, I was alone. And had opportunity to think and ponder. And wonder how my father was getting along over there at NATO, living amid Belgians and negotiating with Germans. It was pleasant being alone for a change, alone without being lonely. I had a capacity for self-entertainment and didn't always need people around. Nice for once to have been abandoned by friends. Cowboy was enjoying ministrations and recovering among his entourage, while Alix and Fruity, and everyone else concerned, were off attending a dinner the Buchanans were hosting at the Shinnecock Hills Golf Club, overlooking Bullhead Bay on the north side of Southampton, not quite as posh as the neighboring National Links but pretty fine.

"A command performance this time, Beecher," she'd told me. "They'll brook no excuses or diplomatic illnesses. If you're in the wedding party, you dine with the Buchanans tonight. They're being quite stiff about it."

She thought it was marvelous the Shinnecocks had a golf course all their own. "I wonder if Jesse Maine will be on hand. Wouldn't be at all surprised, being tribal shaman, or sachem, and all that. Probably on the dinner committee."

I explained the club was named after its location in the Shinnecock Hills, no relation to the reservation, and was where they played the U.S. Open and it didn't belong to the Indians at all but to some Old Money WASPs and golf nuts and sportsmen like Jack Whitaker, who did eloquently literate things on-air for ABC Sports.

"Mmmmm," she said. "I'd be interested to hear Jesse on the matter of provenance and ownership."

Alix loved to stir the pot and you could almost hear the tumblers clicking and falling in her head. In her absence, I hung out for a time at the Parrot with the lads and went home early to burn a steak, and was marginally still awake when Alix returned.

"Well," she said, kicking off shoes and flinging herself into a chair, "that was something to behold. *Quel* drama!"

"Tell me," I said, brightening considerably that she was back. A day without Alix was one thing; the night quite something else.

"Well, first of all, I actually met the blushing bride, the young woman about to be sacrificed to Fruity's animal lusts."

"Which you assured me were few and far between ..."

"Don't be literal. I'm sure, when the time comes, the nuptial bed beckoning and ready, the sheets turned down, that the Viscount Albemarle will do his duty. If, and I stress the 'if,' if indeed such a propitious moment ever arrives. Men of his breeding appreciate their role, they accept the burdens of rank and class. Eton may not prepare a man for the marital gymnastics, the erotic jumping up and down, so to speak, and just who does what to whom, but it surely instills in one a sense of duty. Just read Wellington on the matter, the 'playing fields of Eton' and all that. But I can assure you, Beecher, this girl is lush beyond all telling. I read *Tatler*, *Town & Country*, *The Economist*; I see the photos; I get about. I know that the Buchanan gels, all of them, are prime. Raised like heifers, prepped for market. But Mandy Buchanan, well, the future Viscountess Albemarle, I can testify right here that if I possessed a single lesbian urge within my entire body, and who knows? one day I very well might, I would leap upon this Mandy and take her to my bosom." Brief pause:

"As well as to other essential parts."

"That great?"

"Oh, Beecher," she said, not arch and amused and above it all now, but deadly serious:

"This girl is lovely. And from what I saw of her, awfully nice. A decent, wholesome girl. Ripe, if ever a bride were!" And, in a typically thrown-away line, acknowledged, "Dumb, of course, dumb as a brush." Another hesitation. "Perfect for Fruity, in some ways, when you get right down to it. But needing someone more earthy than darling Fruits, earthy and male and, well, not to put too fine a point on it nor be gratuitously explicit ... all thrusting virility." She looked into my face. "Am I making myself clear, Beecher?"

I said she was. Though not quite sure where she was headed with all this. The social contract cut both ways and I was still mulling. Besides, the British aristocracy has its own handwriting, its special pleadings, rules and regulations you and I might not appreciate. But enough pondering.

"But what actually happened? All the drama you're blathering about," I asked, by now up-to-date on Miss Buchanan's charms.

Alix licked her lips and was at last prepared to give an account of the evening, having aroused curiosity:

"The evening chez les Buchanans opened with an absolute shocker!"

"Oh? The Shinnecocks turn up demanding a deed to the place?"

"Not at all, and don't be flip. We were confronted with a demand, and a quite outrageous one, from Mr. Buchanan. They're manipulative people, Tom and Daisy; you can see it with the girls. And now with a captive audience, all of us members of the wedding, they set out to bend everyone else to their will."

What was this all about? I wondered. Alix went on:

"Mr. Buchanan wanted us all to sign legal documents pledging that we wouldn't sell our stories of the wedding to the *National Enquirer*. Or the *Star*. Or, God save us, to something called 'The Geraldo Show.' Who might that be? I inquired politely, and was told he's a fellow on the telly who gets into fistfights with guests when he isn't praying over them. Can that be so?"

"Approximately," I said, not being a big Geraldo fan.

It seemed, she said, the Buchanans had already cut their own deals with individual magazines and other media, picking and choosing. *People* magazine had the exclusive among weeklies, *Vanity Fair* the monthly, the *Chicago Tribune*, surprisingly, the daily exclusive (it turned out Mr. Buchanan's worldwide headquarters was in Chicago, in the very building named for and housing the *Tribune* newspaper!). A control freak, apparently. If you can't keep the press out then spin the story your way.

"He admitted he was still dithering over giving the television rights to Entertainment Tonight or Barbara Walters. But leaning toward Barbara."

"Fortunate Ms. Walters," I remarked.

When they'd presented the pledge of confidentiality to Alix Dunraven, she'd refused.

"I said it was a freedom of speech issue and that I'd like to mull it over a bit, consult with eminent counsel, and similar rot. After all, I do work for Mr. Rupert Murdoch and I'm not sure Rupert would be all that pleased to have one of his key operatives signing pledges not to pass on the dish to Page Six and the like. You're a canny sort, Beecher. Do you think I was correct to refuse?"

Whenever Alix called me "a canny sort." Or, even better, "a hardcase," she could do just about anything with me. Didn't even have to use a little finger to twist me about.

"I'm sure you were, Alix. Very shrewd indeed."

"Oh, good."

"Did anyone else object?"

"There were a few raised eyebrows, but no. Not really. Fruity, of course, practically broke his arm signing up right away."

"Why was he so enthusiastic?" I asked.

"Hates the tabloids. All except for *News of the World* on Sundays. That's the best-selling Sunday paper we have, and, as you probably know, specializes in stories about campaigns to bring back the chamber pot in country inns and naughty choirmasters up in the loft with boy sopranos. Fruity loves *News of the World.* By far his fave, simply dotes on it. So does my old pa. But Fruity hates the rest of them. Nigel Dempster in the *Daily Mail* and the *Sun* and the *Mirror* especially, they keep on and on about him, especially since the PM put him in the cabinet. I don't blame Fruity, either. They make him sound a proper twit."

"Well—" I started to say, but she cut me dead.

"Don't be vicious, Beecher. You know he's a former fiancé of mine and a great chum, while you're, well, currently my . . . well, you know what we are."

"Yes," I said, quite pleased.

She went on then about the dinner, which was apparently quite something, and the music after, also first-rate. "For a golf club, it's an appealing old house. No Shinnecock need be ashamed of it. Even the secret agents seemed to be enjoying themselves."

"Secret agents?"

"Fellows in dark suits huddling with the banquet manager and using cell phones. Must have been them, don't you think?"

"Mmmm," I said. So men in suits had descended on Shinnecock Hills, not to play a round of golf but to sniff out the place, and the crowd, lest the president find himself next weekend sailing in harm's way.

Alix picked up the yarn:

"And then came this extraordinary confrontation between Mr. Buchanan and one of the supposedly honored guests, not a member of the wedding at all but someone I assumed was a close family friend, even a relative, a favorite uncle, perhaps, an elegantly plump, pink, dimpled gentleman of a certain age with a shock of white hair. Except that it turned out he was John Fairchild of *Women's Wear Daily*."

"Fairchild!" Now it was my turn to be startled. "What the hell was John Fairchild doing at a bridal dinner for Fruity and Ms. Buchanan?"

Alix bathed me in smiles, terribly pleased to have disturbed my sangfroid.

"Well, that's precisely what I wondered, Beecher. I mean, there's Mr. Buchanan laying down the rules of engagement for the media in general, dictating terms to Barbara Walters and the networks and Time Inc. and Conde Nast, to say nothing of the *Chicago Tribune*, and here at Mrs. Buchanan's elbow, place of honor, practically a member of the family, is the man who runs *W* and *Women's Wear* and makes a positive career out of scooping the world on juicy inside details of wedding dresses and so on."

"What happened?" I demanded, all thoughts of Fruity's sexuality or of Mandy's lush beauty swept from the board by this puzzling and dramatic entrance of an unexpected guest onto the Southampton stage.

"All in due course, Beecher. It's what we all wanted to know. Everyone was mystified. Even Fruity, who I must concede can be dense about such things, was caught up in the drama. Though I did have to explain to him just who Mr. Fairchild was—"

"Alix, what happened?"

"I'm getting to it, Beecher. Apparently the Buchanans were in possession of highly authoritative intelligence that *WWD* was on the case and that details of the wedding dress had already been leaked. You know how fashion designers are. Compared to them, a hairdresser takes positive vows of silence. So information was trickling out of the Maison Karan. Not from Donna herself, of course; the woman's confidentiality personified. But various of her minions came under suspicion. Had Donna's most trusted aides betrayed her? Had money changed hands? Whatever happened to loyalty and such? Being the sort of people the Buchanans are, they didn't so much confront Mr. Fairchild as attempt to co-opt him, drawing him into the family's more intimate circles and inviting him to this bridal dinner. Inviting the fox into the henhouse for cocktails, so to speak, a not awfully subtle attempt at bribery of the most genteel sort. Their assumption, of course, that being a gentleman and having enjoyed their largesse, John Fairchild could no longer, in good conscience, break the story. Not as a Yale man who'd dined at their table and so on—"

"Princeton," I murmured; "he went to Princeton."

"Quite," she said.

"And?" I asked.

"Well that's when the shouting started. Mr. Fairchild's understanding was decidedly *not at all* the understanding of Mr. and Mrs. Buchanan! What had been until then a pleasant enough evening, laughter and dance, decent food and smashing vintages, all bonhomie and genial talk, erupted in challenges and defiance of the most heated sort. I'm not quite sure what triggered it, but suddenly, there was John Fairchild on his feet, looking down the table at his host, bowing slightly to his hostess, and announcing:

"'I am a journalist. Thoroughly committed to our nation's Bill of Rights, the First Amendment and that sort of thing. I refuse to have this country or my newspaper compromised. *Women's Wear Daily* scooped the world with details of Princess Margaret's dress when she married Armstrong Jones. Norman Hartnell never spoke to me again. And I fully accepted that as part of the cost we pay for a vigorous editorial independence. The black dress Valentino whipped up overnight for Jackie Onassis to wear at Daddy O's funeral; the body not yet cold, yet we had the dress on page one. The younger Lyndon Johnson's daughter's wedding dress, I forget her name, not the one who was engaged to George Hamilton, the other one. Her marriage didn't take, as I recall. When the king of the Belgians, that skinny chap in spectacles, when he married Fabiola of Spain, we were there. Balenciaga was stunned at our audacity. But our First Amendment rights were observed. Even the great Balenciaga knew better than to tamper with the American press. And you know that no one, anywhere, cuts a suit or a coat with quite Balenciaga's mastery. Or does a superior armhole. Streisand's awful dress at the Oscars. We had the exclusive there, I can assure you. Scaasi's a nimble little chap who, I must say, neither sulked nor pouted but took it in good humor. The Gore girl's wedding. A rather pretty dress. Simplicity was 'in' last year. And why not? And I must say, I can do without Gore, but Tipper is great fun. We scooped them all. Every one of those wedding dresses out there, and exclusively, on page one. But if you think I can be bought off by a good dinner or intimidated, well, you have another think coming, Mr. Buchanan. That isn't what the Bill of Rights is all about!

" 'So if you can have my car called, I'll be leaving.' "

"Wow!"

"But there's more! You know that Disney owns Fairchild Publications? Well, here was Mr. Buchanan's opportunity. 'I know Michael Eisner!' he thundered, in tones one could only describe as stentorian, 'and I'll report your behavior to CEO and Chairman Eisner in the morning.'

"And Mr. Fairchild shouting back, 'Don't attempt to bully me and the American media, sir. We discuss it often, he and I, and I can tell you Chairman Eisner believes fiercely in the First Amendment. And in the great work *Women's Wear Daily* does and continues to do for the fashion industry and for America!' "

I shook my head. "That's some story," I acknowledged.

"My sentiments exactly," said Lady Alix smugly, delighted to have topped a journalist on his own turf.

## s i x t e e n

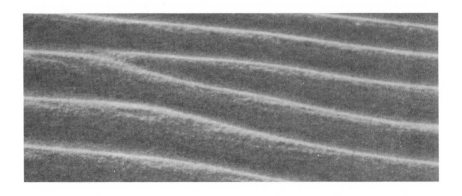

*Bill Blass and Fairchild snubbing each other in the elevator . . .*

John Fairchild on Gin Lane! This was astonishing news. First Cowboy Dils; then feds in their business suits talking surreptitiously into their lapels; now Fairchild of *WWD*.

What had God against Southampton?

None of us (well, maybe God) yet knew much about O'Hara; we learned more later on. This was the first Secret Service operative actually on site, the first carelessly, almost arrogantly, to double-park a car on Job's Lane or Main Street or First Neck Lane and leave it there. Illegally. In order to get out and just stroll around. Looking, watching, taking mental notes. The first to amble into shops and bars and the movie house and begin asking questions. And waiting, *waiting*, until he got answers. An . . . uncomfortable man. The first to arrive, to watch, to ask, to raise a skeptical eyebrow as if to inquire: "Is that so? You really mean that? I find that difficult to believe." There'd been no one like this in Southampton since 1990, when they took the last census.

And those people were sent 'round to the servants' quarters to submit their forms in triplicate. You didn't send O'Hara anywhere. And especially and notably not 'round back!

For all the talk from Daly and others about Job's Lane swarming with feds, laying wires and breaking out search warrants, there was at this stage only O'Hara. He was the opening wedge, shortly to be reinforced by lesser men. And he was beginning to make his presence felt.

You know how small towns are, discreet and nosy at the same time, desperate to maintain privacy while dying to peek into the neighbor's bedroom? O'Hara was a brisk, beefy man, round-faced and sandy-haired, pleasant-looking, who wore nicely cut gabardine suits, oxford button-down shirts and repp ties (the effect more J. Press than Brooks, if you know what I mean), and read deeply in the early Latins, Vergil, Horace and Livy, though most enthusiastically in *Caesar's Wars*, and from all of which he was fond of reciting, by memory, both in the original Latin and (for the less well educated) an excellent English translation. He also was an amateur of Irish lit and enjoyed entering a room with a phrase or two from Joyce, an especial favorite being, "Stately, plump Buck Mulligan came down from the stairhead..."

So, being nosy, bartenders and others inquired—politely, of course—of O'Hara just what work he did and what did he think of Southampton? You didn't snare O'Hara that easily. To one he hinted he was with the Army Corps of Engineers, here to assess the perils of beach erosion. To another he suggested the government was preparing a new geodetic survey and he was making preliminary measurements of the earth's curvature and reporting the calculations back to Washington. To others he mentioned the Department of the Interior and its National Forestry Service and allowed as how he might be here on a "timber cruise," estimating the number of board feet of potentially useful lumber contained in the East End's famous pine barrens.

A few pushy interrogators were fobbed off with "I'm here for my health, Johnny, taking the waters. Per doctor's orders, on a regimen of diet and high colonics."

Some saw sinister motives in all this, usually those who'd actually seen O'Hara talking into a button on his lapel. Others thought he was just another silly man, of whom Southampton already had plenty. A few well-informed people checked him out with sources in Washington and were told he was indeed some variety of government man (no one confirmed he was Secret Service; they prefer to keep those things to themselves down there, and understandably so) here on official business. Beyond that, even the best of "sources" would not go.

And what nobody admitted or even hinted at was the truth: that O'Hara was fiercely ambitious, funny, eccentric, canny, Cal Tech–educated, and possessed (but never boasted of) the highest IQ any Secret Service agent ever scored. At his age (about fifty) he was young enough for active fieldwork and old enough to have a healthy fixation on Nazis.

"Oh, the Commies, sure. The domestic militias. Hezbollah. The Libyans. But when you get down to it," he would inform subordinates, "it's the Nazis you're watching out for, those bastards."

"O'Hara," someone might protest, "the war ended fifty years ago. Any Nazis still around, they got to be seventy-five, eighty at least."

O'Hara would shake his head slowly in regret, fixing his interlocutor with bare tolerance.

"You're so easily taken in. Everyone lives longer these days, why not the Nazis? Don't be naive. There are palliatives, hormone treatments, all variety of nostrums, oils and unguents. Liposuction and cosmetic surgery. Exercise and diet. These fellows are clever. They subscribe to the *Journal of the AMA*, the *New England Journal of Medicine*. They know what's safe, what's effective—"

"But then how can we know which are the Nazis and which . . . ?"

It was then that O'Hara would drop his voice and lean in close, sharing confidences with his men:

"Good question. Glad to see you're asking it. In a beach resort like Southampton, it can be difficult. There are plenty of suntanned Nordic blond huskies. Lots of them wearing shorts. And, being shrewd, you'll find very few Nazis still sporting lederhosen. They're in Bermuda shorts from Banana Republic like everyone else. They may be crewcut, but so are we, and they sure don't wear those armbands anymore."

"But then, how do we tell . . ."

O'Hara's voice fell yet another register and men leaned even closer to hear.

"Hairless limbs. That's the giveaway, that's how you can always tell a Nazi. Smooth, virtually hairless legs. I've never yet encountered a hairy Nazi. You check it out, look it up. They did studies at Nuremberg during the trials. Not a single Nazi ever examined closely had hairy legs. Not one..."

He conceded there were felons other than aging Nazis. But the Nazis were his favorites. Some of his men idolized O'Hara; others thought him a bit of a crank. The Secret Service itself? Well, just consider this; he was assigned only to the biggest, the most complex and difficult cases.

Oh, yes, one other thing: O'Hara was a trained killer.

It was this fellow that Southampton now gossiped about and wondered just what he was up to and why, who sent him and what might be his vulnerabilities and his vices, which his resources and his strengths? Except that none of us really knew the answers to any of this, nor would we, until one late May morning on Gin Lane...

But that was later.

It happened, on the other hand, that I already was reasonably well-informed about John Fairchild. Being Old Hamptons myself, I needed no briefing, knowing at least approximately how Mr. Fairchild truly felt about the place, since he'd lived here and been driven out. And I suspected what his attitudes might be about social climbers like the Buchanans. Clearly, if Alix's information was correct, and on something like this she was uncanny, we were due ferocious moments and high drama before Memorial Day and with the Season hardly begun, there being nothing quite as savage as blood sport among the rich and privileged.

It might be worthwhile to review the bidding at this point. First of all, John Fairchild knew the Hamptons. He and Jill had for some years a splendid place in the Georgica Association in East Hampton. They sold both house and land when a former Fairchild executive had the audacity to buy a house of his own on Further Lane barely three miles to the east. To the Fairchilds, this was equivalent to "there goes the neighborhood." And it was sufficient for John to write off the entire Hamptons, relegating them to "a haven for the second-rate." People here might have money. But what was money when compared to caste and class? Rather showily, and often, Mr. Fairchild quoted Coco Chanel:

"There are people with money and there are people who are rich."

And so Mr. and Mrs. Fairchild sold short on Georgica and left for the south of France and a historic farm in the Camargue.

In more recent years, the Fairchilds had not only that farm in France but a town house in London, a chalet at Klosters, the apartment on Sutton

Place, a Nantucket getaway. The Bermuda house was sold long ago, as was the apartment in Gracie Square and the New Canaan house. They might still have the French farmhouse but I'm not sure about Klosters. The one mystifying purchase? A condo in Vero Beach, Florida. What did John and Jill Fairchild have in common with Vero Beach? Palm Beach, perhaps. Or Boca. But Vero Beach?

That was a puzzlement.

Now the ubiquitous (and surely relentless) Fairchild had surfaced on Gin Lane. The Buchanans, understandably, were at a loss. Panic, fear and loathing, a sense of betrayal, righteous anger, resentment, insecurity, and the vague suspicion they'd been gulled. It was nearly as bad as having the tabloids on your case with shifty little men pawing through your trash and bribing the servants. Or so came the breathless telephoned reports to Alix through the following day. Not from the Buchanans themselves, they were sufficiently astute to keep their mouths shut, but from members of the wedding, young men and women Alix knew. Or if she didn't, Fruity did.

Then Harry Almond called. He was in a decidedly pious Parson Weems mood and couldn't have cared less about John Fairchild.

"Did you see page one of the *Times* this morning? That story from Shanghai about Chinese Communist gays coming out of the closet?"

Yes, I'd seen it. So what?

"Cowboy wants to use it in a skit. He has Fu Manchu mincing around the lawn practicing a Chinese lisp. A Communist Chinese lisp at that, which Cowboy insists that, in Mandarin, has a distinct, proletarian tone to it. I'm convinced the whole idea is racist and sexist stereotyping of the worst manner and sort. I've told him so and that it's in such dreadful taste even I won't write the dialogue. Bad enough we have the president sore at us; we need a billion Chinese plus who knows how many gays on our case?"

"What did he say to that?"

"He said, and I quote him precisely, 'I know it's in terrible taste. That's what's so great about it!' "

Dils even had a working title for the skit: "Mao-tse-Tongue." Harry seemed to cringe even as he spoke the words and I'm sure I groaned.

When I remained mute, Harry said Cowboy wanted to know what Her Ladyship and I thought.

"He respects you, Stowe. He may not admit it but the fact she has a title and you went to Harvard made an impression. In New Mexico, they don't have many Harvard men or titled Englishwomen..."

I promised that Alix and I would get back to him.

I called Karl Lager on Scuttle Hole Road with the news. Not, I assure you, about the gays coming out of Shanghai closets, but about John Fairchild's appearance at the wedding banquet (was it Banquo or Macduff who crashed the party in *Macbeth?*). There was that long-standing feud between Fairchild and Lager and I knew Karl would want to know "the auld enemy" was in town.

"I've already heard," he said morosely. "Half a dozen phone calls late last night and this morning alerting me. People so enjoy spreading the bad news."

Here was a man the OSS parachuted behind German lines during the war and he'd gone into a funk over the arrival in Southampton of John Fairchild.

"Cheer up," I urged Lager, who'd not shown a collection on Seventh Avenue for years. "You're out of the business."

"And a good thing, too," he agreed.

Karl Lager had all the money he would ever need and the license deals coined money and pretty much ran themselves and he spent his time painting and boating and writing books. So one would think he was well and safely out of the reach of Fairchild's critical pen and of hard feelings dating back years. But this was the fashion business and who ever understood such matters, the whys and how of feuds and dislikes?

"And this time," I reminded Karl, "it's not you that Fairchild's tangling with. It's Buchanan and Bill Blass."

I threw that in, about Blass, to cheer up Lager. Fairchild had, just recently and rather publicly, broken with his old pal Blass over some real or fancied slight. And since the two men owned apartments in the same Sutton Place building, this made things somewhat sticky. Karl brightened marginally and his eyes crinkled into something of a merry glint. Perhaps he was imagining the two gentlemen, Fairchild and Blass, encountering each other in the lobbies or, better still, being isolated together in an elevator, neither man speaking and each refusing to be the first to remove his hat.

At the very notion, Lager seemed metaphorically to be rubbing his big hands together.

But he was hardly cocky. "I don't believe Fairchild came out here simply to bedevil the Buchanans."

"Of course that's the reason. Alix said there was a very ugly scene over dinner. A shouting match. Accusations made. Action threatened, legal and otherwise. Fairchild hurling defiance and Buchanan digging in. Each of them claiming to have the ear of Michael Eisner out there at Disney in L.A."

"Don't be taken in. I don't deny there may be hostility over *WWD*'s coverage of the Buchanan wedding. But I'm convinced Fairchild's gotten word of what I'm up to, our campaign to save the raceway. And is out to embarrass me, sabotage our efforts—"

"Rubbish. John Fairchild's no land developer. With no interest at all in auto racing. What possible motivation—"

Lager pounced.

"Didn't you see last month's issue of *W*? The one with that pretty Paltrow girl on the cover?"

"No."

"Well, then, you missed the Suzy Knickerbocker column with its very favorable reference to a dinner party hosted by Wyseman Clagett! When Suzy starts writing about Long Island land developers, I smell funny business at the crossroads. Society hairdressers and interior decorators and the loftier fund-raisers are one thing; but a man who builds shopping malls? Don't tell me you don't sense Fairchild's fine Italian hand at work here."

Although Mr. Fairchild's motivation was still mystifying, I actually knew more than I wanted to know (it had been all over the local weeklies for several years) about the battle over the old race course, a parcel of some five hundred acres: lawsuits were pending, the owner was refusing to sell, Clagett and his backers were floating grandiose schemes, and both county and state had concerns about protected groundwater and the Peconic Estuary Watershed.

But you don't want to know about that unless you live out here or have a piece of the speculative action.

And now when I asked just why an outsider, John Fairchild, would take sides in a local land matter, Karl Lager spoke, his voice ice-cold now and steady.

"Except for the difference in style, he and your friend Cowboy have something in common: They enjoy making a fuss."

I see, I said, not quite sure I did.

Nor was Karl convinced government could be trusted to preserve the land and fend off development. "Sometimes you have to get up on your hind legs yourself. I learned that a long while ago when my family got out of Germany. Your father would understand, despite being in government."

I knew he and the Admiral were, if not friends or colleagues, aware of the other's work. Almost as if Lager read my thoughts, he murmured, "You know, the Great Game..."

"Yes," I said, knowing precisely what he meant. Yet how long it had been since I'd heard the phrase...

"The Great Game," once played by the secret services of Britain and Tsarist Russia over India and Afghanistan and Kurdistan and all those other little "-stans" in between, a deadly game played out in the last century, Kipling's time, and then in Lager's time, against the Nazis, and finally in our time during the Cold War, yet another brand of Russians and ourselves, the Yanks this time. Old OSS men like Karl Lager, younger men like Clair George in the CIA. The Great Game...

Karl shook himself as if to clear the air of memory, and said, almost sheepishly, "Silly, isn't it? Bunch of old farts not willing to concede their obsolescence. Driving fast little cars and playing the fool. Fact is, we don't give a damn about the land, just hate to see our youth paved over." Oddly, admitting foolishness seemed to cheer him up considerably.

I didn't say anything right away, chewing it over first. Extraordinary, here we were in May, the Season not quite launched, and all this was going on: Cowboy Dils the victim of a hit-and-run. Federal agents in the streets. Jesse Maine and the Shinnecocks menaced by a rival tribe. Her Ladyship striving to rescue Fruity from an unsuitable marriage. *Women's Wear Daily* kicking up rows. Wyseman Clagett throwing his considerable weight around and threatening to break crusading local journalists. Race car drivers planning demos and snarling holiday traffic.

"Well," I said, and not sheepishly, "maybe it is all foolishness. But I think it's actually pretty great."

And I did. Old men hanging on to youth. People battling against progress. Morning drive guys challenging the White House. Native Americans snarling at each other. The British aristocracy maintaining class distinctions. Maybe it was just talk on Lager's part, bravado, with nothing behind it. Maybe all the others were simply talk, as well. Somehow, I didn't think so. Men who'd played the Great Game for real, when you might well get killed at it, had a tradition of living up to their talk. And so did the great Indian tribes and British Miladys and men as gifted, and mad, as Cowboy Dils.

Before I slept I phoned Harry Almond. "Lady Alix and I [I hadn't even discussed the notion with her, fearing she might actually like it!] feel your 'Mao-Tse-Tongue' skit would be pushing the envelope."

Harry sounded pleased. "Cowboy came to that conclusion on his own, I'm happy to say. He told Maguire, 'Shitcan Mao!' " Then, more subdued, "He's muttering about something even more clever. Which has me shuddering in anticipation."

When I hung up I was firmly convinced that, all things being equal, this year's Memorial Day weekend held out enormous promise for mischief of all variety.

## seventeen

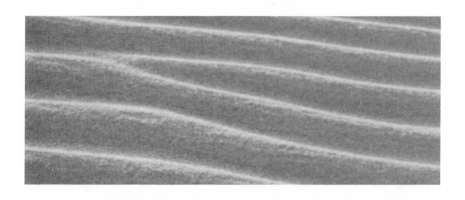

*"Cowboy!" I called. "Quiet," he shouted. "I'm here under an assumed name."*

It was that same morning that Cowboy Dils's golf cart somehow contrived to spring into life and roll itself into his own swimming pool and very nearly drown Cowboy in the process. . . .

"Accidents happen, right?" an irate Maguire demanded, "but they don't happen twice in one goddamned week to a man so many people hate!"

Okay, Dils's producer conceded, the hit-and-run that broke Cowboy's leg and tossed him into the lake might have been innocent. An accident compounded by panic. Or driver guilt after having had a few drinks. No premeditation. No intent. Didn't prove a thing. But now, a second "accident" happening within a week on Gin Lane to the same widely and cordially despised outsider? And less than two months since his helicopter crashed and burned. Maguire was no paranoid like his boss but even his threshold of skepticism had been crossed. Tom Knowles was on the case now. Suffolk County police for the first time were taking Cowboy's difficulties seriously. Alix and I drove over to the hospital to see how badly hurt he was. Maguire was outside, pacing the parking lot, waiting, still angry but by now seeing the black humor of what could have been Dils's death.

"He'll live," he said.

The problem was how long Dils had been underwater.

"That's what scares the doctors," Maguire said. "How long his brain was starved for air. They don't think it was all that long. And Cowboy's brain works on a seven-second delay anyway."

Alix, being British, gave Maguire a look. She tugged at my sleeve for emphasis.

"Isn't that the Irish for you. His employer near death yet being dissed by this fellow. Not awfully good form, that."

Just because she'd learned to use Americanisms like "dissed" didn't mean Alix yet understood us as a people. She had no conception of the fraternal bonding on "the Dils Team."

"Maguire's devoted to the guy, Alix. There's real love there. Believe me."

"Odd way of manifesting it," she insisted, her native distrust of the Irish instinctively in play.

I asked Maguire if we could go up and see the great man.

"Sure, the rule is immediate family only. Harry's in there with him. He and Fu Manchu."

"See," I said.

"But they're not family, are they?" Alix protested.

"That's what I mean," I said. "With Cowboy, everyone's family. They define a concept like 'family' in different ways than hospitals do or we might."

Maguire gave us the room number and we went inside and, without checking in with anyone, waited for the big freight-sized elevator to come down to the lobby to take us up. Except, when it did, we couldn't get on, blocked by Dils's wheelchair and an entourage.

"Cowboy!" I cried out, recognizing his Stetson.

"Quiet," he shouted. "I'm here under an assumed name."

Which may have been true because just below his accustomed hat he was wearing a slim black Lone Ranger mask over his eyes, and was propped up in the wheelchair with an IV still in his arm, the by-now familiar broken ankle stuck out stiffly before him in its plastic brace. A nervous-looking nurse was holding the intraveous tube and pushing (and complaining aloud at the same time) while Harry Almond, strolling alongside, strummed a stringed instrument (a ukulele?) as Fu Manchu and Jersey Fats shuffled a reasonably competent soft-shoe in accompaniment. It was left to the poor nurse to power the wheelchair. Except for the tube in his arm, Cowboy looked pretty good.

"Where's the Rolls?" he growled at Maguire. "You're probably going to tell me along with everything else, someone stole the Rolls. You know what that'll do to my auto insurance rates?"

"Guzik is bringing it right up, chief."

Dr. Fu Manchu was wearing green scrubs and had a serious-looking stethoscope around his neck. Did "Cowboy in the Morning" have a properties department; did they just steal these things? Addressing the nervous nurse, Harry Almond said:

"You'll be mentioned in despatches, Nurse Cavell. Prime Minister Asquith himself has been fully briefed on your gallantry in Flanders Fields. Kitchener will be informed. At Buckingham Palace they await further word."

The woman had no idea what he was talking about. But she knew about hospitals, knew about rules. Jersey Fats took her by the waist and attempted to dance her away from Cowboy.

"Stop that! This man is in my care!"

"I can't keep my hands off you," Fats told her lecherously, twirling an imaginary waxed mustache. Nurse Cavell slapped at him and resumed her plaint:

"There are regulations . . . the patient has to . . . papers, release formalities. Documents have to be signed. I don't know his Social Security number. Insurance forms filled out. The government . . . signed in triplicate . . ." She rattled on pedantically, deferentially, a proper bureaucrat despite her terror (Jersey Fats was again twirling mustaches, all the while snapping his fingers and dancing gaily, his large belly moving like Jell-O in a bowl, to the strains of Harry's uke). And still, ever the faithful practitioner, the nurse was hanging on gamely to her patient's dangling intravenous tube and bottle.

"Of course, of course," Almond said soothingly. "Dr. Fu comes to us direct from the Mayo Brothers Clinic. We'll be delighted to seek second opinions, engage in consultations with competent men. It's a tradition

with the Mayo brothers, all four of them—Chico, Harpo, Groucho and
...Bruce," he concluded weakly. "Dr. Fu'll see to it."

Alix and I attempted to blend in, trying to look as if we belonged. I
thought of waving a press card about but concluded Cowboy and his
merry pranksters were doing quite well on their own. So we just tagged
along, through the lobby and out the door by now, patients, visitors,
hospital personnel and idlers standing back, getting out of our way. Polite
deference or an instinct for self-survival? It wasn't quite clear. Especially
when Dils shouted out, his great voice resonating and echoing off walls:

"You may fire when ready, Gridley!"

People didn't just hang back then; they began to scatter.

Cowboy, still on the IV, still in a wheelchair, now broke into song,
what was apparently the theme for a long-forgotten (though not by him)
radio serial, *Jack Armstrong, All-American Boy:*

"Wave the flag for Hudson High, boys/Show them how we stand/
Ever shall our team be champions/Known throughout the land..."

Harry Almond picked up on it with the uke and they did several
choruses, with Dr. Fu now joined by Maguire and Jersey Fats, soft-
shoeing along as well. At that, Greasy Thumb Guzik screeched to a halt
in Cowboy's Rolls, followed closely by a large white van bearing gaudy
illustrations of pumpernickel bread loaves and the slogan "Don't loaf. Get
Funk's—the freshest breads."

"The wheelchair ought to fit inside, just barely," the Sports Geek announced, wielding a tape measure as he burst through the large rear doors
of the baker's van, opening to all of us the hot, delicious smell of good,
freshly baked bread.

"Funk says get this back ASAP," said the driver, a fat-necked German,
"he got delivery schedules. Fresh bread they want; stale bread, who needs?"

"Sure, Fritz," Maguire told him, "anything you say."

"My name is Otto."

Jersey pumped his hand enthusiastically and in turn introduced himself.

"The fellow will be rewarded handsomely," Harry Almond promised,
peeling off a couple of twenties and shoving them into the bakery driver's
breast pocket, calling him "my good man" and assuring him, as the nurse
had earlier been assured, "The Kaiser himself will hear of your feats today.
Also, your knees, your hips, your..."

He and Maguire and Greasy Thumb lifted the wheelchair containing

Dils and rolled it through the open doors into the bread van, as the nurse, hiking up her starched skirts and still gripping the IV tube and bottle of fluids, leaped aboard, terrified but fiercely unwilling to abandon a patient.

I don't know how it was arranged but Cowboy's Rolls was equipped with a highly official-sounding siren and flashing lights, like a chief's car or one of those sedans the Secret Service ride around in, and Ed Guzik now set both of them to working as he burned rubber pulling out of the hospital's parking lot, followed closely by Otto and his pumpernickel van and its precious cargo of Dils, the IV, and the nurse. As they roared away you could still hear Harry's uke...

I took Alix to lunch at the Candy Kitchen on Main Street in Bridge-hampton, where we sat on a couple of stools at the counter. Let the Dils gang sort itself out. Alix and I asked for menus and then after considerable study she asked:

"Might I have one of those lovely thick shakes with two scoops of American ice cream and whipped cream and cherry? We don't have anything like them in Europe and the menu makes them sound glorious."

"Sure."

Alix leaned across from her stool and kissed me lightly on the lips.

"I have missed you, darling. I kept telling chaps in Paris; I do wish Beecher Stowe were here! And purchasing thick shakes for me."

Sure, I thought, remembering her coded encomiums to the vin rouge and dancing the night away in smokey boîtes.

After lunch we drove back to Gin Lane. Enough time had elapsed that they must have Cowboy settled down by now and I was still curious about the whole affair, not the least of it how he'd gotten into the swimming pool in the first place and what the Southampton doctors told him before he absconded with their wheelchair, their IV and most significantly, their Nurse Cavell.

Fu Manchu was in his "faithful manservant" role, amid scurrying maids, Central American and illegal by their look, and led us out to the patio that gave onto the offending swimming pool and past the pool, to the dune and the ocean beyond. It was startlingly beautiful and drew, even from Alix, an impressively inhaled breath.

"Honorable master awaits esteemed guests," he said, bowing us into the Presence.

"I'll fight it out on this line if it takes all summer, Mr. Lincoln!"

Cowboy shouted out in one of his accustomed greetings. Which, for some reason, always seemed to cheer him up even if others found them pretty corny. He was reclining with apparent comfort on a chaise with his injured leg stuck out in front of him and a large beach towel tossed impatiently aside, a notebook and several ballpoints conveniently on his lap. The intravenous tube was nowhere to be seen and Nurse Cavell, fitted out tastefully in a swimsuit borrowed from Annie Willow, was enjoying the pool, swimming a very competent backstroke. "Fetch the drinks trolley, Fu. No reason for my own painful abstinence to be visited cruelly on others . . ."

When the gin and tonic was served and Cowboy had an iced tea, he shouted something in Spanish at one of the hovering maids and she scuttled away. "You grow up on a ranch in New Mexico, you speak Spanish," he said in explanation. "Half our cowboys were vaqueros."

I asked what they'd told him at the hospital.

"The usual. Take it easy for a day or two. Take a sleeping pill tonight. Very gloomy as to just what might have happened. But didn't. If I hadn't somehow gotten untangled from the golf cart and out of the water that quickly, I could have been in real trouble. A couple of minutes without air getting to your brain is all it takes. Five minutes, say, and if you're not dead, you're a vegetable." He lifted his glass in modest salute to Alix and asked, "If you had to be a vegetable, Your Ladyship, what would it be? I'm inclined toward brussels sprouts, myself."

"Oh, no, not I, Mr. Dils. Asparagus in season, tepid and with melted butter. That's the ticket. As they do it at the Connaught. Or the Paris Ritz. And eaten with the fingers and never a fork. Definitely not brussels sprouts, not for a Brit; the Belgians being awfully sticky on the matter of agricultural subsidies. And you, Beecher?"

Cowboy was scribbling frantically. Alix was like that. We'd been here only a few moments and she was once again being written into skits.

"Are tomatoes vegetables or fruits?"

We bickered over that for a little and then I asked Cowboy what I wanted to know most: "How did you get into the damned pool in the first place?"

He'd been lazing in the sun after breakfast right out here on the ocean-and-pool-facing patio in the golf cart he'd chosen as his vehicle du jour since breaking the right ankle. This despite its being awkward to drive with his left foot. But he was getting the knack. Then, having eaten and with the warm sun working on him, Cowboy fell asleep.

"You get up at four A.M. five days a week, Your Ladyship, you get into the habit of a quick nap now and then. I can fall asleep standing up, like a horse. Except that while I was asleep this time, in the golf cart, it somehow got rolling and the next thing I knew I was underwater, and trapped. The plastic brace on my right foot and ankle had caught somehow on the gas pedal and the brake pedal—"

"But it's electric," I said. "An electric cart."

"Damned right. And don't you know the instant I woke up and realized I was in the water, I started thinking about electrocution. You know, like if you drop a radio into the bathtub, you're toast. Every bit as much as if it's electric chair time in the Death House at Sing Sing. But I knew I wasn't dead and it didn't feel like I was being electrocuted, so I started fishing around down there to free my foot. It was caught on whatever you call the pedal that gets it moving; it had me pinned. This plastic cast they gave me is lighter but bulky, just like a ski boot. Straps and buckles and Velcro. Damned thing hooked onto something."

"But how did the cart start rolling? Was the key in the ignition when you fell asleep? Or was the motor running when you nodded off?"

"The key's always in there. Where else would the damned key be? I don't know if it was running. The key is always turned on and then you hit the pedal and it starts. That's how it works, doesn't it? Seems to me that's how."

He was getting testy. Hell with it, this was my trade. I kept asking questions.

"Who else was around? Who was in the house or on the grounds?"

"You sound like that cop at the hospital this morning."

"Knowles? Tom Knowles?"

"That's the guy. He asked me all that."

"And what did you tell him?"

"Just what I'm telling you: Claude Rains was on the case and the usual suspects were being rounded up."

There was a hostile edge to his reply. Not playful, mischievous, suggesting rascality where none existed. Cowboy was normally a libel lawyer's dream. But now, he was in no mood to be questioned closely. Instead of his usual paranoia, cataloging enemies and ascribing motives, Cowboy was taking the blame on himself. He'd fallen asleep, gotten tangled, nearly killed himself, and the resultant embarrassment had Dils uncharacteristically subdued. He didn't like being made a fool of; and here he'd made a fool of himself.

No one to blame but me, he acknowledged morosely. What he really wanted was to be able to stand up and declare, "I name the guilty men!"

Peter Jennings! George Stephanopoulos! Senator D'Amato! Roger Champion! Cardinal O'Connor! Ivana Trump! Jesse Jackson! Hillary Clinton!

So many rascals, so much guilt. Such villainy, such perversity. And here was poor, flawed Dils, who had, in his wounded innocence, sworn off drugs, turned from the bottle, intermittently embraced chastity, a potential saint in any creed, falling asleep and driving his trusty golf cart into his very own pool.

"I did everything but clothe myself in sackcloth and take ashes, as Catholics do in Lent, and am I rewarded? Not a bit of it. Choppers crash on my lawn, I have my leg broken by hit-and-run drivers, I'm tumbled into my own pool by golf carts, policemen invade my privacy and bring out the rubber hoses. Reporters move in and tug out notebooks. Captain Dreyfus didn't put up with this shit. . . ."

Then came an odd and in ways jarring moment. It began as Alix attempted to provide solace.

"Do try to pull yourself together, Mr. Dils . . ."

"Cowboy," he said, still grouchy even to her.

"Well, then, Cowboy."

"I am pulled together and do I go on calling you by titles or what?"

The question was stupid and also rude, since he knew the answer. My own fists clenched and I got up, snapping back, topping his rudeness, "Just a damned minute here, Cowboy. I—"

Alix anticipated me, as, with an icy politeness, she responded, proper but cold:

"Since I'm a friend of Beecher's and he's a friend of yours, it seems the sensible thing is simply to call me by my name. Alix."

Cowboy cooled down as suddenly as he flared up and he reddened now, knowing he'd been an ass.

"Sorry," he said. "Sorry, Alix. Sorry, Stowe." Cowboy liked people who didn't panic or cut and run. Alix, clearly, was one of those. And he recognized that he was off base snapping at her. The awkward moment passed. But why was he so touchy? That still wasn't clear. Unless it was a hangover from his latest accident. Or the medication.

"Not to worry," she said. "My own pa is the sweetest old thing. But when the wind is in the east, oh, dear! One doesn't want to be in the same house. Rum, the moods chaps have."

Dils went on about it a bit more.

"You're gracious to say so. My problem is I'm like a whodunit where the last page is missing. I don't always know just who I am or why. I shout at the people I like best. I lash out. I'm not a bad person yet I can be a miserable son of a bitch. It's why people are forever suing me. There are times when I'd sue myself."

At the fringe of the argument, I relaxed. This was a Dils I'd heard about but not seen, with motivations confused. And since I loved Alix and liked Cowboy, I would hate to have had a fight because he'd been rude to her. You don't want to fight a man you really liked with a broken leg who'd just nearly drowned.

And who was our host. In our family, at the schools I'd gone to, you learned deference and respected your host. Besides, I thought, more pragmatically, if we fought, Maguire and Fu Manchu and Harry Almond and the well-armed Greasy Thumb and the rest of them would surely have set upon me. Even the Sports Geek. The illegal maids. Maybe Nurse Edith Cavell. Otto the pumpernickel man. And I certainly didn't need that.

It was Alix, cleverer than either of us, who brought the moment to the most cordial of closures, pledging never, ever to sue Cowboy, and that he ought to feel free to "lash out" as often as he wished.

"You're an honest man, Cowboy in the Morning," she said. "And I for one like honest chaps who lash out."

"Thanks, Alix," he said, being offhanded about it but pleased. "And if you or Stowe ever get to the last page of the whodunit, let me know. Even a schizo wants to reconcile contradictions. I'm kind of curious just who I really am."

# e i g h t e e n

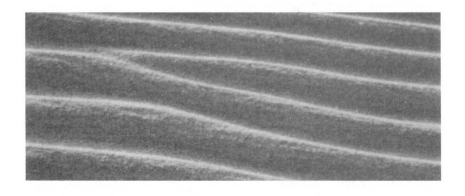

*He let me leave a message on the prime minister's voice mail . . .*

Jesse Maine called. "For the moment, Beecher, I and the Pequots are observing a truce. They've let up on me temporarily and no casinos are expected to open on Shinnecock land any time this week. Is that viscount pal of yours still game for a day at sea in pursuit of the great shark?"

"I'm sure he is, Jesse. But you know it's too early in the season for shark."

"I know that and you know it. But if we bring in a nice mess of mackerel or a few cocktail blues, who's the loser? Anyways, I got a boat for us. And a skipper. Call me back in an hour if you want to make up a party."

We met Jesse on the west side of the Shinnecock Canal about eleven. Again, Alix was impressed: "My, a canal as well. Your chaps do themselves well indeed, Jesse."

The boat was called *Sachem*, a big, beamy Bertram, which was a good thing for size since I'd gotten Dils to agree to come along. "Anything to get him out of the house," Maguire told me, sounding like a sorely put-upon wife. The fishing boat was helmed by Captain Bly of Hampton Bays. Fruity pumped his gnarled hand enthusiastically.

"Bligh! Bligh! Oh, I say, are you related to the famous Bligh who . . ."

"Spelled bee-ell-why. And, no, I ain't. Nosy bastard."

Bly had encountered similar confusions previously and for him any amusement had long gone from the situation.

"Sorry, no offense intended," the viscount murmured.

Cowboy and his crew drove up now, still in the Funk's pumpernickel van, a long-term lease arrangement apparently having been negotiated with the bread man. Otto was driving and I wondered if they'd leased him as well. But when Captain Bly saw them lifting the golf cart out of the back, with Dils in his cowboy hat perched up there, the Red Ryder air rifle nestled in his lap, he started up.

"Golf carts? I didn't sign on for no golf carts on board." Then as Dr. Fu emerged from the cab, "Japs, too?"

Cowboy, now on the wharf, carted over to the captain.

"My compliments, sir. Dr. Fu is ambassador-without-portfolio to the United States representing His Holiness the Dalai Lama and the Tibetan government-in-exile, and I'll thank you to show the usual courtesies."

"Well," Bly said sourly, "some of them Japs is good tippers. I guess it's okay. Did you say he's a monk? He ain't planning to pray over us out there or nothing, is he? I don't want no monks praying and setting theirselves afire over some injustice or other in Third World nations. You don't want fire on a small boat at sea, y'know. And what's that BB gun for?"

"A Red Ryder air rifle isn't your ordinary BB gun," Dils told him with considerable indignation. "In the Marine Corps we—"

I cut him off while we still had the charter, and assured Bly we were there only for the fishing. Yet when we had Cowboy and the cart winched aboard and settled into the roomy stern, Dils got the captain started again with his recitation, and it was a good one, of Captain Ahab's famous speech to the crew of the *Pequod* when he nailed the gold coin to the mast to be awarded to the first man who saw the Great White Whale and gave cry:

"Thar she blows!" Cowboy called out now, his deep, booming voice startling gulls and setting them into panicked, wheeling, squawking flight from the piles and stanchions of the dock.

"Damned few whales you'll see this time o' year," Bly responded sourly.

"I thought you said Frank Mundus was ill tempered," I told Jesse in an aside.

"He is," said Jesse. "This boy mellows out after a drink or two. . . ."

We were soon away from the dock and heading south across Shinnecock Bay and through the inlet of the same name toward . . .

"Mystifies me why it's called the Atlantic," Alix said, "considering everything else they have is named after the Shinnecocks."

"An oversight," Jesse conceded. The sun was near its height and with a slight quartering breeze it was very pleasant for May. The water would still be pretty cold. Bly knew his stuff, Jesse said, and we headed due south out into the ocean.

"How are the in-laws?" Alix asked Fruity.

"Haven't seen them, actually. Not since dinner at the golf club. I thought it best to make myself scarce what with all the drama. Mandy and I chatted by phone yesterday. I thought about asking her along this morning when you said Jesse had arranged a boat. But I'm advised these things work out better when bride and groom maintain their distance leading up to the, well, zero hour."

I thought there might be a more felicitous euphemism for "wedding day" but held my tongue.

"Do you think that Fairchild fellow was talking rot, Alix? I mean, who gives a fig if the wedding dress is lace or satin and has a train or not?"

"Means a good deal in the rag trade, I'd wager," she said. "Those chaps knock off a frock by the thousands overnight if you let them. Girl like Mandy doesn't want to see herself coming and going, y'know. Too bad the Buchanans didn't give the assignment to Hardy Amies. Sir Hardy's a stout fellow and not likely to blab to *Women's Wear Daily*."

"I should hope not," said Fruity, "now that he's got his *K*."

"Yes. Knighted for services rendered Her Majesty over the decades . . . though he might well have done something about those dowdy hats she insists on wearing."

"See them birds, miss," Captain Bly announced. "You see birds wheeling and swooping like that, it means baitfish."

"Oh, good! Is it baitfish we're after?"

"No," Bly said, and let it go at that.

Jesse took up the slack:

"Baitfish is only little bitty things, Lady Alix, not worth catching. The birds show where the baitfish is close to the surface. 'Cause usually that means bigger fish, macks or blues or whatever, are under the baitfish chasing them to the surface and feeding on 'em. It's bluefish we're after, and the birds and the baitfish will lead us to 'em. Ain't that right, Captain?"

"Yup. And they'll take off your goddamned finger if they get half the chance as well. Mean bastards they are."

"Yes," Alix agreed. "*Pomatomus saltatrix*, to use their official name, the bluefish is one of the speediest fighting fish in the sea, ranging in weight to over twenty pounds. Most gourmets think the flesh a trifle oily."

It was extraordinary the things she knew, the random knowledge in which Oxford clearly excelled.

Bly carried a mate who baited and put out rods now, umbrella jigs rigged for trolling, each of us taking one except Cowboy, who might still have been feeling the effects of yesterday and was alternately squeezing off shots from the air rifle at flotsam and dozing in the morning sun. Dr. Fu and Harry Almond were amateurish as anglers but Maguire seemed to know what he was doing. Fruity looked quite pleased. "I've done my share of fly-fishing for trout and salmon but I've never been out on an actual ocean with a rod in my hands. What d'you call the bluefish again, Alix? Something *saltatrix*? Hate to lose a finger to the filthy beasts but I'm awfully keen to catch something. Next cabinet it'll be all the talk—"

"I'm sure," Alix said. Then, to Captain Bly, "You know Viscount Albemarle is Her Majesty's Minister of Ag and Fish. As such, he's responsible for fisheries, fishing and angling throughout Great Britain."

"If it was me," replied Bly, "I'd be back there in England hanging out with dukes and earls and horseracing with the queen instead of looking for shark out o' season in Hampton Bays, the silly bastard."

It was a logical, if sour, remark and quieted Her Ladyship for the moment.

Mention of the cabinet reminded Fruity:

"I spent most of the morning trying to get through to Downing Street. What with the president coming to my wedding, I thought it timely to inquire of the PM if he wanted me to pass on any information or queries, you know, informally and out of channels, during the reception."

"And what did Tony say?" Alix asked.

"I didn't actually get through. Spoke to a secretary chap who didn't seem to feel the matter was all that urgent. Let me leave a message on the prime minister's voice mail."

We caught a few mackerel and a cod which for reasons no one could explain, not even Bly, was surface feeding instead of running deep. The savage bluefish were being coy.

"I so hoped we'd see a shark," Viscount Albemarle told the captain.

"Well, we didn't," Bly said.

Fruity took me aside. "Have I offended him, somehow? Ignored protocol or something?"

"No, I think it's just his manner. Might be a New Englander. Some of them moved down here years ago. Nothing personal about it. They just don't say much."

"Oh?"

"Is my nose getting sunburnt, Beecher?" Alix asked. "I love an early tan but can't abide a red nose."

She looked perfect to me but then you know how I am about her, though I do try to tell the truth.

"Just slightly rosé, like the wine."

Bly, without a word, handed over an industrial-strength tube of 30-power sunblock.

"Why, how considerate of you, Captain."

"Yes, ma'am. Keep it aboard against the skin cancer."

It was the lengthiest response any of us had yet gotten out of him. Not even the stoic Bly was proof against her charms. And by the time we were back at the dock, and after half a dozen beers, Bly was almost genial, at one point borrowing Dils's Red Ryder to pop away, and quite accurately, at a floating beer can.

Cowboy and his bunch had plans, most of which seemed to revolve around getting Nurse Cavell and the illegal Hispanics to clean the fish they'd caught. Alix and I took the viscount to dinner. We asked Jesse but he had plans. A new lady friend, it appeared, though he was vague about that and might simply have had an evening's poaching in mind. I called ahead and we got a table in the barroom of the American Hotel in Sag Harbor. Fruity was very keen on it. "Splendid wine list," he kept saying, smacking his lips over the vintage clarets. We had the brandied duck and with the evening coming off slightly chill, they lighted a fire. Which made everything approximately perfect.

And so did the endearing remarks and imaginative little moves Her Ladyship put on once we got back to the gatehouse and went up to my bedroom and got undressed.

# n i n e t e e n

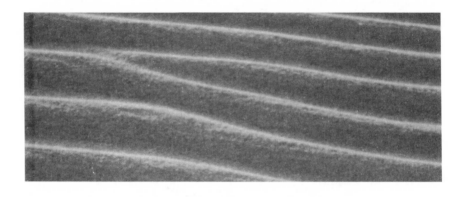

*"Charlie Rose hates you." "I hate Charlie Rose..."*

These were pleasant interludes. But along Gin Lane the question still floated menacingly in the air, unanswered.

Was someone trying to kill Cowboy Dils? If so, who? He himself, when I'd first interviewed him, acknowledged he was difficult: "I have my lawn mowed early Saturday morning. Which annoys weekenders that want to sleep in. I like loud music. I admit I ain't totally housebroke and I shoot at dogs that pee on my property. I can be uncomfortable if you live next door."

There was that Dils, ornery and crude. And another. One who spoke a refined and even cultivated English, who was capable (when in the mood) of something approaching eloquence. Never mind who was trying to bump him off. Who was there, friend or foe, who truly understood Cowboy Dils?

He was not, of course, the only irritant the Hamptons had this spring. I experienced my own ugly moment when I came out from shopping at the Caldor up there at Bridgehampton Common and found Wyseman Clagett's car blocking my own.

"Hullo, there, Stowe," Clagett called through the rolled-down window from the back of the car, yet another black Rolls, I noted. For Clagett, he sounded almost friendly. In the front seat sat henchman Riddle, brow creased and his little pig eyes watching me as he ground his teeth.

"Hello, Mr. Clagett. Hi, there, Roadkill. There's a lovely sight, Attorney Clagett and his strong right arm, taking the air on a spring morning. Warms the cockles, just to see you both, all good cheer and civic improvement."

I enjoyed being more satanic than the devil; it annoyed people. The ruder they were, the more mannered and elaborately polite I became. Up front, through the polished window, Roadkill kept an eye on me but left the conversation to his employer. The pair of them could have been Sidney Greenstreet and Elisha Cook Jr. of *Maltese Falcon* memory.

"I worry about El Niño," Clagett began, "and here's a big-time journalist like you wasting his time messing about with Baymen. Drunks and wastrels, junkies and womanizers, the lot of them. You're missing the big picture, Stowe. There's a lot better story in how the Army Corps of Engineers, and some nobly motivated local folk, are concerned about this summer's hurricanes, trying to halt erosion, save our Hamptons beaches, and protect women and children and the elderly from having green water again go sloshing up into the town."

"That going to happen, you think?"

"Possible. If no one else around here has the sense to worry about it, I do. That's why we're putting in revetments, replenishing the sand."

Riddle was looking out at me, still grinding his teeth.

"Some local people don't think so, Mr. Clagett. They think you and Packer are making a killing. They think—"

"El Niño's coming but only a few of us are on the alert. We could use some positive ink, Stowe. You write for a big magazine and you're smarter than the rest of them," he said, striving to be amiable.

"Just another local, Mr. Clagett. Just another Bub . . ."

"You know that ain't so," he said, rewarding me with a deep boom of his most phony laugh. "How many Bubs go to Harvard and are born in Paris, eh?" Then, "Let's get down to it, Stowe. We need hurricane protection on the beaches. That worthy project and the Bridgehampton raceway development could increase the tax base, mean a thousand jobs out here—good, well-paying, blue-collar jobs. Maybe fifteen hundred. Your Bub pals could use the work, use the pay. You know that, Stowe...."

I did. Grant him that. But didn't say so. Instead:

"A man for all seasons, you are, Mr. Clagett. Saving the beaches, creating jobs, confronting hurricanes, a regular Father Christmas..."

He was steaming now but tried sweet reason one more time.

"Just think of those little tots with their pails and shovels down on the beach this summer and here's El Niño coming. Someone's got to face reality and save those kids, Stowe."

I looked into the front seat of the Rolls.

"You losing sleep over it, Roadkill? I mean, those tots and their pails and shovels with El Niño coming and—"

Clagett had had enough. He hit a button and the tinted window flew up, shutting me out. I got a last look at Roadkill's tiny, cold, near-dead eyes before he turned and gunned the motor, getting both of them out of there, lest they be exposed to something contaminated.

You could smell the stench of burned and very expensive rubber as they went. Surprising the pickup you got with a Rolls.

I called the Dils compound when I got home. The great man was pretty much recovered, CAT scans and MRIs having all come back negative. Or so reported Nurse Cavell, who while seconded to Cowboy's mansion was staying in touch by phone with the hospital. Things had been regularized with the authorities and she was now on Dils's payroll as a private attending nurse practitioner, specializing, as Dils said, in "bloodletting and the application of leeches." She also helped out with canapés (possibly illegal Hispanic maids were notoriously weak on canapés) and mixed cocktails (straight fruit juices and iced tea for Dils) and danced with guests and members of the entourage during the cocktail hour's "the dansant." As for her employer..."The chief is feeling fine," Maguire assured me when I called. "Normal. Which means he's rotten as ever."

When Alix and I arrived at Gin Lane to pay our respects, Dils had convened his entourage (it filled and waned like the moon, varying in size and scope, in conjunction with the planets and Cowboy's emotional needs) in a full-blown council of war out on the patio.

"Check your sidearms with the adjutant," he called out as he saw us being ushered from the house and onto the patio by Nurse Cavell. The few introductions necessary were made while Harry brought us up to speed, briefly reviewing the violently diverging swings in Cowboy's moods and suspicions.

"Now that he's feeling himself, Leicester is more than ever convinced this isn't simply his morbid imagination at work here, but that there are actual cabals and plots, conspiracies and menacings, all targeting him personally." The tone of voice indicated Harry Almond was hardly convinced. But Cowboy was.

"Absolutely," he said; "this isn't my usual paranoia. There very well might be someone out there trying to bump me off." Then, remembering his role as host, he nodded toward Alix and me. "Disport yourselves, the coffee is hot, the OJ is cold, there are sweetmeats and refreshing sherbets, spicy mangoes and rare botanicals to hand, breadfruits and coconut milk."

There was coffee and some orange juice. No sweetmeats or sherbets or botanicals I could see.

"Oh, splendid," Alix said, as she took a chaise, reclining prettily with her tanned, bare legs glistening in the morning sun, and I took a share of chaise by her feet and sipped black coffee.

"Look," Dils said, "I know I'm often confused and contradictory. In my case it's probably brain damage from the cocaine and vodka years. But so was Alexander the Great sort of screwed up. And he'd conquered the known world before he was thirty. Was also dead by then, as well, I'll admit . . ."

"And gay, too, chief," Maguire put in, never missing an opportunity to make a point. "Don't forget that."

"No call here for your trademark homophobia, Maguire," Cowboy scolded. Then, regaining the thread of his thought, "Or T. E. Lawrence. He was pretty much a whackjob but he and a couple hundred towelheads drove the Turks out of Arabia. U. S. Grant was a drunk. And he beat Lee, who was sober but spent his time praying. Van Gogh, which incidentally, is pronounced 'Hock,' cut off his own ear and presented it to a woman of the pavements. So it's quite possible for a man to be confused and yet to—"

"Wasn't Lawrence of Arabia gay, too?" Maguire asked. "Him and the Turks, y'know, getting it on there in their harem pants, dancing and . . ."

Dils glowered. "We have a substantial broadcast audience of our gay and lesbian friends, Maguire, and with very attractive demographics, I'll thank you to remember."

Greasy Thumb was on his feet and, when we arrived to interrupt, had apparently been reading something aloud. He'd fallen silent on our arrival.

"We're compiling an enemies list," Maguire explained, "starting with members of the staff, all of whom qualify as suspects without saying. Plus the other people who hate the chief and might want him iced."

"Oh."

Now Guzik, with the training and style of a flatfoot, but in the mournful tones of Mr. Gloomy, resumed reading the enemies list from a spiral notebook:

"Donald Trump hates you."

"Donald Trump hates everyone," Cowboy responded airily.

"Well, yeah. Rock Newman, the boxing manager. He says you're a racist."

"Rock's okay. He thinks everyone's a racist. Next?"

"Senator D'Amato. He doesn't like the pidgin Italian accent we do him with in skits."

"He's not supposed to like it. We're making fun."

"George Stephanopoulos—"

Dils interrupted Guzik, holding up a cautionary hand. "What the hell's he doing in New York, that little fink?"

"Teaching at Columbia," Harry said.

"You're so easily taken in, Harry. The man's a born plotter and the president's creature, besides. The Borgias employed such men. Remind me to retain a qualified food taster. And beware of Greeks bearing gifts..."

Former detective Guzik resumed his list of suspects: "F. Lee Bailey. Madonna. Mr. Guerin, the sexton at Saint Andrew's Church, because you shoot at their belfry. The Bosnian Serbs. Bill Parcells, because you said he's too fat—"

"He is. And grow up, Bill!"

"The Scientologists. Peter Jennings. Liz Smith—"

"Time!" Maguire called, interrupting Greasy Thumb. "Liz and Cowboy made up, remember?"

"Right. We like Liz these days," Cowboy confirmed.

"Charlie Rose hates you."

"I hate Charlie Rose."

"Wash!" declared Maguire, striking a name from the roster.

"Your boss, Roger Champion..."

"He wouldn't kill me. We make too much money for the network."

"Rupert Murdoch. Nigeria. Wyseman Clagett because you call him 'seersucker white trash' on the show. Newt Gingrich. Tom Buchanan and his wife. Giorgio Armani. Lots of Southampton people: the Toppings, Mrs. Bass, Robert and Georgette Mosbacher..."

"They're divorced I believe, chief."

"Which one gets custody of hating me?"

"I'm checking with Raoul Felder, chief."

"Whitney Flippen, whom you're suing by the way, Pennington Phlar, Culbreth Sudler of Time Inc., Archie Reeve, the Dillons on First Neck Lane. You shot at their dog, too. Mica and Ahmet Ertegun..."

"Who are these last people, honored sir?" Dr. Fu Manchu inquired.

"Rich people, Fu. He's Turkish and runs a record company."

"Ah, so..."

"Yeah," Dils said, "and I ought to trying making up. You don't want the record industry on your case. Remind me to send flowers to Mrs. Ertegun."

Greasy Thumb snapped his spiral pad shut, not needing to read the final entry: "And the president of the United States."

"Ha!" Cowboy exploded, his powerful, broadcast-quality voice setting coffee cups and juice pitchers to tinkling. "Now we're getting someplace."

The case against the president could be briefly put. Showbiz personalities like Dils were accustomed to crank threats. It went with celebrity. But the frequency and viciousness of the threats had increased exponentially since Cowboy gave his National Press Club speech this past winter, the one in which many thought he had gone beyond reasonable good taste in twitting the First Family. Including the kid. "Sure, I went too far," Cowboy conceded afterwards. "I always go too far. It's what they pay me for."

He felt it was unfair and unrealistic for the Washington press corps to book him as speaker and then to expect he wouldn't take advantage of the opportunity to trash the First Family. "They know my act, they know who I am and what I do."

There was something to that. Something as well to Dils's theory the president was focusing on Cowboy so as to duck more serious questions. Simpler to have feuds with a radio talk show host than respond to congressional critics and the special prosecutor.

But the pious inside the Beltway who castigated sinners while praising their own virtues had turned on Dils in righteous wrath. Even those who privately held the president in contempt and wished earnestly for his destruction. There were calls for all Americans to rally 'round the president and to denounce Dils as a hissing and a byword. The hypocrisy couldn't be more smug, more blatant.

"The scribes and the pharisees," declared Harry Almond, who knew his Bible and read it, "stoning the woman taken in adultery, casting aspersions on the apostles. Didn't they entrap Jesus Himself? There are false prophets and sychophants ever among us."

"Amen to that," said Cowboy just as piously, though he was not much for Bible studies, a chant then taken up by Maguire and Harry: "Aaaa-aaaa men, Aaaa-aaaa men, A-men A-men." It was right out of an opening reel of *The Blues Brothers*.

"I say, Beecher," Alix remarked as they broke into another soft-shoe, "they are good, y'know. Spontaneous, as well. Like the choir at Westminster Abbey."

But could a sitting American president seriously be considered an actual threat to one of his countrymen, no matter the provocation? Do chief executives conspire to commit murder? As Maguire rather stylishly put it:

"Would the president ice a fellow American?"

It was an irreverent question but seriously put. This was substantive stuff; this was Watergate or even bigger. An uneasy silence fell upon the scene.

Then Alix had an idea.

"Forgive a foreigner for putting in an oar, but you might consider this. You know how our British prime ministers get to know your presidents rather well. That historic 'special relationship' they speak of that dates back to wartime, Lloyd George and President Wilson, our Churchill, your Mr. Roosevelt? It continues even today, I'm reliably informed. We could have Viscount Albemarle, our Minister of Ag and Fish, phone the PM and ask him his opinion of your president, his potential for murder and that sort of thing. Subtly, of course."

Dils looked interested. Until now, his capacity for mischief had been limited to our own shores. Here, conceivably, was the making of an international incident. You could see he liked the idea, the potential it held. Shrewdly, not wanting to appear anxious, he asked, "But would Tony Blair level? Be sticky as hell diplomatically if it got back to the White House. Whatever he told Fruity, I mean, the viscount."

Alix bit her lip.

"There is that," she conceded. Then Dr. Fu offered a suggestion, his wily Oriental mind working cleverly.

If the Tony Blair approach wouldn't fly, why not sound out John Major?

"Honorable John Major no longer in office. Cannot lose face. Must have informed opinion on honorable president's capacity for manslaughter. And is in position to speak honorable mind."

The rapidity of Her Ladyship's reaction astonished all of us.

"Just a mo there, Fu! You've come up with a brilliant idea. But you don't take it far enough."

"What does Honorable Lady Alix then—"

"Bugger John Major!" she cried. "Go right to Maggie Thatcher! Go right to Baroness Thatcher of Wellfleet or whatever her full title and panoply may be. Surely she wouldn't mind giving the viscount the benefit of her years of dealing with the Yanks. Ask Maggie right out, 'Baroness, do you think the president of the United States would commit murder, given appropriate provocation? Is the chap homicidal?' If there's a Brit who speaks his or her mind, well, there's the Baroness Thatcher for you, thank you very much. And they can say anything in the House of Lords, you know, libel and slander included, and can't be prosecuted. My old pa says in any event half the peers are quite dotty."

Opinion was divided, with Cowboy intrigued sufficiently to say he'd like to think about it, sound out Fruity and so on. Harry Almond continued to grumble. It was all foolishness, he insisted. "This is absurd, calling prime ministers and suggesting American presidents are in the business of bumping off people. They don't! Not even on Gin Lane!"

"Ha!" said Dils thoughtfully, "then why is he coming here Memorial

Day weekend and why is the village lousy with Secret Service? And just why is George Stephanopoulos lecturing in Manhattan, so convenient to Southampton? If any president ever had a Cardinal Richelieu, it's that mop-haired little conniver."

Then, becoming agitated again, he turned to Maguire. "Tell them about the other attacks."

Now it was my turn to be incredulous. "What other attacks? The chopper crash in the fog, the hit-and-run, and the golf cart in the pool. Am I missing something.?"

Cowboy looked maniacally triumphant. "Little you know, Stowe. We've had other attacks! *Animal* attacks."

"Tell him, chief," Maguire urged, happy to make trouble but preferring Dils to recount his own story firsthand.

"I will, then. Countess Crespi's silver-gray miniature poodle. Went for me twice. Biting me once on May third. Then again on the sixth. Went for my throat. Savage little beast."

Harry protested. "That dog is fourteen years old, Leicester. The countess carries it around in a wicker basket. Its hind legs don't work. That dog's even more decrepit than her husband. But that's another story. As for the dog, it may have growled. At worst, it was gumming you."

"Yeah? Well, a determined poodle could gum a man to death."

"And only after you tried to hit it with your BB gun."

"I don't *try* to shoot things with my Red Ryder air rifle. I damned well *hit* them. I hit the bastards. Ask the Marine Corps about my marksmanship, check the roster of sharpshooters if you have doubts. If I take a shot at a poodle, I hit the damned poodle!"

"And what about the raccoon?"

During the past winter there'd been a raccoon in the chimney. What was that about?

"Raccoons are all over the place in the Hamptons," I said, "and during cold weather they take chimneys for hollow trees and climb inside to enjoy the hot air rising. Nothing malign about it at all."

Except to the fevered brain of Cowboy Dils:

"Tell me this, then, about your raccoons, Stowe. With all the beaches and golf courses and woods around here, farms and open fields and school-yards and that big shopping mall at Bridgehampton, all those thousands of acres of open space, then why do raccoons have to go up on my roof to take a crap?" He looked over at Alix. "Sorry, Your Ladyship, but it isn't reasonable. I've had the house for a year and it's been eating at me from the very start. When my leg ain't broken I go up there to take a look. I go up there to shoot at things. Or just stroll about on the widow's walk as the old whaling ship captains' wives once did, looking for a sail. And I can testify without fear of contradiction, 'cause I seen it, up there on my own damned roof. Raccoon poop! All those raccoons on the roof in the middle of the night taking dumps. Hell of a thing, lying abed nights and having to think about what's going on right over your own damned head on your own damned roof! Drive a normal person nuts—"

"Never mind one like you, chief," Maguire murmured.

"I heard that, Maguire! And what about the field mice. Spreading Lyme disease? What about the damned mice? Don't tell me someone isn't waging biological warfare around here. The bubonic plague was spread by rodents. Killed half of Europe. Just recall that if you will, half of Europe killed by rats and mice. Another thing about raccoons, I forgot to mention, they're rabid, some of them. Rabies? No cure for it. You get bitten by a rabid raccoon, that's all she wrote! And don't kid yourself about mice. Those bastards..."

He settled into a combination of muttered curses and vague mumblings.

Almond, gently, meek as Parson Weems, picked up Cowboy's burden:

"Until late this winter he rarely saw a mouse in the house. Since then, a half dozen mice showed up in traps in the pantry and kitchen alone." This muted explanation got Dils started again.

"And if it's not the government behind infected mice, who is it? Microsoft and Bill Gates? DuPont and the chemical cartel? How about GE? Neutron Jack Welch?" Cowboy sort of calmed himself with the ridiculousness of that notion and knocked it down himself.

"Nah," he said. "Neutron Jack might blow you the hell up. He wouldn't stoop to sending mice...."

We declined an invitation to lunch. As we drove off, Alix said, "You know, it may not have been very astute of me suggesting we get Fruity to call the PM and ask if your president is, even potentially, a homicidal maniac."

"No," I agreed, "puts Fruity in a dicey position. The president might resent such questions from a member of Tony Blair's cabinet."

"You're right, Beecher. I should have offered to call Tony directly myself. Whether they'd have told me is another matter entirely."

I said that indeed it was.

But she hadn't yet entirely abandoned the idea. "Would it be possible for your old dad to ask around? He must know Mrs. Thatcher. And what would Yeltsin think of the notion? Or Chirac? Could the president possibly—"

"No, Alix, my old man isn't going to start asking questions like that."

"Just an idea," she said defensively, "don't be so testy. Absolutely no harm in asking."

I was going to explain to her what a "ring-knocker" was and how Annapolis men didn't do such things. But the day was too pleasant for that so I took her out to Montauk to buy a six-pack of cold beer and then lunch on lobster rolls at Perry Duryea's outdoor seafood place overlooking Fort Pond, you know, where the Duryeas and the town were forever arguing over the zoning and just who really owned Tuthill Road and the Duryeas were periodically barricading it to the rest of us and the town was suing to get it opened again? And then we went back to the house and wiled away a portion of the afternoon making love.

"Why, Beecher, you are a sly dog. Pretending to be concerned about that nice Mr. Duryea and his barricaded road when all the time you were harboring dirty thoughts. Or did you know I was thinking precisely the same thing myself?"

## twenty

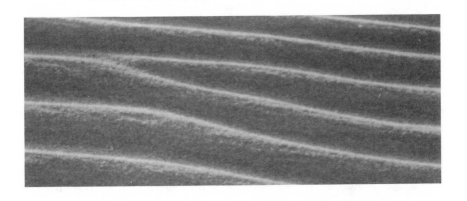

*Mustachioed chaps drinking daiquiris and dancing*
*the tango, eh?*

It was early in the Season for serious polo but in Bridgehampton there was a card of matches to benefit Paul Newman's Hole in the Wall Gang Camp for sick children, attracting a good crowd to the field off Hayground Road.

Fruity Metcalfe so enjoyed a good polo match, he got tickets at fifty dollars a head and invited the RAF along.

"They don't seem to do much actual flying, do they?" Alix said.

"It's liaison chores mostly," Fruity assure her. "Vital to the Alliance and terribly hush-hush. They liaise to people and people liaise to them..."

I thought it sounded like Hollywood—"My people will get back to your people," that sort of thing. The viscount and Alix dismissed the idea, both regarding me narrowly. Then Fruity resumed:

"I've proposed to the PM we revive that grand old wartime slogan about security. You know, 'A slip of the lip/Can sink a ship.'"

"Why, that's awfully clever of you, Fruits," Alix said. "I'm sure Tony will take action along those very lines. They'll not have you pigeonholed for long at Ag and Fish, I'd wager. It'll be the Foreign Office next. Or chancellor of the exchequer."

"That had occurred to me as well, Alix. Awfully decent of you to say so, though. I do wish we still had colonies so I might go to the Colonial Office."

"Mmmmm," Alix said, dubious.

He wondered if he ought to tell Mandy Buchanan about his idea, reviving wartime slogans and rebuilding the national morale. "After all, she is my fiancée . . ."

"And a splendid girl, Fruity. But a Yank. When it comes to the RAF and Ag and Fish and cabinet matters, as well as the Colonies, might be best not to tell foreigners. After all, as you so deftly put it, 'a slip of the lip . . .'"

"Right-o!" he said cheerfully, relieved, I suspected, at not having to have substantial conversations about anything with his future bride quite yet.

Alix leaned her left breast winningly against my upper arm and whispered, "Do poke me or hiss or something if you spy Paul Newman, Beecher. I never miss one of his films and must admit I'm mad for him. Though your eyes are awfully pretty as well."

I promised.

The feature match at the polo would be White Birch versus Revlon, both of them first-rate sides, and to no one's surprise, the viscount's connections had provided us entree to the VIP marquee sponsored by *Hamptons Magazine* and LeSportsac.

"This is posh, Fruity," Alix complimented him. "Do let's order some champers." The RAF had fallen in with four attractive young women whose names and faces seemed interchangeable but when the champagne arrived, they all tucked in. "Cheers!" Fruity called out. "I do so enjoy a few chukkers of decent polo."

"Do you play yourself, my lord?" one of the enlisted men asked.

Fruity grimaced, gripping his right elbow.

"Have done. Played with the Prince of Wales. Or used to. Bad shoulder. Sidelined for the year, I'm afraid."

"Bloody shame," the wing commander murmured. Then: "I say, we could use a little more champers over here." He was very egalitarian about it and didn't seem to mind drinking with the enlisted men. My father would rather have gone dry (the Annapolis years, of course; they formed a man!) and in the Hamptons he wasn't the only one, the tradition of the Officers' Club holding up very nicely out here.

"Hi, ho!" shouted the wing commander as they passed around a fresh champagne.

Donald Trump was there. So was Jerry Seinfeld's former girlfriend, Shoshanna Lonstein, she of the bodacious ta-tas. Some of the prettiest women and the richest men in the Hamptons had turned out for the polo. None of them seemed to know very much about the game but that hardly mattered, did it? The rich men all seemed to be substantially older than their women friends. Then two of the married Buchanan girls came in, the mararajah's wife and the one wed to the Tyrolean graf. They seemed to be with men other than their husbands. Fruity, noticing this, reddened in embarrassment and called for more champagne, trying not to make eye contact.

"Damned awkward, y'know. Prefer not to have to make introductions." After all, these were his future in-laws and he was nervous about making a gaffe. If his future sisters-in-law were committing adultery, well, that was their concern, wasn't it? Hardly up to him to draw conclusions and make moral judgments, was it?

He was saved from all that when a preliminary match began.

Revlon had defeated White Birch the year before in the Mercedes Benz Cup final in August with both teams fielding several ten-goal international stars. But May was early for really top quality polo. Or so Fruity, who knew the sport (I didn't), assured us. I admired Shoshanna Lonstein and her bosom from our excellent seats. It was amazing, a girl that young and otherwise so svelte, the sheer exuberant grace and thrust of her breasts . . .

"Oh, Beecher," Alix cried, "did you see that goal? Smashing stuff!"

Despite what was, inarguably, a marvelous goal, the prelims were hardly life and death. Until Rex Magnifico and his Argentinos trotted out for a second preliminary match and were introduced over the PA and the wing commander realized just who they were.

"Oh, I say! Damn my eyes! It's the ruddy Argies!"

Fruity was immediately swept up into another dilemma, one that had nothing to do with in-laws or family but with patriotism and love of country. Here he was, host to these RAF heroes of the Falklands War, and beyond that, himself a member of the Blair cabinet. Yet now came to the field a team representing, at least in large part, a country against whom his country and his guest, the wing commander, had fought a war. And gallantly so.

"Exocets up the old bunghole!" Fruity could hear the RAF hero now. Just who was this Rex Magnifico chap, bringing these fellows in for a match? Damned cheek.

"He sells advertising space in fashion magazines," I explained.

I was close enough to hear the wing commander myself, a sort of stream of consciousness plaint, fortunately out of earshot of most the those in the VIP marquee, occupied as they were with young girls and sodden with drink, if not closely following the sport.

"All very well for chaps to swagger about Long Island twirling their mustachios and wiping daiquiris from their lips, preying upon Anglo-Saxon women and dancing the tango, conjuring up their dark-eyed señoritas at the same time."

"It sends shivers through one," Fruity agreed, "just imagining the possibilities. Suppose the Argies actually won the Falklands War. What next? London? The Isle of Wight? The Lake Country? Yorkshire and Lancashire? Cornwall and Devon? Eton itself; they'd have Eton co-ed in a sec, I'd wager."

The wing commander took it from there.

"Right you are, sir! There's no limit to their mischief. Not an Englishwoman safe. Not a village cricket pitch secure from the prancing hoofmarks of their polo ponies, our pubs reeking not of stout and hearty English ale but of their daiquiris. Argentinos dancing the tango at Quaglino's with Chelsea's blondes. And never mind that, what of the true spine and heart of England, our provinces? Chaps doing the tango in Liverpool and Manchester, in Preston North End and Hartlepools? Eh?"

By now the RAF was into a rhythmic chant, led by the wing commander: "Ex-oh-cet! Ex-oh-cet!"

I thought I could hear Shoshanna Lonstein picking up the chant, and melodiously so, but there was no sign of Mr. Trump. Perhaps he was suiting up and would shortly be trotting out astride a pony himself. Rex, who'd fallen off his horse right away during the warm-ups and was nursing a bruised tailbone on the sideline, looked over at us in confusion. He certainly hadn't expected hostility right here in Southampton, where he was among friends, and from the VIP pavillion at that, where major advertisers to his magazine could be expected to muster. Who were these people and what was this little chant?

The three Argies seemed up to the challenge and with a pickup player filling in for Rex, were easily four goals ahead after a chukker.

Alix and I left the RAF to its champers and chants and gathered up the viscount and got out of there halfway through the second prelim and without a single sighting of Paul Newman. Or his eyes. Revlon and White Birch would have to play the final without us. At the Blue Parrot no one seemed terribly curious about the polo. The surfers had their own concerns and everyone else was occupied by the Dow or last night's baseball, while Buddy Pontick was holding forth about a blight threatening the bamboo. Alix and I commandeered a couple of bar stools between Richard Ryan and Dave Lucas, "the lawn king," and ate some tortillas with salsa, washing them down with Pacifico beer.

Fruity Metcalfe enjoyed it aloud:

"With food and drink as tasty as this, you'd think the Mexicans would be perfectly content with their lot and not forever migrating, wading your Rio Grande to Los Angeles and such places," he suggested, his grasp of both economics and geography leaving something to be desired. "And think of the bullfights. And Acapulco, as well. If I were a Mexican, I'd never leave. I've had grand times there."

I was sure of that, I said, quite convinced Fruity's chances of ever becoming foreign secretary in Tony Blair's cabinet were rather slim.

And then, about six, Rex Magnifico arrived. With his Argies, the four of them plus the substitute, taking a large table in deference to Magnifico's wounds, borrowing a soft pillow for Rex to sit on.

"Oh, shit."

"What was that, Beecher?" Alix asked.

"Nothing." But I knew trouble when I saw it. Especially with the viscount at the champers once more.

The wing commander and his squadron came in about seven, quite drunk. I steered them over toward our piece of bar and propped the wing commander himself on my own stool, keeping them as far removed from Rex and friends as possible, and buying a first round.

"Bloody Argies," the commander muttered, hearing a few words of Spanish spoken and glimpsing them over there by the window. Turning to me, quietly but with considerable emotion: "You can't know, sir. You weren't there! You never saw the Exocets fly, eh? Or watched a shepherd mourn his ewes and lambs on the hillside after a firefight. They say war is hell, well, there it was. Peat huts demolished and little lambs wandering about, stunned and motherless. Bleating. The Argies did that, in between tangos. Devastated a gallant little island nation. Did they cock an ear to the bleating? But you can't know, can you, sir?"

I admitted I couldn't, no.

"Place like the Falklands," he went on, with Fruity listening intently at my elbow, "a few sheep on a scatter of barren rock and peat moss in the South Atlantic. Easy enough to laugh off now as worthless, eh? You know what Wellington said, about Eton. That Waterloo was won on the playing fields of Eton! By God, he didn't mention polo fields in the Hamptons, did he, sir?"

I shook my head. Was there anyone in England who didn't quote Wellington? "No, you're right. It was Eton, Commander."

" 'Course it was!" Fruity weighed in, being an Old Etonian, "and not Harrow! It was Eton, by God!"

"Right-o!" the wing commander agreed. "Don't expect the Argies to appreciate that, not a bit of it. What glorious military traditions do they boast, eh? Sheltered a few tattered old Nazis through the years, that's the extent of it, eh? And as for being worth fighting and dying for, well, if you're a man—*and* an Englishman—those islands weren't much but they were *ours*. Our rock, our peat moss, our sheep! And not all the mustachioed chaps in Argentina and their dark-eyed señoritas drinking daiquiris and dancing the tango will ever change that! No, sir."

"Golly," Alix said, "put it that way and you realize what war does to a young man. Though we've a few sheep grazing at my pa's place, filthy, smelly beasts I, for one, could happily do without. And the ram, a surly fellow, he'll go for you..."

The viscount was brushing away a tear as Roland fetched us another round.

"It's on Joe Kazickas," he said. Joe is in real estate and is the tallest good golfer I know at the Maidstone and we thanked him, and the wing commander resumed.

"I mentioned tradition, sir. Trafalgar. The Somme. Mons. The relief of Ladysmith. Old Baden-Powell at Mafeking confounding the Boers.

Kipling and that lot. The Sepoys, settling their hash! That took guts, y'know. To say nothing of Monty in the desert. A grandstander and an egomaniac, they said of Monty, which is as may be. Well, he showed Rommel and those chappies. To say nothing of our own crowd, the RAF, 1940 and the Blitz and Churchill's salute to 'the Few...'"

There was a moment of silence, broken finally by Fruity.

"Sends a shiver through one, just thinking about it," he said, clearly moved.

The fight began a few moments later. I was never quite clear who threw the first punch. The Argies, I suspect, the RAF being as drunk as they were with reflexes drastically slowed. Alix and I got the Viscount Albermarle out of there just in time. He struggled with us in the alleyway, trying to get back inside to join the sport.

"I say, Stowe, my duty, y'know. Englishmen under attack! Foreign elements..."

"Sure, sure, Fruity. We'll talk about it later."

We got some coffee into him at John Papa's and then drove him back to the Mauve House. By now he'd cooled off.

"Wouldn't have been a terribly good idea, Fruity," Alix consoled him. "You can see the London headlines now: 'Peer's Heir in Pub Brawl/ Cabinet Minister Punches Dago.'"

He looked pained. "No, we don't need that," he agreed.

"Nor do I think Argentinos ought to be called 'dagos,' Alix," I put in.

"No, nor I, Beecher. Quite the contrary. But that's how Fleet Street might well put it. Good Lord, I've been in the States often enough to know you can't call people 'dagos' anymore." Pause. "Not even when they are dagos, like the Argies."

It was impressive, how Her Ladyship's sensitivity training was progressing.

# t w e n t y - o n e

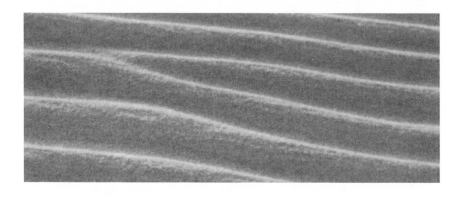

*A young girl dancing atop the table, a ring of men*
*enjoying her legs . . .*

In the morning I needed a little work done on the Blazer and when I called Gordon Vorpahl he told me if I could get to the garage early he'd take me before the rush began.

"Come on," I told Alix, "I want you to meet one of the town trustees."

"How impressive. What ought I wear?" She was sitting cross-legged and naked on the bed, brushing her deep brown hair until it glistened.

"Well, nothing elaborate. But I'd slip into something."

"Right-o."

She got up and went into the bathroom to shower. I enjoyed watching her go. The first time I'd ever seen her, at Hannah Cutting's lawn party, I'd thought how beautiful her back was. Nothing had happened to change that opinion.

I read the *East Hampton Star* while she washed and dressed. A judge had handed down a preliminary injunction against Karl Lager and the sports car drivers. A lawyer for the drivers said they would appeal. Where all this left the Memorial Day weekend protest march and traffic jam was unclear. I made a note to phone Karl Lager and ask. How would Lager and Cowboy Dils get along? I didn't think they would but you never knew. Then Alix came out and kissed me, smelling of good soap and clean water and freshly brushed teeth and nothing else mattered much. As we drove east on Further Lane I set the scene.

"Gordon and Billy Vorpahl run the best truck and auto garage in town. It's about three miles from my house on the Montauk Highway in Amagansett. Between them, they can practically build a car. Gordon's an absolute genius. He'll listen to an engine idling and tell you how many miles you get to the gallon and when you last had your wipers changed."

"My, you do know the clever people."

"I do, you know. Anyway, the Vorpahls've been servicing my cars for years, and my father's, and you can trust those guys to do the job and charge a fair price. If you have to leave the car, they drive you home and come back later and deliver your car. They don't take plastic but they'll take a check. Billy's also the village fire chief and Gordon was elected a trustee of the town a couple years back. People said there was confusion that it was his cousin Stuart Vorpahl running and that's how Gordon got in. I don't know what the facts are but Gordon ended up a trustee and a good one. Trust him with my wallet; my wife, if I had one."

"I say!"

"When Cap'n Dishman's fishing boat capsized in the gale a year ago and he drowned, the Vorpahls were out there, both of them, on the rescue, bringing in the body. And later on when they beached the boat, Gordon flat-bedded it back to the Dishman dock on his own time and at his own cost. Just being a good neighbor. During the hard freezes, he and the other trustees go down to the town pond and shovel the ice clear so it's good skating and get a fire truck to hose it down so it freezes again overnight to a good, smooth surface. No one pays 'em to do such things; they just go out and do them. Gordon says he likes the kids to have decent ice. That's the strength of this town, people like that and lots more, besides."

"You said things like that last summer, too."

"I guess. Sorry. I get tiresome at times, I'm sure, proselytizing about this place, preaching its merits. People think it's all rich phonies and we have plenty of them. And we have plenty like the Vorpahls, wonderfully solid local folk as well."

"I don't find you tiresome at all, Beecher," Alix said.

She put a hand on my thigh and patted my leg. It was fine being with her again driving in the Hamptons together. A few good words, a patted leg. I please easily, I guess.

Gordon Vorpahl performed as advertised, listening to the engine and, as if by magic, figuring out which one of the spark plugs was missing. Or off-timing. And within fifteen minutes he'd put in a new part and tidied up and wiped the grease off his hands and charged me $32, parts and labor both, and when Alix told him she'd heard about his shoveling of the pond for skating, she got an invitation to come back next winter.

"We got even better ponds, Lady Alix. Ponds like Long Pond up in the woods hardly nobody knows. So the ice is always perfect, if we get a good cold snap. Hans Brinker himself couldn't beat skating like that."

She promised to bring her skates.

I had a Bayman to interview for *Parade* that afternoon and she wanted to talk, "and seriously so, Beecher," with Cowboy Dils about whether he'd be interested in a London edition of his next book. She wasn't sure herself that Cowboy would travel well or that the English would appreciate his humour (it was my suspicion she spelled *humour* that way even in conversation!) but she thought HarperCollins would like to think about it and here was an opportunity to open the bidding.

Why not?

It wasn't yet officially the Season. But with Memorial Day weekend closing fast, there were plenty of "summer people" in town and more coming. At the marinas of Sag Harbor and Shelter Island and Montauk and Three Mile Harbor, the season's first yachts, large and small, freshly painted and sleek, or sea-worn and battered, were coming in, from Palm Beach and the Virgin Islands and beaches and ports you never heard of in the Caribbean and along the Gulf Coast and the Redneck Riviera. Just reading their home ports painted on the sterns was like paging through an atlas of the soft, sweet places people with a few bucks and a boat go in the cold months. I drove Alix up there that evening to see them sailing in and tying up. I'm not a big boater, except for the canoe, but she'd rowed at Oxford and knew boats, having sailed aboard more than one rich man's yacht, and it's always fun to see boats maneuvering and docking, especially early in the year when sailors are rusty and may knock a chunk out of the dock, or their own bow, in the process.

"They do tend to colorful oaths, don't they?"

I agreed that they did. "It's part of the fun of watching them."

We got a table out on the porch at Monterey Grill for dinner and watched the sun set on the distant shore of Three Mile Harbor while we smoked and finished off the Merlot. She'd changed into Italian glove-leather jeans and a Hermes print silk blouse and now, with the sun down, had pulled a tan cashmere sweater from her tote and pulled it on over her head. It mussed her hair a bit but she didn't primp or worry about it, just sort of pushed it back into place with two hands without consulting mirrors. Her hair was very soft and behaved well, falling easily into place. I knew how soft it was; I knew very well how soft. She seemed to sense my mood, what I was thinking.

"Let's go dancing, Beecher. I want you to hold me."

"Yes," I said, and called for the check.

This early in the year the only place I knew where you could dance was Boaters. And that was strictly illegal. But no one in memory had ever complained and no fine had ever been levied, and so that's where we went. "I remember this place," Alix said. "It's where Leo Brass threw you out the door."

"Don't remind me."

"But you did awfully well until then, Beecher. All those clever feints and stratagems of yours. I was enormously impressed. For a time there, you had Mr. Brass totally baffled."

I remembered more vividly than she. And now Leo had been dead, what, eight months?

We pushed in to the bar through the dancers. Only a jukebox, no band or anything, but there were maybe a dozen couples dancing and a few pairs of young women dancing together. Short of men, I guess. Most of the people were locals and I recognized a few and some said hello. Others, remembering Leo Brass and my difficulties with Leo, turned coldly away. There were new people there as well, people off the yachts and in from the marinas, some of them very tan as if they'd just come up from down south or the islands. Young, most of them, but some older men, who smelled of money, and their younger wives or girlfriends, who smelled good, too.

When we got to the bar there was another barman I knew from the Blue Parrot, Michael Farrell, working a shift for someone who was off, so we got a couple of cold beers and were caught up on Michael's adventures during the winter and some of the local gossip, and then there was a bit of commotion behind us somewhere and when we looked around there was a young girl dancing alone atop one of the tables with a ring of men on the floor around her, watching her dance in her short skirt, enjoying her legs. She was enjoying it, too, and laughed as she danced.

"Pretty girl," I said. "And she can dance."

"I told you," Alix said.

"Told me what?"

"How pretty she was. That's Mandy Buchanan, Fruity's fiancée and the future Viscountess Albemarle."

# twenty-two

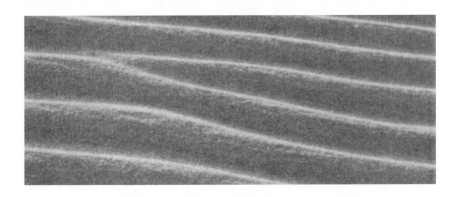

*Captain von Trapp blowing his whistle and the kids singing 'Doe, a deer . . .'"*

I got us a table near the window and ordered some beer from a waitress who knew me from before while Alix went off in quest of the bride. "I think I must, y'know," she told me, "showing the flag for Fruity, so to speak."

When they got back to my table, the two most beautiful women in the crowded room, there were plenty of men looking in my direction. Good. Let 'em look.

I hoped that was all they were intent on doing.

"Mandy, may I present Mr. Beecher Stowe, my very good friend and a famous correspondent. Not, I assure you, from the beastly tabloids. Beecher, this is Ms. Mandy Buchanan."

I stood and we shook hands and she joined us. She was more than pretty; she was superb. And while it was not unknown at Boaters for young women dancing on tables to have been drinking, Ms. Buchanan seemed to be, and indeed was, dead sober.

"I'm learning to drink an occasional sherry," she said, "for when I'm living in England. But otherwise, I stick pretty much to Gatorade and diet Dr Pepper and stuff."

She had what I thought might be a Texas accent.

"You're right!" she said enthusiastically. "We're from Chicago but I went to Texas Tech, at Waco, for two years. I have that kind of ear, I guess, where you pick up on the local accent. That's what happened to me."

"Texas Tech?" I said.

"Yeah, I thought about Northwestern and the Sorbonne but Texas is nice and dry, much better for your hair."

"Your hai—" I started to say but Alix, far wiser than I, cut me off.

"Mandy's getting married next week. Or she will, if all goes well."

The girl laughed.

"I guess I got an attack of the nerves. They say all brides go through it. I've never been married before, not even once, and Mom says don't let it worry me. I'm almost the last one left they haven't married off so I guess she's scared, too. That something might happen, I mean."

"What could possibly happen?" Alix asked innocently. She sounds like that, I know she's got something devious in mind. I waited, suspending judgment.

"Well, y'know, one of my sisters lives out there in Kashmir, India, in a palace. And another is an Austrian grafin now, that's like a countess in German, and they live in this big place they call a *schloss*. And another one's married to this Italian fellow the commendatore in Rome. And another, well, now it's my turn and I'm marrying Lady Alix's old boyfriend Viscount Albemarle—"

"Well, hardly that," Alix said, distancing herself. "In childhood we were chums . . ."

"Whatever. But I've seen my sisters in their palaces, commanding people, ordering the servants around, and having titles, with everyone bowing and scraping, in all these strange and alien foreign surroundings, and I keep asking myself, is that what I want?"

"Though it does solve the inbreeding problem, give the Buchanans that," I said, half to myself.

"Beecher!" Alix said, and forcefully so, scolding me for levity. Then, to Mandy, she began, soothingly, "Well, Mandy, I think it's really up to you to—"

But the girl was off:

"When I first went to Waco my mom took me aside and she said to me, 'Now, Mandy, there's one thing you gotta know out there in Texas,' and I said, 'Yes, Mamma, what's that?' and I thought it was going to be something about sex and stuff, but it wasn't, 'cause we got sex and stuff in Chicago like they do almost everyplace, but what it was my mom wanted to make sure that I was aware of, I mean, being a young girl and pretty and going to be in Texas for the first time, was this. She said, 'Mandy, always remember, there are cowboys. And there are ranchers' sons. And there is a big difference!' "

Mandy looked into our faces to see if we understood. We did. Even back then Mother Buchanan had been planning ahead and trying to insure that her next-to-youngest and quite possibly most beautiful daughter would not marry below her station in life.

"It does your mother credit," Alix remarked. "Good counsel at an impressionable age, nothing better for a girl."

I resisted the temptation to roll my eyes. When Alix began issuing pious little truisms, watch out.

"I thought we came here to dance," I murmured, wondering just where all this was leading.

"All in good time, Beecher. Mandy and I are having a little heart-to-heart."

"And I appreciate it, Lady Alix."

"Just 'Alix,' please, Mandy. In another few days, you'll have a title of your own, far grander than mine. 'Viscountess.' Doesn't that sound nice?"

"Could I have a sherry?" Mandy asked, surprising all three of us, I think.

"I'll ask. But I'm not sure Boaters..."

"Oh, forget it. I don't really want one. Just that for once in my life I might want to get drunk. Do all brides feel that way?"

"I'm sure."

I tried to shift moods a bit. "How did you find Boaters, Mandy? A bit off the beaten track from Gin Lane."

"Oh, I heard it was a wild, fun place, and you could dance. I love to dance. Fruity dances but not that much, I guess. Over there the viscounts don't have time. Daddy filled me in on it. They got so much on their plate already, ribbon cuttings and agricultural shows, and horseracing and judging cows and pigs, and fox hunting and going to the palace on the queen's birthday, playing cricket and being in church and wearing wigs in the House of Lords and marching in parades. Tradition and stuff. My sister in Kashmir, India, says that's how it is there, only worse, the maharajah and all, and sacred elephants, with untouchables to be avoided and the other castes bowing to you, and joining processions to visit temples, burning incense and not killing cows, and funeral pyres and dumping ashes in the Ganges and things. In Austria, too, there's no rest. My sister, the grafin, says peasants are forever coming into the courtyard in Tyrolean costume, step-dancing and yodeling and stuff. All in German, which sounds frightful. She says it's a remake of *The Sound of Music* with everything but Captain von Trapp blowing his whistle and the kids singing 'Doe, a deer...' And Rome? Oh, God, my sister in Rome, the commendatore's wife, she says they're forever at the Vatican being blessed by the Pope. And being handed out souvenir rosary beads and holy pictures and getting ashes on their foreheads. And she isn't even a Catholic!"

"Rank has its privileges, Mandy. But you're quite right, there are also solemn duties and weighty responsibilities." Alix rarely sounded as solemn, as weighty.

Just then a good-looking boy who might have been off one of the boats, fit and tan as he was, came over to ask Mandy to dance. She literally jumped at him.

When Alix and I were alone, I said, "What are you up to with this kid? I know you, Alix. You've got a game afoot."

"Beecher, you do me an injustice. I am simply attempting to prevent Fruity and this delicious young girl from committing a mistake of mythic proportions."

"On grounds that she's too young and naive and not very smart?"

Alix stared at me, shaking her head.

"Beecher, on grounds she's far too good for Fruity! Did you see the way she went for that boy just now? I thought she was going to begin chewing on his shoulder. Fruity will be staying at his club in Mayfair just to get away from her before the honeymoon is over. The girl wasn't raised to manage a great home in Surrey and a town house in Mayfair and dance primly at Quaglino's and sip sherry and observe protocol and bone up on constituency politics and shake hands with Tony, the PM, I mean. She's far too simple and uncomplicated and, I think, just too nice for all that."

"But—"

"Let her sisters marry commendatores and maharajahs and grafs. I say, leave her alone; let her find a boy herself. Here at Boaters or in Waco, Texas, where it's good for hair."

There was a passionate note to her argument that had to impress you. "So you're not just saving Fruity from that 'social climbing heiress from New York'?"

"Beecher, you ought to know me better than that by now," she said, very quietly. When the boy brought Mandy back, Alix and I were both subdued. She, in turn, was revivified. The music, the boy, the dancing? Who knew?

As she reclaimed her place at our table and drank off half a glass of Gatorade against the thirst of smoke and dance floor heat, Mandy said, "Please stop me if this is boring. But in Texas a very smart woman with a good marriage told me, the secret to being happily married is very simple. And of course I said, 'Oh, then tell me!' And this woman said, 'During the day, it's okay to wear clothes you can throw into the washer. But when your husband comes home, always wear something that you have to have dry-cleaned.'"

I didn't know precisely what that meant. But Alix, who'd probably never washed or dry-cleaned anything, nodded.

"As profound a theory as I've recently heard," she said.

"Because I do want to be a good wife," Mandy went on. "The viscount deserves that. Even though..."

"Even though what?"

She came near to breaking down then. "I've seen my sisters in their palaces. I don't want that. I don't want to be Viscountess Mandy. Can't I just be...me? And in love?"

She might not be very bright; she touched us. Neither of us said anything and she resumed. "But then I think of Fruity. How sweet he is. And where does a kid like me get off hurting a member of the British cabinet and rejecting a great old historic title and stuff? How can I do that to him? And to England?"

Her agony was manifest.

"Darling Mandy," Alix said, "if that were your decision, after seriously pondering the matter, to back away and rethink your marriage, we'll manage somehow to pull Fruity through, I promise you. And England, as well . . ."

# twenty-three

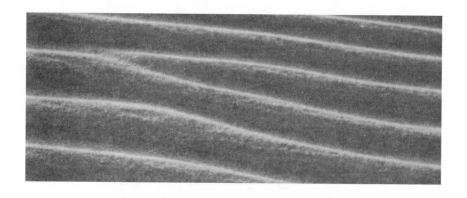

*Senator D'Amato may yet go down in*
*the legends . . .*

We got back to the gatehouse just after eleven, having seen Mandy safely off in her BMW convertible and pointed approximately in the direction of Gin Lane. Whether she was really going there, well, that was another matter and there were places like the Wild Rose, where people danced, between here and Gin Lane. She was of age and who could say? On the late news there was a bulletin from Southampton:

"An explosion, possibly a propane tank, has damaged the Gin Lane home of broadcast personality Leicester 'Cowboy' Dils. A small fire was quickly extinguished by local volunteer firemen and damage is limited. One casualty, a visiting Tibetan dignitary, Dr. Fu Manchu, in this country seeking support for Tibetan Freedom Fighters. Dr. Fu was pulled from the fire by heroic Nurse Edith Cavell. Mr. Dils said only Nurse Cavell's dedication and courage prevented tragedy. Dr. Fu reportedly is planning to meet with the president during his Memorial Day visit to Southampton, seeking Washington's support for the Dalai Lama and Tibetan independence."

The hell with it. If I woke him up, I woke him up. I phoned Tom Knowles at home. The detective sounded sleepy and sore.

"Beecher, it's a propane leak. Not the World Trade Center bombing."

"Tom, last month his chopper crashed. Ten days ago we had a hit-and-run. Then the crippled man ends up in the pool and practically drowns. Now an explosion and fire. Wasn't it a 'routine' gas leak that killed Vitas Gerulaitis in Southampton a couple of years back? Does Dils have to end up dead for the cops to do something?"

"Beecher, you know the man. He's accident-prone. Paranoid. Some people think he's a whackjob. And you're starting to sound like 'Mr. Gloomy' on the bad news hour. I talked to the Southampton guys on this one. Propane tanks blow every so often. They took this one with them for tests but so far the fire isn't labeled suspicious. I'm keeping on it, Beecher. Just as soon as I get some sleep, I'll be back on it."

I called Maguire but got the answering machine. Hell, maybe they were trying to get some sleep, too. Alix and I seemed to be taking all this harder than anyone else.

In the morning, both John Fairchild and Jesse Maine had surfaced....

I went up to Dreesen's before seven to get the papers and the doughnuts. *Women's Wear Daily,* in that day's edition, had broken the story of Mandy's wedding dress, along with what appeared to be a fairly detailed sketch. The headline was typical. Bitchy and brilliant:

"Fruity's Bride/Donna's Lemon."

Mr. Fairchild, still bristling over his run-on with the Buchanans, and never overlooking the opportunity of giving Ms. Karan a tweak, had dictated the accompanying story himself, signing it, as was customary, "Louise J. Esterhazy." It was lethal. The wedding gown was cruelly dismissed as "loving hands at home," one of John Fairchild's favorite labels for a fashion look that fell short of his rigorous critical standards. As for sources, the paper claimed these were "key associates of Donna Karan."

Nice. That'd get the Buchanans down on poor Donna. Who, from her own East Hampton place, was busily issuing denials in somewhat desperate language.

The story went on to say a few nice things about Mandy's beauty and the Viscount Albemarle's distinguished lineage before updating the several previous "arranged" nuptials of Buchanan girls with the world's relatively impoverished nobility (the suggestion being, Mr. and Mrs. Buchanan were in the business of "buying" titles for their girls).

"The maharajah's wife is locally celebrated throughout Kashmir for pig-sticking, having become quite adept at the ancient local sport of hunting down wild boars from horseback and pinioning them to the turf with steel lances."

The daughter in the Tyrol was described as "somewhat odd in that she has organized a juvenile chorus of village children whom she puts through daily scales and other musical drills, much after the manner of the late Maria von Trapp."

The commendatore's wife in Rome was praised as "pious, forever telling her beads, a confidante of His Holiness the Pope. Said to be consulted by him on papal appointments and women's issues."

Mandy, the soon-to-be viscountess, "enjoys showing her superb legs in the briefest of miniskirts and, though a teetotaler, dancing on tables in redneck bars and biker saloons."

Alix was impressed despite herself. "But how does Mr. Fairchild do it? It was only last evening that she was dancing on tables. Could he have been among us at Boaters in disguise and taking notes? The man is astonishing!"

"He does it," I responded, "because he's a great reporter. He's indefatigable. Relentless. And he's been goaded into it by that fool Buchanan. A challenge was flung down and Fairchild's responding. But the real reason he does it is because he's seventy years old and wants to prove he can do it! Like all the great reporters, he wants the world to know he can still get the story, write it, and put a head on it."

Alix thought that one over. Then: "When you're seventy, Beecher, will you?"

"I'd like to think so, Alix."

She kissed me lightly on the cheek. I didn't know precisely whether that meant "Good for you, Beecher!" or "You poor dear."

We were on the lawn having coffee when Maguire called. "Cowboy's on the *Today* show at eight-thirty if you want to tune in. They sent a crew out to ask about the fire."

Katie Couric, from the sidewalk studio in Rockefeller Center, did the story on a split screen with Dils. "I'm bonkers for Katie Couric," Alix said. "There's simply no one like her on BBC. So feisty, such a dear girl."

Cowboy was on the Gin Lane lawn with the Atlantic as backdrop, the surf rolling in and sliding back as he sat casually astride his famous golf cart, the one that rolled into the pool, the familiar cowboy hat jauntily tipped back off his face. After acknowledging the cause of the propane explosion and fire was still being investigated, he launched right into one of his doomsday modes.

"Dr. Fu and his Tibetan Freedom Fighters have long been a thorn in Beijing's side. Those red fiends would love to silence the man's eloquent voice."

"You suspect China's complicity?" Katie asked.

"Suspect? I'm asking Secretary of State Madeleine K. Albright to make representations. To recall our ambassador for consultations. I expect the Pentagon to be moving a carrier group into the Taiwan Straits even as we speak. And I'm reliably informed consultations with our NATO allies are to begin shortly. Especially with the gallant Poles, who have little taste for Godless, atheistic communism, let me say."

"But Mr. Dils, there are reports Fu Manchu is neither a doctor or even Chinese. That he's a former Vietnamese boat person."

Good for you, Katie, I thought. But Cowboy wasn't having any of it. Tolerantly, though with a grudging patience, he said:

"How little we Americans understand the Orient. The mysterious and inscrutable East works its wonders in strange ways and wearing many masks. Always remember the eternal verities. And the sacred chant of the Tibetan lamas as they contemplate Chomolungma, Goddess Mother of the World—"

"You mean Mount Everest," Ms. Couric put in helpfully.

But Dils went on as if she weren't there:

"*Om mane padme hum* . . . the holiest of Tibetan chants, which your viewers are probably aware, translates out to 'the jewel is in the lotus'."

They went to commercial after that.

I called Maguire to find out what they thought about his performance on Gin Lane. Harry Almond got on. "He did splendidly, we thought. And you?"

I said he was entertaining. But was there any truth to . . .

"Of course not. It was a pleasant evening and we were out on the patio grilling some swordfish steaks for dinner last night and poor Fu had gotten into the Chardonnay and worked too close to the gas in dashing on the soy sauce. Nurse Cavell's quick wits really did save him from a bad burn."

I told Alix. She looked thoughtful.

"Still," she said, "you can't really trust them, can you? The Chinese, the People's Republic, I mean, not *our* Chinamen, but the Reds. You know, how they're mucking about the stock market in Hong Kong. Wouldn't surprise me at all if they tried to silence a charismatic spokesman for the Tibetan resistance."

"We're not supposed to say 'Chinamen' anymore, either," I reminded her.

"Oh, all right then," she said impatiently. "Chinks!"

"And Fu *is* Vietnamese, Alix. A guy who does radio bits."

"Well, yes. But as Cowboy in the Morning says, the East wears many masks. . . ."

She had to go into Southampton to Saks to buy a dress. There was another bridal dinner tonight. Must she attend each of them? "Wouldn't miss this one, Beecher. Mr. Buchanan's sure to be out of sorts about Mr. Fairchild and that sketch of the wedding dress. Frothing at the mouth and biting people. I can't wait to see him. It'll be like your friend Wyseman Something, the one who tries to eat his own ear."

Before she'd left, Jesse Maine drove onto the gravel and parked his truck. "I could use a black coffee," he informed me, throwing himself heavily into an Adirondack chair.

"What's happened?" I said, knowing his moods.

"The Pequots."

"Not again, Jesse," Alix said. By now she was as fed up with the Pequots as he was and quite ready to enlist if someone, anyone, would agree to start up a second Pequot war. I went inside to get the coffee. Alix was the best possible roommate but a simple cup of instant coffee could occupy her for an hour, finding things, choosing the cup, fiddling with the stove, pouring, selecting the right paper napkin. And if milk and sugar were involved, half a day. When I came back out with the coffee Jesse was helling and damning at a great rate.

"You don't mind them owning the occasional alderman or town trustee or member of the assembly or state senate. But when Senator D'Amato takes the side of Connecticut Pequots versus patriotic local Shinnecocks right here on Long Island where he himself was born, and in his home state, well, I begin asking pointed questions, Beecher."

"What d'you mean, 'owing' politicians? You mean bribes?"

"Not concerning Senator D'Amato. They don't bribe the senator, no way. No money changes hands; they're far more clever than that, them Pequots. And he's above chicanery, Senator D'Amato, and above bribes as well being a Republican and all. Not unknown for someone to buy a Democrat. But Republicans . . . ? No, Beecher, I'm talking about what the Pequots up there in Connecticut at the casino is planning: a kind of Pequot Hall of Fame. Great men and women through history who furthered the Pequot cause, right back to Uncas, last of the Mohicans. And his daddy Chingacook. A regular Cooperstown of heroes. Notable fellows like Nathan Hale and Herman Hickman the Yale football coach. Natty Bumppo and James Fenimore Cooper, Governor Wentworth, Elihu Yale, them fellows. George Bush's daddy the late great Senator Prescott Bush, long a partner in the Wall Street firm of Brown Brothers Harriman. The mayor of Bridgeport. Calvin Hill who went to Yale and played for the Dallas Cowboys. Lads like that. And there'll be busts and plaques of the finest metals and sculpted stone, attractively arrayed where the twenty-five-cent slot machine players and old ladies in housedresses that go up there on tour buses can gaze on them and admire. Cut flowers in little vases at the foot of the plaques and maybe some votive candles, lit and flickery in the breeze of all them housedresses going by. And there amid them, a handsome bust or plaque of Long Island native son and current United States Senator the Honorable Alfonse M. D'Amato, noted friend and supporter of the Pequot cause."

"What'd he do to earn such recognition and high honors?"

"It's what he didn't do, damnit! We had a bill working its way through Congress down there that would recognize the Shinnecocks as a sovereign and official Indian nation, with all federal rights and privileges, just like them Pequots have had for a time and God knows how they slipped that one through to a vote so swiftly. Except Senator D'Amato never pushed them colleagues of his to call up the Shinnecock bill and bring it to the floor for a vote. Didn't horsetrade or twist a single arm or even whisper promises of imaginative log-rolling into no shell-like ears down there in the damned lobbies of the You Ess Senate. Hell, he didn't do nothing. Just sat on his ass . . . pardon my lingo, Your Ladyship. So our bill stipulating official nationhood to we Shinnecocks, that one curled up and died, and the Pequots, who now see their way clear to establishing casinos here on the East End as the dominant tribe, without no pesky Shinnecocks casting vetoes or distributing petitions, nor sharing in the considerable profits, they're walking very tall and preening, admiring theirselves in sidelong glances as they pass the reflective show windows of Cadillac agencies and the sales rooms of Mercedes and Beamers. Which is what them boys is driving these days whilst us of the Shinnecock Nation is big customers in the secondhand pickup markets or tooling about in Yugos."

"And there's nothing you can do, Jesse?" Alix inquired solicitously.

"Sure, Your Ladyship. I could go out and get drunk. And may do. Or I could go on a hunger strike. Which I won't on account of I can't survive till noon unless I have half a dozen eggs and rashers of lean bacon and a mess of fries for breakfast. Or I could say to hell, and do nothing. But what I *am* going to do over the coming holiday weekend of Memorial Day is to remind folks there ought to be some memorials to us Shinnecocks. And to that purpose, I intend to call out the entire Shinnecock Nation in a grand demonstration and protest."

"Oh, Jesse! What a thrilling idea," Alix enthused.

"How many you think you can get, Jesse?" I said.

"There may be eight or ten fellows who'll go along. But prime, whoever we get he'll be prime. And in full gear, I can assure you. Feathers and paint and breachclouts, with fringe and wampum, outfits no living Shinnecock and few dead can remember ever seeing. Not even me. And there'll be drums. That I can promise you, Beecher and Lady Alix, I can promise you drums along the Montauk Highway."

He paused, savoring the vision, every inch of him as proud as Karl Lager and his "auld brigade" of sports car drivers out to save the Bridgehampton raceway.

"Oh, it'll be grand," Jesse said. "Grand and historic, with full martial honors and feats of daring and courage, and enormous pillage and sacking. Why, Senator D'Amato may yet go down in the legends, not as a second-rate fixer of potholes, or briefly and amongst others the betrothed of that Claudia Cohen who does the gossip reports on television, but as another General Custer almost, the one white man who gets credit for starting the last Indian war in this country of ours that there ever was or will be...."

# twenty-four

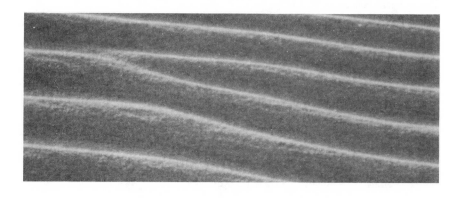

*That's as glamorous as it gets, unless Billy Joel*
*comes in to play piano...*

I drove Alix down to Southampton and while she shopped at Saks I wandered around Main Street and Job's Lane a bit. There was a show of vintage photos in the window of Hildreth's, the furniture store. I admired a shot of James Augustus "Gus" Hildreth in October of 1897, with the rest of the Southampton Town football team that Gus captained. Were ever football players as short-haired and solemn while posing for a team shot? I bet they played pretty good ball, too. Through the years, we all played pretty good ball out here. When I'd thoroughly studied the old shots, sepia and wonderful, I moved on. Daly, the motion picture executive, was right; you noticed a lot more men in suits around town that day and the next. Federal agents, it was assumed, smoothing the way for the president. And not just the familiar figure of "stately, plump" Special Agent O'Hara, who'd clearly been reinforced. It was all reminiscent of last year, when Streisand was supposed to be getting married to Mr. Brolin on Block Island and the First Family were going to attend.

There were reports again now on TV and in the papers that a White House advance party was laying down phone lines. There were flyovers by choppers. And considerable talk of U.S. Navy warships in the area, lying out there just offshore below the horizon, but ready to come in and land the Marines if anything happened.

What could happen? This was Southampton, not Bosnia. Or was I being simplistic?

As for O'Hara himself, he watched and listened and took notes and talked into his gabardine lapel, all this to an extent that he had himself become a part of the Southampton landscape, as if he owned property or, as England was wont to do, had been granted "the freedom of the town." O'Hara drank a little and chatted pleasantly of the weather and of ball scores and, being a strange new element in the village, some women took more than notice and spent time with him, chatting or flirting, luring and being lured. As O'Hara himself was fond of saying, and quotably:

"No man is an island, fer chrissakes."

Various women's names were mentioned at the Meadow or the Bathing Corp. or at the bar of Barrister's. Even Slim Champion's name was mentioned in connection with him. But that was nonsense. What would Mrs. Roger Champion with her wealth and her social standing and her Gin Lane roots possibly want with a transient like O'Hara?

I wondered about things like that, waiting for Alix.

When she'd finished her shopping and filled up the back of my Blazer with packages, I asked where tonight's bacchanal was being staged and she rustled about her Chanel bag to find the invitation, handwritten nicely on creamy Tiffany cardboard. "It says, 'The National Golf Links of America.' Where's that?"

"There must be a mistake. Buchanan belongs to Shinnecock Hills, where you had dinner the other night. The National is another country club entirely."

"No, that's what it says. I guess Mr. Buchanan just joined all the clubs out here. So wherever he goes he can't be snubbed, even if he does own sweetshops."

Made sense. If you thought like Tom and Daisy Buchanan. I wondered if they'd applied to Maidstone and whether we'd let them in.

No, I thought. There were still limits.

"Come on," I said, "let's go see Lager. I want you to meet his wife and see the house." Mrs. Lager was an actress who had made some splendid movies and I wanted Alix to know my friends. It was a glorious day and why not make use of it.

There were four or five red fox pups leaping about in the tall grass, too young to stalk pheasants, but playfully chasing field mice or crickets or something, as we drove up the long dirt road climbing from Scuttle Hole Road to the house atop the hill. I'd phoned ahead and got the okay and when we pulled up both Lagers were out there on the lawn, along with a man I didn't know.

"This," said Lager after he'd bowed Alix a gracious welcome, "is Baron von Kronk. Lady Alix Dunraven and the noted author and correspondent Beecher Stowe. The baron is staying with us for the weekend." The baron had a big grin and we got that and handshakes. Didn't click his heels, I was disappointed to note. There was no indication I could see that he had only one leg.

How long ago was the war? Here was a panzer officer who fought the Americans staying in the home of a Jew who'd fought behind German lines blowing up Nazis as a U.S. Army captain seconded to the OSS. Yet both men, aging now, or aged, were German-born. Maybe those were the ties that bind and not the rest of it?

Sandy Lager and the others made a fuss over Alix, meaning it, and she handled the situation as she always did. This was her turf, titles and wealth and a quality of life you didn't get through mail order catalogs. When we had iced tea and fruit juices and little cakes of some sort, I said, "How goes the campaign to save the raceway?"

Kronk shook his head and Lager made a face. "The preliminary injunction scared off some of the lads. Saw no reason to travel to Bridgehampton for nothing," Kronk said. "Karl and I are still intent on making some sort of fuss. Just what, we can't quite figure out. Something short of kidnapping the mayor and burning down Sandy's lovely house here."

His English was perfect, only the accent suggesting it wasn't his first language.

"I suggested they spend the day playing bad golf. Keep them out of mischief," Sandy Lager said.

"Keep us out of jail, you mean."

But how many drivers really would come through? "Oh, there may be eight or nine of us. If we're lucky, zipped up in our racing suits and tucked into our MGs and Jags and Ferraris..."

Karl didn't sound as buoyant as he had the last time we talked. He sounded, in fact, a lot like Jesse Maine, who might have "eight or ten" Shinnecocks prepared to don war paint and beat drums in dubious battle. Slightly deflated, disillusioned. No wonder Cowboy Dils fought with everyone; the good guys were outnumbered and didn't stand a chance. Wyseman Clagett and his lot, including Roger Champion, had gotten a preliminary injunction; the Pequots had enlisted Senator D'Amato on their side; Rex Magnifico's Argies won the polo match; Dils kept getting run over or nearly drowned and had swordfish steaks blowing up on him; and Fruity's "bride" was out dancing on tables in Boaters.

The "good guys" were losing right across the board. Hell of a note.

Lager took a wry, masochistic enjoyment out of returning to his theme of failure. King Richard Petty was emceeing a shopping mall dedication in North Carolina. Stirling Moss sent regrets. Paul Newman didn't even respond. A. J. Foyt, well, you know about that...maybe they ought to just call off the whole mad scheme.

Von Kronk might lack a leg, but he had guts. "Karl, so to hell with them. I know some fellows who drive, old Germans, not in my league or even in yours. But they drive in rallyes, in local amateur races. It may be Corvettes and MGs instead of racing Bentleys and Lamborghinis, but so what. And don't you have a few CIA boys in your Rolodex who enjoy to drive fast in an open car on Sundays?"

Mrs. Lager took Alix on a tour of the house to get away from all the shop talk and Karl and the baron talked cars and the old racing days. And I told them a few Cowboy Dils anecdotes and about the travails of the Shinnecocks. They mentioned the war only once, when Lager said maybe there were three or four drivers he might be able to reach, old OSS types or slightly younger men from the CIA now retired or gone into other fields, finance or security work or writing their memoirs. The baron weighed in with a couple of names of chaps in Manhattan who drove, men he knew in the war or sons of those men. "And did you say one of the von Ribbentrops lives out here?" It was then that von Kronk said something that stayed with me over the next few days when things got complicated and frenzies of various sorts threatened to shake South-ampton to its aristocratic roots:

"As we sit here on the verandah over tea, hatching good-natured plots, am I the only one," the baron asked half rhetorically, "to wonder with the president about to visit the Hamptons, just what the people in charge of his security must be thinking?"

"What d'you mean?" I asked.

He made an expansive gesture. "Nothing to it, of course. But here you have a former panzer officer of the German wehrmacht suddenly arrived and camping out. CIA men and wartime spies are being rounded up for an illegal demo intended to block strategic roads and snarl traffic. The local Indian tribe is threatening to sound the war drums. Mr. Dils, who fires off a gun from the roof of his home, is unnerving and deviling the White House. A fellow named von Ribbentrop lives down the road. There's everything but a ride-by of lesbian motorcyclists, the Diesel Dykes. If I were your Secret Service, well, I'd be somewhat curious about having all these people in town at one and the same time..."

"But on very different errands, Baron," Lager pointed out.

"Of course, of course. I'm just being silly, talking rubbish," the German said, shifting his leg in the wicker chair as the shadow of pain moved briefly across his handsome old face.

When Alix and Sandy returned Lager piled us all into two cars for an unofficial but authoritative tour of the old race course, stopping at the top of a height of land so that we could get out and look down. "The best view of the bay to the north and the ocean to the south." I took his word for it. For Alix's benefit he pointed out where the Shinnecock Hills club left off and the National began, and where one clubhouse was in relation to the other, just where the Buchanans were holding their series of bridal dinners. And he showed us around the race course. The track was pretty beat up, as he'd said, weed-grown and shabby, but there was five hundred acres of it, sitting on prime Hamptons land atop the aquifer. You could see why speculators might want to take it on.

The baron just went along, looking out, maybe remembering a specific race. Or a specific car. Or a specific car on a specific lap. Old men and obsolescent memories. That's what the Bridgehampton raceway had come down to. Old men remembering and silly people like me gawking.

We drove back slowly to the Lager house and Alix and I thanked them and headed for East Hampton. She had a bridal dinner to get ready for, Fruity to nurture, Mandy to counsel and advise, the wrath of Mr. Buchanan to be confronted. Which reminded me, why hadn't I asked Karl Lager about John Fairchild's latest scoop?

That might have been an enlightening interlude. I wonder what Baron von Kronk would have thought. And whether he might in consequence have asked himself, as a German officer, "How did our side ever lose against this lot?"

When Alix was well and splendidly turned out (the Saks dress was clearly a hit!) she drove off in her Range Rover, with instructions that she should go yet again to Shinnecock Hills but take the second turning instead of the first. In the Hamptons it's vital to keep your country clubs straight. As soon as she was gone I went up to the Blue Parrot and got into a discussion of thoroughbred racing with a tiny man wearing a glen plaid suit and a bowler; he was perched on the next stool and was called "the Colonel" and said he used to be a jockey. He had many fascinating theories on horses and, while never buying a round, insisted on sharing both theories and outlandish stories with us. Finally, someone threw the Colonel out, and we all settled down to talking about surfing and real estate transactions and Kim Basinger and whether Jerry Della Femina was ever going to sell off his commercial properties and what fish were running and how unfortunate it was Richard Ryan had sold his boat with its global positioning device, the boat Alix and Jesse and I commandeered last year after the hurricane to save Mr. Warrender.

That's about as glamorous as it gets in East Hampton, unless Billy Joel comes in to play a little piano. About ten I went home. I don't know what time Alix came home, only that I was asleep when she arrived.

But she woke me up, thoughtfully not until after she'd undressed quietly and in the dark, and then, after brushing her teeth, climbed into bed and curled herself around me and began to lick my neck. I remember that and the sweet smell of her dentifrice.

# twenty-five

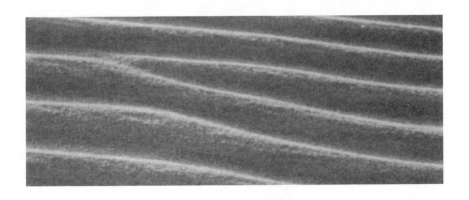

*I'm Lenin at the Finland Station and the tsar*

*says, "Boys, we're outa here..."*

In the morning before we were even out of bed (well, I got up and made coffee for us both and went back), I got a full report on last night's dramatic events at the National Golf Links of America.

"This thing is turning into 'Who Shot J. R.?'" I said.

"Who's J. R.?"

I told her never mind and she began.

"First of all," said Alix, who enjoyed setting a scene, "that's a smashing place. Much posher than Shinnecock Hills, though I'm told the course isn't as testing. Beautiful, but designed for low scoring. Though it seems each of your local country clubs is more lavish than the next. Puts the Royal and Ancient quite to shame..." going on with an account of the drinks and wines, canapés and viands, baby lobsters, fresh fruits and blackened fish, pastries and exquisite sherbets "and little rice cakes the like of which I've never tasted," served before, during, or following dinner, as well as cocktails before and brandies and liqueurs after, with details of hardwood floors and portraits in oil and tall windows and draperies and brasswork and wainscoting and cutlery and scrimshaw work, a description that would have done justice to Paige Rense of *Architectural Digest*. And the staff of servants? They might almost have been worthy of a men's club in St. James.

"... and Mr. Fairchild was there."

I nearly spilled my coffee over that one. "Wait a minute. Buchanan threw him out of the dinner the other night at Shinnecock Hills. And since then, he's run a sketch of the wedding dress, complete with bitchy comments."

"Well, there was a brisk exchange of views about the media. Freedom of the press and the like. Though it clearly was Mr. Fairchild who on that first occasion called for his car and left. No blows were exchanged, I assure you."

"But to crash a second bridal dinner after stalking angrily from the first ..."

"Oh, he didn't 'crash.' Mr. Fairchild had been invited some time ago to both dinners. The Buchanans simply forgot to cancel the second invitation, assuming, one supposes, that Mr. Fairchild had gotten the message and, being a Harvard man, would stay home."

"Princeton!" I shot back. "He went to Princeton. *Not* Harvard."

"Yes, well ..." she said vaguely.

"And what happened?"

"No violence. But a certain chill was discernible."

"I'd imagine."

"And Mr. Fairchild didn't get the favorable table placement he did at the earlier affair. I chatted him up a bit and he turned out awfully pleasant and well-informed. Half the room treated him rather like a leper and the other half seemed to be sucking up. He kept saying he shouldn't really be blamed for every word in *W* and in *Women's Wear Daily*. They practice something called 'group journalism,' he said, invented by a man he called 'Loose.' Who might that be, Beecher?"

"Henry Luce, the man who founded *Time* magazine with Briton Hadden."

"Oh," she said, "I'm sure Mr. Murdoch knows them."

"Not likely. They're dead."

"In any event, Mr. Fairchild flat out denied being the author of that

'Louise J. Esterhazy' story. 'They do these things without my knowledge,' he assured me, the very soul of innocence."

Other than being invaded by Fairchild, the evening went off well. "Fruity actually danced with Mandy. The fox-trot. They looked quite handsome, although the instant it was over she was off dancing to something more contemporary with an American chap. She does have the loveliest legs."

Her Ladyship's legs didn't look half bad either, sprawled as she was across the bed, sipping my coffee, and I stroked one, telling her so.

"You are sweet, Beecher," stroking back, and we kissed and so on for a time. When that was out of the way, I asked, "Any of Fruity's chums there, aside from you? His family? Are they boycotting the wedding, or what?"

"Oh, no, his old pa the earl is quite keen. Apparently, they could use the cash and the bride's family has it a-plenty. He's flying over that very morning via Concorde and being whisked out here by a Buchanan limo. As you know, the earl so loves Britain that years ago he took some sort of sacred vow against America, so he's off again right after the ceremony, flying to Toronto, since that's still part of the British Commonwealth. You know his famous boast, I'm sure."

"I don't think so, no."

"Odd, it's in all the books; I was sure you'd heard it: 'Never fall asleep unless there's a Union Jack flying!' Something like that ..."

"Might it be 'The sun never sets on the British Empire'?"

"Quite possibly," she conceded. "All I know, it's a famous boast of the earl's."

I said I'd commit it to memory. "And Fruity's friends?"

"Several of them were there last night, chinless wonders attached to the UN delegation in Manhattan, and a twelfth Baron Gascoigne. Others are coming up from the embassy in Washington. His banker said he'll make it. Keeping as he does a close eye on Fruity's overdrafts, the banker's a cert to be here."

So despite the best efforts of *Women's Wear Daily* and John Fairchild; the towering rage and fury of sweetshop king Thomas Buchanan, father of the bride; the marital counsel of the absolutely never-wed Lady Alix; the doubts of both of the young people most intimately involved; and any number of negative planetary alignments, the wedding of Mandy

Buchanan to Viscount Albemarle had not yet been canceled. It was still scheduled for Memorial Day afternoon in the church of St. Andrews in the Gin Lane dunes, to be followed by a reception at the Meadow Club, both events to be attended by the president of the United States (POTUS in the jargon of government) and his First Lady. Just what role a shamed Donna Karan might play, following the egregious leak of the wedding dress design, remained decidedly chancey, with no one willing to be quoted.

"Her IPO was better received than the wedding dress," a critic cynically remarked, which was quite unfair. Donna's several attempts to make a successful initial public offering were flops, but she was a fine designer, even if some of her work, including this wedding dress for Mandy, did stray into the category of John Fairchild's "loving hands at home." In any event, the IPO crack was instantly picked up and promptly quoted by Mr. Fairchild's papers.

By now Alix had had enough of the lot of them. "Could we go see Mr. Dils again? I've been dropping the most pointed of hints about publishing his next book in England but he's been terribly evasive."

"Sure, I'll phone ahead."

Alix insisted on buying flowers for the injured Dr. Fu so we stopped at a roadside stand on the way and bought some early spring flowers. The weather was sunny and cool and I hoped it was going to hold for the entire weekend. Instead of jeans or linen slacks she wore a dress, flowery and filmy, also quite short. I think she liked hearing about her legs and was rewarding me by showing them off. When we were ushered into the Presence, Cowboy, from his golf cart, sounded less than joyous.

"If they mean to have war, let it begin here," he said.

Dr. Fu was whistled up and presented with an enormous bouquet. Which he took in bandaged hands, inhaling deeply their fragrance before passing them on in a sharing gesture to faithful Nurse Cavell.

"You poor chap," Alix murmured.

"The jewel is indeed in the lotus when Your Ladyship's smile ushers in the consoling warmth of a new sun's innocence."

"Yes, quite, I'm sure," she said vaguely.

We all lazed about, chatting about meaningless things, only Alix focused on anything, and not getting very far with Dils on her book proposals. Sensing this, she shifted to anecdotes about the Buchanans and

Fruity and the earl's refusal to spend a night anywhere but snugly tucked in under his own flag. There was some pickup on that, idle chat about a skit starring the earl.

"We've got one Brit skit in the works already, chief: 'The Bridge on the River Liffey,' where the Irish force British POWs to build a bridge in Dublin."

No one was enthusiastic. And then:

"Why," inquired Cowboy of a small audience that included Alix and me, "do people still get married?"

This wasn't just the usual raging of Dils against the world. This was philosophical inquiry. Something had happened. Someone or something had gotten to him, was gnawing at him. Harry Almond noticed, I was sure he did, and Harry knew Cowboy better than anyone. And appreciated, for all his bravado and noise, how vulnerable Cowboy was.

"I mean," Cowboy went on, "it usually doesn't work. Look at me. I got to thinking about it when I saw that Shoshanna Lonstein on the evening news, the kid who was going to marry Seinfeld. Now she's hanging out with Trump. I mean, you look at that girl and you want to ... well, let's not get into that. But why didn't she and Seinfeld get married? As Harry would put it, being a born-again Christian, 'two nice young Jewish people ...'"

"Now, just a min—" Harry responded.

"They probably knew it wouldn't have worked for them. You see a couple that look perfect together. But they're not. I know couples, one's cheating or the other's cheating and lying about it." He looked around at the rest of us, didn't see the usual reaction, realized he'd left us somewhere behind in a dust of confusion.

"Ah, the hell with it! What gets into me? It's like the other day when I lashed out at Alix. I'm not even married anymore ..."

That broke the ice and soon he was himself again, telling us that all he really wanted out of life, professional life, was to replicate what John Houseman and Orson Welles did in the late 1930s, creating the Mercury Theater, building a neat little repertory company and doing stage plays and radio shows and even movies, from original scripts and using the same little elite corps of actors and directors and technicians.

"Harry and Maguire and Dr. Fu and Annie and Greasy Thumb. Even Nurse Cavell. And Jersey Fats. Talented people. I mean that. But am I taken seriously? Hell, no! Because every time someone begins to say nice things about the work we do, I shoot off my mouth and play the fool and get into a war with somebody, challenging them to fistfights, the church even. Or the town or—"

He broke it off then.

"I'm depressing myself. Man was meant to wage war. Look at chess, maybe the greatest game ever invented. And what is chess? War without splintered bone and intestines trailing in the dirt." Cowboy raised his voice then, and beating time on the dashboard of the cart, to declaim, and accurately so:

"By the rude bridge/That arched the flood/Their flag to April's breeze unfurled/Here the embattled farmers stood/And fired the shot/Heard 'round the world..."

"Oh, I say, that is stirring stuff," Her Ladyship called out, applauding vigorously. "What's it from?"

Harry Almond told her.

"Oh," she said, considerably deflated, "I see. But it's still bloody good stuff. Even if it did signal rebellion against king and crown. Bunker Hill and all that..."

Dils seemed to be giving me some sort of a high sign. Or else he'd suddenly been taken with a facial tic very nearly as ghastly as that which afflicted Wyseman Clagett and his ancestors.

"I've got to talk to you. Don't want my bunch to know. Confidential stuff. Tell everyone you need some info for the magazine and can we talk privately. Okay?"

"Sure," I said, not sure just what this was all about.

An elaborate game of polo with four golf carts had begun on Dils's grass, the ball a vast, inflated beachball, and rusty old golf clubs as mallets, with Her Ladyship advising on the finer points of technique and explaining to Nurse Cavell what a "chukker" was, all the while calling after me to promote her book-publishing schemes if there were time, as Cowboy and I, the two of us aboard his cart, drove across the vast lawns toward the ocean.

I knew he'd speak so I didn't pester him with questions.

"Look, Stowe, you were fair with me in that piece you wrote this spring. I'm not good about saying thanks. But I appreciated it."

"Sure," I said. I waited, letting him make the running.

"I worry about bra straps showing. Don't you?"

That rattled me out of my cool, waiting mode.

"What?"

"The *New York Times* fashion pages say that's the new thing, bra straps that show. And underwear worn outside. I can take bra straps or leave them, but that's what the experts are saying. I thought we might do a skit on it . . .

"I'm not sure that I—"

"Not important. Look, Stowe, I've made a lot of enemies along Gin Lane in the last year. Sometimes I'm just teasing, getting their goats. Mostly it's that I'm a pain in the ass. Partly the fault of these stuffy bastards. More people hate me than Leona Helmsley. Compared to me, James Carville is St. Francis of Assisi. The odd thing is, with all the feuds and firing of BB guns, I love Gin Lane. This is the best house I ever owned. Real friends, special people when they come by, I show them through the house, looking into rooms one after the other, like Gatsby did for Daisy and Nick." He paused, as if seeing those rooms now, was again with "friends" and "special people." Then, abruptly:

"You read this latest book by Erica Jong? *Inventing Memory?* It's pretty good, much of it. But then she gets started on the Hamptons and you never heard such crap. I was so sore I practically committed it to memory, all about how the Hamptons are everything she hates about her genera- tion. Greed, display, cynicism. 'From Poland to polo, from Grossinger's to the Hamptons,' something like that. And she ends up saying this place 'makes me puke.' "

"She wrote that?"

"Yeah, Erica Jong."

"A little self-loathing is all," I said. "I wouldn't worry about it."

He bit his lower lip in thought, the way the president does when the cameras are on him and he wants to looked concerned, and went on:

"The old farts don't realize how I feel about Gin Lane. That I know how fortunate I am to be here. A reformed drunk from some ranch out west and here I am in Southampton with a twelve-million-dollar spread on the ocean. They take me too literally and they're frightened. When I say we're going to stage a rodeo on the front lawn, or have black men in dreadlocks smoking ganja, I think it's hilarious but it scares Gin Lane.

"So when the president of the United States flies in here to attend a wedding, to the local WASPs, that's comforting and consoling. They're all Republicans so it has nothing to with the president himself but the office. The symbolism. They think if the president and his wife come here, that makes everything okay. That the Hamptons matter, that they themselves count, that the Establishment hasn't yet fallen off the wall and gone smash. There's Humpty Dumpty and there's the Episcopal church. And Gin Lane knows the difference.

"If it's just 'that asshole Cowboy Dils' living here, the place is at risk, we're all in danger. The president flies in, hey! that's cool. It's the final reel of a Jimmy Stewart movie, all touchy-feely like *Mr. Smith* or *A Wonderful Life*. I don't give them love and soothing assurance and that makes me a threat. They hate it that a jerk like me makes millions of dollars and can afford to buy this damn house and tell them all to go to hell. That's what really scares them. I'm Lenin pulling in to the Finland Station and getting off the train, and the tsar gets the bad word and sees Lenin coming. And the tsar knows the ball game's over, and he calls in the grand dukes and says, very quietly, 'That's it, boys. It's the bottom of the ninth and we're outta here.'"

He slid awkwardly from the golf cart now and limped to the dune to stare out at the easy, rolling ocean.

"You have any idea what I'm talking about?"

"No."

He laughed. A hard, rasping laugh that carried no joy. "Does you credit; anyone who understands Cowboy in the Morning is as nuts as he is."

I stood there next to him looking out at the Atlantic. I knew he'd brought me down here to tell me something and not just to philosophize about social tensions. I didn't know what it was. And I was starting to suspect he himself wasn't quite sure if he ought to tell me. Or just how to do it.

So I took a chance. Said things good journalists don't tell people they write about.

"You're okay, Dils. Whatever's eating at you, I can't say. Not even sure I want you to tell me. So let's just leave it at that."

He gave me a cockeyed look and laughed again. This time there was more joy in it than bitterness.

"Good! So if you hear some bad shit about me one of these days, Stowe, suspend judgment. Give me the benefit of doubts. Okay?"

"Sure." I nodded. Then I asked my favor:

"And if you do a new book, let Alix have a crack at British rights. Help her score some points on the job back in London. She made me promise to ask. And I have."

"Deal," he said, getting back in the cart. "And now, let's go cheat some people at golf cart polo. . . ."

# t w e n t y - s i x

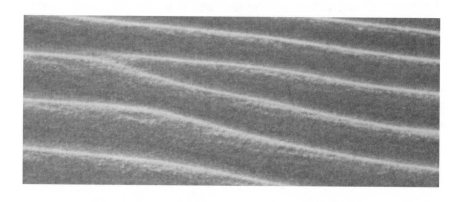

*I love your Bentley. A morning like this one calls
for convertibles...*

"Mr. Stowe? My name is Slim Champion. I'm Roger Champion's wife."

It was a telephone call, like any other, except that it wasn't. Just after seven in the morning and I was in bed with Alix, who was still asleep, or seemed to be, on the dawning of a fine day. Or so the low sun working its way through the bedroom windows seemed to promise. We get a nice morning sun here along the East Hampton beach. You don't usually need alarm clocks. I can hear Alix now, remarking it. "My, but you are fortunate..."

"Yes, Mrs. Champion, I know who you are. What can I do for you?"

I know I'm supposed to say "Ms." but when I'm taken by surprise, I forget the niceties. And this was surely an occasion on which I'd been taken by—

"I have a problem," she said, not waiting for me to finish the thought.

Fine. I'm only half awake and Her Ladyship is curled against me and another woman, also quite beautiful, and married to one of the most important men in America, a man who's one of my heroes, calls at dawn and says "I have a problem."

It occurred to me to protest. To explain that I hadn't recently hung out a shingle. That I was neither a shrink nor a cleric nor, God help me, a marriage counselor. Just a magazine correspondent.

"Where are you calling from?" I asked, a bit wary. I recalled that time I'd seen her at Bobby Van's, and how she'd been the one talking. Had turned her husband's face to stone. Was Champion listening or was this a private conversation? And what was it she'd said at Van's that—

"Do you know the luncheonette on 27-A just east of Main Street in Southampton? It's on the south side of the road and they do very good thick shakes and..." The voice was low, beckoning, throaty, conspiratorial. Easy to understand how she drew men, drew Roger. I wasn't going to be drawn.

"Mrs. Champion..."

"Slim."

"If this is a confidential matter, I'm not sure I want to—"

"Oh, but you're stuffy. I guess it goes with the territory. I thought since you were a reporter and live in East Hampton and not on Gin Lane, you might be more relaxed, a human being, even. Not quite as uptight as the Southampton crowd. People assured me..."

My, but she was cutting. Did I really rate this? I knew I was stuffy. So's my father. And his old man. We're like that. The Stowes are raised stuffy. Runs in the blood. Abolitionist Harriet Beecher freeing the slaves; all those reverends blossoming on the family tree. We're a genealogical treat for academicians. Stuffy's in the genes; we have the Episcopal Church and Harvard check us out twice a year, making sure we're still stuffy. Otherwise, fire and brimstone, hell and damnation. Even worse, black-balled by the Maidstone Club...

But here I am still in bed and a woman I don't know calls to tell me I'm stuffy. Talk about cheek!

"Who's on the phone?" Alix asked sleepily. Her eyes were closed and her lips only slightly parted, her long glistening brown hair all over both pillows.

"Walter Anderson," I lied. "He wants to know about the Baymen story."

"Oh," she said, "those nice fishermen of yours," and went back to sleep, yawning and stretching nicely first, the whole, lovely nude length of her.

"Mr. Stowe, are you still there?"

"Yes." It's her call, let her to do the running.

"It's a matter that concerns me. And someone you know quite well. I don't want to say more over the phone."

Alix had fallen back into sleep, breathing lightly, her face very beautiful. And young. I'd never lied to her. A few boasts and evasions perhaps. But no lies. I wasn't going to start now. Not even for Roger Champion's wife.

"Fine," I said, my voice cold, controlled. "I live on Further Lane in East Hampton. I think the most sensible thing, the most circumspect thing, would be for you to drop by here and we can discuss the problem. I have a friend staying with me. She might be of some assistance . . ."

What I was really thinking was I didn't want to be alone with this woman in case she turned flaky. I wanted a friendly witness to whatever happened or whatever she said. Was that paranoid? Or simply prudent with all the sexual harassment cases in the paper? I gave Slim Champion the street number.

"Yes, well," she said, as if unsure.

I wasn't going to make it any easier.

"We'll be here. About ten A.M.? The gatehouse. We'll be waiting."

I hung up before she could say more. If she came, fine. If she didn't, well . . .

When Alix woke again, about nine, I gave her coffee and a cigarette.

"My, you're the active one. Up and about, brewing coffee, talking on telephones . . ."

"Drink that and take a shower. We may have company in an hour or so."

Alix loved intrigue. "Tell me, tell me." I told her a little.

The light blue Bentley with its tan top and upholstery rolled off Further Lane and onto our gravel at ten precisely. Alix, for once, was fully dressed. She looked as good as Slim Champion's car.

There were introductions and some chat and then we went through the gatehouse and out onto the courtesy patio that led to my back lawn and when I served the coffee Mrs. Champion took the floor. Alix, wide-eyed, for once was mute. Which didn't mean she wasn't listening.

"I could ask that this be all off the record. But I don't think we need to fence. I'm here as a private citizen. Asking questions."

I wasn't about to tie my own hands so I didn't commit to anything beyond "You've got the floor, Mrs. Champion."

"Slim, please. Just Slim."

"Yes, Slim."

What she was getting to was the profile of Cowboy Dils I'd done for *Parade* magazine a couple of months ago. Specifically, "Did he talk about his wives? About relationships he'd had? Other women? There was none of that in your story. I read it a half dozen times and was astonished none of that saw print."

"That's right. I didn't get into it."

"Why not? The man was married twice. Surely there was a story there. Surely there were other—"

"He told me flat out. I asked and he said 'Ask away, I don't want to talk about it. That's history.'"

She looked thoughtful, brow creased and all that.

"Nothing? Nothing he might have told you about other women that you didn't include? The outtakes? Anything he might have..." She seemed to be having difficulty accepting what I told her.

I could see Alix off to the side, wrestling with herself, trying to keep shut but tempted to offer a little advice. She looked agonized but beautiful. Mrs. Champion looked frustrated but beautiful. The sun was way up now and the light did neither of them any harm. Further Lane rarely looked better than it did right now on a spring morning. Except that I was being grilled and becoming slightly fed up about it, I would have enjoyed the scene.

"Nothing," I said. "We didn't get into it." I don't outright lie, but I admit to withholding a little. Not even the *Boston Globe* said you couldn't do that and stay within the rules of the journalistic canon. And the *Globe* was tough; they had standards. Anderson at *Parade* was the same. He had standards, but he'd understand.

"I'm told you and Cowboy Dils have become friends."

"Acquaintances is more like it. I've been over to his place in Southampton a couple of times. May I ask why you're asking all these questions about Dils? He works for your husband. Wouldn't Mr. Champion be a more direct conduit to Dils if you want information? I'm just a reporter who interviewed him once. Never even met Cowboy before this year."

"I prefer not to bring my husband into this. It's a private matter."

Then something seemed to occur to her. "I knew I'd seen you and Lady Alix before. At Bobby Van's the night of the writers' fair. Across the room. Are you doing a story on my husband?"

"No." I let my answer hang in the air, just like that, a flat "No" that was more unsettling than a "Yes."

"Good," she said, "I don't want my husband dragged into things."

Uh-oh. There it was. There was something, or she thought there was something, between Dils and her that she didn't want Champion to know. I could hear Cowboy's voice. "If you hear some bad shit about me one of these days..."

And Slim's urgency level had risen. At first, she didn't want me to "bring" her husband into anything. Then, she didn't want him "dragged" in. It wasn't quite panic time, or was it? Slim seemed to realize she was unraveling so she slowed, taking a few deep breaths, and then resuming. She was hardly Marcia Clark but she bombarded me now with a series of questions about Dils, interspersed with references to her own bona fides, her impeccable connections. If I had doubts, I could ask Senator D'Amato about her, ask Charlie Rose, Cardinal O'Connor, ask Pat and Bill Buckley. I'm an Episcopalian and when they start citing Cardinal O'Connor, enough is enough.

I got up.

"Sorry, Mrs. Champion. Slim. Whatever I intend to say about Dils I put in the story. Reporters don't send out faxes of their outtakes. Not part of the ethic. And what's between you and your husband, or you and Dils, I'd rather not know anything about."

She got up, too. Furious. But struggling to control it.

"This entire morning has the stench of piety about it. I thought you might be of assistance. Clearly you can't help. Or won't..."

As she turned back toward the driveway Alix said, turning on the famous Dunraven charm, "I love your Bentley, Ms. Champion. A sunny morning like this calls for convertibles with the top down. Don't blame you at all for leaving the black Rolls at home. All very well in town or at night, but on a brilliantly sunny spring day such as this, so unsuitable, so dour..."

"I never drive the Rolls. The chauffeur does. And my husband. Far too big and heavy for me, I assure you."

"Oh, quite," Alix agreed cheerfully. "Your Bentley suits you splendidly. Sorry Beecher's been so stuffy. He's heaven when he chooses..."

"A shame he didn't choose," Slim Champion said coldly. Then, fixing her gaze furiously on me:

"A person, well brought up, classically trained, never missed a performance, may find herself in difficult circumstances. Desperate measures called for. Actions taken that under other circumstances, no! Absolutely not! Out of the question. Let's be candid. If you're not there yourself, experiencing those same pressures, well, then, how dare you sit in judgment? Treachery everywhere. Lies and false witness. The erosion of morality and the rise of the gossip web site. How can you criticize without gauging the tensions? The answer is, you can't. You mustn't. You dare not!"

She wheeled on us then, jumped into the car, slammed the Bentley's door behind her, and drove off, spraying gravel as she went, gunning the big engine and performing a competently controlled skid as she bent her way out into Further Lane running west at considerable speed past the old Bouvier place where Jackie and Lee grew up....

"Now what the hell was that all about?"

"Haven't the foggiest," Alix said. "A bit odd, wasn't it?"

"Totally nuts."

"Not a bit of it, Beecher. Quite shrewd, in fact. Gulled you thoroughly, I'd wager."

I cleared my throat, a bit huffy, not feeling the slightest bit "gulled."

"She's attractive, Beecher, isn't she? For a woman her age, I mean..."

"She's forty. Not much more," I said quickly. When you're thirty-something yourself, forty doesn't seem as old as it once did. "And why cast me as villain in all this? Siding with her, chatting about cars. She was the one insulting me when coming here was entirely her idea."

"Oh, Beecher. It's you clever chaps who are always so obtuse. There's been something between Cowboy and that woman. Maybe still is. She's transparent as can be..." Then: "Her husband, the poor dear, how old did you say he was?"

"Eighty. Maybe more. Quite a man."

"Just think of it, a cuckold at eighty. My..."

I stifled questions. Knowing that with Alix, answers would come.

"And she lies," Alix said quietly. "I'm sure you caught that. About the Rolls being too heavy and too large for her. Being very careful to assure us her husband drives it occasionally. Putting him clearly in the shadows, so to speak, if homicides and other dirty work are contemplated."

"What d'you mean?"

"As you well know, I'm firmly supportive of a favorable U.K. balance of payments and as far as the export markets are concerned, when it comes to autos, 'Buy British and drive with confidence,' I always say. Having made something of a study of the matter, I happen to know a Bentley of that marque, with its additional convertible machinery and bracing, is as much as one hundred pounds *heavier* than Mr. Champion's Rolls. And with an equivalent wheelbase and turning radius. They have, in fact, the very same chassis and power train. Bentleys and Rolls differ only in detail and ornamentation. Anyone who can drive the Bentley ought have little difficulty if any in driving the Rolls."

"You're losing me, Alix."

"Mr. Dils was hit and run down by a black Rolls. The Champions own a black Rolls. But she, as she made abundantly clear, never drives it. I accentuate the 'never.' Although her dearly beloved husband does. Suggest anything?"

It did. Though still only vaguely.

Alix bathed me tolerantly in the sweetest smile.

"So as Hercule Poirot might put it in the *policiers*, with all his accustomed Gallic nuance, there's something here not at all *comme il faut*. Or, as Holmes, being Anglo-Saxon, might more bluntly have cried out, 'Watson, the game's afoot!' "

"Oh?" Not being the fan she was of detective yarns, Alix often lost me.

"As for me, I firmly believe *cherchez la femme*. Slim Champion suspects that you, rather cleverly, have sniffed out the trail, very much like an Allan Quartermain, and are following her spoor. A broken twig here, a severed vine there, a bruised leaf, a still-warm dropping in the bush. She's jumpy, she saw us at Bobby Van's, she fears you're getting close, Beecher, and is out to divert you. Casting suspicion on her dear, doddering old husband."

"Hardly doddering," I said. "The man recently broke eighty at the Maidstone."

She ignored my clever (at least I thought so) sally and pressed on.

"We know that Mr. Champion's a keen man of business. Mindful of shareholder equity. Does such a chap put his shareholders at risk by killing off Cowboy in the Morning, one of the corporation's major assets? I would think *not*."

Which led Alix inevitably to this conclusion:

"Yes, Beecher, I think I can state almost positively that if anyone in the family tried to bump off poor Cowboy, the wife is very obviously suggesting the gendarmes ought to seek out Roger Champion. And not her. Doesn't it occur to you 'the lady doth protest too much'? Since his good wife has an alibi in that she never drives black Rolls-Royces?

"Or so she claims?"

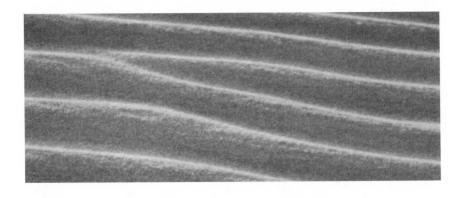

*John believed fiercely in Lobb shoes, Princeton,*
*and fresh lemon squashed atop his head*

As Memorial Day weekend closed in on us (there was a faintly claustrophobic aspect to it even out here on the open beaches and broad lawns
of the Hamptons), corporate and private jets seemed to be landing every
eight or ten minutes, bearing wedding guests and gifts and columnists
and the more distinguished members of the press (mere reporters and
those revolting paparazzi came by car or Jitney bus) to the rustic East
Hampton airport, where there was rash talk of perhaps buying a new
wind sock (the authorities soon came to their senses, checked the bank
balance, and nothing was ever done about it).

These were *our* equivalent of those royal weddings of (so much simpler
and happier) years before and no one wanted to miss the show.

Liz Smith arrived. And Michael Gross from *New York* magazine. Paul
Colford of *Newsday*. Cindy Adams from the *Post*. Jeannie Williams of *USA
Today*. Billy Norwich. A man from the *Daily News*. Bob Collacello and
Andre Leon Talley (not together) and SWAT teams from *People, Enter-*

*tainment Weekly, US,* and the TV shows. Everyone you might have expected was on site but Robin Leach.

John Fairchild with all his connections had, as usual, beaten most of them to the draw, establishing a forward command post at Gin Lane's the Bathing Corporation, the big old Spanish hacienda–looking beach and bath club. It was the old-fashioned, traditional sort of place that Princeton men like Mr. Fairchild favored. As, far from returning in triumph to Manhattan after having disconcerted the Buchanans and scooped everyone on the wedding dress, he was determined to commit additional *betises* (beastlinesses) on Southampton and the Buchanans. John had lived long in Paris and had a weakness for sprinkling French into the most ordinary of conversations, even with other Americans. He was going to be here at least through the wedding, put up in a marvelous Further Lane place owned by in-laws, but with his every waking hour spent at the Bathing Corp.

Mr. Fairchild crouched by days in a vast, ancient wicker beach chair, wearing sunblock on his nose and dressed in the best-cut Savile Row blazer and creamy flannels you ever saw, with a repp tie from Jermyn Street that lacked by a millimeter being the Coldstream Guards, and squashing fresh-cut lemon halves into his hair. People came and went being received at the beach chair, the favored among them being offered tea and cakes, others simply to take dictation or receive or deliver dispatches to and from his newspapers, the unfamiliar among them staring incredulously as he squashed lemons.

Reinforcements having been summoned, his henchman Patrick had come out; he was a tall, gawky young man everyone swore was brilliant, who told John gossip and giggled a lot, and who wore (as John did) a watch on his right wrist (there was good reason for Fairchild's doing this in that he was left-handed; Patrick did it in tribute to the boss). He was always Patrick, never Pat or Paddy. He would no more be called "Pat" than one might have addressed President Wilson as "Woody." Patrick's chums were exceedingly well connected and artsy, precious men and ferociously chic women, all of whom spoke a terribly arch and "inside" jargon and, like Patrick and Mr. Fairchild, did their share of giggling (even the "ferocious" women). On Wednesdays Patrick played bridge with Pat Buckley, whose charities and good works were legendary—and generously plugged and promoted in the pages of both *W* and *Women's*

*Wear Daily.* But that was while he was in Manhattan. Patrick's work here on Gin Lane at Mr. Fairchild's elbow had caused his Wednesday sessions at the tables with Ms. Buckley, temporarily, to be suspended.

John Fairchild believed fiercely in a very few things. English tailors, Princeton University, Lobb shoes, the Union Club, French cooking, the sanctity of marriage and love of his wife and four children, Rossignol skis, and the efficacy of fresh lemon juice squeezed on one's head. As a young man he'd been blond and lemon juice was recommended on grounds, he believed then and ever since, that it improved blond hair. Fifty years later and white-haired, John saw no reason to alter a lifetime's habit and continued to squeeze the occasional lemon, squashing it by halves atop his head and vigorously massaging the resultant juice into his scalp. Thus causing him occasionally to sport, for the rest of the day, lemon pips among the strands.

Patrick squeezed lemons as well, though his hair was dark brown.

Cowboy marveled at having such exotic people on Gin Lane and welcomed their arrival, enjoying the lemon squashing and other eccentricities, distracting as they did attention usually and unhappily focused on him. He admitted saying and doing queer things himself to mask the fact he was acutely shy, socially inept, ill at ease with strangers, and lacked small talk. Having people like John and Patrick capering on Gin Lane enabled Dils to fade back into the scenery and an unaccustomed but most welcome privacy.

I'd not been invited to the viscount's wedding ("You can give me a blow-by-blow afterwards," I told Alix, assuring her I wasn't hurt to have been snubbed), but almost everyone else had. Alix, of course, as Fruity's chum (and saboteur without portfolio, intent to derail the vow taking if she could and save the groom from making a fool of himself). Rex Magnifico pulled various publishing strings to wangle an invitation and planned to show up with the three Argentinos (they'd been instructed to mill about outside, since they didn't have tickets themselves, togged out in polo gear so guests would know they belonged to Rex). Roger and Slim Champion declined, Tom Buchanan not being to their taste. Martha Stewart accepted, wanting to take a fresh look at the Meadow Club for a feature her magazine was working up. Wyseman Claggett wouldn't miss the affair, nor any other opportunity to network among the power brokers who could help advance his plans to sell sand and steel revetments and develop the raceway. John Fairchild and his man Patrick had their press cards. And since so far they "owned" this story, it would have been anticlimactic not to be there at the kill.

So to speak.

By noon, when a Buchanan limo rolled into town bearing Fruity's pa, the earl, just off the morning Concorde from London, four RAF men crisply turned out in dress uniform as a sort of guard of honor were there at the Bathing Corp., where Fruity was giving a small lunch.

"A chap I knew at Eton told me, 'Don't ever get married on an empty stomach, Fruits. Bound to faint right there at the ruddy altar.'" So he and the earl and the groomsmen were gathering for the smoked salmon and cold veal chop and a glass or two of Dom Perignon. Being the generous sort (one reason the earl kept urging his son to marry wealth!), Fruity also asked me, Jesse Maine, Cowboy, the several gay young men who ran the Mauve House, Roland and Lee from the Blue Parrot, Captain Bly (for having enabled him to carry back to London a good fish story), and the RAF. Bly never even bothered to call back his regrets; most of the others declined with thanks, and the Mauve House boys and the four fliers accepted.

"I'd go," Cowboy said, "if the president hadn't threatened to thrash me within an inch of my life. And if he doesn't, the members of the Bathing Corp. will."

The actual wedding guests, of course, were officially ID'd some time ago for security purposes but the viscount's lunch at the Bathing Corp. was informal and not to be attended by the First Family. I tried, without success, to convince Cowboy he stood in no danger there or anywhere else from the president.

"I'll stay safely within the compound, thank you very much. If they come for me we'll fight 'em on the beaches, we'll fight 'em in the towns we'll fight them on the polo fields and the Meadow Club, and we'll never, never surrender..."

Dil's Churchill was pretty good.

Not to brag, but I just happened to know the president. In 1988 we'd played ball here together at the artists and writers softball game on the field behind the A & P, Plimpton and Ben Bradlee and Tom Knowles and Ken Auletta and Jesse Maine and me, plus the late Leo Brass. The president (he was only a governor then) didn't actually play but called balls and strikes. We all got along pretty well and went together to the Laundry for cold beer after, out back of the restaurant at the open-air bar with the bocce alley, and all had a good time, his wife not being along.

I don't know why I drove down into Southampton Memorial Day morning. No reason for me to be there and I could have stayed home on Further Lane and gone fishing and maybe put the canoe in the water or watched the Yankees on television. But it was in Southampton that everything would be happening, where the holiday really would be cele-brated, the brave flags out and the spring sun as well, with Lager and Baron von Kronk driving their Ferraris through town and Jesse and the Shinnecocks in war paint on the Canal Bridge and the president and the old earl of Bute there on Gin Lane to solemnize the marriage of Viscount Albemarle to Mandy Buchanan. All that going on, a guy at least ought to be in town that day just to say he was there. Sort of the way Henry V told the troops how fortunate they were to be with him at Agincourt, even if they were likely going to die along with Harry the King on Crispin's Day.

And Alix would be in Southampton and maybe that was all the reason needed to get me to Gin Lane.

She was up early, torn between wanting to save her childhood chum the viscount from his "social climbing heiress from New York" and not wanting the dear chap to be embarrassed or play bounder or the cad. Or, indeed, to hurt or embarrass Mandy, who'd turned out to be of far better quality than her calculating parents. "Beecher, do you think we ought to get Fruity to the pub first and pour him a stiff one?" she inquired of me. "You always know things like that."

I was half pleased by her confidence in my savoir faire, half uneasy she was suggesting I spent all my time in gin mills.

We chatted about how best to sustain the viscount in his hour of need and then Alix said, "On another topic, Beecher, for some reason I can't quite explain, the prospect of a wedding, perhaps, or simply that June starts in an other day or so and you're looking especially toothsome this morning, but it has me feeling randy. Might we, I wonder, sport about in bed a bit before I shower and such? Would you mind, awfully? I mean, once I bathe and do my hair and start to climb into that bridesmaid's dress, which is quite dreadful, I must admit, with all the underpinnings and things, the fun would have gone out of it." She paused. "Y'know what I mean."

"Yes," I said. I was certain I did.

"Oh, good!" she said with admirable enthusiasm.

After we'd sported a bit (her phrase, and one I rather liked), she broke off to bathe and dress, and while she did I phoned Maguire to ask if I might hang out there at Cowboy's for the day.

"Why not?" he said amiably. "All the other whackjobs are here."

I took that for encouragement and said I'd be along shortly.

## twenty-eight

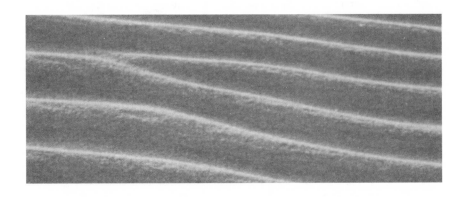

*He may be sexually dysfunctional and probably
served in the Marines . . .*

The United States Secret Service is assigned, among its other responsibilities, the task of protecting the president and his family. Over time, and especially as technique, knowledge and high-tech equipment have improved, the service has been able to fashion a highly specific and widely respected psychographic and demographic profile of potential assassins and their methods of operation. The MOs may differ, but the profile of the theoretically most dangerous threats to the chief executive remains remarkably predictable, and almost always includes many if not all of the following elements (passed on to me in confidence by a "friendly" sub-committee source on Capitol Hill):

The presidential "assassin" is a white male bordering on middle age, a westerner, manic-depressive, easily irritated, a possible drug abuser and/ or reformed alcoholic. He enjoys dressing up in odd attire, fought in Vietnam, frequently assumes identities different from his own, has been known to issue threats to neighbors, acquaintances, family members or to total strangers, collects guns and may be a crack shot. He hates authority, bickers with fellow workers, resents his boss, hatches harebrained plots to discommode superiors, and lies to cover up complicity. He is receptive to conspiracy theories, including the possibility aliens are already here and entrenched in government. He is a complainer, paranoid, divorced, given to loud tantrums, curses habitually and will accost passersby and inquire of them if they, too, are unhappy. He surrounds himself with an odd lot of acquaintances and colleagues, many of whom may also manifest curious behavior. He is trying to quit smoking, uses pseudonyms, is accident-prone, may be sexually dysfunctional and quite possibly served in the Marines.

It did not escape theorists at the Secret Service that there were resemblances here to Cowboy Dils.

Despite reinforcements, the senior federal agent assigned to the president's visit to Southampton and attendance at a society wedding and reception on Gin Lane was still O'Hara, first man on the scene days earlier. And it was O'Hara who postulated what came to be called "the theory of the widow's walk."

Just who it was (possibly the aggrieved pastor) who complained that Cowboy was taking shots at the belfry of St. Andrew's Dune Church, we are not sure. But O'Hara's people checked it out and came up with corroboration from unnamed witnesses. The weapon in question wasn't considered all that deadly, being a Red Ryder air rifle, but with a vantage point from which an innocent might fire a BB gun, couldn't a potential assassin just as conveniently fire a high-powered rifle? And wasn't the Buchanan-Albemarle wedding scheduled to be solemnized at St. Andrew's? And didn't the widow's walk atop Dils's house at number Ten bis offer a perfect line-of-sight vantage point overlooking both the little church atop the dunes and the Meadow Club, just to the west of Gin Lane, where the president would be joining other guests following the nuptials?

"I'm no intellectual," O'Hara was fond of saying (no subordinate would dare to have agreed with him on that!), "but I can put two and two together and get . . . Cowboy Dils or someone close to him."

"Yes sir."

O'Hara ordered a tap on the Dils house phones (they could get a court order later if they needed to use the tape), twenty-four-hour surveillance of the property, and a smash-and-grab raid on the day the president would actually be in the area. "Once POTUS hits town, I don't want Cowboy or any of his people moving around that house anywhere but on the ground floor. I want four men on the widow's walk. You can come up with something plausible. The lightning rods need to be upgraded. The TV dish wants servicing. And I want men in the living quarters chatting with Dils. Asking directions, talking about his show, getting autographs, measuring for wall-to-wall carpet, whatever.

"Hard to believe a cult figure this rich and famous could be thinking about shooting the damned president, but there it is; Cowboy Dils sure fits the profile."

That profile did not include eighty-year-old billionaires driving along Gin Lane in a chauffeured Rolls.

# t w e n t y - n i n e

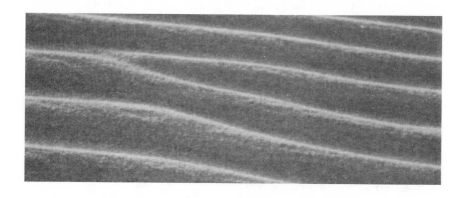

*Falling, sprawling atop of me, shotgun and all,*
*one shot gotten off . . .*

I was standing out on the gravel of Cowboy's house having a second cup of coffee and enjoying a platoon of Secret Service men, business-suited federal agents, pretending to be trees, imitating shrubbery. They were deployed across Gin Lane, which is only about eight yards wide, alert and waiting. If the president really was going to come past here on his way to the church and the Meadow Club reception, I understood their presence. But why couldn't they just come over and say hello and explain they had to be there on guard for a few hours and stop playing at being invisible? Surely my father the Admiral could have explained. I suppose they had their reasons.

It was mid-morning and traffic was moving along at its usual pace, a car now and then, a delivery van, a gardener's pickup with lawn mowers in back. The feds' eyes followed all of them, heads swiveling as if watching a tennis match in slo-mo. Her Ladyship had gone off, after we'd had our sport, being picked up by a Buchanan limo, something to do with the prewedding preparations, and after she was gone I'd driven over to see Cowboy and the crew and ended up having coffee with Annie and Nurse Cavell at poolside and then took a second cup out here when they went upstairs to get their swimsuits. Maguire and Greasy Thumb were playing cards—gin, I believe—with Guzik the ex-cop cheating. Fu Manchu was teaching himself croquet, to the amusement of Dils, perched in a refurbished golf cart with his splinted leg sticking out so as not to foul the gearshift again.

"One if by land, two if by sea..." Cowboy called out in greeting. Then, nodding toward the feds, "I don't know whether to laugh or send out a pitcher of lemonade. I suppose for a change I should just shut up and mind my own business and be grateful they're watching over the property."

Dils whispered to a halt alongside me on the gravel in his electric cart, looking down the drive toward Gin Lane at the traffic and the federal agents showily concealing themselves across the road.

"They are pretty absurd. Lurking in plain sight. But I guess it's work that's got to be done," I said.

I finished my coffee and was about to go back into the house to get rid of the cup when Cowboy said, "Well, now, lookee here. Is that one of my exalted neighbors coming to call?"

A swell black Rolls was coming west along the lane toward Dils's place, the car slowing and its left directional blinking in our direction, so I stayed there next to Cowboy's cart to see who it might be. Who knows? It was a black Rolls that whacked him, wasn't it? The big car turned slowly onto his gravel driveway and came toward us before coming to a halt. A chauffeur got out, nicely attired in livery that matched the car, and I thought maybe he was there delivering an invitation to cocktails or something, but instead he went around and opened one of the passenger doors and out stepped Roger Champion in flannels and a blazer, a Panama hat rakishly smart atop his leonine old head.

"I'll be damned..." Cowboy said quietly, more to himself than to me and certainly not to Champion. I was looking at the car, rather than the man, remembering having seen it outside Bobby Van's, and curious to see if Slim too were...

The broadcasting exec leaned back into the car reaching for a package of some sort, wrapped in brown paper, couple of feet long, and stood there looking at us, wondering, perhaps, who I was, standing a dozen paces away and still not saying anything, his hands working at the crisp, brown wrapping paper. And then, conversationally, I heard Dils say, calmly, quietly and not at all in alarm:

"Good Gawd A-mighty, he's got a gun . . ."

He did, too. I could see it now, a rifle or a shotgun. It—

"Man with a gun on Gin Lane!" an amplified voice crackled out from just across the narrow road, as three or four federal agents sprinted toward us. Champion had the gun clear of its wrappings and was lifting it now, but distracted by the shout, he half turned, wanting to see who was coming. It gave me my chance and I went for him, aiming low so as to go in under the muzzle, hoping to hell I could get to him before he fired, that if he got off a shot I'd be plenty low enough.

He was a tall old man and when I hit his shins with my shoulder and head, he hadn't yet fired, and he went over forwards, knocked off his feet by the tackle and falling, sprawling atop of me, shotgun and all, and only then getting off a shot. Just the one, though it damned near deafened me, being that close, but hadn't hit me, not that I could feel, and for small blessings I was duly grateful. Somewhere behind me I could hear Cowboy's golf cart jump into forward gear as the Secret Service men sprinted across the gravel toward us, and there were shouts and a curse and a cry of pain, and then someone else was on top of Champion, who was still on top of me, and my face was in the gravel and being ground into it.

Still, there'd been only the single shot. I couldn't move but I knew I was okay. Had Champion hit someone? He was supposed to be a crack shot. Had I thrown off his aim? Who'd been hurt? Who'd yelled out in pain?

By now more vehicles were pulling noisily onto the grounds, skidding to a stop loudly on the pebbles or more sibilantly on the grass, and you could hear men running toward us and shouting orders. It was all very confused and I hoped Mr. Champion's finger still wasn't anywhere near that trigger.

"Get that son of a bitch in the golf cart!"

That must be Cowboy.

"He damn near broke my damn leg!" someone called in loud complaint.

That, too, must have been Cowboy.

I lay there with my face in the gravel and I could hear another voice: "We got the bastard; knocked the golf cart into the hedge."

Fine. It was Roger Champion who'd dropped by with a shotgun, maybe intent on killing someone, and firing off a shot, and the feds were beating up on poor Dils and his broken leg, while I was buried under what felt like six guys.

Finally they started unpiling us, the way the officials do in the NFL when there's a fumble down there somewhere near the goal line and they peel guys off until they come across a fellow with the ball. Then Roger Champion was pulled off and the shotgun as well, but instead of congratulating me for swift thinking and grace under pressure stuff and all that great Jake Barnes–Harry Morgan–Robert Jordan performance of mine, a pair of hands grabbed my wrists, slapped on the cuffs, and spun me over so I was lying on my back looking up at the sun and into some hard, decidedly hostile faces. And the black menace of their gun muzzles pointed in my direction.

"Okay, bright boy, just don't make a move," someone told me, as another agent patted me down.

"He's clean. Was he the one with the Purdey? Or the old guy?"

"I dunno. Maybe bright boy here. Your gun, bright boy?"

That's my life; federal agents who lift their dialogue from Hemingway.

"Look—" I started to say.

"Shut up," I was told, and a big man sat down on my chest to give a little weight to the order. Out of the corner of one eye I could see Cowboy. In deference to his broken leg, no one was sitting on him. But he, too, was cuffed, and the golf cart rested on its side, one wheel still idly spinning.

You could just hear Cowboy's voice: "Wave the flag for Hudson High, boys/Show them how we stand/Ever shall our team be champions/Known throughout—" and a hard, unfamiliar voice calling out, "Shut the hell up, *yoo!*"

Champion's driver was also in custody and so, for no apparent reason, was Nurse Cavell. I couldn't see her but I could hear her keening whimper:

"Serves me right for abandoning the hospital. I was always happy there. I loved my patients. I had a career, respect, a Ford Taurus, the medical profession, friends, my 401K..." The rest of her plaint was lost in loud sobs. Maguire, also unseen, was cursing. I assumed they had him cuffed, as well. I wondered where Greasy Thumb Guzik was. Annie Willow. And Fu Manchu.

As for Roger Champion, he was on the grass, apparently unhurt and active, and as a trio of burly Secret Service men attempted to subdue the eighty-year-old Champion, the old man continued to mutter, angry but chillingly calm:

"I'll kill that womanizing bastard. I'll kill him..."

"What's he saying?"

"That POTUS is a womanizing bastard."

"Jesus, so it was POTUS he was after!"

"Make a pass at my wife? I'll get him. I'll..."

"POTUS was hitting on this guy's wife, too?"

"You gotta take your hat off to him, POTUS, I mean, to find time for babes what with running the country and all he's got on his mind..."

"But a guy this old? How old's his goddamned wife if POTUS is boffing her..."

Only O'Hara was still thinking clearly.

"For God's sake," he shouted, "someone read the old fart his rights before he says another word. This is the collar of a career! You want to compromise a historic collar like this on a technicality? You want Sandra Day O'Connor and Clarence Thomas overturning this case because you schmucks didn't read a presidential assassin his effing Miranda?"

One of the quicker-witted young men pulled out a plasticized little card of the sort nuns pass out to good children in the lower grades of Catholic schools with a picture of the Virgin Mary and a little prayer, and began to read:

"Sir, you have the right to—"

At that point Roger Champion fainted.

"For chrissakes!" O'Hara ordered his men, "don't kill him. That's all we need, another Lee Harvey Oswald offed in the police station."

"Then you better call an ambulance, O'Hara."

"Yeah. And backup, to take in the rest of these perverts..."

The agent sitting on my chest got up to light a cigarette and for the first time I could both breathe and speak.

"O'Hara, I'm Beecher Stowe of *Parade* magazine. My press card's in my wallet. The rest of these people—"

"A cabal of perverts, that's what you are, a cabal..." he muttered darkly, but then, sensitive to the Freedom of Information Act and not anxious to get the media down on him ("Those bastards, they get half the chance, they'll crucify a decent public servant!"), he said, "Get his wallet out. Lemme see if there's a press card."

"These others, too," I said. "Mr. Dils is a famous broadcaster who—"

"I know all about Cowboy Dils, mister. Don't you lecture me on the Cowboy. That's why we're damn it here. The threats he's uttered against the president of the United States. The shots he's fired at church property. The foul language he uses in front of decent women. America doesn't need shit like that. Don't you instruct me on Dils, mister, I know this guy chapter and verse."

Harry Almond, still pinioned but with no one sitting on him, joined in now.

"He shoots at dogs as well, Officer," Harry said, trying to be helpful. "Shot a poodle last week for peeing on the lawn. He—"

"Who in hell are you?" O'Hara demanded.

"Name of Harry Almond. Simply attempting to be a good citizen, sir, assisting the authorities in their inquiries."

"Chief," one of the agents reminded O'Hara, "the ambulance. You gotta call an ambulance or maybe we're gonna lose this old guy..."

"I'm Mr. Dils's on-air sidekick, though in this matter an entirely in-nocent bystander," Harry continued. "Happily married as well, and in the church, whatever alternative lifestyles these other people may espouse or just what their sexual orientation..."

To an agent, O'Hara snarled, "Shut him up. But first read him the rights, too. Gimme that cell phone."

"I have a Bible in my things. King James Version. If you could please—" Harry was cut off before he could say more.

"I'll 'Bible' you, mister," O'Hara threatened. "That Cunanan down in Miami, he probably had a Bible. Waving the old Bible around and whack-ing fashion designers and South Beach gays with an assault rifle. When we slap the cuffs on, you bastards all have Bibles?..." Then, into the cell phone:

"Special Agent O'Hara here, number Ten bis Gin Lane, Southampton. We have in custody eight or ten people, mostly male, on suspicion of menacing and perhaps attempting to kill POTUS. Need heavy backup plus ambulance. One perp may have had a cardiac."

"That's alleged perp," Dils shouted, pleased to have caught the feds on a technicality.

An agent came out from the house, running, followed by several frightened, scurrying maids.

"Listen, there's Hispanic illegals in here. Cali cartel stuff? And there's a Chinese guy. We chased him out back and he dove into the pool. Tried to swim away."

"Chinese? You get him?" O'Hara demanded.

"Sure, when he got to the end of the pool. He ran out of water."

Fu Manchu, I took it, had reverted to what boat people did in extremis: they tried to swim to safety.

"A *conjuratio* if ever I saw one," O'Hara murmured.

At his elbow an agent asked, "A what?"

"A *conjuratio*. Don't you people study Latin anymore? Read *Caesar's Wars*? Read Cicero and Livy? A *conjuratio*'s a conspiracy. You read Caesar you'll know about *conjuratios*. Read *Caesar's Wars* and you'll have *conjuratios* up the giggy!"

O'Hara was back talking now on the cell phone.

"There's Third World participation here as well. Undocumented Hispanics. Drug connection possible. At least one Asian. Chinese probably. I think you ought to steer POTUS away from here. I don't know how many are involved. You get the Chinese in on it, this could be huge. I never saw anything like this."

When one of his men trotted up asking a question, O'Hara was patient. "Look, you've seen the movie *Air Force One*, right? Then you know, that's all it takes, a handful of determined zealots. A bunch no bigger than this one. What's needed on our part is vigilance! Unblinking goddamned vigilance. Nothing less than the country's at stake, sonny. Remember that when it hits the fan. You understand?"

Impressed, the man nodded, asked no more questions and trotted off. Then, more unblinking vigilance than patience, O'Hara roared into the cell phone: "Where the hell's that backup? Give me an ETA, pronto!"

He listened for a moment and then, as if stunned, his knees sagged and from my vantage point, I thought he might fall.

"Chief!" one of his men cried out, seeing the distress in O'Hara's face. "They can't get any backup here for a while. No ambulance, either."

"What happened?"

"The roads around Southampton are closed down. We're cut off. HQ thinks this isn't just an assassination plot; they think it's bigger than that."

"But the roads, O'Hara, what's with the roads?"

"They've arrested a bunch of guys driving old-fashioned race cars, checked their IDs. Some of them retired CIA men and a few from the old OSS, who've thrown a cordon around Southampton, blocking the roads. There's some sort of Nazi general, too. Guy with one leg. HQ thinks they want to kidnap POTUS..."

"Jesus," someone said in a low voice, almost reverently.

The cell phone buzzed again and O'Hara slapped it smartly to his ear, listening intently.

"The bridge over the canal's been taken. Now we're cut off from New York." Then, getting more information through the phone: "Some goddamned Indians. War paint and drums. They've taken the Sunrise Highway bridge over the Shinnecock Canal. Local traffic cops are on the way."

"Jesus," one of the feds whispered, again making the word sound truly more like a prayer than an oath, so impressed was he.

"You can say that again," O'Hara said. "Sending traffic cops up against this bunch? It'll be a bloodbath. The cops won't stand a chance."

Another agent with his own phone called out. "Some men in British army uniforms are fighting a bunch of illegal aliens in the Driver's Seat Pub on Job's Lane. What do you think that's all about?"

"British army uniforms?"

"As you were. RAF uniforms. They're fliers."

"Fighting illegals? What kind of illegals? More Chinks? Get that Chinaman out of the swimming pool. I want to question that bastard. If we got to start pulling fingernails..."

"No sir. Argentinos, they say. Armed guys in riding britches and boots with shiny helmets. Sounds to me like neo-Nazi uniforms, chief."

"Don't tell me, Peters. Where the hell d'ya think Bormann ended up after the war? Buenos effing Aires, that's where!" Then, after a breath: "What are they armed with? Automatic weapons?"

The agent on the other cell phone asked. "No, sir. Sticks of some sort. He said something about polo—"

"Bolos, not polo," O'Hara shouted. "Bolos are weapons Argentine gauchos use, heavy balls like for billiards connected by cord. They throw those bastards at you, they'll take your head off right at the shoulder! They're experts at it, them gauchos."

"It's a *conjuratio* for sure," a boyish agent remarked, hushed and respectful of O'Hara.

I'd begun to relax. Why not, since I couldn't move anyway? Damned shame about Alix being at the wedding. She was missing all this.

O'Hara nodded, making a major effort to exert self-control, and then, more calmly, and in a voice that was almost steady, he told his men:

"What we have here is a full-blown conspiracy to bring down the government of the United States. With foreign hostiles linked to subversive domestic elements and neo-Nazi militia groups."

There was a low whistle and then, as if on cue, Cowboy Dils called out to O'Hara, very calm and in a take-charge mode:

"They'll be sending choppers in next, O'Hara. I suggest you get your men on the roof, ready to be airlifted out. It may be your only chance. You know, like Saigon on that last day, right off the roof of the embassy..."

"Oh, my God," O'Hara said. Then, to an aide with a cell phone: "You heard what they told me, about ex-CIA men blocking the roads? This isn't just a presidential assassination plot. Get me Air Force One. This is a full-blown, goddamned coup d'état..."

He broke off, right then. As if Cowboy had whistled them up, out of the south and over the ocean here came the choppers, coming low and coming fast.

O'Hara, his face tomato-red, again lifted the cell phone. The words came out slowly, articulated carefully. He wanted no misunderstanding. Not on the most important message a government agent could ever send:

"Now hear this, Air Force One. This is Special Agent O'Hara of the United States Secret Service. I am ordering you, Mr. President, not to, repeat *not*, to land at Southampton, New York, where at this hour unidentified aircraft are approaching and where you, sir, may well be taken captive by hostile elements, domestic and foreign..."

I could barely see Dils's head and shoulders from where I lay helpless, but an enormous grin was communicating sheer bliss.

## thirty

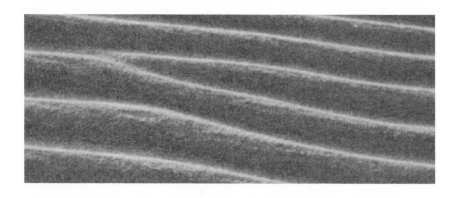

*Cowboy was chatting with the Marines about firefights at Da Nang. And signing autographs . . .*

"Jesus," said Maguire in respectful awe, looking out to sea, "it's the second reel of *Apocalypse Now.*"

We could all see them now, even those of us pinned down, even without the field glasses the feds now wielded, a small fleet of military helicopters heading our way off the ocean, three choppers hovering low over the property at number Ten bis Gin Lane, others higher up and way off to their rear. By now they were close enough; you could see by the insignia they were ours.

And it was sheer Hollywood, all Francis Ford Coppola. All that was lacking was Brando and his montagnards. Two of the choppers, gunships covering the third, continued to circle slowly overhead, hovering and alert, so low you could see the faces behind the machine guns and crouched over the rocket launchers, even their eyes, while the third landed noisily and with windblown clouds of sand and dust, on Cowboy's front lawn. Three fire teams of Marines tumbled out before the craft had securely settled down, efficiently setting up light machine guns with fields of fire that effectively covered the entire lawn. The chopper's rotor slowed to a halt as the Marines watched. And waited. No one spoke. No one seemed even to be breathing. Not even the sulfurous O'Hara. Then, at the door of the single chopper already on the ground, there was movement.

"So this is Southampton," said a lean gent in a well-cut tropical worsted navy blue suit, standing in the doorway of the chopper, before he stepped from the helicopter and dropped nimbly to earth, looking about him with a half-amused smile, and placidly announcing, "I am Special Agent in Charge Vittorini." Then, seeing all about him a half dozen or so people lying prone and cuffed, with Secret Service agents sitting on us, he asked sensibly, "And what's all this about now?"

There was nothing of the romantic about this fellow, none of O'Hara's Gaelic dash. Vittorini was instead one of those brilliant men the Ivy League still throws up now and then, a smooth, handsome individual with prematurely white hair, clear testimony to the heavy burdens of office, yet the kind of man you suspected would age well. And from the deferential way in which O'Hara hastened to his side, you knew Vittorini was the boss.

"I think your men can safely get these people back on their feet and stop sitting on them, O'Hara."

"Right away, sir."

All of us again vertical, Vittorini said, "I'm waiting."

Roger Champion, revived and still furious, was by now incapable of doing more than grinding his teeth and when I stepped forward, to try to make sense of it all for Agent Vittorini, Cowboy cut me off.

"I think I can straighten it all out, Colonel."

"And which one are you?"

"Leicester Dils, cowboy in charge," he said, gently mocking Vittorini, who took it in good humor, smiling his appreciation.

"Go ahead, Mr. Dils," Vittorini said pleasantly, though with the hint of steel in his voice.

"Yes sir," Cowboy began, gesturing toward Champion. "This gentleman's wife and I were good friends years ago, long before their marriage. Recently, when we encountered each other here as Gin Lane neighbors, I attempted, perhaps unwisely, to rekindle an affection she clearly no longer felt. The business is entirely my fault and Mr. and Mrs. Champion are the injured parties in all this. What was simple kindness and good manners on her part toward me, I in my crude western ways took mistakenly for encouragement and I pressed myself on her, even knowing that she was married, and happily so, to my employer, Mr. Champion. That may even, subconsciously, have been part of it. That I was hurling down the gauntlet. His reaction was the act of a gentleman. When he came down Gin Lane with his shotgun, it wasn't the president who was his target, it was I."

"So you hit on the guy's wife and he came after you," said Special Agent in Charge Vittorini.

"Exactly. Couldn't put it more precisely myself."

"You rogue!" Roger cried out, and attempted vainly yet again to attack Dils.

"He's more than justified in his righteous anger, Agent Vittorini," Cowboy said quietly. "She's a beauty, Slim is. Always was. Despite lechers like me, he's the one that possesses her. Not only a beautiful woman, but a virtuous one. . . .

"I don't believe it's overstatement to say that Roger Champion is a most fortunate man."

Once it was established that network CEO Champion had no hostility toward the president (and that POTUS had not been cracking on his, Mr. Champion's, wife), the question was: Had any punishable offense been committed? Apparently so. But not against POTUS or the United States government, no matter how many illegals and suspicious people had been rounded up. If old Roger had gone cruising Gin Lane with a shotgun in his lap and he wasn't out to kill the president, the logical targets were reduced to one, to Leicester "Cowboy" Dils. That was Cowboy's statement and Champion admitted as much now while an agent who until moments ago had been seated on his chest rapidly took notes:

"That bastard Dils was after my wife. A man won't stand for that. Not here in Southampton, not on Gin Lane, not anywhere. There's still something called 'honor,' you know."

Nurse Cavell, whose hands were free, wiped away a furtive tear before breaking into applause, and from somewhere just east of me, I could hear Harry Almond call out, "Hear, hear!" The illegals were sobbing (on general principles, which is what apprehended illegals do) and Maguire was cursing. But by now, Cowboy was very much at ease, handing around cigars, chatting with the Marines and signing autographs, recounting tall tales of the Old Breed at Camp Pendleton and details of firefights fondly recalled from jolly days and nights at Da Nang and the Mekong Delta.

It would take the rest of Memorial Day to get things sorted out here on Gin Lane and elsewhere in Southampton.

# thirty-one

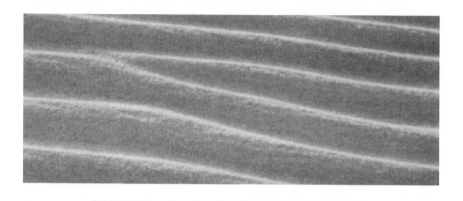

*How does one "ease into" admitting your girl's gone off?*

And that included another event taking place that day along Gin Lane: the marriage of Fruity Metcalfe, the Viscount Albemarle, son and heir to the earl of Bute and member of the British cabinet, to sweetshop heiress Mandy Buchanan, the very rich, long-legged, and healthily sexed (table dancing and all that) youngest daughter of the Chicago Buchanans.

Well, that would turn out to be quite a story as well, though those of us caught up earlier that morning in O'Hara's dragnet at Ten bis Gin Lane knew very little of what was going on with Fruity and Mandy and never got it all until later in the day or that evening and then only secondhand.

The ceremony was, as you recall, to be solemnized by an Episcopal clergyman of extraordinary bearing and piety at St. Andrew's Dune Church. Thanks to the earl of Bute's connections in the House of Lords, where he took counsel on the matter with no less than the archbishop of Canterbury, who didn't hesitate for a moment. "Thigpen's your man,

Bute! Cecil Thigpen. Old Harrovian who migrated ages ago to the States. Presides over a parish at Kansas City, Michigan, I believe. He's the sort of chap to give your boy a sound service and a jolly good blessing, besides. Who's the lucky girl, eh?" The wedding was to be followed by a reception at the Meadow.

And the earl of Bute would not be the only late arrival, the earl who long ago had vowed never to go to bed (unless while seriously ill or during a romantic liaison) except in a land that swore fealty to the Crown.

There was also Mr. Cudlipp, a managing partner (and one of their finest cutters and fitters) in the Savile Row men's tailoring establishment of Henry Poole Ltd., who'd arrived the evening before and been chauffeured to Southampton, Fruity's new cutaway securely in his own garment bag, the final seams basted up and ready for a try-on. Such haste was hardly to Mr. Cudlipp's taste. He liked to have a fourth or even a fifth leisurely fitting, and often suggested that a client, before accepting a new suit, crawl about on the shop floor on all fours, testing the fit lest it bind anywhere. This was the tradition at Poole's over the years. Had they not gone out to Addis Ababa to garb Haile Selassie in his new coronation robes as emperor of Ethiopia? Had a predecessor of Cudlipp not outfitted in the snuggest tweeds and warmest woolen underwear the famous alpinists George Leigh Mallory and Sandy Irvine for their gallant, though tragic, assault on Everest? Had not a tailor from Poole's smoothed many a weskit over the ample belly of Victoria's son, the Prince of Wales (later Edward VII), for the annual tours of the bagnios, boîtes and bistrots of his beloved Paris?

"Nipper" Gascoigne, the twelfth baron, got there a day or two ahead of schedule. He was, like Fruity, an Old Etonian (and reputedly a hot boyhood "crush") who now worked in Singapore as an abritrageur and was enormously wealthy, which annoyed Earl Bute no end. "All very well to be in the cabinet and flaunt status; but there's young Gascoigne out there in the bloody countinghouses coining the old rupee, eh?"

Wully Fitzdale, the notorious rake and 'round-the-world sailor, another school chum, broke off his latest circumnavigation by docking his yacht in Peru and flying to New York for the wedding. Nipper came stag; Wully decidedly not, accompanied as he was by a gloriously nubile Inca maiden who couldn't keep her hands off him, licked his face in public, and with her severely limited English called him *"mi capitán."* She might have been fifteen. It was not so much to solemnize Fruity's wedding but an opportunity to suck up to Tom Buchanan that fetched Wully. He had a new scheme and needed financing; a kayak trip up the Nile to prove that neither the Blue Nile nor the White were definitively "true" sources of the world's greatest river. And when potential backers skeptically eyed his companion, Wully explained that "Señorita de Playa" would be kayaking as well, giving her credentials as those of "a junior official of the Pan-Andean Society and a leading candidate for the Peruvian Olympic kayaking team. Stroke the callus of her palms, just look at her pectorals. This is a girl at home with a paddle."

"I'm quite sure," Buchanan remarked coldly, having nubile daughters of his own to marry off and not welcoming the competition. Especially one this young and randy, and boasting those inarguably impressive pecs.

You know how it is there on the lawn in front of old St. Andrew's, with the bell in the belfry above and the anchor and the old cannon flanking the path up through the Episcopally groomed grass to the church door. That was where the wedding party now gathered pleasantly in the May sunshine, including the groomsmen and Fruity himself following his premarital luncheon, and other guests. From three corners of the world had come the in-laws, Mandy's sisters and their impressively titled husbands. From Rome, the commendatore and his Buchanan wife, in the company of their own personal chaplain, a Dominican friar in sandals and brown sacking, loudly telling his beads; the graf and his Buchanan grafin, he in lederhosen and traditional Tyrolean jacket, she in a flowered dirndl, prettily redolent of the younger von Trapps; and from Kashmir, the maharajah and his Buchanan ranee, he in brocaded robes and jodphurs, the toes of his bejeweled velvet slippers turned dramatically up, she in a silken sari to the floor and with a crimson caste mark on her forehead, very nicely setting off the green of a heavy emerald necklace looped 'round her swan's neck.

As the wedding guests drove up and made their way, there was considerable chat of earlier excitements along Gin Lane, the flashing lights of police cars, the pounding din of hovering military choppers, the haste with which several Secret Service men, their cell phones crackling, had histrionically burnt rubber leaving the church grounds for other, unspecified locations.

"Of course it all has to do with the president," people reassured each other. "Wherever a president alights, there's bound to be a degree of chaos."

And when would POTUS arrive? Would he and the First Lady be at the service? Or join the reception later at the club?

"It's security," a knowledgeable fellow remarked. "They keep you guessing, those Secret Service lads. And rightly so."

That might have sat well with him. But not the earl of Bute. "Confound it, Fruity! It's five past. Where *is* that gal of yours? And I thought their president was to be here!"

To mollify the old gentleman, Nipper Gascoigne and Mr. Buchanan whistled up the corps of bridesmaids and matrons, Alix Dunraven among them, all of them garishly splendid in daringly low-cut satin gowns of a sort of pumpkin hue, to be presented to the earl.

"Curtsy as deeply as you can without falling over," Alix counseled her fellow attendants in a confidential tone. "The earl does enjoy a jolly show of boobs, y'know."

Nor had the RAF yet mustered on the dunes of St. Andrew's. Which was a shame, since they were togged out in their dress uniforms, with swords, even though not since '39 had pilots and flight crews been issued swords by the RAF and the wing commander and his men had to make do with secondhand United States Marine Corps sabers rented from a shop in Sag Harbor. And while his polo-playing Argentinos were also among the missing, Rex Magnifico was there on the church lawn, showing off his early tan, shaking hands, handing out advertising rate cards for his magazine, and wondering where his damned polo team might be. On a tango somewhere, he supposed.

What neither Rex nor the others knew was that, not an hour earlier, the RAF men had been laying about them with swords at the Driver's Seat bar on Job's Lane, desperately defending themselves against a trio of exceedingly fierce and mallet-wielding polo players from the Pampas and, in the process, had gotten arrested. Both sides.

By now the earl had been generously curtsied to, and was consequently in a much improved mood.

"By Gad, Buchanan, there's some lovely pastry there. My hat's off to you chaps, turning out such a crop of gels. Haven't seen as handsome a tit show since last time I attended a matinee at the Windmill."

Tom Buchanan, eager to ingratiate himself with his future in-law, thanked the earl for his graciousness and regretted having advised his wife, Daisy, against wearing a push-up bra herself.

"Jolly good, jolly good," the earl murmured, looking about him now for another glimpse at that young South American girl attached to Wully Fitzdale. Corking bosom on that one, he told himself; pity the Peruvian dressmakers didn't cut their bodices a trifle lower. The Catholic influence he supposed.

But for all the camaraderie, Buchanan was getting restive. Where the hell was Mandy? He went off in search of Daisy and information. It was shortly after that, with guests already filing into the old church with its cool interior and slightly maritime look, that one of the young men from the Mauve House arrived in something of a state of excitement to hand a sealed envelope to their hotel guest, the Viscount Albemarle.

"This seemed to me important, Fruity. I sped it right over."

"Yes, yes, quite," Fruity said, himself distracted by delay and growing nervier as his "zero hour" approached. He started to shove the envelope, unopened, in his cutaway pocket when the earl, still in a mood of gruff bonhomie and recalling certain pert bosoms, demanded good-humoredly, "What's this, what's this? Despatches from the front, eh? Better read it, Fruity. Might be some rival claimant to her hand's turned up, what?"

The viscount retrieved the envelope, broke its seal, and began to read.

"Oh, I say, Father! It's from Mandy!"

Once the earl, the father of the bride, and the groom had all huddled, Buchanan white-faced, the earl in something of a rage, and the groom surprisingly the most controlled of the three, it was left to poor Fruity to march into St. Andrew's and down the center aisle to the pulpit, there to turn, cough for attention, and break the news that his wedding was off.

"I have the honor," he began uncertainly (which was understandable, since he'd never before been jilted at the altar), his father the earl at his side, "to announce that, well . . ."

"Stiff upper lip, lad," the earl hissed encouragement. "Never forget that you're a Bute! Remember the third earl, by Gad, sir!"

Since Fruity recalled all too well that the third earl lost his head, quite literally (a broadax did the job) at the sixteenth-century Battle of Houndslow Plain, this was of sparse encouragement. But he soldiered on:

". . . to announce that the bride, my fiancée, that is, the Honorable

Amanda Buchanan, is . . . well, indisposed. There will be no wedding this day. And thank you all very much for your jolly good wishes and for coming."

Then, recalling Eton and his boyish reading of Shakespeare, the humiliated and near-desperate viscount reached into his own scholastic past to retrieve a dismissive Latin phrase from the Bard, one that five hundred years before traditionally cleared an Elizabethan stage:

"*Exeunt omnes.*"

There were, as you might imagine, tears, shock, a communal gasp, several faintings, and any number of loud oaths. Daisy Buchanan wept as her husband ground his teeth, both thinking perhaps of lavishly annual stays at Bute Castle never to be enjoyed. John Fairchild of *Women's Wear Daily* dashed off for a phone to order a remake of the front page for tomorrow while his aide Patrick remained behind, taking additional notes and seeking comment, Wyseman Clagett being one of the few guests willing (and sufficiently gross) to go on the record.

Nipper Gascoigne, the best man, sidled up censorious and oily, to the jilted groom.

"I say, old boy, well done and all that. But you might have eased into it a bit, eh? Bit of a shock, that."

"But how, Nipper? How does one 'ease into' admitting your girl's gone off? Left at the bloody altar, what does one say?"

The anguish in his voice, the confused mix of embarrassment, regret, and, harsh as it may be to say so, a degree of actual relief, must have surprised Nipper, who went rather mindlessly on for a bit:

"Desh it all, Fruity. I mean, tell a charming anecdote or two about Mandy, you know, spin a yarn. What a jolly gel she is, how you two met, that sort of bosh. Bit hard on the wedding party to be told flat out that the bride's done a bunk on you. Might have thought of the rest of us in breaking the news all that abruptly. That's all I mean, don't y'know."

For once in his life, Fruity Metcalfe rose to an occasion.

"Yes," he said politely, the sarcasm at precisely the correct note, "quite right, Nipper. I certainly should have thought first of the rest of you."

Wully Fitzdale, his carefully laid plans for a financial heart-to-heart about kayaking costs on the Nile with Tom Buchanan dashed, was in no mood for politesse, and angrily stalked from the church, followed by a befuddled and clearly alarmed Señorita de Playa, crying plaintively after him, "*Mi capitán! Mi pobre capitán!*" her excellent pectorals bouncing as she ran.

As for the father of the groom, he might have been the most distraught of all. He was an old man and had come a long way and now, as he informed anyone who would listen, "I can take a wedding or leave it. But to be cheated out of a good reception! I had so looked forward to the dancing. All those jolly bridesmaids. I do enjoy a good orchestra and a hearty gallop about the old hardwood with a young gel in me arms. Don't often get the opportunity, not at my age, don'tcha know."

And the Reverend Thigpen, who'd come all this way from Kansas City (which turned out not to be in Michigan at all) at the urging of the archbishop of Canterbury, and whom no one had bothered to tell just what happened and why the nuptials were off, sadly changed back into his black traveling suit and shed his vestments in the vesting room of the old church, wondering again about Divine Providence and why theology permitted fate to confound him so? Or, in Cecil Thigpen's own, earthier terms, "Just why the devil do people so muck me about?"

Now, as the guests politely or petulantly said their good-byes and began to drift away, to their parked or waiting cars, from First Neck Lane and downtown Southampton itself came rolling slowly past along Gin Lane a curious caravan of the most extraordinary mix:

The last of Karl Lager's Ferraris and Jags and MGs and Bugattis, his "auld brigade," being led home from their demo by a Southampton prowl car, red roof light revolving slowly, the sports cars followed in turn by an open-backed police truck with a half dozen painted Shinnecock Indians happily beating their war drums, their leader Jesse Maine waving to familiar faces among the wedding guests emerging from the church, and then another similar police vehicle with a decidedly more lugubrious mixed bag of RAF fliers and Argentinos in polo gear, both groups somewhat the worse for wear, their swords and polo mallets securely in police custody for the moment.

One of Fruity's groomsmen, slightly sodden with drink and somewhat befuddled by American customs, thought this curious procession might be a local equivalent to the Trooping of the Colours and raised an exultant cry:

"The president! I say, it must be your president arriving, what!"

It was at that moment that from the direction of Ten bis a bearded man came running, desperately, breathlessly crying out apologies and grabbing at departing wedding guests. "No, no! Go back, it's all right. I'm late, I know, God forgive me. Not my fault! Please go back. Think of the bride! We'll get things started immediately..."

People shied away, giving him wide berth, assuming here was the local madman, and not wanting to be accosted.

"Please," he cried, "the wedding! It must go on! Tell the rector, so sorry, so very sorry! We'll be under way any moment..."

This was the hired organist, who, being heavily bearded, fit certain security assumptions and profiles, and who, in passing Dils's gate on his way to early practice at the church nearly two hours ago, had been detained, sat upon and and severely interrogated by O'Hara's men and was only recently cleared and released. It says something about the vanity of artists, especially musicians, that the poor man thought the wedding had been canceled due to his tardiness and the lack of a rousing rendition on the pipe organ of "Here Comes the Bride" and the other traditional wedding tunes.

The organist knew nothing of the high drama occasioned by Mandy's letter to the viscount at his digs in the Mauve House and subsequently delivered by hand at the very church.

# t h i r t y - t w o

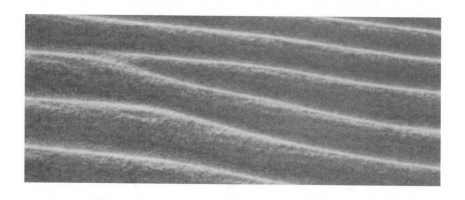

*You can tell a good deal about a person from his
or her notepaper*

In the end Roger Champion was fined $250 for discharging a firearm in
the village but hailed in the *Southampton Press* and elsewhere for his gallantry
and exemplary behavior in defense of hearth, home and Mrs. Champion.
Several committees were gotten up and money pledged toward design of
an appropriate plaque or perhaps a partial scholarship in his name at
Southampton High. The virtuous Slim, as well, was saluted for having
beaten off the unwanted advances of that licentious rascal Dils. Who was
in his turn cited for reckless endangerment in using his golf cart to run
over O'Hara's men. Although for political reasons, the White House
quietly told them to drop the charges and not give the SOB yet another
opportunity to get on the front pages. Nor were prosecutions sought
against the Shinnecocks, Karl Lager and his drivers, or even the RAF or
Rex's polo players, and, in point of fact, the unfortunate organist served
more time in official custody than anyone else. Nor was he ever paid his
usual fee.

Jesse Maine had certainly helped return Southampton to normal, calling off his embattled Shinnecocks after a largely ceremonial and symbolic war dance and drum beating on the bridge across the Shinnecock Canal. Once the first town patrol car arrived, driven by a cop who'd arrested Jesse several times previously and considered him a friend, the barricades came swiftly and efficiently down, and after names and addresses were taken, a police truck was whistled up to transport the Shinnecocks back safely to the reservation.

By then Lager and his civilly disobedient "auld brigade" of race car drivers, having accomplished their demo, agreed to return to Scuttle Hole Road after a lap around the houses and the issuance of traffic tickets, led by a police cruiser (to make sure the lads really were going home) with its revolving lights. Melisande Lager, who dearly loved her husband and tolerated his cronies, would be waiting with a nicely chilled Dom Perignon and caviar, for a round of genial reminiscence and a few outright lies.

The RAF and Rex Magnifico's Argies had eventually succumbed to drink and fatigue and been thoughtfully carted away by the local constabulary, not to be booked but simply to avoid further mischief.

So that, in the end, no one was shot or even wounded, the president (POTUS) hadn't ever left Washington, while only Roger Champion was even fined. Although several of Cowboy's illegal maids were given appearance tickets and Dr. Fu was warned against traveling outside the jurisdiction until his bona fides were established. As for citing Cowboy for vehicular assault, for having rammed his golf cart into three Secret Service agents, a sympathetic magistrate bought his claim that the cast on his right leg, once again, had become tangled in the controls, causing misadventure, and dropped the charge. A summons issued for careless driving and a reckless endangerment rap were both in the end quashed by executive order.

Although confusion as to the identity of Champion's intended victim had been cleared up to Vittorini's satisfaction, O'Hara of the Secret Service still took serious convincing. Few federal officers get an opportunity, in the very same day, to save a president's life and put down a coup d'état. Now both of these glorious career-making events had proved ephemeral and O'Hara was not taking his disappointments gracefully. Despite Special Agent in Charge Vittorini's generously having promised to look into mentioning, in dispatches, O'Hara's swift and efficient response, arresting any number of (largely innocent) people while seeing to it they were read their rights.

The wing commander, deprived of his sword and sobered up, was provided a police escort to Westhampton airport. The understanding was that, glad to be rid of them, Southampton would permit him and his crew to transport the earl of Bute from Gin Lane to Toronto and the comforting embrace of a friendly British Commonwealth nation where His Grace might that night sleep beneath a proper Union Jack.

None of this did much to mollify O'Hara, who fell into a sulk, gave up quoting Joyce, no longer read Vergil, Horace and Livy, either in translation or the original Latin, and never again paged through his beloved *Caesar's Wars*. Within six months Special Agent O'Hara was drinking heavily, putting on weight, and had submitted to the service a resignation of honor.

I expected Fruity to be crushed, humiliated. That, or wrathful. In a towering fury and hurling imprecations, reduced to weeping and sobs. Or consulting solicitors about an action for breach of promise. But when Alix finally produced him next day but one at the gatehouse and I poured us all some champers, he seemed almost relieved.

"Mandy was such a good sport about the whole thing, y'know—"

"I should think you were the sport, Fruity," Alix interrupted. "She was the one left you standing at the altar!"

"Yes, of course, but she sent the nicest note. It arrived by hand at the Mauve House. Jed took it, he's the tall one, gave it to me himself. 'Thought it might be important, m'lud,' that sort of thing. Y'know, Beecher, you can tell a good deal about a person from his or her note-paper. I get mine made up at Henningham and Hollis of Mount Street in Mayfair, W1, but I'm sure there are excellent stationers here in the States as well—"

"The note, Fruity," Alix said. "What did the girl say?"

"Well, all her fault, terribly sorry, begging forgiveness. Hit all the right notes. Not every young woman today would have the decency or the breeding to take all the blame on herself. Especially when you consider her father runs sweetshops and she was educated in Texas. Awfully generous girl and I say, no disrespect to you, Alix, but she is a piece! Has the most gorgeous legs. Despite myself I was rather looking forward to the wedding trip and having her jumping about. I said that to her, on several occasions, I said, 'But you *are* a piece, Mandy.'

"Even told Beecher here, didn't I, about her legs?"

"You did," I said, proud of him for taking it like a man, and poured us all a fresh Dom.

Fruity said he was sorry that with all the confusion at the church, with the bride never showing up and Mr. Buchanan in a snit about John Fairchild (who with his man Patrick "took one of the better pews, which was cheeky indeed!"), and with Fruity himself having to make a speech of sorts, that he missed out on "The Battle of Gin Lane," all that excitement on Cowboy's lawn with the Secret Service and Roger Champion and all that.

"Must have been a dazzling show," the viscount said in admiration, "all that chaos and confusion, Dils running amok aboard the golf cart, bowling over federal agents, and old Champion firing off shots and wielding the Purdey over and under, and Nurse Cavell weeping and Dr. Fu attempting to swim to safety, and Air Force One forced to turn back and Secret Service men sitting on you, Beecher. Golly, what a show that must have been!"

"It was indeed," I agreed cheerfully, and poured all three of us a little more of the Dom.

# thirty-three

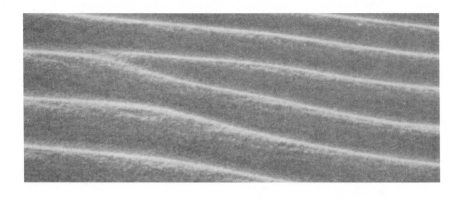

*I was thinking of you, laying down the basis for*
*an insanity plea . . .*

I didn't get to see Dils again until Thursday morning. I phoned ahead and then went over to the house. Here it was, only the first week of June, the Season hardly begun, but at Ten bis Gin Lane there was a final act curtain feel to it, the fin de siècle come a year or two early. The impeccable lawns had grown somewhat long and untidy, the long, curving gravel drives were littered with trash and marked up by tire scars from the government vehicles and the media. The daily papers and the local weekly had been delivered but had gone uncollected and unread, until a wind off the ocean scattered about the pages so that the place, house and grounds both, had an unkempt and vacant look, a house nobody loved and where no one lived. All it lacked was graffiti and Mrs. Danvers at the window peering through curtains.

The Hispanic maids had gotten out. Nor did the twice-a-week gardeners show up or the pool boy. Scared off, I guess by the feds, suspecting the Immigration and Naturalization would be coming in next, and in the

Hamptons in Season, who didn't have an illegal worker toiling away somewhere on the place? Even the entourage was thinned out; dispersed on its own or sent back into the city by Cowboy in the Morning.

I found him out back, alone on the sloping lawn facing pool and ocean. He was on his feet, using a cane, a five iron actually, and awkwardly lifting it from time to time to slap at golf balls raggedly strewn on the grass, missing most of them completely, nudging others but a few yards away. One or two he drove solidly and they vanished over the dune toward the ocean and, well, where was the next hole out there? Europe? The Azores?

"I thought while I was still in Southampton I ought to learn their national game," he said, grinning at me from under his cowboy hat in that lopsided way, a bit embarrassed, I think, to have been caught golfing.

"Yeah," I agreed, "you hit that last one pretty well. Right down the middle. You could probably learn this game, get good at it."

"The hell," he said, but I think he was pleased.

He limped back up to the patio where I'd stood watching and dropped into one of the glistening white-painted Adirondack chairs and I tugged one over closer to him and sat as well. The sun was nice but the morning was still fresh and cool and despite everything, there were worse places to be. Except that on the broad armrest of my chair a gull had perched and I brushed away some bird shit. When no one cleans shit off the Adirondack chairs on Gin Lane, you suspect the place no longer rates three stars in the Michelin Guide.

"What happened, really?" I asked.

Cowboy laughed.

"You're not a phony, Stowe. At least not entirely. And on Gin Lane, that qualifies. And besides that, you saved my life back there when you tackled old Roger."

"Thanks." Typical of Dils's system of values that he considered it more important I wasn't a "phony" than that I'd kept Champion from blowing him away. Was he to be evasive, polite? I'd rather he'd chase me off the way he did most people. No, he was playful. But I wanted him talky.

"You mean what happened Monday? Or from the day I stopped drinking? Or when I first came east?" He paused. "What didn't happen is more like it."

I asked where the guys were, just for openers.

"We go back on the air Monday. We've got a show to do. They weren't doing much good here. Maguire cursing out everyone and Harry reading the Bible and Dr. Fu terrified the INS was coming for him. Jersey Fats has a wife and the Sports Geek, well, I think he has to cover quoits or lacrosse or something this weekend. Annie wanted to stay but I told her no, not without a duenna. Woman's got to watch out for her reputation in this town. Greasy Thumb is still pissed off at the feds for taking away his weapon when he had a perfectly valid license for it. Nurse Cavell, I believe, ran off with Otto the pumpernickel man. He's teaching her German and they plan to live in the van. The soaps don't have story lines like this."

I had the impression he'd chased them away, that except for the servants, no one had actually abandoned him, that for the moment at least, he really wanted to do a Garbo, to be alone. Then Harry Almond came out, lugging a sort of weekend bag and a couple of books, overdressed, for Southampton and the hour, in an actual suit. Polyester or poplin, but a suit and tie nonetheless. Harry, clearly, was a reluctant deserter. If anyone loved Cowboy, it was Harry Almond.

"Leicester, this isn't at all necessary, you know. I—"

Dils cut him off. "I'm not talking to you, you traitor. Compared to you, Quisling was faithful as Dog Tray." To me, he said, "Harry keeps Boston terriers and has a Vaughan Monroe collection needs cataloging. He's the last American who collects vinyl—"

"He's moving up to forty-five RPMs, chief," Maguire said, coming out a few beats behind Almond. "For Harry, that's cutting edge."

"Shut up, you baldheaded geek. I thought you left with Guzik and Fu."

It turned out Cowboy hadn't yet forgiven Harry Almond for having told the feds about the dog he shot. "Talk about betrayal, talk about kicking a man when he's down..."

Almond, righteously, wasn't giving an inch:

"Don't lash out at me, Leicester. Concerned citizens have a responsibility to aid peace officers in their work. And I was thinking of you, as well, laying down the basis for a possible insanity plea. Or at least one of diminished responsibility..."

This drew from Dils an astonishing series of oaths.

"All I can say," primly protested the abashed Almond, "is that you must really love your fellow man when you're as good a Protestant as I am and still go into an R.C. church to pray for him."

Harry's piety, for the moment, silenced Cowboy.

Maguire shrugged. He, too, hesitated to leave Cowboy Dils alone. They knew him far better than I, were aware of vulnerabilities at which I couldn't even guess. But Dils was issuing instructions now, back at the top of his game. Or so it seemed.

"We go back on-air Monday. I want that Dr. Kevorkian skit worked on. And either get 'Vlad the Impaler Meets the Promise Keepers' right or let's can it. Get cracking. Tell Jersey Fats I want his 'Trump' even dumber. You can forget 'Bridge on the River Liffey.' Too subtle. Let's for a change have a really bleak 'Mr. Gloomy' . . ."

Maguire, stubborn, but sensing iron in the words, shrugged, and then picked up his bags and started off. Almond didn't. But only stood there in his J. C. Penney suit.

"Go away, Harry," Dils said, whispering the words.

"Now, Leicester, I think you ought—"

"Harry . . ."

Louder and edgier, and Almond understood. Turning to me, he said, "Grand seeing you again, Stowe. I have dogs, as Cowboy said. I'll be off."

"Sure," I said. "Sure. My best to the dogs."

When he was gone Dils sat there a while not saying anything, which for him was odd.

Then he said, shaking his head, his voice low and even thoughtful, "If you have two people in the world who love you, you're a fortunate man."

I nodded. He didn't have to say who the two were. Then, more briskly, he began:

"It was all bullshit, about the president being after me. I knew that. I voted for him twice. I liked him. A smart man who does stupid things. And in my own way, on the air in the skits, down there at the Press Club, I tried to install a little sense into him. By kicking him in the ass. Being me, I overdid it. I always do. But that wasn't viciousness or envy or resentment or wanting to bring him down.

"It was just trying to, I dunno . . . get his attention." I was still absorbing that when he shifted gears, asking about Her Ladyship and whatever happened to Fruity after Mandy left him at the altar and ran off and they canceled the wedding. Stuff like that. We were fencing, both of us.

"Beautiful woman, classy, too. Educated. Rock stars think they get the best girls in the world? They're idiots. Best-looking girls in the world hang around with race car drivers. You know why? Because they want the thrill of sleeping with men about to die."

"Is that so?" I said, wondering where he was heading, what this was all about.

"No. I'm just bullshitting, Stowe. You Harvard people don't understand when—"

That was unnecessary; that annoyed me. Want to irritate a guy who went to Harvard? Start addressing him as "you Harvards." Or "you Harvard people . . ." Just why that gets to us, I can't say. But I was sore.

"I'm the only 'Harvard people' here, Cowboy. So why don't you quit doing shtick and start telling the truth? There's more to this Roger Champion stuff and his jealous rage than you're saying. Why don't you tell me? Or if not me, tell the world. You've got a pulpit. You've got a microphone. Why are you taking a rap you maybe don't deserve? You never struck me as the type who enjoys shouldering guilt for other . . ."

"What is truth?" he said piously, going into something resembling Harry's Parson Weems persona. Or was it Cotton Mather?

"Come on, Cowboy. You've got a case. I know you have. Southampton's all over you. Phonies like Wyseman Clagett, and you won't fight back. Just why you're playing martyr and refusing to make the case, I don't understand."

"Man suffers." He sighed.

"Man issues bromides," I rattled back. Then, in an inspired moment, or a foolhardy one, I wasn't quite sure which, I said:

"Leicester, what really happened between you and the Champions?"

I got the explosion I wanted. Or thought I wanted.

"Nobody calls me 'Leicester' outside my family. Only Harry Almond. And you ain't no Harry Almond—"

"No, I'm not, Leicester."

He was up out of the chair and starting for me then with the five iron gripped in two fists and ready to swing. I was bigger than him and younger and I was ready. But his leg wasn't back to strength yet and went out from under him, tumbling him to earth.

"You okay, Cowboy?" I said as I helped him up.

"Leicester," he said quietly. "It's okay for Harvards to call me 'Leicester.' It's a new rule I have. But only if no one's around to hear it, like Maguire or Dr. Fu, okay?"

"Deal," I said.

And then Cowboy told me about Slim Champion.

# t h i r t y - f o u r

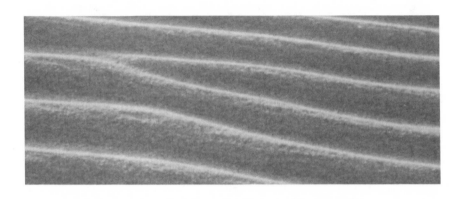

*Glenn Close is indisposed. Her part will be played by Slim Norris...*

"This was maybe ten, twelve years back. I was new to New York working nights as a DJ on an FM station no one ever heard of and even fewer listened to, an out-of-town hick trying to make it, and Slim was a local, a New Yorker, big-city girl, born and bred in Manhattan and pretty hip, in a play on Broadway, and we got together. She was a hell of a lot prettier than me and knew the town. Maybe I had a future and she didn't, but that wasn't immediately evident. Both of us got out of work about midnight. The rest of the evenings pretty much took care of themselves. I was still drinking and she was frisky. We had a lot of fun. And we could sleep late.

"You know how Liz Smith and the columns always refer to Slim as this great star of the American theater who sacrificed a career to marry the legendary Roger Champion? Well, I knew her then; she was no star. Oh, sure, she played all the big leading roles on Broadway, Nora in *A Doll's House* and Maggie the Cat, and Babe in a revival of *The Pyjama Game* and Nellie in *South Pacific,* one of the cats in, well, *Cats.* But she played them as an understudy, the girl who went on every few months when Blythe Danner or Betty Buckley or Kathleen Turner or Glenn Close had the flu or cramps. 'You're the Queen of the Understudies,' I told her once. 'Yeah,' she said, not sore but actually pleased about it, and gutsy, too. 'The producers know how good I am, Cowboy. They can go to the bank on it; my PMS is never too bad to go on.'

"She played Broadway all right. Her specialty was that last-minute announcement at the footlights by an assistant stage manager who came out and announced, 'Glenn Close is indisposed. The part of Nora will be played tonight by Ms. Slim Norris.'

"It must be tough when the only time you hear your name announced in public from a stage, there's a groan. Actors and actresses, they live off applause. Ovations. Curtain calls. Ushers lugging baskets of flowers to the footlights. Autograph hounds outside the stage door, waiting in the rain, Eve waiting for Bette Davis. And all Slim Norris ever got, until Roger came along, was groans. The people who'd paid forty bucks to see Lunt and Fontanne up there were being fobbed off with an unknown named Slim.

"So she took consolation in make-believe. She was beautiful, still is. Got to give her that. Tall and graceful and beautiful. She just didn't have that whatever it is stars have and the others don't. A spark. And to make up for it, she lied. Slim lies like Jordan plays basketball; it comes natural. Only trouble, she's not as good as Jordan. She lies easily but not well. Slim's transparent; her nose grows long, and only someone who truly loves her believes Slim for a minute. That's where Roger comes in, goes right along. She lies and he swears to it. The bigger 'star' she was, the more she 'gave up to become Mrs. Champion,' and the better the old goat looks. He's eighty years old; she's forty. Match made in heaven.

"Or was, that is, until I moved in down the block on Gin Lane."

Cowboy looked me over again then, in that shrewd way he has, as if he were buying a horse or auditioning an act. He saw through people. "Phonies." His favorite insult. "Phonies" were even worse than "weasels." You could be a forger or murder people or bite your girlfriend like Marv Albert or steal your mother's retirement money and still be okay. But a phony? No. Apparently I was still passing the "phonies" MRI and he went on.

"Roger came up here the other day to kill me for sleeping with his wife. That's why he had the Purdey over and under. Fine gun, a Purdey. Champion buys the best, hires the best, he works with the best, that's why the network's so good. The man has style. You've got to be shot? Take a Purdey anytime. No distinction in getting shot with a Saturday night special. But a Purdey over and under? Almost an honor to be bumped off with a Purdey..."

"Sure," I said, knowing more was coming.

"And the feds thought he was after POTUS. What a joke."

"Well, the president was coming and here was a guy with a gun and—"

"Harvard taught you better than that, Stowe. The president never came to Gin Lane, never really meant to. That was just a bone thrown to Tom and Daisy Buchanan. Their kid was getting married to a fancy Englishman with a title and the president of the United States, POTUS, was going to be there. People wet their pants in excitement. Buchanan gave big bucks to the campaign and the prez lent a sort of... what's the word, something like a shine, to the affair..."

"A patina."

"Yeah, a patina. A gesture to a campaign contributor. You have people in for coffee at the White House. You let them sleep in the Lincoln bedroom. You promise to attend the bar mitzvah, go to their kid's wedding. And then, affairs of state keep you away. A crisis in Rwanda. In outer space. A crisis in Brooklyn. But the guests are thrilled, anyway. 'The president almost came...'"

"You know what it's like? That the president *almost* came? It's Brando, 'I could of been a contenduh.' Social climbers like the Buchanans can live off it for a month..."

"And did you sleep with Champion's wife?"

"So you've had enough shtick?"

"Yes. Because you don't do shtick. Not very well."

"No."

After a minute he said, "You know, Beecher, I'm a real pain in the ass. I know that. But that's why they started America. So the pains in the ass would have a country, too."

I got up. I liked him too much to push it.

"Okay," I said, "about Mrs. Champion, forget it. Sorry I brought it up. None of my business really."

"Don't go," he said, getting up himself, leaning on the old five iron, the cowboy hat low on his brow, shading his eyes so I couldn't read them.

Then: "Sit down, Stowe."

There was something in his voice and I did. I sat down in the Adirondack chair where the seagulls shit. And Cowboy said:

"No, I didn't sleep with Slim Champion. First time in my life I ever said no to anything good."

I listened, knowing there was more.

"She reminded me of the fun we had. She loved Roger, she was a good wife, but at his age . . . I was here on Gin Lane, she was here. Why not?"

"And?"

"I don't even like Roger Champion. He's a snob and a hard man and my boss. But he created something in this network and earned his billions and he's not a phony and he loves this girl. This woman."

"And?" I said again, feeling stupid, but I said it.

"She said he was failing. The land deal with Wyseman Clagett for the racecourse. That was just Roger showing the world he still had muscle, could still pull off a big deal, make even more dough he didn't need. If he couldn't function in bed, well, there were other places he could still push people around, swagger a little, still get an erection.

"But I said no. I wasn't going to screw Roger Champion by screwing his wife. Not for her pleasure or for mine. For once I was going to walk away and not do something."

I thought back.

"But Champion thought you and she were . . ."

Cowboy shrugged.

"Sure, she told him we were."

"*What?*"

Cowboy tried to be patient with me.

"I told you. She was an understudy. All her life she wants to be the star. So she lives in a dream world. She lies. She lies to her husband that guys are chasing her. Maybe even suggests she's cheating on him with other men. His rage is like applause. Like curtain calls. His jealousy is an ovation. The only thing she can't take is that groan of disappointment when the stage manager tells the audience, 'Tonight's leading role will be played by the understudy . . .' Better that her husband shoot people than she has to go through that again."

"You really think this?"

"I'm speculating. But don't forget, I know her. Of course, no one could anticipate that Roger would get out his Purdey and try bumping me off on the day the joint is crawling with feds and we end up scaring POTUS away."

"So you lied when you told Vittorini that you'd propositioned her. To save her face and Roger's. And not your own. All the time, there was nothing to it."

He limped around a bit, on the golf club, as if wondering what to tell me and whether it should be the truth. Good men face such dilemmas; how much truth do you tell?

"Yeah, I said I was the one cracking on her, not the other way 'round. That I stalked her. I'd chased her down and she, to get rid of me, told her husband. Who bought her story. And being a gentleman, defending his wife, his home, and despite age, he came after me with the shotgun. The Purdey. Did I tell you what a fine gun that is? That if you've got to be shot—"

"Yeah," I said, "you told me."

# thirty-five

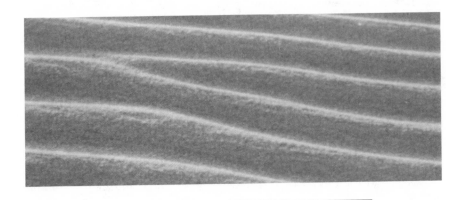

*A chap took her skiing at Gstaad and the competition closed . . .*

The RAF had flown out rather hurriedly to Toronto with the earl, not having quite completed their NATO liaison chores (*our* security people having talked to *their* security people who spoke harshly in Westminster to the Royal Air Force) and it was not long after that someone in Downing Street twigged to what Viscount Albemarle had been up to in the States and sent new instructions. Ag, and not Fish, was to be Fruity's focus for the rest of his American stay.

We met with him briefly, and solicitously, before he went off. He was approximately as unhappy as Greasy Thumb's "Mr. Gloomy." Alix attempted to be supportive:

"Downing Street ought be considerably more understanding, Fruity, and not so down on you for your efforts to smooth things over with the American authorities."

Except that it wasn't Her Majesty's government that was depressing the viscount. "Oh, no, it's not the PM at all. I fully understand his point. It's my gov'nor."

The earl of Bute, from Toronto, had apparently rattled off a stiff letter to his son and heir.

"He was furious. 'Desh it all, Fruity, I come all this way for a damned wedding, I expect to see a damned wedding! Pretty gels in low-cut gowns, handsome groomsmen, the church, a jolly organ, some sort of reverend praying over all of us, the exchange of vows, the music, the flowers, old aunts weeping, and a reception afterwards, the caviar and bubbly, and a gallop around the old hardwood with the bride and the bridesmaids. Damn it, at my age I don't get asked out dancing all that often. Haven't been to Quaglino's in years, never mind the Café Royale. I'd looked forward to a good gallop! Yet here I am, having been bustled off to Canada not six hours after arriving in the bloody States, and with my son and heir still unspliced."

What had the earl of Bute truly irate was snide commentary from his fellow peers.

"You're a trial to me, Fruity. I'm tired of chaps in the House of Lords coming up, all smarmy and interrogating me, 'That son of yours, Bute. He married off yet?' Your cousin Jasper's a year younger and he's been married three times already. Jolly gels, too, all three of 'em. Good dancers, as well."

Before he was through he got on the subject of Tom Buchanan's sweet-shops. And of the bride herself, who'd jilted his son at the very altar.

"They tell me she's not only rich but beautiful, Fruity. I'm assured she's a piece!" said the earl of Bute, who did so enjoy a good turn with a chorus girl.

"I agreed with everything he'd said," Fruity assured us now. "Told him Mandy was indeed a piece. Hits a splendid long iron, as well."

We bundled the lugubrious Viscount Albemarle onto the Hampton Jitney (a window seat, bran muffin, waxed cardboard container of orange juice, and the morning papers being provided) and waved him off. The driver was given instructions that he be dumped at the Flushing airport connection, where a gypsy cab, hired by the Foreign Office, would speed him to LaGuardia and a feeder line's midday flight to Des Moines with stops in Pittsburgh, Cleveland and Chicago (Midway).

"Our geography experts say Eee-oh-wah is about as far from any beach resort town and ocean that you can get and still be in the United States, Prime Minister Blair was assured." Gently, I provided Fruity the pronunciation of "Iowa," preferring he get it from me rather than an indignant farmer out there.

In Iowa (and an agrarian from the Ministry of Ag and Fish was being rushed over from London to see to it!) the viscount was to spend the next fortnight attending meetings of the Grange, visiting a poultry show, awarding medals to 4H Club members, and dedicating a grain elevator. He was also to be instructed in the ways of the pork bellies futures market, shake hands with farmers, discuss crop yields, marvel at irrigation projects, and be briefed on this growing season's outlook for soybeans, hay and the more serious of the legumes.

A highly automated dairy farm where a computer, and the cows, pretty much ran things was also on the program.

As for Mandy Buchanan, far from wasting away or entering nunneries, she turned up in the south of France wearing a shiny yellow jumpsuit in the entourage of a Formula One race car driver from Tuscany, the marchese di Montecatini, and was fetchingly photographed by *People* magazine at his Nice hospital bedside as she cradled his head and solicitously took the cigarette from his bruised lips to knock off its ash before reattaching it to his singed but undeniably handsome Tuscan face. It was to this hospital that the marchese had been taken after pranging his Lamborghini during trials and practice for the Grand Prix de Monaco to be run later in the season. Mandy's parents were said to be all in favor of an engagement if that was the young people's intention. Having been burned, and badly, by Fruity Metcalfe, the Buchanans were not about to let another potential aristo slip through their daughter's fingers and were flying to Nice by private jet. As for Rudolfo di Montecatini, he was delighted to be sleeping with Mandy and enjoying the usual carnal pleasures but was in no apparent rush to wed. Which meant this wasn't going to be the first time that Tom and Daisy "had counted noble husbands before they were hitched," or so went the wag's line famously quoted by Liz Smith in that Sunday's column.

And now I, too, was to lose someone.

The weather held, and gloriously so, and Alix and I lazed and sunned and canoed and borrowed a couple of old ten-speed bikes my father had and cycled to Sag Harbor and swam. Though the water was still too cold for my taste. "Rubbish," she told me, "you want it brisk!" I'd never seen her on a bicycle before and once we'd adjusted the seats and handlebars she was off, those long legs golden (from Barbados, you'll recall, and I was still a bit testy about that) and the faded khaki shorts and old-fashioned ribbed cotton men's undershirt she wore as a tank top just right for Sag Harbor, where heads turned in approval to see her pedaling past, nose practically on the handles and her bottom jauntily up. At Spinnakers, where we went to cool down, three different men bought us beers. When I mentioned, quietly, how they stared, Alix said, sensibly: "It's the chaps that don't stare you worry about. The sneaky type, who peep."

She had a few regrets, not many.

"I do wish I'd been there to see federal agents sitting on you and quoting in Latin from *Caesar's Wars*."

Other than that? "The poet was right," she said. "What *is* so rare as a day in June?"

We differed on the poet. I thought Lovelace; she insisted Suckling. We were both wrong and laughed to realize Harvard and Oxford were producing the half-educated.

"I should have known, you know," she said. "Didn't I very nearly capture the annual Newdigate Prize for poetry at university?"

"Why, that's marvelous, Alix. You never told me that."

"And I would have done if I'd gotten my entry in on time. I'd dashed off some absolutely corking verses if I do say so myself. Really first-rate. All meter and rhyme and tropes and things. Delicious figures of speech, similes and metaphor and irony and all that."

"What happened?"

"A chap took me off skiing at Gstaad over Christmas and the competition closed before I got back."

"Pity," I said.

"Yes, wasn't it."

For the rest of that first week of June I spent several days interviewing Baymen and going out on longline trawlers and except for the one time I was at sea overnight, Alix and I partied evenings. "I love your Season," she enthused. "There's dancing and drink and all variety of lovely nonsense. And sunshine besides. The London Season would be so much more jolly if the sun ever shone. Just imagine Ascot with number fifteen sunblock. Or Wimbledon without brollies! And there's absolutely no one in

London who knows anything like as much about bamboo and pandas as your nice Mr. Pontick."

She was supposed to be back at work in London Monday without fail. "They've got me down as absent without leave for sure, darling," Her Ladyship informed me. "They'll be calling up firing squads any moment now."

Each morning she logged in on that laptop computer of hers in its chic Louis Vuitton carrying case and E-mailed the most astonishing lies to her London employers at HarperCollins. When she let me read them over her shoulder I protested.

"But Alix, they can't possibly believe this nonsense. There are no brush-fires cutting off the Hamptons from New York. JFK hasn't closed down. You haven't been asked to dinner by the mayor. No cholera epidemic rages."

"They're awfully good sports," she told me optimistically. "They always give me the benefit of doubts." Then: "And surely when I show up bearing a signed contract for his next book from Cowboy Dils..."

"You don't have a signed contract," I pointed out.

Her admirable chin came up on that, and rather smartly.

"Mr. Dils gave his word of honor, Beecher, and decent chaps don't go back on their word.

"Specially not you Yanks."

"And if he does?"

"They'll have me flogged and keelhauled" she admitted, briefly glum and for once conceding the realities.

"And rightly so," I agreed.

She kissed me then, and fondly. "You hardcases haven't a scintilla of compassion. I'd much rather have you for a lover than an employer, Beecher."

I felt that way as well and on the strength of it, took her to dinner in Southampton, just for old times' sake, at Savanna's on Elm Street, just across from the railroad station. We got a table in the garden, awfully pleasant on a mild night like this, and where we were about to have an extraordinary stroke of luck.

"Your last night in town and we have a Wyseman Clagett sighting!"

"The chap with the tic? Oh, Beecher, you spoil me rotten! Where is he?"

Clagett and three henchmen, none of them (even Roadkill) as ugly but all as sinister, had one of the larger garden tables and were there over the food with their heads together. When I nodded toward them for Alix's benefit, she moved her chair slightly for a better view.

"This is splendid, Beecher. What d'you suppose they're up to?"

"Plotting, I suppose. That's what fellows like Clagett do. They plot and lay plans."

"He's heaven, Beecher. I do wish my pa could be here. When does the tic start, d'you think?"

"Any moment now," I said, not knowing but not wishing her to lose heart.

Karl Lager and his "auld brigade" of sportsmen thought they'd failed. But their quixotic drive through town Memorial Day had attracted an unwelcome glare of publicity to Clagett's proposal to build two hundred houses on land Mr. Rubin and the ecologists felt might safely accommodate twenty. Now questions were being asked at county level and upstate in Albany, in the State House. The governor, looking toward a tough reelection campaign, surely didn't need one of Wyseman Clagett's schemes hung from his neck like an albatross. Roger Champion, with problems of his own, more personal ones, had pulled out of the raceway deal. Not that Clagett was beaten yet; men like him don't go down without a fight. But defenders of the Bridgehampton aquifer, and loyal fans of the silly, crumbling old anachronism of a racecourse, had some reason now to hope.

"Beecher?" Alix said, becoming a bit anxious about the Clagett tic.

"It can't be long now, darling."

It was precisely then, as Wyseman Clagett slammed a big, hairy-backed hand flat on the dinner table, illustrating some point or other, but setting silverware and china to jumping about, that his two great, bushy eyebrows leapt at each other and his jaw, with its yellowed, protruding front teeth, pulled dramatically to one side and seemed to snap voraciously at—

"Good Lord!" Alix said aloud, her hand gripping my forearm in considerable alarm. "He really *is* about to eat his ear!"

He never did, of course; it merely looked that way.

Over coffee and cigarettes (Savanna's was hardly a bastion of the smoke police) Alix kept remarking our luck in having actually seen the Clagett tic in action. He'd gone off with his cronies and their table was occupied now by two perfectly normal young couples laughing and scanning menus.

"I do hope it isn't catching, Beecher. You wouldn't find me sitting at Clagett's table on a wager."

I didn't want the evening to end and took her for a nightcap at the Driver's Seat on Job's Lane, where we sat out back at the outdoor bar and let Sonny Columbo make us Cosmopolitans. He'd been the barman there for years and said he never had seen a Memorial Day like this one.

"Have you had Mr. Wyseman Clagett in recently?" Alix asked, a glutton for divertisement.

Sonny shook his head. The Driver's Seat wasn't Clagett's style. Had Cowboy Dils ever come in? I asked. He wasn't a big fan of the Cowboy, Sonny said, and passed on a Dils story he'd heard earlier that evening over the bar. It wasn't very amusing and from what I knew, wasn't very accurate.

"People like that don't make it in Southampton," Sonny said, passing on the weight of snobbish local feeling as if handing down judgments from the high bench. "Hampton Bays might be more his style."

Neither Alix nor I, who knew what really happened, laughed. That disappointed Sonny, I think, but so what. Cowboy, to spare both Slim and her husband, lost whatever tatters of reputation the people of Gin Lane had left to him. You didn't laugh over something like that.

A car was picking up Alix early the next morning to whisk her off to JFK and BA's noon flight to Heathrow.

"I've been shameless in overstaying my leave," she said, "but we've had such grand adventures. There's simply no one I know, not in this hemisphere, who's half the fun you are, Beecher."

This hemisphere? *This* hemisphere? There was a guarded and highly qualified compliment if ever I'd heard one. But this was no time to quibble. Not on her last night.

"If they sack you, fly back next week. You can bunk in with me. Mary Sexton will see to it," I told her. "Sally Richardson would hire you in a New York minute at St. Martin's. If you bring Cowboy's next book along with you."

"Don't tempt me, Beecher. You know I'm pliable and weak."

She wasn't, of course. Anything but. And when she joined me in bed that night, a certain fine gold chain was missing from her breast.

When I mentioned it Alix said, "Good, you noticed. I love a chap who notices things."

A chain through one of her excellent nipples, or its disappearance, was hardly to be dismissed as a routine "noticing things," but never mind. It was gone.

"Yes," she said. "I concluded it was juvenile of me. After all, the man who gave it me never meant anything."

"And you weren't engaged to him?"

"Not this one, no. And I *don't* get engaged to *ev*-eryone, Beecher, and you know it. But my philosophy has always been that when someone's going through a rough patch, one ought to kiss chaps and such. It rarely does harm and often bucks up a friend. Everyone knows that."

She might wear a nipple ring again someday, she said, "if it came with meaning. From someone I truly cared for. For instance, from someone like you, Beecher."

"Mmmmm," I said, enjoying the moment and the sentiment, though not fully satisfied that she'd accept a ring from someone "like" me. But rather than quibble, I stroked the bare breast in question, admiring it, brushing it lightly with my fingers while she lay back against pillows. I looked down at her, attempting to gauge the size and heft and style of gold ring that might be most suitable. As for quality, twenty-four-carat gold, of course, or what I understand they call in the precious metals trade "99 fine."

Maybe I could call Ralph Destino at Cartier's. You couldn't just go up to the jewelry counter at Bloomies and say to the salesclerk, "Show me something in nipple rings." At least, I couldn't, being an Episcopalian and all. Ralph Destino would surely know about such things and might have an idea that would please her. Be somehow worthy of her. You get Alix Dunraven to wear your nipple ring, you don't deal in shoddy.

# thirty-six

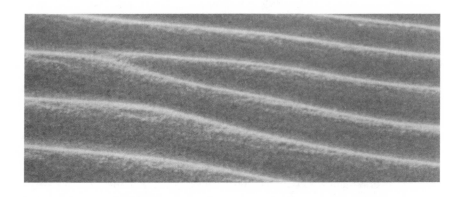

*He held up the old uke. "Leave a light in the window, Mother...."*

I got Dils alone one more time. Too many loose ends not to. There was talk he was getting out, selling the Gin Lane place, with local people boasting how they'd driven him out, that he wasn't their sort and never would be. That brand of pious rubbish. I caught him on the Sunday morning a limo was taking him back into Manhattan. He'd been back in the city on the air for a week and was out here for perhaps this one final weekend. He was rushed, I guess, and short with me.

"I don't have much time, Harvard. Not in the mood for rehashing things."

I ignored protests.

"The hit-and-run Rolls. I still don't understand that. Had Slim already told him you were hitting on her? Was that why Champion ran you down that night?"

"No."

"That's all, just no?"

He shrugged. The fun had oozed out of the story. I was no longer amusing. Okay. So I just said:

"The night you were run over. Just tell me about that."

He thought for a moment. And then he said:

"I'd jogged west all the way along Gin Lane to the Meadow Club, where I turned to come back. A car went by going east. Same direction I was now headed. It passed me, going maybe thirty. Fast enough I couldn't tell much about it in the dark, slow enough they could see me in the headlights. It passed, went maybe four-hundred yards further along so it was in the wide part of the road in front of the Bathing Corp. Right there it threw a quick U-turn and started back. Faster this time. As if the driver forgot something and was going back for it."

He chewed his lip for a minute, then went on.

"What they were coming back for was me. Very fast, now. Blinding me with the lights. Instinctively, I started edging to my left, off the road. But the ground fell away there, pretty sharply, toward the lake. So I had to edge back or fall into the damned water. I was heading back up toward the road when the car got there and I couldn't reverse myself fast enough. I never had a chance. I tried to dive but the car was on me by then and the fender brushed me. Hard enough to break my leg, and also hard enough to toss me out of the way, or it would have been 'all she wrote' and '*arriverderci, Roma.*' Next thing I knew, I was under the water and kicking and scrambling my way to the surface. I guess that's when Maine came along."

"You knew the car."

He nodded. "A black Rolls. Roger Champion's car."

"In the dark, you could be sure?"

"There are some things you just know."

"And he was driving?"

Cowboy didn't say anything. Then: "You know as well as I do, Stowe. It was Slim. Hit-and-run at midnight ain't Roger Champion's style. And whatever else he may be or how old, Roger's got style . . ."

He drew out the word "styyyyle" as if it were spelled that way.

"My fault, of course. I'd rejected Slim and walked away and she couldn't tolerate that. She was still beautiful, still desirable, and she wasn't going to accept rejection without a fuss. She'd read your piece about me, how I was obsessive about late-night jogs, and I suppose that gave her the idea. Whether she meant just to throw a scare or was really trying to kill me, maybe not even Slim can say."

"And when the golf cart went into the pool?"

"Yeah, that was her, too. I must have been asleep in the sun so I can't prove it. Never actually saw her. But afterwards, one of the illegals told me, 'A tall lady is here. She fast running away . . .'

"I told the maid to keep her mouth shut or she'd end up in court and then the INS would get her."

"But why?" I asked. "The woman tried twice to kill you."

"I know, I know. But what the hell. If I told the cops and everyone the truth, where would it get me? I'd be destroying a marriage and bringing down two people: one an old man I respect; the other someone I used to care about. No profit in that, is there, Harvard?"

"So you lied. Blamed yourself. Even though Slim was perfectly willing to shift suspicion to her husband."

"Yep."

"And the Champions end up on pedestals and you're being run out of town by the hypocrites around here."

"'Wave the flag for Hudson High, boys/Show them how we stand. . . .'"

"Don't you care? Your reputation and all?"

Cowboy laughed, a harsh sound.

"That's the thing of it, see. I have no reputation."

There wasn't much more to say and when the limo arrived to take him into town, I helped him with the bags and watched him limp to the front seat. "I like to ride up with the driver," he said.

I wanted to tell him things, then, and didn't. About how in the end there were some of us who thought Cowboy was okay. And maybe more than okay. But I was the only one who came to say good-bye and didn't want to embarrass him. And when the car had turned 'round and was ready to roll out the driveway, he let down his window to shout at me what I assumed would be his good-bye.

Instead, he held up the old uke and began to strum, calling out to me as he left:

"Leave a light in the window, Mother. . . ."

That afternoon Arnold Leo, chief of the Baymen, back from his travels, finally returned my call. Where, I wondered, do Baymen go when they're not being Baymen? Do they go fishing elsewhere? Yes, Mr. Leo said, taking me literally. Sometimes they went fishing for sport and had grand adventures. But they also had considerable grievances which he'd be delighted to air. Against the market, against government, against the environmental lobbies. If I needed to interview him for my story for *Parade* about the fishermen and their work, their lives, he was perfectly willing. Yes, I said, I'd like to do that. I'd already pretty much wrapped it up but Leo could put a cap on it.

"It should make quite a story for you, sir," the Bayman said, quite courtly the way some of these fellows are.

I said that it surely would. And we agreed to meet for coffee and a talk the next morning at the Montauk docks, where the land falls away and the real ocean begins.

The place where the Hamptons end.

# t h i r t y - s e v e n

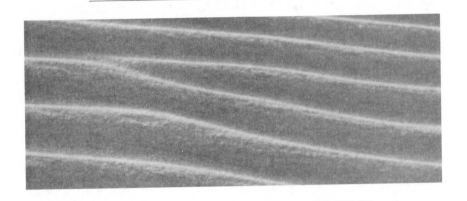

*They called him vulgar and common, and drove him out. . . .*

I drove out again to the Hamptons for the Fourth of July. My dad was home, briefly, from Brussels, and we enjoyed one of those typical, emotional Stowe family reunions where each of us cleared his throat and said something about the weather. If there are people more loving, and more reluctant to demonstrate affection, than we are, I have not yet made their acquaintance. But it was fine to see the old man again on Further Lane and to know that he'd survived both the Belgian haute cuisine and the NATO Germans. My piece on the Baymen had come out. Well received, too. Even by Walter Anderson, who was difficult to please. And Eddie Adams's photos didn't hurt. Eddie had a Pulitzer for his photography in Vietnam and his camera had caught the Baymen just right, their boats, their work, their strong, scarred hands, their tanned, seamed faces, and the sea on which they made their hard living. On the Saturday morning early, before the traffic clogged Route 27, I drove one more time into Southampton, hung a left, near the hospital, crossed Toylsome Lane down to Gin Lane, where I turned right and drove the gorgeous two-mile length of it. To look, to ponder, to remember.

And to marvel at its unaccustomed tranquility.

No Secret Service, no POTUS, no society weddings, no RAF versus the Argies, no sports car legends driving fast cars very slowly, no Shinnecock uprising even, the Pequots and our own local Native Americans for the moment at peace. Mr. Fairchild and the faithful Patrick had moved on to other elegant precincts, scoring their scoops, wearing their watches on the wrong wrists, and presumably still squashing lemons. The only unexpected and alarming news came from Mecox Bay, where Gilbert the portfolio manager was quietly recovering from injuries. Having at last foiled the alpaca cartel and taken delivery of nearly a dozen animals, he had in all innocence entered their corral to go among them, amiably rubbing their heads and permitting the little ones to nuzzle against his stout legs. The trouble was, he'd just finished attending to his hives and was still garbed in his beekeeper's suit, size XXL, and its matching Darth Vader mask, and the poor alpacas, not recognizing their new master, took alarm and attacked him, spitting, butting and kicking. I assumed Karl and Sandy Lager were experiencing no equivalent problems or wounds and were safely at home on Scuttle Hole Lane. But their Season had already been sufficiently eventful and I chose not to pester them.

Back in Britain, pursuing their separate careers, were Fruity and Her Ladyship. The viscount was up in the Outer Hebrides explaining and defending the government's agricultural subsidies to sullen shepherds and drunken crofters, and not doing it all that well, confounding one puzzled audience with hair-raising tales of how gallantly the RAF had fought in the Falkland Islands, "where we also raise sheep, decent, honorable British shepherds all, and don't spend our days dancing the tango and quaffing daiquiris." At a crossroads agricultural rally in Devon, farmers pelted the viscount's car with turnip. You had the feeling from reports that in the next cabinet shakeup, Fruity Metcalfe might be losing his situation as Minister of Ag and Fish.

As for Alix, she was a veritable cyclone of energy for Rupert Murdoch's book-publishing house, busily trying to convince people that the British public would snap up, at twenty quid, the wit and humor of a Yank broadcaster named Cowboy Dils. In the several brief messages in cipher that she rattled off to me either by E-mail or through the post, she was encountering considerable opposition to the project. On the positive side, however, "the new Malraux" was hard at work in Paris on his latest book and thanks to Alix, HarperCollins had been awarded British rights. Delighting Mr. Murdoch, or so she claimed. About which more cynical people might withhold judgment. Her Ladyship also swore she'd not yet again become engaged, whatever Nigel Dempster was reporting in the *Daily Mail*, and assured me in terms too intimate to set down here of her continuing passion for me.

And for sunshine and the Hamptons.

Roger and Slim Champion, I'd been given to understand, were traveling in Europe, their marriage more solid than ever. Mr. Champion, decidedly and very much a local hero for having confronted and challenged the lascivious Dils, and seemingly infused with a randy, new vigor, had swept up his wife and taken her off, his mind once again clearly focused. Roger understood clearly now the motivation that had driven him to finance Clagett's sleazy schemes, making enemies and backing wicked men and evil projects. Just to prove he was still relevant. That had been a mistake. Crazy as it seemed, going after Cowboy Dils, now that made sense. That, Mr. Champion concluded, that was truly relevant, that was what a younger, more vigorous Roger Champion would have done. Tried to shoot somebody.

Despite herself, Slim Champion was impressed. Maybe all the lies and plots had paid off. Gradually, as they made their cushioned way from one five-star hotel to the next, her frustrations cooled, she began to mellow. Slim didn't get quite what she wanted; maybe what she ended up with was something better.

And Leicester Dils had been right about one thing: Whatever his righteous anger and justifiable outrage, Roger Champion didn't fire him from the network. With all the sturm and drang and the personal derision, Cowboy in the Morning had ratings as good as ever. Networks don't fire people who deliver an audience; Champion knew the broadcast rules. He'd helped write them.

I drove Gin Lane slowly, savoring memory. One great, walled house after another. A young woman cycling past or at the wheel of a fine car or a pretty girl briefly glimpsed through wrought iron gatework, very satisfied with herself, on her own lawn. I passed the quietly private lane of Wyndcote Farm, where the Dukes lived, the Bathing Corporation, where parents and nannies were dumping young children from cars for the morning swim lessons, the dull red-painted wooden steeples of St. Andrew's Dune Church, Lake Agawan on the right, all the way to Meadow Lane and the Meadow Club, secure behind its hedges and its stuffy membership rolls. Nothing seemed at peril; all, as Her Ladyship might have put it, very *comme il faut.*

The Buchanans and their daughters, and their daughters' purchased husbands, had vanished, gone to Monte and wherever else it is that such people sport.

At the Meadow Club I made my U-turn to drive slowly back along Gin Lane, one glorious place succeeding the other. Only number Ten bis was significantly changed, Cowboy Dils's house, closed to all but real estate agents and potential buyers. There a hired gardener glumly drove a small tractor around the lawns, moving the slovenly, overgrown grass approximately to Gin Lane standards so that the place would look lived-in, beckoning, desirable, important; might attract a moneyed buyer. Out front, a realtors sign advertised the property as "a gentleman's estate," a claim instantly seized upon as a source of amusement for the sophisticates of Southampton.

People scoffed at the outsider Dils, the pretensions of his being labeled a "gentleman," his dated notions of chivalry, his gaucheries, called him vulgar and common, and drove him out. Oh, it was his decision to leave. No one threatened eviction. But Cowboy was finished in the Hamptons and knew it. And if Gin Lane found him faintly ridiculous, I didn't. But then I knew what they didn't, that Cowboy in the Morning permitted himself to be made the butt of jokes and derision. Not because he was some weird variety of masochist; but taking a beating so that a gallant old man not be humiliated, and that a beautiful but silly woman, with whom he had long ago experienced a passage at arms, not be destroyed.

Out here, where they establish the mores and determine protocol and parcel out judicious opinions, the Old Money WASPs believe they still run the place. And in ways, of course, they do. Though when it comes down to it, if anyone makes value judgments in the Hamptons, it's the real estate agents. They're the ones who assay quality, set the prices, put a worth on location, on a piece of land, a house, an address and a name out front. And theirs were the ads for Dils's place that called it "a gentleman's estate."

If anyone along the whole damned lane turned out to be a gentleman, it was Dils. He never had the class of the Duke boys, of course. But he had something. Maybe he picked it up here, in the house at Ten bis Gin Lane. The Dukes had moved on; Monsieur Pierre was long gone; so were the Conover Girls and the Goldwyn Girls and the Powers Girls; and those gloriously penniless White Russians and Count Vava and Sasha and Serge Obolensky, a prince who knew the tsar. For a time Cowboy shared their house; maybe a touch of class rubbed off as well.

It's the real estate boys who set the prices out here. They know value. And however it came about, perhaps accidentally, they got it absolutely right that whatever Gin Lane thought of him, Cowboy's place turned out in the end to have been "a gentleman's estate."